Praise for *Mr. D*

*FOREWORD MAGAZINE BOOK OF THE YEAR
—Silver Award

"'Wild, bawdy, and utterly enjoyable sequel…Austenites who enjoy the many continuations of her novels will find much to love about this wild ride of a sequel."
—Booklist

"While there have been other Pride and Prejudice sequels, this one, with its rich character development, has been the most enjoyable."
—Library Journal

"A breezy, satisfying romance."
—Chicago Tribune

Darcy & Elizabeth: Nights & Days at Pemberley

*INDEPENDENT PUBLISHER'S BOOK AWARDS
—1st Place HISTORICAL FICTION 2007.

A frothy historical dessert following a meaty entree of a classic, suitable for fans of Regency romance who don't mind a little spice.
—Booklist

The Darcys

The Ruling Passion

Pride and Prejudice
Continues

LINDA BERDOLL

Well, There It Is
Austin, Texas

Cataloging-in-Publication Data
Berdoll, Linda Baker
The Ruling Passion: a novel / by Linda Baker Berdoll
— 1st ed. Well, There It Is

Edited by Terry Monfort
Cover Design Rebecca Bretz

ISBN 978-0-9674817-3-9

Printed in the United States of America
10 9 8 7 6 5 4 3 2 1

Dedicated to:
Ivy Symons Berdoll

*U*nder Heaven

In the year '18, Mr. Darcy remained the tall, handsome-featured gentleman of his youth. The figure he struck remained much admired by other than just his wife. Given the peculiar tribulations he had withstood, society certainly could have forgiven him (even expected) an alteration in his bearing. However, he suffered no stoop, no dishevelment of his costume, nor had he taken to drink.

If he had scars from the wars, they endured indelibly, only examined upon retreat. Hence, there was little improvement in his public mien. Upon social occasions, his conversational skills remained hampered by a continued disinclination to share his private thoughts. Indeed, Mr. Darcy's silences remained near legendary. When he did speak, it was at great personal sacrifice.

The birth of his children did not alter his pride nor meliorate his arrogance. In many ways he was of even stricter sensibilities. Indeed, he made no more outward show of affection for his children than the average man of condition. When unobserved, however, he had a habit of tousling his son's hair and lifting his daughter into his arms that suggested a fondness for them few people of station would forgive.

Until he returned from his sojourn to the Low Countries, his fastidiousness would have required a month's ablution to cleanse him of the indignities of town. Of late he had become remarkably tolerant of the patriciate. Indeed, he had accustomed himself to the notion that one day it would be necessary for him to deliver himself unto The Season on behalf of his children's future. He was happy only in knowing that as an eventuality—a far distant prospect not to be bothered with until the day was at hand.

As for the Darcy marriage, some whispered that few love-matches could withstand the boredom of constancy. Elizabeth Darcy was far too happy to be bothered by those ill-informed opinions. As before, their two hearts beat as one. So abiding was their love that they felt no need to put it on display.

The armies of devotion stood firm, only vulnerable to injury from within.

In the year '18, to every thing there was a season, and a time to every purpose under the heaven.

*H*ow Does Your Garden Grow

It was a fair estimation to say the Darcy marriage had remained… well-tended. Despite their duties to hearth, park, and children, they consoled each others' enduring appetence with great enthusiasm. Time and children had not mitigated their passion whatsoever. If any consternation bedevilled them, it was finding privacy wherein to avail themselves of their desire, not the want of it.

Due to what certain mavens of propriety might have decreed as an inordinate degree of indulgence in their children, it had become the Darcys' custom to allow them to come to their chambers at will. Whereas Mrs. Bennet (and her unheralded intrusions) had returned to Longbourn, they had leave to forswear the heavy bolts placed on their door. Elizabeth had given specific directions to nurse that should her children awake from some night terror; they were free to go to their mother.

This freedom made it necessary for the Darcys to be more circumspect about when and how their conjugal exchanges were enjoyed. When once they had not hesitated to enjoy achievement in a random closet or deserted dining room (enduring the wrath of scattered cutlery and mahogany veneer as they did), such acts were now proscribed. When in want of true abandon, they simply visited the verdant grounds surrounding the estate. (One particular spot so well-used as to be absent of all but the most unflappable wildlife.)

Of course, time was the test of all tribulations, even for the impervious Mr. Darcy. It did happen that his hauteur was challenged—most often from awakening prematurely from his night's rest by tiny toes imbedded beneath his chin. (This happenstance, of course, was better entertained than when small, thrashing feet brought him to that singular grief—the sort that only a man could appreciate.)

This night a passing storm had been accompanied by a huge clattering of thunder. The twins had fled to their parents' bed just before dawn. They had made their way with such haste as to be through the door and in their parents' bed ere nurse caught them. Margaret Heff halted at the doorway, wringing her hands and extending profuse apologies. Elizabeth waved her away, content to quiet their fears herself. Mr. Darcy was less pleased, for as she cosseted them, their cold feet found warmth against his. By the time every tear was dried and fear calmed, there was no question of them returning to the nursery.

By daybreak, Geoff was sound asleep on his father's chest. With well-rehearsed precision, Mr. Darcy betook himself from the bed and carried the boy to the door. Owing to his father's care (or that the boy was simply a good sleeper), he did not awake.

Darcy opened the door but a crack and peered out. Seated in a chair just outside, sat the nurse, still in a fret. He whispered to her and she leapt to her feet, allowing him to hand the boy to her—still without waking him. Nurse began an apology for allowing the escape, but Mr. Darcy put a finger to his lips and shushed her. She nodded and withdrew, Geoff still fast asleep. A stout housemaid stood ready to collect his sister.

It took some time for Darcy to untangle Janie's fingers from her mother's hair. It was his particular wish not to awaken his wife. (Of late, she looked to be well-nigh fordone by half past four.) She must have her rest. Despite his guardianship, Elizabeth awoke before he could transport Janie to the door.

"Does she stir?" she asked.

He shook his head, gave Janie over to waiting hands and closed the door.

As he turned to the bed, he said, "Roused by the slightest bit of thunder outside their window, our children would sleep through Armageddon in the room."

Running her fingers awkwardly through her hair, she tossed back the bedclothes as if to rise.

"I must look a fright," said she.

To him, her mussed hair and sleepy eyes were nothing less than an aphrodisiac.

He announced, "You look nothing of the sort."

As he walked towards her, he drew his nightshirt over his head and tossed it aside. Well-honed and well-hung, he sported a rather magnificent genital tumescence, one that gently swayed with every step he took in her direction.

Was she given to histrionics, she could have managed a swoon. As it was, she had to stifle an anticipatory gasp. She knew well that his sexual capital included, not only immoderately appointed loins, but a penchant for passion that included the bestowal of pleasures upon her person so exceedingly well-executed that her toes curled at the very thought of them.

Without word or hesitation, she quit any thought of taking leave and extended her arms to him. He slid in beside her, nuzzling her behind the ear.

She laughed.

As he serried his body next to hers, the evidence of his affection (at present heavy with morning pride) insinuated itself between her thighs. Overborne by her own indocile desire, she turned to meet his touch. Within their embrace, Mrs Darcy's hand slithered downward to Mr. Darcy's nether-region—to guide, to encourage, or, perhaps simply to admire. Whatever her motive, Mr. Darcy's response to his wife's caress was immediate—and thorough.

As much as they loved their children, languorous longing and supine delights would never be suspended.

The ruling passion conquered reason still.

*S*peaking of Love

There were four dining parlours in Pemberley House. The prettiest was well-proportioned and ideal for summer as it had grand windows opening to the grounds below. It also beheld a fine prospect of the hill Elizabeth Bennet and her Aunt and Uncle Gardiner descended on the occasion of her first visit to Darcy's estate. Every disposition of the park was handsome, but that remained Elizabeth's favourite. It was crowned by a wood, with trees scattered on its banks and the winding of the valley as far as Elizabeth could trace it.

As it was hithermost to the stairs leading to the nursery, they chose there to breakfast. The children took their own morning meal in the nursery. If they did not dawdle with their food, they were allowed to join their parents. Having them attend his table curled, powdered, and dressed was a concession to their father's sensibilities.

Whereas the napery was adorned with a pair of fine silver candelabras and a sideboard that groaned under the weight of china tureens (and a chafing-dish embossed with a scene of Perseus turning Phineus to stone), the children were expected to behave accordingly. It was all much more opulent than anything Elizabeth Darcy had enjoyed at Longbourn, but then, material possessions had never been her heart's desire. As the owner of her heart possessed the finest estate in three counties, she thereby was of the opinion that their children should be witting of their station—but not ruled by it. Consequence had its tax and that included taking care of gilt wood tables and French glass.

Mr. Darcy arrived at the dining parlour behindhand of his wife. Before he seated himself, he came to her ostensibly to bestow a kiss. Whilst engaged in that liberty, he used the morning light to steal a glance at her countenance. Diligent husband of her health, he was a bit troubled by what he observed. Small, dark semi-circle lay just beneath each eye. (Those eyes that once drove him to distraction were provocative still.) In every other way, she seemed fresh as the morning rain. Her hair was glossy and her cheeks pink. Thus he was reluctant to remark on the circles lest she take his observation as censure. It was apparent that she knew they were there for she had taken to dusting her face with a bit of powder. That, in and of itself, was unusual.

He would not have her unwell.

For all their household help, there was great need of another nurse. Obviously, Mrs. Heff needed help. Once another nurse was in place, Elizabeth would be less inclined to take the stairs every time she heard a child cry out. (Their children were, granted, a noisy pair.) When they were young, Mrs. Littlepage, the former wet-nurse had served as nurse as well. However, she had proved far too fatigable to chase the youngsters. Once they were weaned, she had bid take her leave. The search for a second nurse had not been embarked upon in a timely fashion as Elizabeth had braved great travail in finding the first one. She was loath to begin interviews again and he could not help but be sympathetic. (One particularly nasty applicant had tempted him to set the dogs after her.)

In deciding that he should resolve the ongoing worriment for his wife, he began to grumble before he took a plate to the sideboard.

"We must see to obtaining a second nurse, Mrs. Darcy. Or, at the very least, find one a bit quicker than the one we have."

She turned her eyes in his direction. Her expression, an odd combination of relief and defeat, suggested that she was in agreement.

He continued, "Despite the troubling economy, I do believe Pemberley can afford to take on additional help. Indeed, if you would like, I shall be happy to interview them for you myself."

His suggestion was less an offer than a command. Her procrastination, she knew, had provoked his decree. Saving her from the necessity of formal surrender on the matter, their children did gain the room with only a little less cacophony than last eve's storm. As fine a house as Pemberley was, Elizabeth believed nothing above the angelic faces of her children, freshly scrubbed and fed, beaming up at her in the bright morning sun. This day the twins had trooped down the stairs and taken their places looking for all the world as if it was the first their parents had seen them.

Quite as usual, Geoff and Janie were engaged in a disagreement, one Janie wanted her father to resolve. Before being seated, she escaped Mrs. Heff's grip and ran directly to his chair.

"Papa," she asked with great solemnity, "When it thunders, is God angry?"

Geoff interrupted her, snapping, "Oh, do not be such a ninny!"

Once he had entered his fourth year, he had begun to harbour little patience for his sister and even less for her opinions.

He announced, "Everyone knows that it is caused by lightening."

"Papa," Janie grumped, "Geoff called me a ninny!"

Without looking up from his melon, Darcy said, "Geoffrey, do not use such language. It is coarse. Apologise to your sister."

"Yes, Papa," he replied. To Janie, he said, "I am sorry that you are a ninny."

Janie frowned. However, Mr. Darcy was pleased to leave any more reproach to his wife. Content with his success over his sister, Geoff looked at his mother with apprehensive eyes. Elizabeth raised an eyebrow. He needed no other censure. It was uncharacteristic of him to be unkind. Elizabeth wondered if Jane's wild brood was a regrettable influence on him. Neither Jane nor Bingley had the heart for discipline which left their children in compleat want of restraint. Being the second born in a house full of girls, Elizabeth believed it should fall to Darcy to instruct his son.

Geoff was seen to be quite precocious (even to those other than his parents). He was handsome and sturdy, unafraid (aside from thunder) and his favourite possession was a compass. Although he was, at times, uncivil to his sister, no one had leave to tease her but him. Janie was quiet, but clever and very independent. Although it was a struggle to keep a ribbon in her hair, she was as pretty as a porcelain doll.

From beneath his coat Geoff produced a horse that his namesake, Colonel Fitzwilliam had carved for him. He pranced it along the edge of the table without thought to the finish or to his lapse in table manners. Elizabeth thought to correct him before Darcy spied him, but she held her tongue. If she was to err, she would rather it be on the side of indulgence. Time would come soon enough for the burden of his heritage. She was disposed to let him be a boy whilst he could.

"What do you call your horse?" she bid.

He said airily, "I have named him Copenhagen, Mama."

"After the city?" she queried.

He answered patiently, "No, Mama. I have named him after Wellington's horse."

"Wellington's horse is called Copenhagen?" she repeated.

Enunciating carefully, he said, "Yes. Copenhagen. Wellington chased that French rotter, Nappy across the Continent."

His father corrected, "Do not employ that word either. It is coarse as well. A gentleman does not speak in that manner. Enemy or not, the emperor's name is Napoleon Bonaparte."

The boy needed no further chastisement. He suffered under his father's censure above any other. Without compleat submission, he ducked his chin and hid his wooden horse beneath the edge of the table. Usually his parents listened with nothing but pleasure to what the boy said, but it was important that he not become accustomed to employing such language. Elizabeth suspected that he obtained the word "rotter" from the same relation who carved him the horse.

Seeing that the tips of his ears had turned red, Elizabeth altered the discourse.

She asked, "Do you know the name of Napoleon's horse?"

Delighted that he knew, Geoff said eagerly, "Marengo, Mama." Geoff then asked his father, "Did you know that black horses are born with a brown coat?"

Darcy opened his mouth to reply. Before he could utter a word, a servant stepped into the room.

He announced, "Mrs. Littlepage here for Mrs. Darcy."

Without looking towards her husband, Mrs. Darcy told the footman, "I shall see her in the front salon."

As Mr. Darcy was well aware of the service Mrs. Littlepage provided, he caught his wife's wrist as she made for the door.

"Must we speak?" he inquired deftly.

She did not pretend ignorance.

"Perchance," she replied, unintentionally evasive. "One must be prepared for any possibility."

"How possible?" he bid before checking himself. There were, after all, many ears in the room.

Glancing at their children, she only agreed, "We must speak."

4

Passion's Gift

After speaking to Mrs. Darcy, Mrs. Littlepage took her leave directly. Having been sent a bit off-kilter by the woman's unexpected arrival and her husband's observance of it, Elizabeth escaped from his questioning eyes via the back staircase. She was breathless by the time she gained their chamber door. This was only partly due to her dash up the stairs. A frisson of anticipation scurried up her spine as she turned the knob. This day she was especially stirred.

Darcy abhorred schemes and disliked conjecture. No doubt he had been apprised that her meeting had concluded and was on his way thither to hear of it from her own lips. Her obliqueness had been deliberate—and she hoped she would be forgiven.

She thought it only fitting that she inform him of the coming child next to the bed they had laboured so pleasurably in to create it.

All the rooms of Pemberley were handsome beyond measure. The Darcys' bedchamber was sumptuous above all others. Time did not make Elizabeth invulnerable to its august and uncompromising façade. This particular stirring owed less to its magnificent furnishings than the slight scent of her husband's masculinity that clung to the bedcovers. Despite being the mistress of the house for any number of revolving frosts and summer reveries, she had made very few alterations to its décor. The only change of any importance was compleatly hidden from view.

At one time a large pier glass hung on the wall opposite their bed. Now it lay beneath it—concealed from prying eyes, yet at the ready to be brought forth to bear witness to their connubial pleasures. When once it was a nightly voyeur of their intimate embraces, of late it had been gathering dust. That alteration alone should have alerted husband that something was amiss. It had been her design to leave any declarations to the gods. No doubt he would have soon discovered the happy news himself (he was nothing if not a very thorough lover).

Now the pleasure of that special moment—when his hand would cup her abdomen in wonder—was lost. This due all through the auspices of an over-eagre wet-nurse. Elizabeth had done no more than made inquiries as to her availability, not invited her to come. No doubt half the countryside was awaiting a formal proclamation of another child to be born of Pemberley. Once Mrs. Littlepage was announced, there was no call to turn her away. The cat was out of that particular bag. Elizabeth knew the fault was hers. She had procrastinated in hopes of finding the perfect moment; now it had found her.

Her hesitation was with just cause.

She had been taken to the straw three times, each fraught with crises. The first two pregnancies were grave disappointments—one a miscarriage, the second, a still birth. Whilst the third ended quite happily, the delivery took place in a chaise and four on the road between Wigston and Fleckney. Not only was Darcy not at her side, he had been quarantined abroad and she feared he was dead.

Their first two losses grieved him deeply. Whilst the first two were not his to make right, he never quite forgave himself for not being by her side for the last.

Although another birth should have daunted her, her real trepidation was in disquieting her husband. That, however, was inescapable. Launching a wet-nurse at him as an opening salvo did not bode well for the remainder of her watch over his sensibilities. Sitting in a tufted chair next to the balcony, she was lost in that thought when the sound of the door gave her a start. He made his way into the room silently and found his ground midmost of it.

Whereas he did not come to wither she sat, she stood and took a few steps in his direction. When they were perhaps ten paces apart, she stopped and dropped her hands and held them as if in supplication. Then, slowly, she turned a full revolution, allowing him to appraise her figure fully. The cut of her gown made that a useless exercise. His brow furrowed. By virtue of the otherwise slightly dumbstruck expression he bore, she walked to him.

"You must manage your affairs ever more closely," she said.

When she was a step away, she took his hand and held it against her cheek. Said he, "Indeed?"

"I had hoped to make a grand announcement at a more fitting time," she said. "I apologise that my condition was exposed most importunely."

In a move both swift and tender, he turned her about and held her against him. His breath against her neck was steady. As she sank back against him, a small convulsion of relief overcame her.

"You are my sheltering oak," she whispered.

As her head fell to the side, she languorously enjoyed the kisses he gifted her neck.

She wanted to speak reassuringly, but a catch in the back of her throat betrayed her. She turned about and buried her face in the fabric of his waistcoat. After a moment, she looked up at him. His burnished cheeks and adoring eyes compleatly countermanded the unease she had felt not a moment before.

Pushing a curl aside, he whispered in her ear, "Speak to me, Lizzy."

Wishing the moment could last a lifetime, she willed herself not to lose her countenance. Indeed, her voice was artificially light.

"I advise you that you must be ever vigilant of your business affairs lest you be unable to support your ever-growing family."

A smile erupted when she thought of the expression just then.

Embracing her once again, his hands began a slow caress of every hill and valley of her body. She was not in the smallest way fooled by this manoeuvre. He meant to sketch her shape, of course. It pleased her that he was in want of finding the first trace of the coming child on his own. (Moreover, his roving touch was never a burden.) When one large hand paused at her abdomen, she held her breath. The small swell it contained was a surprise to no one at that point. However, when he cupped his hand upon it, she slid her hand to cover his. In concert, they sighed. As they did, it was as if she could detect his worriment burgeoning.

Then he stepped back and bestowed a sweeping bow.

"My fruitful wife," said he.

She curtsied.

In a small, and very unsuccessful attempt at jollity, he bid, "Might you have just one this time?"

"Of course," she replied, curious if he was altogether serious.

"Mrs. Littlepage," he said cryptically.

As Darcy was a veteran of what was known as the "nursing wars" between Elizabeth and her mother, he knew that Mrs. Littlepage had only been employed owing to the problem of nursing twins.

Unwilling to enter into a conversation just then to explain the intricacies of mother's milk, she only said, "One must be prepared for all occurrences. Moreover, the blame of twins falls solely on you, sir!"

"*My* doing? *You* are the one who produced them"

"I could not have done so without furtherance from their father."

"I fancy," he conceded. "We acted in that together."

"Well said," she agreed.

When she placed her hand against his cheek, everything—the air in the room, the sunlight flooding onto the rug and, most important, his countenance—altered. His brows knitted. When she spoke again, her voice was immoderately confident.

"All shall be well," she said.

He nodded.

"Promise me this," she whispered urgently. His expression told her that were the moon his to give, she should have it. "I only bid this—stay with me, do not leave my side again."

He drew her so hastily and tightly to his breast that she left her breath behind.

He vowed, "This I do promise."

She, however, would not allow such a happy moment to be discoloured by those dismaying remembrances. She turned and her hands slid up his lapels and clasped them. At first all she felt was the slight susurration of his breath on her hair. It was unclear who first sought the other's lips. It really didn't matter. The kiss they shared was as deep as any she could ever recall.

In one commanding move, he clasped a wrist in each of his hands and tucked them behind the small of her back. Knowing what was to come, she held her breath lest it scatter away. His lips found her neck, her ear, her shoulders, then forsaking her wrists, he began an undulating exploration beneath her skirts. His long, lithe fingers gently probed her.

As she lost command of her knees, he caught her.

"My limbs have no will. They are limp with want...."

As she clung to him, her hands discovered that he was not.

In a manner more given to lust than love, they slid to the floor.

"Give care!" he urged.

"I shall take great care," she laughed, drawing herself atop him.

Huddling her hips atop his, she whispered, "What, pray tell, is that I feel?"

There was no denying that a very generous concomitant of desire had raised its head—so to speak.

Regardless of the conspicuousness of his tumid member, he said, "I can not imagine to what you refer."

Nestling more firmly, she gasped playfully, "Upon my word, it grows even as we speak!"

"I am free to confess you are right. Another of your doings I would guess."

"In concert, I should think."

With that, she threw back her head and laughed. As she did, the huge door to their bedchamber burst open. Fast behind came their children. Seeing their parents on the floor next to the bed, they shrieked with laughter.

"Mama, what are you doing there?

Without time to think, all Elizabeth could answer was, "Looking for my shoes."

Always inquisitive, Janie asked, "What is Papa doing?"

"Helping me," she answered feebly.

Geoff was suspicious, pointing out, "But you have your shoes."

"Is Papa not a good helper?"

The children agreed just as nurse arrived. Understanding the situation, and the part she played in it by losing her charges, she did a fine job of containing them without any show of knowing something was amiss. Therefore, Elizabeth was spared having to round them up herself and possibly exposing her poor husband to further humiliation.

As the door closed soundly, their ardour remained uncooled. And as they were on the floor next to it, they retrieved the long forgotten looking-glass and put it to good use. Franny Tupin was employed as second nurse by the end of the week.

 olden Eggs

The year '15 had become known as the Season of Waterloo. Although Napoleon was vanquished, that did not put an end to strife in England. The war had a near cataclysmic effect on its economy.

In the following years, vast hordes of the wageless and the famished ran amok in the cobbled streets of London prompting all good society to draw their drapes and think kindly on their country estates. Secret meetings were beginning to be held in Methodist houses and songs of social disorder were wafting up from within them.

As had been then their habit, the Darcys did not season in London. Indeed, they came to town but seldom. Some believed that, like others of his station, Mr. Darcy abhorred the disruption in the theatre district. Those who were better acquainted with the man knew that to be untrue. His dislike of the ton was rivalled only by his dislike of the people who inhabited it.

Once his sister Georgiana was honourably married, they kept to Derbyshire. That county, and therefore Pemberley, had vexation and rioters of their own. Only the direst of events would bring them thither. Hence, when word made its way round the first circles that Charles Bingley was near ruin and Mr. Darcy hied to London to forestall it, the story was widely admired. As he was known to be of above moderate taciturnity, no one dared ask Mr. Darcy to either concede or disclaim the rumour.

In truth, there was another, far more scandalous reason for him to be in town that week. He would have come too his friend's rescue regardless, but the other motive was of such detestable urgency that Mr. Darcy risked life and limb to keep it a private matter. Saving Lydia Bennet-Wickham-Kneebone from herself was hardly a singular event. He undertook that office with no small reluctance, determined to untangle his family from George Wickham's clutches once and for all.

Through considerable monetary compensation, Wickham was persuaded to forgo his undying love and devotion for his child bride and give her up to her second husband, Major Kneebone. As Wickham had charges of murder and desertion from duty filed against him, he had reason and means to make his escape. Whether he did or not remained unknown. Darcy had left Wickham that day alive and well (albeit with a line of vengeance-seekers forming at his door), reported his whereabouts to the magistrate, and wiped his hands of the matter.

After everyone that was in his power to be put to right had been redressed, the Darcys left town and sallied forth unto Pemberley, content to abide there into peaceful eternity.

Their serenity had been shattered ere they gained the portico steps.

They were met not only by their children, nurse, and Mrs. Bennet, but two hand-wringing servitors as well. (Obvious in his absence was their steward, which foreshadowed news of the most disturbing sort.) Having never seen either of these specific servants in such a pother at the same time—at least over events unfamiliar to him—Mr. Darcy was of a mind to take an audience with them directly. There were far higher priorities for Mrs. Darcy. She was quite happy to leave such bad business to her husband and hurried off to fuss over their twins and to submit to her mother's aggravations and spleen.

Neither envied the others' task.

Whilst Mrs. Bennet caterwauled about the impudence of Sir Morland to Elizabeth, Darcy was apprised of the unhappy news that whilst they had been in town, the very privacy Mr. Darcy had striven to protect with his every word and deed, had been lacerated. All the worse, the party guilty of this breach was not a stranger. Nay, the culprit was the man whose very life had been sworn to uphold that privacy.

Advising Mr. Darcy of misconduct within his house should have fallen to the errant Cyril Smeads, Mr. Darcy's steward. As Mr. Smeads himself was the malefactor, there had been a passing (but very contentious) rhubarb between the butler, Mr. Howard; Mrs. Darcy's maid, Hannah; and Mr. Darcy's long time dresser, Goodwin; as to which of them would have the pleasure of tattling first. Mr. Howard held the senior position, Goodwin, trumped them both in longevity. Hannah, however, was both outraged and loquacious. She elbowed passed both men and the story began tumbling from her lips ere either of them gathered their thoughts.

"Smeads, sir—he done sold viewings of our *dear babies*! People gave him two pennies a head to come to the door of the nursery—," her voice trembled with anger and she was unable to carry on. Instead, she held out her hand. In it was the money Smeads had collected. "Poor Margaret didn't know what to do!"

Mr. Darcy's grasp of the situation was remarkable in its rapidity. In the wake of that understanding, his state of mind swerved from well-above angry to just shy of apoplectic. This rage was betrayed only by the barest flicker of his nostrils.

"Where is Mr. Smeads at this time?" he bid mildly.

His economy of language and evenness of his tone did not in any way suggest that his interest in the whereabouts of his steward was casual.

"Gone, sir," sputtered Mr. Howard. "Stole away in the dark of night like the dog he is!"

"He got his comeuppance, I promise that!" interrupted Hannah. "Hit his head and lost a tooth or two!"

Under Mr. Darcy's eye, Hannah's ejaculations wound down, "Fell down the stairs. Tripped over the dog, you see...."

Directly, she hushed herself, curtsied and left the particulars to the men. Tiptoeing out of the room, she hurried away. There was further information that needed to be shared with Mrs. Darcy. Neither Howard nor Goodwin would have a part in that. Although he did not dismiss her, Mr. Darcy did not appear to be offended that Hannah had taken her leave. He was bent upon speaking with Mr. Howard.

"Is there word of Smeads destination?" Mr. Darcy inquired.

"I cannot say, sir," said he.

Here Goodwin felt compelled to interject what he knew.

"It was said that he made for Rosings Park, but was turned away."

"I see," replied Mr. Darcy.

Several weeks would pass before all would be revealed of what became known as "the incident." No criminal charges were sought. Giving leave to sightseers to gawk at their children at a tuppence a head was not, strictly speaking, illegal. (Visitors were admitted regularly.) It was, however, an unpardonable offence against them personally. Had he discovered it for himself, Darcy may have beaten Smeads from the house—Mr. Smeads had to have known that. It seemed remarkable that he would risk all for a few pennies. Something else was afoot.

Although the essential actors were known, aims, schemes, and significations remained muddled. Why Smeads repaired directly to Rosings Park was merely speculation. No one knew absolutely that Lady Catherine or her own butler had any sort of relationship with him. And if Smeads indeed had a second calling of selling information of their household to Lady Catherine, no one could prove it absolutely. Not that Darcy would think his aunt above such chicanery. The single reason he did not seek a confrontation on the matter was her bereavement. Moreover, Georgiana and her child remained under her care. Nothing would induce him to compromise their convalescence.

He was not disposed to share all the gossip with Elizabeth. What she soon learnt was troubling enough.

"How could we have misplaced our trust so willingly?" she exclaimed. "Why would a man risk his position for so little? This is was all quite vexing."

That was what worried Darcy too. He did not say that. He spoke to reassure them both.

"I am reminded of the story of the man who killed the goose that laid the golden eggs."

Raising an eyebrow, she asked, "In this tale, are we the goose or the eggs?"

Other that that drollery, she did not mention Smeads again. As did her husband, she believed it was well and good that the wretch was gone. Darcy saw it as one more distasteful matter to put behind them. Wickham would be apprehended and Smeads would find his own level in town. Whatever satisfaction he might have gotten by having Smeads depart at the point of his sword, he was content to consign such vengeance to his imagination. He would happily leave London and its rats to London. He was satisfied to abide at Pemberley in the bosom of his family for the rest of his days.

Although not readily apparent, happier times were at hand.

*O*pen Arms

Understandably, Bingley's nerves had been in quite a state after his forced retrenchment. Indeed, he had not wanted to remain at Belgrave Square at all. No small thanks to Darcy, he still had a country estate.

In arranging the settlement of his debts, it had been worked out that he would exchange estates with Henry Howgrave—giving that man a seat in Parliament and Bingley a step up and out of his financial morass. Rather than dwell upon the unpleasant recollection of being stripped naked by a hoard of angry creditors, he threw himself into the enormous task of moving his family, bag and baggage, scrip and scripage, from Kirkland Hall to Howgrave Manor. That project came to pass with all the chaos, hubbub, and ado that only their singular household could generate. The Bingley children stayed with the Darcys much of this time. Despite their cherubic aspects, the Bingley children were two parts hellion—with a penchant for making signs of derision at each other behind the notice of adults. When at last they were returned to their own beds, everyone toasted the move.

Darcy pronounced, "Five miles of good road is a perfect distance to make the Bingleys excellent neighbours."

Aflutter with excitement, Jane told Elizabeth, "Mr. Darcy told Charles that it is not Howgrave Manor at all. It was called that only of late. When it was built it was known as Deering Lodge."

Although Jane was wholly unaware of it, Mr. Darcy was very-nearly as pleased to have learnt that information as had she. He liked the Howgrave name no better than the man—and he despised the man. Speaking Howgrave's name regularly would have been a test. Elizabeth shared in her sister's pleasure, for she disliked Howgrave as well. This was in part because Darcy did, but also because Howgrave had contrived to court Georgiana without Darcy's approval.

"I do hope returning the manor to its historical appellation does in no way offend Sir Howgrave," Jane worried.

Elizabeth reminded her sister, "I am most certain that if he does not care for the alteration, he is quite free to call Kirkland Hall any name he chooses."

As everyone else was satisfied with the move, Mrs. Bennet was much in want of someone to scold for it. She decided to find it unfitting to go about renaming ancient homes (and did not care for her opinion to be controverted by the facts involved). In fortune, Mrs. Bennet was unable to deliver her reprimands to Jane in person. She penned missives whilst in repose beneath a stately tree in the park next to Longbourn as the illustrious painter Sir Robert Morland took her likeness. (Indeed, Mr. Darcy's particular instructions to that man had included the proviso that should Morland find himself unable to hurry the portrait; he would be well-rewarded.) Mrs. Bennet had complained of the painter and his habits unceasingly whilst he was ensconced at Pemberley at work on the Darcy commission. However, she minded her tongue when her likeness was at stake.

As he disliked the general lack of elegance of Longbourn and its cramped rooms, Morland took that as good an excuse as any to take lodgings elsewhere. No one, from Hertfordshire to Derbyshire, was heard to blame him.

With that one obstacle to family felicity settled, the Darcys were happy to take each new modification to their number as they came.

The most astonishing came from a most unlikely source.

To the surprise of all, Georgiana had returned from her unexpected confinement at Rosings Park bearing two newborns rather than the one. They were cousins born but days apart. One baby girl was born to the Colonel Fitzwilliams; the other was the child of the late Lady Anne. (In fortune, Beecher had not kept his threat to name his motherless daughter after Elizabeth—that had been another ludicrous ploy.)

As often bechanced, the baby had been called after her grandmother. Her name was Catherine, but they called her Cathy. Both girls would become lovely little toddlers and good playmates for Janie.

Georgiana's rescue of Anne's baby from the cold halls of Rosings seemed to be an equitable ending to that sad event. To those who knew her as a woman demanding to supervise the lives of all those about her (exempting neither kith nor kin), obtaining Lady Catherine's approval of such a scheme had seemed unfathomable.

When told that her ladyship had, indeed, acquiesced to her granddaughter's relocation, no one was more astonished than Elizabeth. (Darcy may have been astonished, but it pleased him to believe that all was well.) She was not so certain. There had never been a detail too small for Lady Catherine's supervision. She gave irrefutable judgements on the clothes others wore, the feathers in their hats, the food they ate, and how many times they chewed it. Indeed, her influence was not limited to her own manor. Cottagers could not have a quarrel over a garden spot without her entering an opinion on the matter.

"Your aunt's finger is in everyone's pie," Elizabeth groused.

She caught herself before she said more. Even in the privacy of their parlour, it was unseemly to speak of her husband's relation in a spiteful manner (no matter how true it was). She took a deep breath and a less strident tone. (Hers was not to hold her peace, just mind how she spoke it.)

She said, "I find it quite inconceivable that Lady Catherine would leave her only granddaughter in want of her guidance."

"You fancy that mere miles shall keep her at bay?" he asked drolly.

Raising an eyebrow, she agreed his point was well taken.

All Elizabeth's motherly instincts were aroused at the notion of Lady Catherine within fifty miles of her children. Georgiana's kindness put Elizabeth in the questionable position of disapproving of what was nothing less than rescue. Yet, she knew she had good reason to beware. During their bereavement visit to Rosings Park, Lady Catherine had cornered her in the nursery. She had been invited there ostensibly to admire Anne's motherless child. Instead, she engaged her in a conversation that, although cloaked with an air of cordiality, was nothing less than an ambush.

Initially, Elizabeth believed the poor woman was overwrought by grief. With Beecher leering at her elbow, her ladyship had attempted to employ sympathy over her daughter's passing as a means to her own ends by coaxing Elizabeth into promising her son, Geoff, to Anne's newborn daughter. Confounded and profoundly dismayed, Elizabeth had taken her leave from Rosings Park with Lady Catherine's plot still ringing in her ears.

Perhaps it had merely been the act of a mother desperately desiring assurance of her granddaughter's happiness. Something about the eerie doings made her believe another, more sinister plot was in the works. Nonetheless, Christian charity demanded that grief not be reproved. Any mother's heart would be wounded to the quick by their child's death. Each mourned in their own way. Lady Catherine's may have been to repair to the most profound aspect of her character—that of harrying her relation.

As it happened, there was even more to that story.

Not satisfied just to rescue Anne's daughter, Georgiana also spirited away poor Mrs. Jenkinson. Her ladyship's unkindness to her after Anne's death was the talk of the back stairs. (Anne had a penchant for lurid novels and when they were found after her passing, Lady Catherine blamed Mrs. Jenkinson). Upon learning that Anne's beloved companion had been banished from the house, Georgiana felt compelled to take her with them too. She and Fitzwilliam hid her away in their coach as they took their leave of Kent, knowing at any moment their deception could be found out. It was all quite stirring to Georgiana. Fitzwilliam, the war veteran, was beside himself with anxiety. No wrath burned hotter than his aunt's and he preferred not to have his hindquarters scorched by her ire. Georgiana, however, was not contrite.

"What was I to do?" she shrugged. "Mrs. Jenkinson was so heartbroken. I could think of nothing but my dear Mrs. Annesley. Such devotion is to be rewarded."

Mrs. Jenkinson was to live the years left to her happily overlooking Anne's daughter at Whitemore. Still, Elizabeth knew Lady Catherine did nothing for sentiment's sake. Tucking her granddaughter away with Georgiana also kept her out of Sir Winton Beecher's sway. One thing Elizabeth knew to be true, the child was much more apt to find loving care in Georgiana's arms than any at Rosings Park.

Who could deny any child that?

The Guests

As soon as the Bingleys compleated their move to the neighbourhood, the Darcys had planned to honour them with a ball at Pemberley. It took above two years for them to relocate. It was no surprise that other events engulfed them.

Upon learning that his wife was again with child, Darcy was quite adamant that they should postpone the event forthwith. Elizabeth would not hear of it.

Unused to his edicts being countermanded, he was less than pleased when his wife did just that.

"I fancy we shall not abandon our plans," she said merrily. "Soaked though I am with nature's fecund blessing, I confess that I should like to dance with my husband one more time ere I become too unduly corpulent to be moved about the dance floor with any part of grace."

Mr. Darcy looked at his wife carefully. For a woman of even temper, her moods had been unusually mercurial. It had been his study that when in doubt, it was often wiser to remain silent. Nonetheless, he spoke his mind.

"Allow us to come to an understanding," he said. "I shall take you in my arms just as willingly when you are great with child."

Accepting the reaffirmation, she gave him an appreciative curtsy.

He continued, "I do not find emaciation attractive. Ladies who are excessively thin remind me of spiders."

As he spoke, he gave a slight shudder.

Upon occasion, his compliments could be somewhat clumsy (just as often, they were sublime). This one was so genuine that she was highly diverted.

"In fortune, I am sturdy as a milkmaid," she told him. "No doubt I shall grow evermore stout with each passing year. If you are as true to your word as I know you are, I am to be assured of your love thenceforward."

Taking her in his arms, he told her in all seriousness, "I care not if you grow thin as Lady Caroline Lamb. So long as there is enough flesh for me to hold you near me, I shall be content."

The spell, which had been cast over her so delightfully, was broken when the seamstress was announced. Stealing a hasty kiss, she bid him adieu to face the most evil of all taskmasters—the measuring tape.

Her husband's speculation in regards to her fluctuating moods was undeniable. She never quite caught him at it, but she had been certain for some time he kept track of her womanly cycle more closely than did she, for he anticipated her in ways that astounded her. Of particular enjoyment was the small spray of flowers that would appear upon her dressing table a day or two before she could expect to become a tad peevish. She knew they were from his hand because they were crudely arranged—and thus all the more treasured.

It was proof that he was much vexed by country, and county political doings, that she had been above three months gone with child and he had not known of it.

Although her coming child had plagued her with morning sickness, she was now in high flutter at the notion of taking the first dance in her husband's arms. It harkened back to the earliest days of their marriage. Her romantic notions notwithstanding, there were far greater reasons not to abandon the ball.

Most important amongst them was that the invitations had already been posted. Nothing short of a death would be cause to withdraw them. As it was, their family had become a veritable fount of gossip. It mattered not that Bingley had weathered his financial crises with his usual good humour. Bankruptcy was only cause for ostracism if one's family did not stand behind the bankrupt party. The ball was imperative to show family solidarity.

Moreover, it was out of season to be in the country. Hence, their guest list would consist of more true friends rather than members of the ton. Amongst others, it would be a welcome opportunity to see her friend, Charlotte Collins. Still, she held out little hope Charlotte would come. It was quite a distance to Hunsford and she had never been a good traveller.

Gazing upon her own fulsome figure in the looking glass, Elizabeth recalled how fragile Charlotte had been when last she saw her. The passage of time disposed every figure to some particular evil, be it thickened waist, drooping bosom, or stooped shoulders. The only form to escape the rages of revolving seasons was her husband. Paunch would never trouble his midsection. Each year he stood a little straighter, forestalling maturity through will alone. He remained as impeccably fit as the first evening they met. Just the thought of dancing with him again made her heart leap.

"Is this to your liking, Ma'am?" inquired the seamstress. "If I do say so myself, the colour flatters you."

She held out her new bisque-coloured gown, seams basted and ready for the final fitting. It was very pretty, if a bit subdued. Elizabeth could hear ladies tittering behind their fans even then of how Mrs. Darcy had lost her bloom. "Vanity, thy name is Elizabeth," she silently reminded herself.

It was imperative that she cease fretting. If she did not, she knew that she would be beside herself with nerves by the time she stepped onto the ballroom floor.

As was her husband's wish, she meant to crown her ensemble by donning the pearls he had bestowed her just prior to their wedding. They were a family piece—a double strand with a diamond and sapphire clasp. The Darcy jewels would improve general opinion of any gown she wore.

This was not a spiteful conclusion; it was fact. The crass were always well-represented at any affair.

Whereas the ball was meant to honour the Bingleys, the guest list had to include Charles's sisters, Caroline Bingley and Louisa Hurst. Mr. Hurst was tolerable in that he over-imbibed and was customarily semi-comatose soon after dinner. Louisa and Caroline were not at all agreeable. They were alternately fawning, demeaning, and outright abusive—particularly to Jane. After Darcy apprised her of their refusal to reduce their own indulgences during Bingley's retrenchment, Elizabeth's dislike was sharpened into outright abhorrence. Indeed, she had not a good thought for either of them. The only consolation was that Bingley no longer harboured any misconceptions concerning his sisters' integrity.

As Miss Bingley was invited, so would be Sir Winton Beecher. Their engagement had been formed the previous year, although they seemed in no hurry to marry. Elizabeth had supposed that as a well-established husband-hunter of unparalleled determination, Caroline was happier to parade a fiancé around the monde of London and Bath rather than a husband. Once they wed, the couple would slide into the semi-obscurity of a married couple.

Jane was apprehensive of the match. Word had it that Beecher was in no way but name a gentleman. Jane (who was in no way a gossip) feared for her sister-in-law's reputation. Fingers clutching his elbow, Caroline followed Beecher into gambling halls of every sort. Darcy had been quite appalled by the man and took the exceptional step of informing Bingley that he considered Beecher little above a fortune-hunter. Bingley shrugged his shoulders. Caroline had her twenty thousand pounds and could essentially marry whom she pleased. He could disapprove of it, but she held the emotional whip-hand over her younger brother.

In allying herself with Beecher so hastily after Lady Anne's death, Caroline had incurred Lady Catherine de Bourgh's keenly-expressed disapproval. Upon any other occasion, such censure would have sent poor Caroline into paroxysms of fear and despair. Teetering on the brink of spinsterhood, it appeared she would brook castigation long before she would forego a marriageable man.

It was another matter whether Beecher might sacrifice his love for his dear Caroline to the Gods of Credit.

Although it was not her place to make a conjecture about another's pecuniary situation, Elizabeth was quite certain that Beecher was financially bound to Lady Catherine. If the mood struck her, her ladyship could cut him off without a cent. As to why she had not done so was a puzzlement to some. Every step that lady took was a manoeuvre; every decision she made, a scheme. What Elizabeth suspected was that by having Beecher join the Bingley family fold, her ladyship had another foothold within the Darcy family as well.

These were machinations worthy of Shakespeare.

Another invitation was extended with even less cordiality than to Bingley's sisters. It was fraught with implications quite of another sort altogether.

By virtue of his former ownership of the manor the Bingleys had purchased, decorum dictated that they invite Sir Henry Howgrave and his wife. It was an honour Elizabeth would have thought nothing of except
for one small bother.

Darcy and Howgrave's wife had once been lovers.

ℱor Better For Worse

It is said that time is a creeping thief.

Juliette delicately patted her plump, honey-coloured locks. Turning her head first one way then the other, she appraised herself in her looking-glass. She was inordinately happy with what she saw. Her nightly ablutions (potions, pomades, rouges, tinctures, rose powder, eye lotion, lemon ointment, and gillyflower water) had kept her in the bloom of youth. Most women her age would need to augment their coiffure with hair pieces. Her hair was still luxuriant—a sure sign of youth. She had a check-book with a formidable balance and a fine footman to follow her.

Her once dwindling finances now replenished through marriage, her life was once again one of opulence and admiration.

For all of her years in England, Juliette Clisson had only lately been in want of status. She was, after all, a daughter of a French Viscount. She would have been there yet had not politics of a *dégoûtant* nature interfered with their exquisite existence, usurping their land and chattels. Her mother died of shame and her father turned to drink. When they died of their weaknesses, they were mourned as victims of the revolution as surely as if they had been beheaded with Louis himself.

Juliette had been left to fend for herself as best she could. Convent raised, she was chaste, but not naïve. Cast out into lesser society, she landed on her feet with all the facility of a brindled cat. As her golden hair and creamy skin were highly desirable, in no time she found a well-fed Marquis to keep her in the style to which she was accustomed. Indeed, he put her in an elegant house around the corner from his wife. Unfortunately, the political winds soon shifted against all nobility and her temporary *inamorato* was arrested. A trial was only a formality and it came to pass that she stood next to him in the tumbrel as they were carted off for a hasty execution. She escaped by a hairsbreadth, but it was a nasty business all-round. The episode influenced her to betake her charms to a less volatile climate.

When she first observed the pasty-faced Englishmen traipsing up to St. James Palace, she deduced that her fellow Parisians had been quite correct. London was a backwater hamlet full of self-satisfied shopkeepers. Her opinion of London and its tiresome citizens was much improved by reason of one spectacular point. In London it was very unlikely that she would hear the singularly disturbing words, "Off with her head!"

Indeed, the good people of England looked evermore lively as they came to honour her noble status and admire her voluptuous figure. Her patrician beauty brought her the proper patronage a fortnight of her arrival. Ere long she was the toast of the ton, universally admired as London's most accomplished courtesan.

It pleased her no end to have the ladies of the court looking upon her with a confusion of loathing and envy. Their husbands (oblivious or uncaring of their wives particular dislike) crowded about her, begging for her attention. Pressing their cards into her hand, they gazed upon her lasciviously whilst whispering indecent suggestions in her ear. It was uproarious fun!

She despised them all of course. Had she not, she still would have never allowed an emotional entanglement. They were superfluous and untidy.

She wanted for nothing. She kept a *tres elegante* house in Mayfair, had gowns beyond counting, and bijouterie to rival that of any mere duchess. Her celebrity was limitless. She travelled in the first circles and often dined at Carlton House. True respectability, however, escaped her. That was part of her cachet. When she was young and vaunted, that hardly mattered. Of all the many things she owned, her most prized possession had been her independence. Self-determination, however, was expensive. In time, she lost her most lucrative clients through the attrition of old age and bad health. Rarely was she remembered in their wills—an indelicacy which left her finances in shambles. The new young bucks were *déclassé*. They desired nothing but young, fresh flesh.

Much could be hidden behind a fan, but the lack of elasticity in one's gluteal furrow was uncompromising.

Indeed, time was not only a thief, it was outright cruel. Her living was her face, her figure, and her charm. With more than a nodding acquaintance with the second half of her fourth decade, only her charm defied earth's gravitational pull. When she took uncompromising appraisal, she admitted that her jaw line had begun to soften and a few crow's feet worried the corners of her eyes. Her waist was still waspish as a seventeen-year-olds'. Her bosom had begun its inevitable droop, but she could counter that through proper stays. As for her complexion, it had not yet failed her.

She did not take to the street in the daylight, but if she did, she held her chin just a little higher. In bed, she made certain she lay on her back. Granted, morning callers would find her drapes lowered. Eventually, she would see no one until half past four. Time was at hand for her to engage in an enduring association—one that assured her financial security. She did not delude herself in this regard. It was probable that she would have to settle for a man wanting in one capacity or another. Good manners, handsome bearing, and ready capital were rarely united. Of the three, wealth was the one necessity.

When she cast out her trawling net, her spirits were not particularly high.

As expected, proposals were offered from an assortment of gentlemen (some of them were even sober). As it was necessary to narrow the field to a manageable number, she pondered three of the most lucrative proposals. Each had their own merit.

One was from an elderly widower who owned an estate in Somerset, a house in town and had no relatives.

The second struck a fine figure, but he had a fondness for buggering his footmen. She did not object on moral grounds, but was loath to weather the tittering.

The third suitor was an unctuous little man of questionable ancestry. His wealth was recently acquired, but substantial. His valour during the protracted hostilities with Napoleon earned him a knighthood. In a bid not singular to him, he hoped to parlay his heroics into a seat in Parliament. A handsome wife would be an asset to him. When introduced, she found nothing notable about him save one small thing.

When he explained his particular situation, her eyes did not flutter, her throat did not flush. She betrayed absolutely no indication that his neighbours were of the smallest interest to her. Under most circumstances, she would not even think of staying anywhere but London despite the grandness of a country house. His proposal was offered with all the finesse of a plough horse. That was of no importance to her.

Their marriage was already foreordained the moment he spoke of his estate in Derbyshire and his good neighbour, Mr. Darcy, not five miles away.

In Wickham's Wake

As they lived in a festering warren of poverty, the friendship between Daisy Mulroney and Sally Frances Arbuthnot had grown stronger with each season. It had reached its apex when they, united by desire for revenge and a determination to escape the muck-crusted streets of the Dials, exacted vengeance on a certain Major George Wickham.

Yet not long after that purification rite, they parted ways. This separation was not due to any disagreement between them. If anything, satisfaction of a wrong made right gave them further commonality. They trotted off, each carrying more money than they had ever imagined. Both had their scruples, but only Sally's path was clear.

Whereas their attack on Wickham was just in everyone's eyes but the law, Sally took a hasty leave from Mrs. Younge's boarding house—and Daisy did too. His howling could be heard clear to Newton Street. It was certain to bring attention. Mr. Darcy would not want his name brought into such a conflagration whether Wickham deserved his fate four times over or not.

Wickham was the devil incarnate. That rogue had done more evil than any murderer in Newgate—Sally was sure of that.

No doubt that was why Mr. Darcy paid the man the better part of a King's ransom just to leave his family be. She and Daisy were only happy to have the chance of relieving Wickham of those funds (it was a monstrous amount of money). In truth, she did not need encouragement to shoot that bastard in the vitals. With any luck, he didn't die of blood loss. If there was a God, which she sorely doubted, Wickham would die a slow and painful death like her brother had. One thing was certain, whether dead or dying, George Wickham would never sire another offspring to abandon.

Sally never doubted that Daisy had made good her escape. She was faster than a mouse and twice as wily. With the money they took, there was no reason to return to her bawdy house. Indeed, Daisy could live in any manner she chose—and there was little chance she would remain a harlot.

Daisy was more clever by half than any other wench, but Sally Frances was not stupid. Whatever the temptation a poor girl might have to crow over her windfall, years on the street and innate good sense told them both to keep it quiet. Dyot Street was known for citizens on the game. St. Giles Breed they called them. There was no law in that parish. She had to make haste.

Once Sally Frances passed the last urchin and blood-scabbed beggar, she knew she had escaped. She kept her head down and poke stowed until she reached the edge of Chelsea. There she would be taken for a simple maid-of-all-works, or the like, on her way to her place in one the fine houses.

Only then did she allow her breath to overtake her mind. She vowed not to ponder what Daisy meant to do. Keeping ones own council on matters such as that kept a body from harm on the streets. In her heart she envisioned Daisy buying a house in West End and keeping an opera box. The thought of her friend sitting in finery enjoying Italian singers made her laugh. As for her share, Sally knew from the beginning that she would not keep it. She had taken it just to nettle Wickham. There had been no time for a plan. For all her artifice and intrigue chasing the man down, the entire event came to pass due to the perverseness of life as anything else.

No, such a bounty was not hers to keep.

It was not right to take someone else's money, especially to do that which she would have happily done for free. Such dishonesty would plague her conscience forever. Her scruples did not always agree with her wishes. Now that she had settled her brother's affairs, the thought of her poor grannum, Nell, was all-consuming. Sally did not know if the old woman was alive or dead. She concluded that she would keep a few sovereigns to take care of the old woman. No harm in that. One could say it was for services rendered.

Given her druthers, she would not have returned to Chelsea and Mrs. Kneebone's house at all. She went there only to locate Mr. Darcy. It was in the early hours and therefore little challenge to slip into the house unseen. She knew the most efficient way to collect any intelligence of the doings of the quality folk was to ask the help. In doing so she learnt quite expeditiously that Mrs. Darcy had taken leave the evening before and not returned. Undoubtedly the Darcys had not tarried in town but rather had made haste for Derbyshire.

As if a sign fell from above, she saw that her first obligation was to take care of that which was closest at hand. Nell was but a half-day's walk. If luck favoured her, she could catch a ride there on the back of a waggon.

She took just a minute to look in on baby Susanna. She was a sweet child—favoured her father no doubt. Being nursemaid to her had been a joy. Had it not been for a rancorous employer like Mrs. Kneebone, she might have been tempted to stay. Mouthing a silent goodbye to the child, she attempted a covert leave. Sheer accident also saw her meet Mrs. Kneebone on the staircase. Lydia's bowels had been nagging her else she would never have arisen at such an early hour. (Given that the servicing of chamber pots was a good part of a maid's duties, the intricacies of their employer's innards were quite obvious.)

"A-ha!" Lydia cried. "Where have you been?"

Sally looked at her with the blankness singular to a servant hiding compleat contempt. Receiving only silence, Lydia snorted and announced that Sally's absence that night would be deducted from her wages.

"I get no wages, ma'am," Sally dully reminded her.

Sally had accepted the position for its propinquity to the Darcy family, certainly not for remuneration. Lydia was not only ill-tempered to those she saw as beneath her, she was notoriously tight-fisted. She lay out no more than room and board to a nursemaid. Major Kneebone objected to such parsimony. His protestations were ineffectual. Lydia scoffed at his presumed benevolence.

"Throw them a few old dresses every year and they shall be quite happy to have them."

It was a sign of the shuddering economic times in London that a line formed to hire on for such meagre compensation.

Sally was relieved to see that Lydia was more concerned that Sally was gone rather than wither she went. Sally was undecided whether to tell the part she played in saving Lydia from Major Wickham's clutches. She decided to keep Mr. Darcy's confidences. Lydia was indiscrete. Moreover, Lydia was not the sort who cared to be saddled with gratitude. Although Lydia had been troubled, Sally believed it was unlikely that the affair had altered her character appreciably—certainly not enough to include gratitude.

As she had her employer's attention, Sally gave her notice.

"I'll not be back," she said, clomping down the stairs.

Lydia was dumb-founded (an unusual state of affairs for her, for certain).

"Well, why not?" Lydia finally asked.

Leaving her gaping, Sally was off. She had to find her grandmother before the scythe of poverty saw her carted off to Potter's Field.

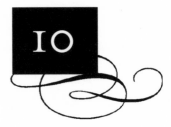

*O*ld News

Elizabeth Darcy had observed Miss Clisson on three separate occasions. Each of these encounters, while singular, were similarly disconcerting and Elizabeth had not yet taken a full and uncompromised measure of her countenance.

It was the first year of their marriage and she and Darcy had walked arm in arm along Regent Street when they chanced upon Miss Clisson. Elizabeth had caught no more than a glimpse of her patrician profile; however it remained quite clear in her recollection. The subtleties of that small exchange held dual offices. Firstly, that her husband had once known the lady. (Somewhere within her heart she realised that acquaintance had been of an intimate nature.) The second was that in exposing the long-passed connection, her husband told her that the woman in question was no threat to her.

As she stood for her seamstress, Elizabeth observed Cressida, Darcy's aged wolfhound sneaking into the room. Generally the dog was consigned to the downstairs now that she was too arthritic to take the stairs. Cressida turned in several circles until she found just the position to lie down. Elizabeth looked upon the dog with fondness, for she had been her constant companion and great comfort whilst Darcy was away on the Continent. That reminded her of when she actually met Miss Clisson.

It was the height of the hostilities with Napoleon. She was great with child and desperate for word from her husband. Although Elizabeth would have come to town regardless, she had not known that she would meet Miss Clisson that day. She had been taken aback, uncertain whether or not she was victim of a rather cruel joke. Being seen in her condition in public was an offence meriting a verbal stoning by the dutiful decorous. Sitting in that manner, in the company of a woman of ill-repute, insulted all that was holy. As she had always taken great care to conduct herself in a manner befitting her position, the lengths she went to learn of her husband's fate was testament to her alarm.

Seated on a public bench in a small park, they spoke for ten minutes full. She had but one cause—to learn if Darcy was alive or laying in some blood-soaked battlefield injured or dead. Indeed, Elizabeth had been sick with worry, desperate for intelligence, and so compleatly flustered that the particulars of Miss Clisson's complexion was not of the smallest interest.

It was only on the long journey home that her mind was sufficiently settled to contemplate Miss Clisson's connection to her husband. Only then did she truly wish that she had paid closer attention.

Although Juliette offered her a plausible explanation of it at the time, all Elizabeth's womanly instincts told her she was not to be trusted. (No lady of innocent motives would have dared allude to a past connection to one's husband, much less imply that it was not consigned to the past.) At the time, Elizabeth had not given a fiddler's fart whether they were lovers or not. She had been happy enough just to learn that he was alive.

Once he was safely home, she was no longer magnanimous in regards to that acquaintanceship.

Admittedly, her interrogation of her husband on that particular matter had been a bit disputatious. His defence, however, was exceedingly thorough. Thereby any connection he had with Miss Clisson was long over—and of no importance. It had remained forgotten (well, perhaps not forgotten, but certainly of no concern) until she happened to see Juliette on the steps of Howgrave's house on Regent Street the following year. Elizabeth might not have recognised her then had she not been standing on the broad steps in the middle of the day conversing with Darcy. As often bechanced such events, their meeting had been as fortuitous as it was innocent. The information Miss Clisson had extended had been a very present help in settling certain affairs wholly unconnected to her.

Juliette Clisson had not vexed her thoughts again. Indeed, when Elizabeth had learnt she had married, she was quite happy for her. Elizabeth's regard for the lady was only as a personage who had twice been the agent of assistance to her family. Her opinion would remain as it was until she had reason to think otherwise. As she was fitted for the gown she meant to wear to their upcoming ball, her husband's former lover did not trouble her thoughts.

Not in the least.

She would have looked at her reflection in the cheval with the same critical eye regardless of who would or would not be in attendance.

Derbyshire was a lifetime away from the heart of the ton—which was the very reason her family enjoyed abiding at Pemberley. Upon the occasion of their ball she did not care to be accused of being a dowdy country housewife. Had it not been for the visits of Caroline Bingley, she would be altogether unwitting of what was fashionable. Caroline's life was dedicated to the au courant. She was not, however, always faultlessly attired. Miss Bingley was often adorned with more ribbons than a Maypole (and upon one famous occasion an ear of Indian corn), but she kept apace of what the ladies of Paris were wearing.

With the ball a fortnight away, Elizabeth looked longingly at the lovely satin gown she had chosen. She touched the embroidery and shook her head with perturbation. It suddenly looked pale and uninspired. It was a useless business. No frock in time immortal could perform to her expectations. And even if her gown had been fit for a queen, she feared her figure would not do it justice. Pregnancy may have enhanced her bosom, but her waist was thickening far more hastily than she anticipated. She could tighten her corset only so much before it caused her to hiccup.

As the seamstress pinned a flounce to the bottom of her skirt, her thoughts turned again to the former Juliette Clisson. She recalled that although she was one of the most stunningly exotic women in three countries, Juliette was older than Darcy—by perhaps five years. The new Lady Howgrave was entering what the cognoscenti liked to call the "years of danger."

Elizabeth stopped herself from such ruminations. She was perilously close to celebrating what might be construed as another's misfortune. That was cruel. Rather, a different notion pleased her. There was a chance that the Howgraves would send their regrets. Lady Howgrave was known to be a woman of town. As Elizabeth knew well, it was far easier to be magnanimous from a distance.

Mrs. Darcy had great confidence in Mr. Darcy's fidelity. His good leg and handsome fortune, however, drew forward women like moths to a flame. Interceding on his behalf when they made pests of themselves was not her favourite occupation. Most were just innocent flirts. Lady Howgrave, however, was not a mere flirt and she most certainly was not guileless. Elizabeth did not for a moment believe that was a threat to their marriage. Regardless, the woman had employed unforgiving wiles in an attempt to make Elizabeth believe otherwise. There was no mistaking her designs.

That was why when Elizabeth learnt of Juliette's sudden marriage, one singular possibility troubled her.

Those unsuspecting of Juliette's past might have concluded that in marrying Sir Howgrave (a certified war hero), hers was a love match. Perhaps it was. As Elizabeth was not much of a believer in coincidences, she had come to another, less cheerful conclusion. Sir Howgrave's charm may not have bewitched Juliette half so much as his manor—which lay not five miles from Pemberley.

The manoeuvre might have vexed Elizabeth more had she not already known that an exchange of estates had been arranged between Howgrave and Bingley. There would be thirty miles between them, rather than five. She should not have desired such a reassurance, but she enjoyed it all the same.

"Worry," she reminded herself, "is the price one pays when borrowing trouble."

Her life was far too happy not to heed that caution. Unfortunately, it was a sad truth that when it came to arts and allurements, there is no device too paltry for some ladies to employ for captivation. Indeed, she held no fear for her husband's affections. It was just another gambit that she would prefer not to have to deflect.

For there were times when, despite all our finest defences, trouble not only comes to call, it draws up a chair.

$\mathcal{T}$he Cost of Fame

$\mathbf{S}$ir Henry Howgrave, lately of Howgrave Manor, and Miss Juliette Clisson had an understanding. He would make her rich and she would make him famous. Each kept their promise.

When a deal is made with devil, however, one can often end up sitting squat in the middle of Hell.

Upon learning the principal reason for marrying Sir Henry Howgrave had evaporated beneath her tiny feet, Juliette threw herself into a well-hidden rage. She was almost ill with regret. In time, she stopped reproving herself for that which she could not alter (snits, after all, were generally unproductive) and took an account of her situation.

Odious though the notion was, it had been imperative that she marry. Moreover, the match she had made was not without merit. Quite the contrary. Howgrave was a man of ambition. He meant to stand for the House of Commons, but confided that his ultimate aspiration was to become Prime Minister. That was not just hubris speaking. A Prime Ministership was not unfathomable. With demands for reform, the House of Lords would soon become as irrelevant as the King—or so Howgrave and his cronies claimed.

Juliette gauged Howgrave's merit as a husband much as she would have had she been allowed to vote. He was a landed gentleman, knighted for courage displayed in battle (his valorous conduct meriting him several mentions in the Gazette). He owned a hearty laugh and a commanding voice. Despite his short stature (and near torporific gait), Howgrave was, indeed, an imposing orator. He had lacked but one asset to win any election he chose—a handsome wife by his side. The common folk loved to mingle with ladies of class and culture.

As she had nothing to lose and much to gain, Juliette decided that she would forward her husband's political aspirations in any way she could. His success would be her success; the power he obtained, she would share.

Her chosen path meant pledging herself to the tedious electioneering circuit. It behoved Juliette just then to be in the public eye. For all of her life, circumstances had kept her to the shadows of society, more notorious than famous. As a courtesan, she might be seen on a gentleman's arm at the theatre or soirees. When he was to be lionized, his wife shared in his glory.

If she was to give of herself, Juliette meant to do more than adorn her husband's arm. She meant to be the jewel in the crown of his campaign. She would shine whilst Howgrave waved at the unwashed masses. With her first whiff of fame (notwithstanding the stench of those unwashed masses), she was smitten. To everyone's astonishment, she leapt into the political fray enthusiastically. Wearing velvet slippers and sporting a silk parasol, she flounced into each second-hand store on Monmouth Street, shaking hands and giving out sweets to ragamuffins. Finding that a great triumph, she increased her rounds, inciting wild melees as children fought over candy and shopkeepers and their wives vied for a chance to see Lady Howgrave's hat.

Whilst this attention was pleasing to Howgrave's backers, ladies of condition were unamused. They deemed Lady Howgrave's avid interest in her husband's campaign unseemly. (As ladies did not vote, they were largely ignored by politicos on all sides.) Others gossiped that the Howgraves' marriage was not a love match—that each was the other's prize. This was a conclusion that Juliette encouraged. She did not care to be immortalized as a doting wife. She despised wifedom and those who inhabited it. If she had to play that role, it would not be as a *faux dévot*—pious hypocrite.

Word soon spread beyond the ton that Lady Howgrave's past was a tad chequered. Scandalous talk only added to her allure, adding a multitude of followers to Howgrave's camp. This was just as well, for standing for Parliament was an expensive undertaking. While on the speech-making stump Howgrave laid out thousands of pounds for just beer. Bribery cost far more. Some of the expense he shouldered himself. (Much of it he did not, thus incurring what was euphemised as "obligations.") Lady Howgrave's charms were put to good use in persuading others to loosen their purse-strings.

Notwithstanding her vow against it, when her husband stood at the podium and spoke fervently of God and country, she gazed upon him with semi-adoring eyes. So eloquent was his oration, upon one occasion she gave herself leave to be brought to tears. (She had once contemplated a stage career, but doing so would have necessitated a reduction in circumstances and a loss of several social tiers.) By the end of each of her husband's speeches, the crowd roared with approval for them both. A touch of her handkerchief to the corner of her eye was such a success that it became an oft-repeated gesture.

Engaging in such theatrics lost much of its impact if it went without notice in newspapers. The Howgraves could not stand on their laurels. To command more newsprint, Howgrave had to fashion more grandiose promises and craft more scurrilous accusations. At some point, even he knew he was flouting libel laws. Hence, his wife concocted the *ne plus ultra* of public performances all on her own.

"I shall award each man a kiss in exchange for his vote."

"No!" commanded her husband. "You shall be called a harlot!"

"I have been called worse," she reminded him. Then with finality, she said, "I shall do it!"

His advisors were more intrigued than he, but they wanted limitations.

"Only gentlemen should be kissed, of course!"

She replied, "Gentlemen's votes will not win this election. I shall kiss whoever shall promise their vote, be they dustmen, farrier, or Yeoman of the Guard."

Thereupon, the beautiful Lady Howgrave, velvet shoes, silk parasol and all the other finery Howgrave's considerable fortune could afford, set about her mission. Keeping her pledge, she bestowed a kiss upon the cheek of each man she encountered (and their number were legion) in exchange for their promise of support. The tactic was outrageously successful. It also further scandalised society. Notwithstanding a few fisticuffs and free-for-alls in vying for her favours, she excited nothing less than boisterous approval. Hence, any indignation was handily overruled.

Breathless with appreciation, the newspapers reported not only every word Juliette said, but recounted the turn of her countenance and each twitch of her lovely brow as she spoke. Her garb was described carefully, no detail of her hat or button on her coat too trivial to relate. Some writers went so far as to chasten London's ladies of station, insisting that they follow in Lady Howgrave's well-appointed footsteps. One might have expected such impudence to be met with expressions of appalled incredulity. It was not. Ladies of the aristocracy were emboldened to copy Lady Howgrave's sleeves, gloves and shoes. Indeed, parasol wielding women began to appear at Howgrave's speeches, standing on their tiptoes just to see Lady Howgrave's latest ensemble.

Such notability was highly intoxicating. It was understandable that when Lady Howgrave's husband actually won the election it was a mite anti-climatic for her.

Sitting in her London mansion, ennui ruled Juliette's days. Not only was she bored to tears, she knew that her position as beloved wife was in grave and immediate jeopardy. To secure her situation and have continued access to Howgrave's fortune, she had to give him a child.

Juliette's fertility was a tenet of their marriage contract.

Howgrave was unforgivably crass when he inquired of her age and questioned her ability to bear a child.

She lied to him, of course, on both counts.

Howgrave's unblinking acceptance of her fabricated answers told her just how unworldly the little fig-piddler was. A man of experience would have been witting that a lady was not held to the same principles by society as that of her male counterpart. A gentleman was only as good as his word. A lady was only as good as her inventions.

She had to keep him benighted at all cost.

Although no one could say absolutely, she knew there were habitués of the demimonde who would not be loath to betray her. They would not hesitate to lie (or, God help them, tell the truth) about her age. To keep them at bay, Juliette lay out significant bribes of her own. Each well-placed coin assured her that such talk remained hushed. (And did it not, her time within the political sphere meant that she knew more than one man whose occupation included silencing those who would not do so of their own volition.)

Nonetheless, she disliked falsehoods. The truth had a way of being uncovered at the worst possible moment.

What she did know was that if she did not supply her husband with an heir forthwith, he would go elsewhere. Indeed, Howgrave's own father had procured an heir through the agency of a mistress (and not a very elevated one at that). Word had it that her husband was already visiting the beds of several other women. The thought irked her. Considering her past, the position of a wronged wife was an ironic one. Had it happened to one of the women of her circle, she might have laughed. Her predicament, however, was quite without mirth. Was she not impregnated soon, she would be cast out of Howgrave's house with no more than a fiver and fare-thee-well.

It was quite paradoxical.

She became a courtesan when was but a girl. Her very life depended upon not falling pregnant. In doing so, she had made use of pennyroyal and other ghastly substances to protect against it. Such means were not infallible. Courtesans often had children tucked away in other counties (one or two kept them in back rooms). Over the years, Juliette had managed to elude that complication. There was only one affair that tempted her to throw purgatives—and thus caution—to the side. She had dared hope that a child might come from it, but it was not to be. The gentleman came to her far too seldom. After that, she had kept to men less virile—and alluring.

Those lost years could not be retrieved and she shed no tears for them. Once again she took stock of her situation.

Although her figure was as voluptuous as ever, she knew her fertile years were in decline. Had she married more wisely, all would not be lost. Regrettably, her husband had particular sexual predilections. By virtue of this disposition, she had to resort to measures to sate him that were not conducive to conception.

It should have come to no surprise to her. Henry Howgrave was not only a bastard by birth; he was also one in practise.

*F*ictional Freddy

Sir Henry Howgrave saw himself as ripe with promise. His ambition knew no constraints. He meant to become the Prime Minister of England and would let no distraction alter that goal. Driven by the lust for power and cowed by the fear of failure, this Hero of Waterloo pursued his place in history with an astounding sense of purpose. Each day, he met with constituents, plied the wealthy citizens of his county for support, and dictated his memoirs.

Each night, he beat his wife like a cottage rug.

Juliette Clisson had been a rapturous selection as his betrothed. And, as it happened, she was a damn fine political partner. He had understood the cleverness in wagging around a beautiful wife (men inherently admire a man with a handsome woman beside him). No one would have guessed such a delicate blossom would have thrust herself unto the masses as she had. The people, of course, were delighted. When she began the kissing business, the filthy rabble was near frenzied with admiration. He liked to believe that he would have won the election soundly without her. But she certainly gained him some productive attention from the mephitic press.

As for employing the whip, Howgrave was not a compleat savage. He was not one of these ham-fisted country oafs who thrashed his wife and beat his dogs. His preference had a higher purpose. He lashed his wife's bare buttocks only as a means to satisfy his carnal urges. There was nothing wrong with the practise. It was one of kings. Why, the Prince Regent was said to be a great whip in his day.

Flagellation was hardly a method singular to him and the King. Indeed, there was an entire guild of flagellants in London. They gathered in darkened chambers and engaged in all manner of debauchery. Such voyeuristic exploits were beneath Sir Howgrave. He saw himself as a gentleman of the highest order (despite all indications to the contrary).

He had first accustomed himself to the sting of a whip between gut-hauling military engagements across the water. He had becalmed himself through the agency of an agreeable camp-follower (who accommodated him between her laundry duties). When he married, he chose his wife with his particular proclivities in mind. It would not do for him to wed some virginal maiden. The first time a strap was produced she might have run home to her mother (or besoiled herself—he had known that to bechance an unwitting chit). No indeed, he selected a woman not only for her beauty, but her sophistication. He must have a wife who would not be taken unawares by such habits—a woman of the demimonde.

Although he had selected her for her urbanity, Howgrave held out hope that she would be able to gratify his passion in the customary fashion. Initially, she did. Regrettably, the many burdens of his office (infested as it was with ungrateful rioters and cunning compatriots) had coalesced into a teeming mass of agitation, depriving him of the ability to obtain amatory consolation unless aroused in some perverse fashion. Hence, it had been necessary for Lady Howgrave to employ evermore elaborate manoeuvrings and manipulations to bring him to achievement. Only when she did not succeed in those ministrations was he forced to take the whip to her. He did not take delight in it. He was left with no other choice.

He must have a child—a son to carry on the family name (such as it was).

However, he vowed not do as his father had done. He would not take a child from some low mistress. His son would not bear the disgrace of bastardy. He would be suckled at the breast of a proper wet-nurse not consigned to the scullery with the likes of Bess Dumpstitch.

Dear Bess was his mother and a lowly maid in the service of Howgrave Manor. He was called Frederick, but was not allowed to take his father's surname. The master of the manor had a wife and, as mistress of the manor, she looked upon his bastard son with disapproval. Hence, poor Bess received no compensation for giving birth to the master's child. It was enough that she was allowed to keep her position (and was happy that she was not struck from the house due to her disgrace).

Until he was ten, Freddy slept in the same bed as his mother at night and helped in the kitchen by day. He had to sit outside upon the steps to partake his meals and was beaten for every dish he dropped. Called Fictional Freddy by the other servants, he grew up altogether baffled as to why he had to suffer the envy of others for a position that netted him absolutely nothing.

No education—letters or numbers—had been squandered upon him until the day he was sent off to school. His classmates abused him mercilessly. This came to pass as much for his lack of learning as his dirty fingernails. He received no quarter from the schoolmaster either. If given an incorrect answer, he laid the rod across every boy's knuckles. (Hence, Freddy's were perpetually swollen.) Two hours a day were dedicated in prayer and introspection. Each week, they bared their buttocks to accept a switching just on general principle.

If Freddy was not a particularly astute student, he was a magnificent learner. He hastily uncovered the most important lessons the school had to offer—and he did not have to attend a single class to learn them. By undertaking distasteful chores, befriending stupid boys with wealthy families, and falling prostrate with reverence in the presence of the most despised schoolmasters, he ingratiated himself to those who mattered. One did not have to be good; just have the appearance of it.

Upon his final year he had grown fat but not tall, yet his adiposity was no longer the target of unkind pranks. For the first time in his life, he felt approval. He arrived at school a shunned dunce and would leave a clever young man, having gained an extraordinary education in finagling, connivance, and collusion.

Just when all seemed right with his world, word came of his mother's death. Freddy did not sally forth to Howgrave Manor to watch her being tossed into the cold, dark patch of dirt set aside for the servants' graveyard. He remained at school and was believed to be bereft. He was not. His pitiable mother and the inhospitable place he had called home was nothing to him but a reminder that he was ignored by his rightful father.

After taking his degree, Freddy Dumpstitch was anxious to escape to London. There he could put his many new skills to work. His visit to Howgrave Manor was perfunctory, born of the faint hope that his success in school might earn him some sort of financial consideration. It was a fortuitous decision.

Unbeknownst to Freddy, he had been cast in a drama not of his making—but one in which he was quite happy to have a part.

As it happened, the Howgrave estate was to be entailed to the male line. Due to past misdeeds, Freddy's father had been removed from the line of succession. If a male progeny was not produced ere the eldest Howgrave died, Howgrave Manor would go to a cousin in Aberdeen. Mr. and Mrs. Howgrave would then be tossed out on their tuffet. Freddy had been sent off to school as a precautionary measure. He had been held in escrow—a spare heir—should plump (and seemingly fertile) Mrs. Howgrave not produce a legitimate one. It eventually fell apparent that her womb was as inhospitable as her heart.

Post-haste, the matter of a child born of his housekeeper was suddenly not the indignity that it had once seemed. Mrs. Howgrave still despised Freddy, but she liked her situation well enough to overlook the personification of her husband's adultery. Freddy, being the sole natural son of the Master of Howgrave Manor was suddenly in a most happy position. He owned an adoring father, a boatload of servants, and with little fanfare, an admirable new surname (Dumpstitch not being a particularly melodious appellation to adorn his future campaign signs). No longer was he the bastard child of a scullery maid. He was a gentleman.

Young Henry Howgrave was presented thusly to society.

Regrettably, to society he was still the Son of the Left Hand.

He wanted more—much more.

Refusing to be turned away, young Howgrave polished his manners and attended every party, fête, and bull-bating to which he was admitted. Having been slighted all his life, his rise was not with undue humility. (Granted, his ascent was not with any more sense of entitlement than other young bucks in the county.) He refused to be satisfied with what society deemed within his grasp. A modest country estate and marriage to the daughter of a hapless squire would not suit him.

His ambition was keen, so much so that he overstepped all sensible boundaries. Making a bid for the hand of Miss Darcy was societal (and very nearly literal) auto-da-fé. With what Freddy saw as unnecessary peremptoriness, Darcy rebuffed his overtures to Georgiana. Freddy was humiliated, causing him to believe that Miss Darcy may have fifty thousand, but she was a mouse. He sniffed derisively, vowing to find a wife worthy of his ambitions.

Deep within his breast, however, Freddy was cut, not just publicly, but to the core. His dislike of Darcy was not because of his haughtiness and station. It was for the same reason the schoolmaster administered the whippings—on general principal.

It was just as well, Henry told himself then and ever after. When opportunity struck, he took advantage of the war. It was a gamble that paid off magnificently through a knighthood and wild acclaim. When he did finally marry, he secured the most desirable woman in England.

Yes, one day the Prime Ministership would be his.

He vowed that his son would not have to bear squalid surroundings and the sniggering degradation of his lessers.

Fictional Freddy was no more.

At Your Service

Lord Humphrey Orloff was quite a man of town.

He had foul breath, inelegant habits, and a protruding tooth. He had also obtained a fortune (and an indelicate disease) whilst settling his father's affairs in the West Indies. Now a widower with a wandering eye, he enjoyed entertaining in his house in Pall Mall. It was an exquisite place, one he had inherited upon his wife's death. Despite the persistent rumours that his wife died in consequence of his faithlessness, he was still considered a man worth knowing by those who held sway over such judgements.

As a young man, Orloff was known to cut quite a swell in the iniquitous pathways of nocturnal trampers and brothel tourists. It was no surprise that when his bad blood left his doodads a tad ineffectual, he became enthralled by the backroom antics of Parliamentary politics. The Napoleonic wars had kept a tumultuous hold upon gentlemen for a decade. Those least likely to see battle were always the most eagre debaters. Forgather three men in a room and fill their glasses, they would argue over the battle strategy for days.

Orloff delighted in inviting the opinion of the working class. They had odd thoughts about taxes and levies. One must be kept abreast of common notions regardless of its absurdity. Whilst having measurements taken for a new pair of boots however, he asked his boot-maker, "Edmund, what say you of Wellington—good man or fool?"

Edmund O'Reilly kept his head down, clearly disinclined to debate him.

Orloff harrumphed and turned to a well-shod gentleman having his boots polished for an answer.

"What say you, sir? Do you believe the cabinet seat Liverpool gave Wellington will propel him on to even greater political rewards?"

The man took a breath before answering giving Orloff to understand his response was well considered.

He said, "Wellington speaks his mind untroubled by who might take offence. For a soldier, that is an admirable quality. For a politician, however, compromise is essential. It is unlikely that Wellington's sympathy for Catholic emancipation shall endear him to his other Tory cabinet ministers."

Orloff raised an eyebrow. Then he spoke to Edmund.

"Listen to this man, Edmund. He knows whereof he speaks."

The man added, "I suspect that our friend, Edmund O'Reilly had an opinion on that issue, he merely chose not to speak it."

As he worked, Edmund smiled. Orloff was too pleased with himself to notice the point the gentleman made. However, they did introduce themselves. Curious, Orloff inquired if he had special knowledge of Wellington.

Alistair R. Thomas replied, "I was Wellington's political attaché during the Napoleonic hostilities. I served my country in several campaigns and have now sold my commission to enjoy the peace at my leisure."

Orloff gasped at such fascinating information. Alistair was reluctant to speak of the specific conflicts, but loquacious Lord Orloff was bored and begged to hear more.

"Waterloo? You must tell me of Waterloo! You were there?"

Alistair nodded. Orloff, ever the raconteur, loved to learn anecdotes he could then pass on as his own. He begged Alistair to tell of battles and intrigue. Alistair reluctantly admitted to having been wounded.

Alistair insisted, "Mine was nothing but a scratch."

Just then, Alistair attempted to stand, but wobbled as he tried to put his walking stick to use. Orloff leapt to help Alistair to his feet. Alistair suppressed a groan as he stood and put his weight on one foot.

"Your country owes you a great deal!" Orloff gushed.

Alistair demurred, saying, "I am but a slave for my country, happy to have given what I have for its honour."

"I stand in awe," said Orloff.

Only admitting to being a middling officer before Waterloo, Alistair did say he came out of that engagement with a chest full of medals. Although Orloff was much in want of seeing them, Alistair declined.

"Put away," he insisted. "Like my uniform, I shall not look upon them again."

Such impeccable credentials meant Alistair was welcome into the best company and the finest clubs. Ladies were always in want of a charming gentleman to make a fourth at cards and fill out their table at suppers. His white hair and well-tanned countenance made Alistair a most distinguished-looking man. As it happened, Orloff knew how to fill a table. Twenty ladies and gentlemen joined him that evening. Some of them were witty; all of them were rich.

Orloff announced, "I must have you come round tonight."

Alistair's suspiration was deep, but he seemed agreeable, "Although my Brothers of the Blade have my compleat devotion, I must admit I am much in want of other society."

Orloff pressed his card into Alistair's hand.

"Do come round. There will be gentlemen there who would be much in want of hearing what you have to say."

Although he did not promise, Orloff was pleased when Alistair appeared at his door. His coming was a great coup. Orloff liked to sprinkle his soirées with gentlemen of different stripes. A self-deprecating gentleman with a noble countenance and decent wit was difficult to find. As they talked, Orloff learnt that he was correct about Mr. Thomas. His greatest assets lay beyond the card table. They shared an eagre interest and keen understanding of the political climate.

When the gentlemen retired from the ladies and their interminable rounds of Whist, they escaped to Orloff's handsomely appointed smoking-room for cigars, serious drinking, and brash talk. Affairs of the state were the preferred topic. Orloff was backing a coming man for Parliament and was in active pursuit of good heads to join him. To gain everyone's attention, he was not above agitation.

He announced, "The rioters taken to streets after the Westminster elections were equal to what was seen in Paris."

As no one else had a comment, Alistair replied, "It was said had they been well armed and well-drilled, the mobs might have done real damage."

His remark was greeted by a scattering of laughter, no one quite certain if he spoke in jest.

Now that a common enemy was left to die old and alone at St. Helena, another ogre had to take his place. The emerging Labour movement gave the defenders of the probity good reason to panic. Any call for change in the existing order was viewed as a wedge opening the door for a French-like atrocity. Any alteration in social rectitude was tantamount to erecting a guillotine in Hyde Park.

If the French had taught them anything at all, it was that change—of any sort—was to be fought at all costs.

Therefore every gentleman hushed when another man reported, "Lady Hatton had forty windows smashed by a collection of rock-wielding children. My wife says we must board up our house at Brighton lest it be torn to bits."

Alistair spoke again, soothing, "Tell your dear wife that Dragoons have been stationed in every town from Coventry to Bristol. I am certain we are all safe"

Despite alleging a great distaste for politics, Alistair had an eagre opinion on each point—including Wellington. He stood solidly behind him.

He explained, "I owe the man a great deal. Had he not learnt that I attended Eton, my epaulettes would have been scorched off my shoulders in the Peninsular War." He furthered his point by saying, "A classical education is a necessity for all officers."

There were murmuring nods of approval from all. Lord Orloff, however, saw Wellington as remiss.

"Why have you not been given a knighthood, sir? They have handed them out like flower petals to men of far less standing. I shall speak to Wellington on your behalf."

As everyone knew, Wellington's success in Spain won him many honours and, more importantly, large estates and cash awards. He was the man of the hour.

Alistair insisted, "I fear that in the peninsular conflict I was merely a scribe of Wellington's greatest achievements, not the author. Indeed, with the resumption of hostilities I spent more time interpreting his missives to Blücher than upon the field of battle."

"Still..." said Orloff.

"If you please," insisted Alistair. "I beg you do not speak upon my behalf."

Orloff was keenly pleased. Alistair was well-educated, well-spoken, and well-dressed—a gentleman of the first order. He did not give up Alistair's part when it came to Wellington either.

"The Duke was fortunate at Waterloo," Orloff insisted. "The French cavalry showed up quite well during that great battle."

"Yes, and they went down very well too," rebutted Alistair.

The laughter was infectious. It was only natural that when Sir Henry Howgrave arrived, he was immediately introduced to Alistair Thomas. They were each given a brief history of the other and understood instinctively that they were similar animals.

Howgrave asked Alistair, "Did you happen to attend Wellington's welcoming festivities after his triumphant return from France? I do not recall seeing you there."

"I saw it only in passing," Alistair replied.

Howgrave was aghast (or seemingly so), "I am astonished that the duke forgets his loyalties with such haste."

"With cashiered soldiers filling the streets with their disgruntlement, the Duke has far greater concerns than one poor gentleman," said Alistair.

With a sly, sideward look, Howgrave bid Alistair, "Come with us tonight, Thomas. After Almack's closes, we like to finish the evening in the East End with good, plebeian company—low men and loose women."

A smattering of snickers were heard at his remark.

Alistair R. Thomas was quite conscious of the young blood's penchant for rubbing elbows with the motley lowborn on Nightingale Lane. He also knew that Howgrave was born of a left-handed union and his wife was once a courtesan. A voucher to Almack's was a dearly held commodity and the ladies who extended them thought far too highly of themselves to sell their company that cheaply. One could be assured that Sir Henry Howgrave was not invited to Almack's. Yet, he implied he was. If Alistair's nose sniffed the winds of speculation, it went unremarked.

With real or feigned reluctance, he begged off from that night's carousing.

"Then tomorrow morning, do to take a turn with us around Rotten Row," urged Howgrave. "You must join us Mr. Thomas. We solve all of England's many problems as we take the Serpentine."

Alistair declined this offer as well, but explained his refusal.

"Although I once took a rail quite handily, I fear that since I took my wound I no longer look to advantage in the saddle."

Howgrave said, "We shall enjoy watching those who do through the auspices of my landau. This, I insist."

Alistair bowed in acceptance to the invitation.

It was in the landau that next day that Howgrave bid Mr. Thomas to oblige him by joining his campaign. With gracious good humour, Alistair again demurred, saying that there were far better qualified men than he. It took a great deal of arm-twisting to convince him to accept the proposal. Orloff was quite pleased to have obtained him.

Alistair's own ambition had been temporarily satisfied to sit in a shared carriage around the Serpentine. It was apparent that Howgrave hoped to trade on his connection to Wellington. He was not offended. Any man of good sense knew inherently that one must use all one's strengths.

When Howgrave once again invited Alistair to join him upon his nightly prowls, Alistair agreed. It would not do to appear too depraved or too priggish. They spent most of their evening at Vauxhall Gardens and finished that night at White's. Engrossed in conversation, they took no note of the servitors therein.

Discharged from Pemberley without a letter of recommendation, Cyril Smeads stood behind the bar polishing glasses. Through previous connections, he had found a suitable position at the well-known watering hole for the aristocratic drinkers and their failed sons. It was a situation that many might have believed as beneath them. Truth be known, it was an office over which prospective agents fought tooth and nail. The wages were poor, but a man with a sharp mind, discrete tongue, and a total want of character could earn a substantial stipend.

For Smeads, procuring female companionship for members of the esteemed class took only the smallest adjustment to his already compromised ethics. He should have paid far greater attention to the patrons within his purlieu. There were those who would have paid him handsomely for the information.

The Breeching

The hours before their guests began to arrive for the ball were full of bustling activity and, especially for Pemberley's mistress, rife with angst.

Although the household was as well-prepared as any seasoned military battalion, Elizabeth was a bit out of sorts. They had not entertained so vast a number of guests for longer than she could recall. Fortunately, Mr. Howard was a master at dousing last minute fires of all sorts. One round through the ballroom and dining hall soothed her nerves. The frills and folderol were well in hand. Fresh flowers were in place and the floors gleamed as if glass. A pyramid of grapes, nectarines and peaches were excellently presented and the partridges were ready for roasting.

Whatever the gossips might have been whispering apropos the doings of certain members of their family, when they wanted to, the Darcys knew how to present a united front.

The only thing not quite ready for scrutiny was Mrs. Darcy herself.

In not yet ten years of marriage, they had held many galas, soirees, and parties. Such was their position in the county, it was their duty to host all manner of events, be it religious observations or harvest fests. As Mistress of Pemberley, Mrs. Darcy saw them not only a duty, but an honour. Although her husband was not, she was sociable by nature. Upon such occasions, it was she who clasped his arm to quiet his discomfort. Their upcoming ball, however, burdened her nerves. She felt unbecoming and lacked her usual self-possession. This state of disorder was of her own making. After all, it had been her husband's wish that the ball be delayed.

Feeling bloated and tired, she wished that she had allowed him have his way.

Whilst sitting at her dressing table, she could feel the bulge in her belly. She stood and turned sideways for glance in her cheval mirror. What she observed was not promising. It had been necessary for the seamstress to let her gown out another inch. Had she not, The Mistress of Pemberley might have looked as if she was lately stuffed into a sausage casing. Just returned from a last minute pressing, her gown hung on a hook next to the window. Elizabeth prayed it still fit.

She slumped to her stool and looked glumly at her reflection. Wearing nothing but her chemise, she felt quite vulnerable. Hannah twitted about arranging her hair, but that made her even more fretful. Looking at the clock with apprehension, she knew she must prepare herself. It was a ridiculous vanity to be in low spirits. She attributed it to womanly melancholia. She was the owner of far too many blessings to be anything less than compleatly content.

Her thoughts were overtaken by what she observed in the corner of her looking-glass. She saw Hannah duck her head deferentially and withdraw. Elizabeth's eyes followed her maid quizzically as she scurried through the door. Only then did she spy what sent the maid on her way.

It was Mr. Darcy.

He was still in his shirtsleeves and wearing knee breeches. It was a rare occasion for him to be seen without his coat when others were about. If he appeared thusly, he was in want his wife—and all that implied. It was not Hannah's to question. It was Hannah's to beat a hasty retreat.

Once the maid was gone, her husband's frame filled the doorway. Beyond him, Elizabeth could hear doors opening and closing as servants scuttered from one dressing room to another with pressing cloths and hairpins. The house was full of guests and their many wants taxed maids and the corridors. Instinctively, she held a handkerchief to her bosom lest she be espied in déshabillé by other than family.

That was unlikely. Darcy broad shoulders blocked anyone's observation of her person. Still, one would expect him to close the door forthwith. Rather, he remained still as a statue, making no move to come into the room. It was as if, perchance, he awaited her to bid him enter. He stood with one elbow resting on the doorjamb, the other hand at his side. He drew the back of his fingers to his lips and as did, his chin lowered. His gaze was penetrating—enough to make her drop her hand mirror. Had he been a bull in a field, she would have fled. Because that inclination struck her so strongly, she stood. As she did, she did not notice that her handkerchief fell to the floor.

Had she mentally furthered her metaphor in regards to her husband and the bull, her reason would not have returned with any greater haste. There was certainly no ambiguity in this gaze. His expression was copulatory. Her hand fled to her bosom as if to quiet the pounding in her heart. As she did not speak, he did—and his eloquence on the matter before them was unparalleled.

"*Lizzy*," he said.

Her riposte was simply, "Eh?"

Had she the composure to rally and offer another, finer éclat, it was lost in the moments that followed.

He kicked the door closed. It was a full ten foot from thence to where she stood. He crossed them in no more than two steps. As she stepped backward, she was stopped by the edge of her dressing table. It mattered not, for he had overtaken her.

Before his fingers touched her, she anticipated him. Closing her eyes, a blissful foretaste of the pleasures he would bring to her body made her sigh.

But he did not caress her.

Rather, he did something just as familiar and, if possible, more esteemed.

Taking her face in his hands, he whispered, "My lovely Elizabeth,"

In that she had felt quite unlovely not minutes before, these simple words repaired her. She gave herself leave to enjoy his sentiment, basking in his devotion so compleatly that when his hand crept beneath the hem of her chemise, she was expecting it, desiring it, but not witting of it. His fingers often prowled the soft flesh of her thigh just above her stockings. It was a region particularly vulnerable to his touch. His encroachment stopped quite abruptly.

She opened her eyes.

His eyes were looking directly in hers and his expression was not... salutatory.

"Pray, good wife," he queried carefully, "What is that?"

It took a moment for her head (and other portions of her person) to be free of all manifestations of passion before she could answer that which he—most probably—knew. His finger hooked the edge of a two-legged garment worn by women of fashion.

They were all the rage on the Continent.

They were not at all common.

The most elegant ladies in London wore them, even Princess Charlotte (which she knew, truly, did not excuse them). The ladies of fashion made a show of flashing them when they stepped into their respective carriages.

They were made of lawn and some bedecked with the finest Belgian lace available.

It was said if they are to be worn at all, they are to be handsome.

She did so not want to be out of fashion....

Mrs. Darcy had silently practised every argument in favour of lady-breeches for some time. With her husband's unflinching inquiry, those good reasons and explanations fled from her consciousness. When she spoke, she endeavoured to speak with authority. Her voice, however, suddenly turned on her and all she could do was squeak.

"They are all the fashion."

His retort was short and to the point.

He said, "I do not like them."

That was no great surprise. Mr. Darcy did not care to follow fashion. At least he did not admit to it. As she gathered her thoughts for a rebuttal, she considered whether to point out that the buff waistcoat that was a favourite the year passed had been cast from his wardrobe. Moreover, he no longer wore knee-breeches except upon formal occasions. Had she wanted to win the day, she could have reminded him of either of those facts. However, she thought better of it.

"Pray, how do they offend, sir?" she asked mildly.

The answer to that was most probably that they were on his wife and not another. Lest either forget, his hand encircled her calf; his finger, loosed from the offending garment, stroked her just below the back of her knee. Whilst engaging in this most pleasing activity, he gave her a plausible, if entirely erroneous, reply.

"The garment is immodest and worn only by women of easy virtue."

She dared to laugh, saying, "They are said to be au courant for years in Paris...."

With that, his indignation knew no bounds. Indeed, he took his hand from her leg and turned his back to her. She placed the flat of her hand just below his shoulder blades. The one thing she did not care for was to engage in a disagreement over something so trivial. She would have thought he would have been amused—even impassioned. In a moment, he turned towards her again. His brows were knitted and his mouth was grim.

"So this is just another coruscation from the dashers of the haut ton? How is it that every time some abomination is instituted, it is always said that the French have been doing it for years?"

She sniffed, "I am sure I do not take your meaning, sir. However, I recall a time some years ago when so meagre an impediment would not have deterred you in the smallest way."

He retorted, "I dare say that it does not upon this occasion either—was I so disposed."

She raised her eyebrow—a blatant invitation. Accepting the provocation, he reached for her ankle and she made a small game of trying to keep him at bay. As she wriggled away, the tabletop rattled and a bottle of perfume was in danger of tipping over. Their skirmish was just that. Brief, but impassioned.

Clasping her fingers on the back of his neck, she said, "I am not inflexible upon this subject. Given the proper argument I am quite certain that I can be swayed."

Having corralled her ankles, his hands began to search upward. It was a difficult expedition as are most into unknown territories heretofore uncharted. The expression upon her countenance was flirtatious, bequeathing him with the understanding that, in this quest at least, he was on his own. It was her prerogative to know how she got them on and therefore up to him on to how to remove them. Ere exasperation set in, he found the end of a ribbon.

"Hark, the bell-cord," said he.

When he grasped it, she smiled, ready to explain how the garment met the needs of nature. Ere she could, a look of triumph overspread his countenance. But it only lasted a trice. With great haste another expression replaced it. This one was not foreign to her whatsoever. It had been several winters, however, since it had last been seen. It was at once seductive and impish.

He did not tug the ribbon. Indeed, he let go of the ribbon altogether. When he grasped the legs of her newly acquired drawers, she was a bit surprised, but not unduly so. Her husband was but making his preference known. This predilection, along with his unfettered desire, was set forth with undeniable vehemence. (And the predilection, the desire, and the vehemence, were accompanied by the very willing instrument wherewith he meant to employ all three.) The fine, thin fabric of her fashionable new drawers was easily conquered by he who desired most vociferously to conquer them. With one quick, almost fierce tug, they rent.

Alas, her lawn delicacies were shredded by his passion; her passion, their passion together.

Her thighs were then engirthed in soft gauze leggings as they engirthed him. Breathless, she felt her body sink as if melting, her trembling calves useless in want. Fluttering from her heart to her lips came forth the words of that affirmation.

"Yes. Yes. Yes, oh, yes! To be *sure!*"

Conspirators and Concubines

"Please—not my *face!*"

To cry out was a severe humiliation.

Not once in her life had she ever begged. Indeed, Juliette had refused to plead for her life whilst pitching about in the tumbrel as it lumbered towards the guillotine. Therefore, when she was finally driven to throw herself upon the mercy of a mere man, it was not a passing event.

Her face was her fortune. Was her husband to despoil her delicate visage, the loss would be ghastly for them both. Howgrave knew that. In the throes of sadistic heat, it ill-behoved him not to take heed of her caution. To her great relief, her cries did reach him. When he came to his senses, she turned her head, determined to hide her disgust and abhorrence of both him and her capitulation.

"Bourgeois fool," she hissed behind his back.

Having spent more than half her life being pursued by men of all nationalities, Juliette had come to question the average Englishmen's voluptuous habits. (If those sons of aristocracy slouching about the clubs of the West End were utterly gauche in the nuances of pleasure, those born in the provinces were absolute louts.) Not unlike many men of his ilk, her husband was not schooled in the art of love. He had hopped on top of chambermaids and widows at will, confusing quantity with proficiency. Therefore, his ego was easily offended. If he happened to fail in the furrow, he cried like schoolgirl. She had to coax him to continue by employing evermore imaginative means.

Her gamesmanship in the boudoir was excellent. In her life as a courtesan, Juliette had engaged in all manner of services (wielding a variety of props). Thus, she was able to arouse her husband to heights previously unknown to him. It was unsurprising that he (like many before him) became quite devoted to her.

Bliss had an unhappy knack for abandoning those who come to expect it.

However eagre he was for her to keep his wick well-lit, his manhood began to fail him once again. Thus, she doubled her efforts, engaging two candlesticks, a pair of tongs, and a pretty Rambouillet ewe. But even those persuaders did not keep him satisfied for long.

She did not recall which of them introduced the notion of the lash.

When sheep and dildos did not bring him to achievement, she recognised that the time was at hand to whip his buttocks. It was a remarkably effective tool. Employing it, however, was a delicate business. When applying a cat-o-nine or the likes, one had to strike only the buttocks. If care was not taken, a scar would result. It was all in the wrist. Juliette was a veritable virtuoso with the switch, the lash, the rod. With the merest flick, her tiny hand had Howgrave howling like a she-wolf or shivering like a just-plucked pullet. Indeed, he took the instrument with more enthusiasm than a vestal maiden. (Had she been in want of her own desires enflamed, the sight of his pink, steatopygian bottom was not an encouragement.) As time passed, she had to ratchet the pawl ever more tightly.

Eventually, whatever her method, laying the strap to him was not enough to bring him to orgasm. To her great unhappiness, he desired to inflict pain—upon her. (She had proposed that they hire a surrogate, but he would have no one but his wife—Juliette saw that as quite touchingly pathetic.) Hence, a train of intolerable degradations encompassed her evenings—made even more so by the unhappy fact that he had no idea how to wield such an instrument. Understanding that her screams requited his passion, she employed her well-honed skills of pretence, elevating and sustaining her cries to maximum effect.

When her screams did not avail his pleasure, he expressed his disappointment with a braided whip—and a backhand across her cheek. Together, the two brought him to a spectacular orgasm. He fell to his knees, lowing like a cow.

The next morning her head pounded with the weight of a thousand disappointments.

She avoided her looking-glass, knowing that she would see a new test for her talent with cosmetics. It was crucial that she cover the contusions. Touching her cheek gingerly, she winced. At one time her looking-glass had been her dearest friend. Now it had become an ever-encroaching enemy. She ceased to gauge her general decline and merely looked at herself to see what repairs had to be made. After her subtle application of powder, her bruises were barely detectable. She sighed with relief. Even her severest critics would not have deduced her true age—or the extent of her husband's blundering brutality.

She set to fluffing her curls over her forehead and around her magnificent cheekbones. In the months that she had been arranging her hair in what was essentially a contrived fashion; other ladies of the ton began to copy it. What a laugh. She twisted another curl about her forefinger and placed it just so. Her greatest prayer was that her dunce of a husband would not accidentally blacken her eye. Even her talent could not disguise that.

Satisfied that she had done all she could; her hands fell helplessly to her lap. With Howgrave's seat secured, seeing to hers was an ever-pressing concern. Unfortunately, the sands of time were flowing faster than her erratic menses. Without thinking, she caressed her abdomen. It felt youthful, plump, and fertile. She sighed.

Her husband had begged her forgiveness, presenting her an enormous floral apology. She had accepted it, for she could not afford to turn him away. She must conceive. That left her on the prongs of a nasty dilemma. Upon those occasions when she could bring him to achievement, more and more frequently he cast his seed across her blistered buttocks and not inside the increasingly-arid terrain of her womanhood. She had been reduced to the most demeaning measures to overcome this particular obstacle, but to no avail.

A child was imperative. Without one, she would be cast aside, penniless and alone.

As it became evermore unlikely that Howgrave would do the job, she saw only one way out. She must take a lover with more customary inclinations. To that ends she began to fill her idle hours by enumerating likely candidates and imagining intrigues. From the comfort of her chaise lounge, she took stock of her footmen. They were a fit lot, but far too lowborn to further the thought. As Howgrave was bent on begetting a true heir, she dared not dally with the men of their London circle either. Should word get back to him, no doubt he would exact the ultimate revenge upon her. He was no more disposed to be cuckolded as the next husband—unless the interloper was of a royal strain.

That was the only officially sanctioned liaison. A duke would not do, the gentleman in question would have to be in line for the throne. She investigated the Carleton House set for possible lovers, but was disappointed. The Prince Regent was more interested in his dinner plate than her charms. Copulating with the corpulent monarch was uninviting (so much so that it took the sting out of any rejection she might have otherwise felt).

Her search led her to the young man assigned to ghost-write Howgrave's memoirs. He was a handsome boy. He had an aquiline nose and aristocratic accent, but he was easily excitable. Ere she could compleat his seduction, he lathered the front of his trousers. The phenomenon was not unknown to her. If one was too young, he went off in the bush. If too old, he could not maintain the saddle.

Meeting with repeated defeat, the manoeuvring incumbent of such an enterprise looked to be increasingly tiresome. Moreover, she dreaded the ordeal of submitting herself unto another sweating male body. Any spark of passion she still harboured had been all but extinguished by her husband's weaknesses. This frustration ultimately led her down the familiar road of decadence. More than once she fell to prowling gambling dens and low theatres (accompanied with men-friends who enjoyed the all arts save that of admiring the female sex).

To have no occupation but to look handsome led to morosity. Her gambling debts began to mount, but her husband covered them, boasting that he had the means to do so. She was never seen without a glass of wine in her hand. Knowing full well that a woman of her age should not partake of wine in abundance, she still welcomed that escape. She did not stop even when she began to trip. She did not curtail her drinking until her husband removed a glass from her hand, reminding her that she must not pollute the vessel with which he would attain his son.

She nodded complacently. Guarding her womb was a perfectly good excuse to sleep half the day (and she did so by way of successive doses of laudanum). When she arose and the weather permitted, she fled to the air of Kensington Gardens. Anything was superior to overseeing the tedious drawings for the renovations to Kirkland Hall. Her husband insisted that they finally take possession of the place. As it was not a mere five miles away from Pemberley, but thirty, she had lost her enthusiasm for the project. Still, Howgrave insisted they tarry in Derbyshire whilst he trolled the surrounding towns for political support.

Having taken to her bed for a fortnight upon learning that her husband had traded estates with Charles Bingley, she despised being reminded of it. As Howgrave had understood that his wife did not enjoy country pursuits, her reluctance seemed quite reasonable.

She eventually acquiesced to a visit to Howgrave Manor, lying, "I look forward to seeing your ancestral home."

"It is hardly that," he said. "My grandfather took it in a game of cards."

The moment passed without further comment. (He was happy to be untroubled and she was happy for him to remain unwitting of her dashed designs.) Howgrave had always spoken of Darcy with derision. She was convinced that his hatred for Darcy was both personal and longstanding. Therefore, it was wholly unconnected to her. That was to be expected. Her husband had been far too busy attempting entrance into the first circles to know what went on within them. Few women dared flaunt past lovers in their husband's face. Juliette kept her own council about hers as well.

Her *affaire* with young Mr. Darcy was, at his request, one of the utmost privacy. One might have called it clandestine. Those few people witting of it did not know that to Juliette, theirs was more than just an *arrangement*. Darcy was more than a handsome man of good leg and handsome equipment—he was one that she had never quite given up.

When the winds shifted in Juliette's quest for an estimable lover, they swung about gently.

Upon the reintroduction of Mr. Darcy's name into their conversation in regards to their Derbyshire estate, her expression did not alter. Sipping a cup of tea, she noted demurely that, for political considerations, it would be a shrewd move for him to have a man of Mr. Darcy's influence in his camp. Indeed, once the seed was planted, the notion of it had Howgrave all but salivating to secure the man. Howgrave saw the invitation to the ball at Pemberley as fortuitous.

Juliette did as well.

16

A Ball for the Bingleys

The Howgraves arrived at the Pemberley ball just late enough to serve fashion.

When they gained the room, guests parted before them as if by Moses' hand. It was a momentous appearance. Fresh from London, Howgrave was the man of the hour—at least in Derbyshire. Those gentle-people, who had cut him cold in his youth, now squabbled to have his ear. The last whiff of Freddy Dumbstitch's shameful stench had been expunged. He took the room with a swagger worthy a West End fop.

His wife tugged at his sleeve, whispering, "For God's sake remember yourself."

That was enough to bring him to his senses and his airs hastily evaporated. Still, he only perfunctorily presented himself and his wife to his host. Mrs. Darcy was in an animated conversation with an ageing dowager with mulish teeth and freckled arms. Mr. Darcy stood firmly at her side, but spoke little. As Howgrave took his hand and began to pump it, Juliette looked away.

As well-rehearsed as Lady Howgrave was in all regards, one would have expected that her lowered eyes were meant to serve some higher design. As it happened, it did not. She did not look at him because she was unprepared to brazen out that particular encounter. Like her husband, she needed time to collect herself. She left Darcy with no clear vision of him, but with an exceedingly strong desire to secure one.

The Howgraves could not tarry in the receiving line, and Howgrave begged away.

At any gathering, the moneyed class was always much in want of reassurance that their wealth was not endangered. Upon this or any subject, Howgrave was happy to hold forth—thereby cornering possible campaign contributors whilst doing so. This prototypically was a two-part procedure. First he would explain that their fortunes were in dire straits; and second, he would convince them that only his re-election stood between them and all out ruin.

With great dispatch, Howgrave divested himself of his wife, eschewing her company for that of a contingent of local squires. Being abandoned was

neither a surprise nor a disappointment to her. Social functions were for
being seen, not to be entertained. And seen she was. As was expected, word of
her arrival undulated through the crowd as if a small quake. Every pearl in her
hair, every thread of her gown was inspected and remarked upon to another.
She was quite satisfied that in reference to her handsome aspect, there was
nothing that anyone—man nor woman—could find wanting. For a moment,
she was blissfully happy. But then knowing oneself to be perfectly turned out
was a consolation seldom found—even in prayer.

Renewed purpose engulfed her as she looked about the ballroom. It was
the peak of the evening and a crowd still congregated near the door. She could
see Darcy's head as he towered over everyone else. It took her only a moment
before she was certain she caught his eye. She hastily looked away. It was
enough that he had seen her.

The Bingleys, of course, were midmost in the room. She would allow them
to find her.

Juliette was unacquainted with the northern counties. She had gone twice
to Bath and once to Brighton. (She once spent a fortnight at a forbidding estate
in Hampshire—it was so dank that it put her off of the country altogether.) The
northern ladies were as she expected. Openly envious, few of them dared to
converse with her. That was no great loss. Juliette disliked making pleasantries
with fat-necked women of little breeding and no taste. They spoke of nothing
but incorrigible cooks and dull parables. To her, conversation should be like a
very graceful edition of a society newspaper—anointed with a large dollop of
malice.

The silence was excruciating to those poor ladies who awaited her ladyship
to deign a remark. At last, one lady (wearing a serpentine bracelet and abused
expression) asked another about a mutual acquaintance, saying, "I dislike
spreading rumours, but...."

"What else is one to do with them?" interrupted Lady Howgrave.

Before the tittering died down, Juliette lifted her skirts just above her
ankles and made her away. The ladies were left in fluttering admiration,
thrilled beyond words to have been privy to one of her ladyship's outrageous
witticisms.

Happy to escape, Juliette took a glass of (rather good) champagne and
allowed herself a more detailed observation of the house. She had never set
her pretty foot in either of Darcy's homes. (When they were... acquaintances,
he had always come to her.)

It had not been difficult to convince herself that propitious fate had
rekindled their affair. Despite being thrown in Darcy's path, she had conceded
that due to the throng of guests, a private chat was unlikely. Hence she saw
herself on an investigatory excursion. She did not care to admit to curiosity.
A woman of her sophistication should be above such banality. However, she
was curious—*exceedingly* curious. Had she been a cat, her tail would have

twitched with anticipation.

Other than their brief encounter across the channel, she had never known Darcy in any milieu save her house in Mayfair. They did not dine out nor attend the theatre. No one saw them together save a smattering of servants. He never stayed the night. At the time it had been a distinct vexation that she could not be seen on his arm. (Indeed, that vexed her yet.) Although he had never invited her there, she had observed his Park Lane house from the street. It was a handsome home, but not above others.

Pemberley, however, was of great repute. A number of sources had described it as quite *élégant*. With one expert glance about at the painted ceiling and alabaster doorcases, she saw that it had not been over-praised. The house was testimony to what good taste, centuries of attention, and a substantial fortune could achieve. It was certainly not Versailles, but it bettered the battered Kirkland Hall twenty-fold. She could see how Darcy influenced and, in turn, was shaped by such a home. Seeing Pemberley made her believe she knew him better.

Her good opinion did not pass as an expression on her countenance. It had long been her practise to claim compleat impassiveness as such aloofness piqued the interest of admirers and allowed her forehead to remain unvexed by loathsome creases. As time marched on, she was even more mindful of such seeming trivialities.

Observing Pemberley's august halls pricked another vanity.

She was given renewed incentive to restore Kirkland Hall. Its parquet floors and rosewood wainscoting had been beaten to its knees by the Bingleys' ungovernable offspring. Fortunately, the damage looked to be mostly to the paint and finishes. (Mr. Bingley or his minions paid good heed of the roof.) If she were to inhabit such a wreck, it would take a half-year and a hundred men to refurbish it. She would not settle for anything less than the magnificence surrounding her then.

Juliette had taken a visit with Mrs. Bingley at Kirkland Hall just days before, ostensibly about their removal. In truth, Juliette wanted the opportunity to sketch her character without the intrusion of others. Their conversation had been most enlightening. Jane was nothing like her sister, either in looks or manner. She was soft-spoken and graceful, emanating an inner beauty equal to her countenance.

It had been a test not to inquire after the Darcys. But then, that was not necessary. Jane warbled on over the felicity of the Darcy household with an easiness that meant she was both a most genuine lady and that she was entirely unaware of Juliette's connection to them.

Jane's opinion notwithstanding, the likelihood that the Darcys' marriage still flowered with any portion of its original passion was remote. It had been a compleat astonishment to her that Darcy had formed such an unlikely alliance in the first place. Miss Elizabeth Bennet was decidedly below his class. At the time Juliette saw it as a sort of insanity—one of such violence that she had no power to divert him. Never in her life had she had such little influence over a man. It confounded her then and for some time thereafter.

For years after she travelled the Continent, often spending winters in an Italian Palazzo. When the Napoleonic wars intruded, she and an entourage quit the place to make their way back to England. Consequently, it had been beyond astonishing when she chanced upon Darcy one evening in a chateau near Lille. It had been at the trembling culmination of the war, therefore the last person she expected to see there was an impeccably-dressed and haughtily-composed son of the English aristocracy. In a bat of an eyelash, all her feelings and wants had been excited once again. Unfortunately, he had been in the middle of a single-minded pursuit. (It was a reprise of the behaviour that had so bewildered her the night he had ended their affair.) In Lille, he had been quite alone and altogether distracted. The desire to reach out to him—to becalm his brow, arouse his spirit, enjoy his touch was almost too much to bear. To her great chagrin, she found that she still had no rule over him. He spoke only of his wife and his need to contact her. In the end she agreed to carry a missive, full of dear words, no doubt, to his wife.

The letter was destroyed.

When she returned to London, an odd whim overtook her. She decided to meet with the woman who had stolen Darcy's heart. Simply by professing to be in possession of a letter from Darcy, she commanded Elizabeth Darcy to hie to town to meet her. *Tres enciente*, Mrs. Darcy had not hesitated to come, leaving Juliette almost chastened to have enticed her on what could have been accused of being a pretence. After their talk, Juliette harboured a certain admiration for her. No other gentlewoman would have gone to such lengths merely to hear word from their husband. (Therefore, there were few gentlewomen who had Juliette's good opinion.) Theirs had been an unusual encounter, leaving Juliette with an odd sense of need. For a while she became the self-ordained champion of the Darcys' union. It was an odd caprice, nothing more. Her life's work had been to avoid encumbrances such as friendship and affection—especially when one's own interests were at stake.

Time, it is said, makes more converts than reason. And in time, another conviction comforted her. It was the unassailable truth that time was any marriage's most insidious enemy. To maintain steady ardour for so long would have been unthinkable. To sustain passion, one must create unease, cause jealousy, cast spells. No doubt the Darcys' wedded bliss would be on the wane. Nothing Mrs. Bingley said altered that conviction.

It was that thought that fed her eagerness to attend the Pemberley ball.

As guests moved to and fro, she could see Darcy more clearly. Time had not altered his bearing or his countenance. As if entranced, she stepped in his direction. Then, abruptly, she turned away, wholly thwarted.

For standing next to Mr. Darcy was Mrs. Darcy, her arm clasping his.

Juliette did not fault her for that. Had he belonged to her, she would be just as chary. Although marauding ladies were circling him even then, his wife seemed oblivious to her competition.

Whilst taking delicate sips of her wine, Juliette took a moment to scrutinise Elizabeth Darcy. Albeit begrudgingly, she admitted that Elizabeth had gained in countenance. That afternoon in London, her face had been drawn and worry troubled her expression. Tonight, her cheeks were flushed. (Either that or she was not above applying a bit of rouge.) A bit smugly, Juliette opined that Elizabeth was not near the beauty as her sister, Jane. Fancy that. Mr. Darcy not only married beneath him, it was to a second, less desirable daughter.

Slyly, she looked at Elizabeth again.

Through further study, Juliette decided that she approved of Elizabeth's gown. Although it was pale, it complimented her, almost as much as the exquisite necklace. It was a significant enough piece to arrest everyone's attention. Juliette did not envy it, for she had been bestowed exceptional pieces of jewellery over the years. She wore them only to impress other women. When gentlemen were about, she disliked adorning herself with anything that might compete with her own countenance.

As the Darcys stood side by side, oblivious to any menace, Juliette carried on planning a seduction with an air of purposefulness. She told herself that her quarry was merely that—a means to an end. It did not cross her mind that, by harbouring an abiding and all-consuming yen for this man, she breached every tenet she had ever held dear. There was but one thing Juliette thought of nothing else from that moment thenceforth.

She must have Darcy again or she just might die of want.

$\mathcal{O}$ld Friends, New Chapters

Within an hour of opening the doors, the ball would have been deemed a success by anyone's standard.

Mrs. Darcy's eyes were lively and her cheeks rosy with pleasure. Even her husband (so often out of humour) responded favourably when asked of his children's progress. It did not go without notice that Mr. Darcy looked upon Mrs. Darcy with easy affection. Their happiness was a joy to their friends and a bane to the few who were not.

Although Jane suspected, Elizabeth had told no one of the coming child. That secret was behind her only true regret of the evening—her husband had not taken her on the dance floor as much as she would have liked. When Bingley bid her to take a turn, Darcy did the unthinkable—he shook his head (granted, almost imperceptibly). Bingley was not one to take offence, he was a bit surprised. A word from Jane and he smiled agreeably and withdrew. Everyone was pleased save Elizabeth.

Although her husband stood as if wholly consumed by watching the others dance, Elizabeth was not deceived. She knew he was standing guard lest another gentleman ask her to dance.

Upon her tiptoes (the only way she could whisper in his ear), she said, "If you come between me and another turn, I shall pout."

He pretended to ignore her, but leaned over and said, "I am most happy for you dance. If you please, pray, not with Bingley."

"Why, pray, do you deny me Mr. Bingley as a partner? Save for you, dear husband, there is not a more admirable man in the room."

He said, "He is far too lively. He all but lifts Jane off her feet. It is my opinion that if you must dance, let it be a less frolicsome number...."

"Or a less frolicsome partner—say, one in his dotage?" she retorted.

"He can be of any age so long as he does not bound about. Mr. McNeely or Master Squires both appear to be in want of a partner," he replied.

She replied, "Mr. McNeely lost a leg last year. Master Squires is all of fourteen and much in want of dancing with Miss Amelia McGreevy, who is but twelve. To make the poor boy stand up with a woman twice his age would be a torture for him. It might ruin his love life for all his days...."

"I surrender," Darcy whispered, "Dance with whoever pleases you, but do not look to me to rub your... feet at the night's end."

At his capitulation, they shared a gaze. From the discrete caresses his hand gifted hers throughout the evening, Elizabeth suspected that he had other misgivings—most likely over their assignation in her dressing room just prior to the ball. Granted, he had left her breathless. She recovered with remarkable haste. He had yet to understand that she was not depleted by his attentions—quite the reverse. Time would come soon enough when caution would rule them, but not yet.

With a saucy glint in her eye, she took his arm reassuringly.

"Do not trouble yourself, sir," she said. Then in a low voice, she teased, "I am a strapping wench, happy for you to make free with my person at any opportunity."

Her protestations notwithstanding, to be looked after by her husband pleased her in a way she could not explain. Perhaps it was because he had been away during her last confinement. Regardless, he felt the need to cosset her and she enjoyed his guardianship—so long as he did not mean to keep her from dancing.

When the music stopped, the Bingleys returned to their spot next to the Darcys. After a moment, Darcy made a surprising announcement.

Bowing to his company, he said, "I am to do my duty."

He then disappeared. As the music began, Elizabeth saw that her reticent husband's partner was a stout widow of reduced circumstances. Seeming a bit flustered, the lady beamed once he led her onto the floor.

Full of pride, Elizabeth watched him as he betook the woman about the floor. Darcy's dancing was not particular, but he moved with enough grace to be a pleasure to watch. As she did, Elizabeth was reminded how few men had the leg for breeches. With an inward sigh, she made herself quit such selfish entertainment. She had duties to perform as well.

In answer to Pemberley's gilded invitations, friends travelled thither with all due anticipation. Many of these friends the Darcys had not the pleasure of seeing for several seasons. In some instances it was an intentional declension; in others it was with genuine regret. At one time, Charlotte Collins's was one of Elizabeth's dearest friends. Their friendship was tried by the many miles between them and not any particular dislike of her late husband. (This unadulterated fallacy Elizabeth chose to believe long after Mr. Collins's untimely demise.)

Charlotte was neither fair of face nor romantically disposed. Therefore, she married the first man who asked her.

Mr. William Collins had the good fortune of being recommended to

Lady Catherine De Bourgh when the living of Hunsford became vacant. The veneration he felt for her as his patroness, mingled with a very good opinion of himself as a clergyman, made him an unhappy mixture of obsequiousness and conceit. He was also Elizabeth's cousin. For Elizabeth, there was no greater testament to Darcy's love than that he married her after his introduction to all her relations.

There was some good in Mr. Collins's match to Charlotte. He did supply her all that she truly treasured—a comfortable home, a warm hearth, and one semi-adorable offspring, Chauncey Charlemagne Collins. Although Mr. Collins death was premature, the circumstances of it lent it far too much ridicule to mourn him properly. Therefore, remembrances were unusually brief. Charlotte took to widowhood with grace and good cheer. Indeed, she appeared almost relieved.

When Elizabeth spied Charlotte across the room at the ball, she was delighted. It was as if they were once again at Netherfield almost ten winters passed. That night Charlotte admitted that she was not a romantic. It was then that Jane knew that she truly loved Charles Bingley. It was also the evening that Elizabeth became fully witting of how much she despised the arrogant, punctilious, and singularly seductive Mr. Darcy.

That evening had been the rise, the root, the spring, the threshold, and the dawn. That had been the beginning of it all.

Jane and Bingley took to the floor again before Elizabeth could tell her that Charlotte had come. She did not hesitate to rush to greet Charlotte by herself. Charlotte's pale face alit with delight when she caught sight of her friend. They laughed and kissed each other's cheeks as if schoolgirls. It was only after admiring each others gowns and coiffures that Elizabeth observed Charlotte's companion. The new vicar of Hunsford, Mr. William Henry Pratt stood in nodding approval of their joy.

After Mr. Collins's death, he had been Charlotte's single consternation. When Elizabeth last called upon Charlotte, she had been critical of his sermons, the tithes, his relentless veneration of Lady Catherine, and the abysmal condition of his coat.

Clearly, Charlotte's opinion of him had improved.

"Mr. William Henry Pratt, at your service," he clicked his heels like a member of the Green Guard. "I am a faithful servant of God, dedicated educator of Hunsford Parish, and grateful vicar under the condescension of the illustrious Lady Catherine de Bourgh."

They had met previously, but he had introduced himself as if they had not. Elizabeth did not know if he enjoyed the repetition of his presentation or fancied that she did. When he spoke, only his lower teeth showed

"It is good to see you again," Elizabeth said.

His offer to fetch them some punch was quite agreeable to her for she was much in want of speaking candidly with Charlotte. Yet, it was a test not to stare at him as he went. There was a prissiness about him that was unnerving. He was tall, but knock-kneed. His height did not preclude the beginnings of a paunch. It had grown since last she saw him. The buttons on his waistcoat strained to keep his stomach in check. Perhaps he favoured Charlotte's cooking. When he walked, he looked as if he was attempting to withhold an expulsion of gas.

The moment she looked at the besotted expression on Charlotte's countenance, she was ashamed of her criticisms.

Without ado, Charlotte announced, "We are promised."

For the first time in Elizabeth's recollection, Charlotte was bathed in the glow of happiness. When last she saw her friend, her five-year-old son, Chauncey was still attached to her breast as if it were a cow's teat. Seeing Charlotte happy at last gave Elizabeth a shiver of contentment. She remained pleased despite Mr. Pratt's return. For once he began to talk, he did not pause—not even for a bit of air. It seemed there was no limit to his pomposity. His voice, when taken at length, was a monotone. Sunday sermons must be a severe test on his parishioners not to sleep. Indeed, she had to make herself listen attentively. When she did, she was horrified.

The man had taken up, and was preoccupied by, beekeeping.

Mr. Collins had met his demise by means of an enraged swarm of bees. They had chased him into a pond where he had the misfortune to drown. Elizabeth had no idea if Mr. Pratt knew that or not. She decided he must have been insensible of it, for who could drone on as he had otherwise. Elizabeth dared to glance at Charlotte. Her face was still a mask of contentment. Mr. Pratt's voice, however, became quite animated when he began to speak of his avocation.

"I have found what I fancy to be an exceptionally handsome honeybee colony. It was quite in shambles, left to ruin, no doubt, by the previous tenant. Beekeeping is a most ancient occupation. It is said to have originated in Egypt. Thousands of years ago, Cleopatra traded honey and beeswax along the Dark Continent."

Here he took a deep breath before continuing, "Although I fancy that beekeepers do earn a tidy living through the honey and mead it produces, our most important contribution is through fertilization. If it were not for honeybees flitting about across this flower and that cabbage, our children would starve. Chauncey is particularly fond of honey and bread. And in what other county is there such an abundance of clover and flowers than our own?"

Here he lowered his voice so as not to affright any ladies in earshot, "I must confess that beekeeping is quite a dangerous undertaking. Those proud men who fought Napoleon's legions have little on us who must keep the vicious honeybee at bay. I myself have been stung ten, nay twenty times in one day. But one must put one's fears aside when it to the betterment of society. Mankind avails himself of the instincts of the inferior animals to his own advantage. We shear sheep, gather eggs, and use oxen as a beast of burden. Thus sprang the art of keeping bees—and I flatter myself, apiculture is indeed an art."

"Indeed," Elizabeth answered.

Turning to Charlotte, she said with enough energy that Mr. Pratt could not but help hear her as well, "I pray this discourse does not injure dear Charlotte?"

Charlotte replied, "Indeed, I am not offended. It is good to have the hives put to use. I could listen to Mr. Pratt's intelligence on the subject for hours on end."

That, of course, was to Charlotte's advantage, but most especially to Mr. Pratt. As he began his digression into the history of apiaries, husbandry of the honey bee, hives, and pollination, his conversation wandered into (and then camped out in) mythology.

"Aristæus, the son of Apollo and the nymph Cyrene were the first apiarists," he explained. Then, unaccountably, his eyelids fluttered and he began to chant, "'O mother, the pride of my life is taken from me! I have lost my precious bees. My care and skill have availed me nothing, and you, my mother, have not warded off from me the blow of misfortune.'"

Charlotte sighed.

Others surrounding them were less impressed. Indeed, Mr. Pratt's sudden falsetto caused a number of people to quit their own conversations and see what wounded beast had found its way to the ballroom. Although Elizabeth was acutely aware of this notice, Mr. Pratt was not.

"Forsooth, his bees were damned due to Aristaeus attempt to seduce Eurydice, the wife of Orpheus. She fled from him and suffered a fatal snake bite—which is neither here nor there. It was his mother's nymphs who punished his sin by causing all of his bees to die; but he vowed to appease the nymphs by sacrificing his cattle, from whose carcasses emerged new swarms of bees."

"And let that be a lesson to us all," pronounced Charlotte.

Ignoring her remark, Mr. Pratt finished his story in his own time.

"Aristaeus was learned in the arts of healing and prophecy. Wandering over many lands, he shared his knowledge of curing the sick. He was widely honoured and was often depicted in our art as a youthful shepherd carrying a lamb."

"Yes," agreed Charlotte. "Mr. Collins and I always agreed that bees, especially honeybees, have an innate sense of purposefulness. Beware, Mr. Pratt, lest lofty self-regard obscures your path."

At that, Elizabeth almost choked on her own saliva. However, Mr. Pratt seemed to take no notice of Mrs. Darcy's near strangulation. He spoke only to Charlotte.

"I am a man of books and peaceful habits...."

"As was my late husband," said Charlotte.

"Whose loss we look to God and his infinite wisdom," Mr. Pratt retorted.

"He too had a good stomach and good temper and was not perplexed over much by fatigue of the brain," replied Charlotte.

Mr. Pratt snipped, "I did not attend the funeral but sent a nice letter saying I approved of it."

Charlotte turned to Elizabeth, remarking, "Mr. Pratt likes to say that he is a self-made man—and he worships his creator."

Mr. Pratt said, "Nature did it's best to make Mrs. Collins's a wit, but nature was sadly thwarted."

Thereupon, the repartee ceased.

Charlotte turned to Elizabeth, explaining, "As you see, Lizzy, I have once again given up all projects that cupid has any share."

A laugh erupted from the back of Mr. Pratt's throat ere he could quash it.

Not fully pleased to be the intermediary over whom they conducted their carefully designed abuse, Elizabeth found herself there regardless. She begged her leave. The nexus of Charlotte's forehead, Mr. Pratt's chin and their clasped hands was a posture that Elizabeth felt altogether forgiven to quit. They smiled contentedly as she made her away. And as she did, she attempted to recall the many twists and turns that bechanced the conversation as she was much in want of recalling their exact words when she told her husband of it.

Mr. Pratt was not the man either of them had supposed. He was pompous and servile. It took a very special humility, however, for a man to be happy to laugh at himself.

$\mathscr{T}$he Belle of the Ball

$\mathbf{M}$r. Pratt had been a frugal bachelor, but now needed feeding regularly. Hence, Elizabeth beckoned them to several tables groaning with food. He held a plate as Charlotte heaped it full. Satisfied, Elizabeth returned to the dance. She did not stand there long, ere several neighbours had joined her. In time, Mr. Darcy found his wife and nodded his greetings all round. Then, he took his usual stance (one foot foremost, hands clasped behind his back). With both of the Darcys together, the topic of conversation was the success of the evening. All believed it as an unparalleled triumph. Mr. Darcy again accepted the compliments with only a slight nod. Hence, once again it fell to Elizabeth to speak on their behalf.

Before she could, they were all overtaken by Bingley's sisters. They were not a welcome sight to anyone there, but they were in want of an audience and any three people would do. Elizabeth braced herself for Caroline's cackling and Louisa's dull-witted snipes. Elizabeth often wondered how they could be siblings to sweet Charles Bingley.

Most of the county knew that Caroline had clung to Darcy's coattails for a half a year hoping to secure him and was barely able to contain her joy when he asked for Elizabeth's hand instead. Despite that, Elizabeth had never rejoiced in her triumph. That would have been unkind. Caroline, however, did not recognise kindness as a viable social strategy. Indeed, Caroline had devoted much of her time to looking down her nose at the situation and conduct of others.

Upon this occasion, the sisters were flushed with excitement. They had not only Mr. Hurst in tow, but also Sir Winton Beecher. As Mr. Hurst was in want of wine, he left his party directly. (They did not seem to notice that he was gone.) The Darcys knew Mr. Hurst and his proclivities, therefore made no inquiry of him. At the end of an evening he could often be found asleep in odd places, but so far as Elizabeth knew, he had never caused any harm.

As innocuous as was Mr. Hurst; Caroline, Louisa Hurst, and Beecher were the triumvirate of vulgarity.

Beecher's marriage to poor Lady Anne had been a mockery of true love.

Their nuptials were hasty. The birth of their daughter (hastier still) was more than Anne's poor constitution could stand and she had not survived it. Beecher's grief was easily consoled at the gaming tables in London. As he was no better a widower than husband, he was seen with Miss Bingley gracing his arm before the month was out. After attaching herself to Beecher, Caroline found it more and more difficult to locate persons morally inferior to her.

Despite the talk, Caroline held fast. Some matches were meant to be and she was not one to deny fate its due. (Beecher disliked petty trials like death and she liked nothing more than a widower with a title.) With the leading lights of propriety glaring at her through their quizzing glasses, she bowed at the altar of her own one true love—the latest fashions. The grand gowns, trimmings, trappings, and accoutrements soothed her in ways that might have given regular folk pause.

Having made her rounds in London, Caroline had deigned to enjoy her brother's new country house. Her attendance at Pemberley that night was less to greet old friends than to assess their frocks. What had once been a favourite occupation now filled her waking hours. Louisa happily accompanied her on these stalking excursions about any gathering. They liked to titter behind their fans when they spied a truly tragic gown. The Pemberley ball had left them breathless with anticipation as country frocks were rarely tolerable and therefore always good for a giggle.

If they were critical of the lack of invention in the gowns, they drew a few odd looks in return. Both of the sisters had their hair combed down around their faces. Caroline had a long nose and the effect softened the outline of her face. Louisa's round face, however, was not improved. They were quite pleased with themselves regardless. No other lady at the ball dared such a coiffure. Nothing was more rewarding than to know oneself above one's company.

Having learnt that the incomparable doyenne of hairstyles and mode, Lady Howgrave was in attendance, the sisters had breathlessly sought her ladyship out. Once they had her in their eye, her ensemble left them all but giddy with adulation. Anxious to share, they had hurried to the nearest group of persons to exalt in the details of the lady's fallals. Regrettably, those they happened upon were the ones least likely to be in want of hearing them.

Caroline announced, "We have seen *Lady Howgrave!*"

A pause gave Elizabeth leave to understand that it was hers to reply. She said, "Indeed?"

"Have you had the privilege of observing her costume?" Caroline queried.

Elizabeth replied in the negative (having had only a glimpse of the lady when receiving). In fortune, Louisa was there, else Caroline would have been loath to find someone to participate in the conversation.

"Her gown is far and above every other attempt in the room, Louisa! The skirt is bell-shaped, the shoulders... dare I say it? *Dare I say it?*"

"Yes, yes, *yes!*" said Louisa.

Louisa gasped with such inflection that had one heard her from the other side of a door, her utterances might have suggested something unseemly was in progress. As Caroline and Louisa gushed, Beecher engaged in his own separate discourse, wholly indifferent to theirs.

"Ah Darcy," he said, "I am happy to see that your fine repast includes French fare. Some of society believe that it should no longer be done. I say, pish-tosh. When it is done well—as your table attests—our palettes enjoy all its many pleasures."

Without drawing a breath, Beecher said, "I spied Colonel Fitzwilliam's brother just across there. Matlock, is it not? The man has grown quite stout. I must give him my man's name. He does wonders with a Cumberland corset. It is altogether miraculous. I fancy it is the whalebone back and what has been come to be called the "Brummell" bodice."

When Beecher addressed him, Darcy's lip curled ever so slightly (betokening his particular dislike).

Unwilling to stand next to anyone conversing about undergarments, Darcy said, "Desist, sir."

Obtuse with wine and ego, Beecher was unwitting that Mr. Darcy was deciding whether to have him led away or simply ejected. Whilst he pondered each possibility, Mr. Darcy's gaze remained somewhere in the mid-distance, just above Beecher head. He took a sip from his cup of punch. It was his habit to ignore all discourse other than that of the weather and condition of the roads.

Beecher was still determined to speak of corsets.

"Mr. Brummell had nothing to do with that particular model, I promise you. You are a fine, tall fellow, Darcy. However, if you are to retain your figure you must wear your stays on the hunting field."

When Beecher put forward his forefinger as if to poke Mr. Darcy's middle for emphasis (or to determine if his lean figure had the help of a corsetière), it was unsurprising that Mr. Darcy was displeased. Only the inebriated or the truly stupid dared to touch Mr. Darcy's person. With great economy of movement, Darcy positioned the back of his hand so as to parry Beecher's finger.

Ignoring the deflection, Beecher snickered on, "Caution to the unwary—when Lord Fiddleback's wife dropped her glove and he, the gentleman, stooped to retrieve it the thing gave way...."

"I say, belay that, sir!" Darcy very nearly barked.

Startled, Beecher bowed into retreat. His boorish remarks were hastily over-spoken by Caroline who was still crowing over Lady Howgrave's gown. In a quandary as to whose conversation was least pleasing, Darcy glanced at Elizabeth, searching for escape. Regrettably, Elizabeth was (much to her personal dismay) intent on hearing the particulars of Lady Howgrave's ensemble without having to trouble herself with conversing with the woman whilst she did.

Caroline's praise was effusive.

"The shoulders of her gown are dropped! We shall not see them in *La*

Belle until next season. To think we were here to observe it first...."

Into this confabulation stumbled Lydia Bennet Wickham Kneebone. Her husband, Major Kneebone and Colonel Fitzwilliam were sharing accounts of the Peninsular Campaign and war stories bored her to tears. Finding the wine punch to her liking, she tarried at the bowl long enough to leave a bit tipsy. When she found Elizabeth, she wobbled noticeably. Darcy introduced her to those who were not of her acquaintance (admittedly leaving them to extrapolate that Lydia was his sister-in-law). Already acquainted with Lydia and her indiscretions great and small, Caroline was gleeful at the prospect of obtaining fresh gossip.

Beecher returned to their party, having trailed Lydia from the punch bowl. He took her hand and said, "Charmed beyond measure, I am sure."

"Why, hello little man," Lydia replied.

Although he had not had the pleasure of understanding Mrs. Kneebone's connection to the esteemed Mr. Darcy, Beecher did not respond to her affably gauche greeting. Vain in many things, Beecher was especially miffed by her reference to his lack of height and might have taken greater offence had she not displayed an alarmingly bounteous bosom. As his short stature made him eye-level with her décolletage, he took his time assessing it. However, he had firmly held prejudices against portionless creatures of inferior connections— at least in the presence of ladies of condition. Hence, his eyes soon quit her. Still gazing at the top of Beecher's head, Lydia swayed ominously.

In all ways alert to her youngest sister's indecorousness, in the faint hope of circumventing it, Elizabeth bid, "Shall you not sit down?"

"I think not," Lydia replied merrily. "I have already landed in more laps than a napkin."

As he put the back of his hand to his lips, Mr. Darcy coughed once.

Thereupon, he leaned over to his wife and said, "I shall locate Major Kneebone."

In the intervening time, Elizabeth took Lydia's elbow. She was much in want of leading her away from the Bingley sisters and Beecher. They were happy to have someone else to natter on about, and Elizabeth happier still to leave them to it.

All the tugging of a team of oxen couldn't have hurried Lydia on her way, but Elizabeth refused to admit defeat. Somehow, Lydia seemed smitten with the diminutive Beecher and looked upon him as if a poppet sitting on a children's bench. Caroline refused to relinquish the floor to Lydia regardless, and continued to expound upon her very favourite subject—fashion and its victims.

"Lady Howgrave's gems are exquisite. She wears a single strand of pearls offset by rubies, for anything above a single strand is *tres passe*. Still loops of them are seen everywhere—even in the most fashionable of neighbourhoods." Not so vain as to care for the opinion of someone she disliked, Elizabeth was uninjured by Caroline's comment disparaging her double-strand of pearls. They had belonged to Darcy's mother and she treasured them. She thought no more of the information than she did the source. Other ladies seemed uncomfortable at the slight and shuffled their dancing slippers a bit. Caroline was undeterred.

"Ladies of no taste are everywhere. Indeed, if every vulgar girl in Bath were laid to end—"

"I shouldn't be surprised!" Lydia snorted.

Those who could disguise their guffaws did. Beecher was particularly amused and Caroline shot him a glare of reproach—one he felt free to ignore.

Turning on Lydia with a withering gaze, Caroline bid, "Where, pray, is your husband?"

Tittering, Lydia responded, "If you see two people talking and one is bored senseless—he's the other one!"

Elizabeth refused to have the good Major Kneebone maligned, especially by his wife.

She said, "I believe Major Kneebone is a most agreeable and estimable man."

With precision, she then clasped Lydia's hand firmly in hers and dragged her away.

Suddenly aware that the size of Elizabeth's bosom now nearly rivalled her own, Lydia loudly declared, "Why, Lizzy, you are so *fat!*"

Once they were out of earshot, Elizabeth pinched Lydia hard on the inside of her arm. At this offence, Lydia yowled.

"Quit it, Lizzy! You shall leave a bruise!"

Fortunately, another allemande was in progress and Lydia's outrage went unnoticed. Behind her fan, Caroline whispered to Beecher, advising him of Lydia's unlikely connection to Elizabeth Darcy. He raised an eyebrow at the information, reassessing Lydia's worth in the world. Indeed, his West End pretensions could be put aside with utmost haste when it suited him. He only quit his observation of Lydia's strut when her sister had her well out of sight.

Lydia was so often in want of conduct, Elizabeth had very nigh given up defending her. If she were to embarrass herself, Elizabeth would have much preferred that she would not do so in front of the worst magpies in Christendom. Yet, Lydia's silliness did one good—it ridded Elizabeth of unpleasant companions. It was her sisterly obligation to chastise Lydia despite that, so she did.

"Really, Lydia!" she whispered. "Why must you insist on bringing us all to ridicule?"

Lydia whimpered, "What do you care, Lizzy? You hate Bingley's sisters. "

"It is unChristian to hate. That is too harsh a word. Everyone has some disposition to admire."

"And what, pray tell, do you possibly find to admire about Caroline Bingley?"

"She does her hair well," Elizabeth replied evenly.

Lydia was unmoved.

"You hate her and that is a sin—although not one of the "thou shalt nots.""

"You mean the Ten Commandments?"

Elizabeth was incredulous to find herself standing in the middle of a ball, conversing in such a stupid manner. However, speaking of the Bible and its admonitions sobered Lydia a bit.

She observed, "Say what you shall about the Ten Commandments—there are but ten of them. Think of what other evil deeds that could be added... thou shalt not speak ill of Caroline Bingley; thou shalt not break wind at the supper table; thou shalt not overspend one's purse... oooh, there's the punch bowl."

She turned in that direction as if caught by a spell. Elizabeth caught her hand and redirected her. The last thing Lydia needed was further libations.

"Your strict integrity and delicate sense of honour astound me," Elizabeth said as she pushed her towards the door.

To her great fortune, Darcy had found Kneebone and Kneebone then found them.

"Perchance, she needs fresh air," Elizabeth suggested.

"Perhaps we shall retire for the night," he wisely proposed.

In this, they thought quite alike. Lydia looked as if all the spirits she drank were to be cast out. As she was in grave danger of soiling a very fine Aubusson carpet, Elizabeth handed her to her husband. He nodded gratefully. With good fortune, Lydia would sleep until noon.

Happy at last to know Lydia was no longer a danger to their dignity, Elizabeth was much in want of sharing that intelligence with her husband. He could not be far, she was certain. After being delayed to speak and be spoken to by several guests, she eventually saw him.

He was not alone.

Posit and Presumption

Charles Bingley believed his wife was the handsomest lady in England. There were those who agreed with him—especially if goodness had its say. Yet, Bingley was all but rendered a gibbering schoolboy under lovely Lady Howgrave's alluring gaze.

Another wife might have been piqued. Jane, of course, was not. Indeed, she found Bingley's befuddlement adorable. (Granted, there was little that Jane did not find charming of her husband.) After all, Bingley was not forward in his admiration. It was a matter of judgement. Effusiveness was not frowned upon as long as he did not fall headfirst into her ladyship's bountiful cleavage.

Juliette's special gift was attracting attention from both sexes and she revelled in that notice at Pemberley. Her severest chore was finding discretion. When need be, she was mistress of heedfulness. Those who clamoured for her eye and hearkened her every sigh were unhelpful. Therefore, she had become adroit at pretending to be engrossed in conversation without actually having to participate. A nod here, a smile there and those in her company were happy to know that she was entertained by them. Albeit, she did smile more brilliantly at Mr. Bingley. Even after his reversals, he remained a man of financial consequence—and of happy temper, not that she had any designs on him. To her, he was a bit of a buffoon.

Some innate instinct told Juliette that Bingley knew nothing of her long passed association with Darcy. Bingley was some years younger than Darcy and they became acquainted when the affair was on the wane. As they were both gentlemen, Darcy would never have told him of it regardless. Darcy, terse on all matters, was silent as the grave when the subject was intimacy. Had there been any question, Juliette learnt the truth absolutely when their paths crossed upon the steps of Howgrave's apartments in London. When she spoke to Darcy, Bingley's expression had been exceedingly inquisitive. He had wanted to know of their connection, but was far too daunted to inquire.

Shaking away such recollections, Juliette's gaze expertly swept the room. It was important to have Darcy in her eye and gauge those about him before she bechanced him. Her initial objective of simply being an observer had been set aside for the possibility that she might gain a private word. To do so, it was important that he believe that accident brought it about. Was she seen to go to him, scandal would ensue. (In truth, she would have adored scandal, but a whiff of it would turn Darcy away.) In order to achieve that specific conjunction, she knew she must continue to oblige herself to the Bingleys' company.

As Darcy's closest friend, it was important for both the Howgraves to groom his friendship. Hence, Howgrave was near her elbow obtusely attempting to ingratiate himself to Bingley by publicly reminding him of a very private financial embarrassment.

"We had the income tax repealed, did we not?" Howgrave insisted on having Bingley's agreement. "You sir, would still be retrenching otherwise."

Well-mannered as he was, Bingley ignored that Howgrave made mention of his reverses. He looked to entertain Lady Howgrave instead.

Couching his voice for jollity, he bid her, "Pray, what distinguishes knowledge from stupidity?"

After a well-timed pause, she responded, "Knowledge is *finite*."

"Yes, yes," he explained to one and all, "Stupidity knows no bounds!"

Everyone laughed. Bingley allowed her to own the jest. It was, for all that, an old joke. If all of Derbyshire had heard it, they were too polite not to applaud. Juliette had good reason to fear that was to be the apex of wit for the evening. Had it not been for the sweet anticipation of encountering Darcy, she might have pled a headache and fled. Not unlike other much-touted virtues, she had never admired patience. It had always seemed an excuse for hopelessness. But she had begun to learn it—that and optimism.

Eventually her newly acquired forbearance was rewarded. And when it was, she had Charles Bingley to thank for it. It was he who spied Darcy and beckoned him.

No one, not even Jane, realised that Bingley was not merely overawed by Juliette's beauty, he feared her. She flustered him. When disconcerted, his loquacity was known to run amok. He feared that once unfettered, his effusiveness just might expose information that he knew he should keep to himself.

Not that he held any intelligence of Darcy's past. No, not at all. Bingley suspected, but he did not know. Suspicion was enough to test his tongue. Heretofore he had barely kept it in check. He could not think of another joke suitable for ladies' ears.

Desiring escape at all cost, when Bingley espied Darcy, he saw reprieve. From across the room Darcy saw Bingley raise his hand and betook himself in that direction. Half the distance was crossed ere Darcy's countenance altered. So little did it change, however, only Bingley was witting of his annoyance. Despite his good friend's displeasure, Bingley experienced only the smallest regret. In some instances, it was every man for themselves.

Before Darcy could retreat, Bingley bid, "Tell us, Darcy, what is your opinion of the current economy? Shall it remain on the mend? What say you?"

At this inquiry, half of the listeners gave an inward groan. Few (and that included Bingley) cared to speak of politics. A few others were happy for a chance of contention—that which all political discussions were certain to bring. Everyone awaited Darcy's response.

Darcy paused before answering Bingley, weighing his words. He disliked giving his opinion on such matters in public and Bingley was well-aware of that disinclination. Therefore, he did his best to remain vague and glowered at his friend as he did. (Wisely, Bingley gazed with great interest upon his toes.) Whilst equivocation was demanded by the onlookers, Darcy only said, "Unemployment looks to remain a source of agitation."

"Yes," agreed another, "I defy you to agitate a fellow who has a full stomach!"

That simple theorem incited an all-out political debate—arguments defending order and those who believed in the working class movement. This reignited Bingley's interest. Granted, Bingley's sensibilities were innately kind. However he had come very close to compleat financial ruin, so his understanding on this issue was sympathetic. The only thing that kept him in new waistcoats was that he had retained interest in his coal mines.

He said, "I must say that time in Fleet Prison has cured no man's financial situation. We need good men of the people to represent us...."

Here he was interrupted by another, "There is no such thing as a good politician or an honest thief!"

Howgrave had better sense than to harrumph, but his laugh was hollow. A hint of a smile tempted the corner of Darcy's mouth. Others whooped and laughed enough for twenty men. The group ebbed and flowed as those uninterested in political unrest repaired to other corners of the room, and those who enjoyed the possibility of fisticuffs, or at least a good argument, joined them.

"If you pick up a dog to feed him, he won't bite you," said a cadaverous man with a pock-marked face. "This is the main difference between dog and man."

Unadvisedly, Bingley said, "If we are to speak of beasts, I beg a question." He paused and then asked, "Pray tell, why is it that there are far more horse's asses around than horses?"

When he issued that vulgarity, Bingley hastily glanced at Jane. Her countenance trembled, thereby advising her dear Charles that he overstretched his humour. Regrettably, her admonition was too late by half and the discussion was propelled into an arena better suited for other, less dignified, venues. A man named Feakes (who had nothing to promote of himself but a fat stomach and a wife with property) was most vexed upon the havoc the unrest had played on wages.

He announced, "When once a well-made woman in Haymarket was had for six shillings a year ago, now her time cost five pounds...."

"I *do* beg your pardon, sir," said Bingley.

Mr. Darcy's jaw clenched. When he did speak, it was in a low, precise voice. "Indeed, Mr. Feakes, you forget yourself, sir."

The man did not wait for the rebuke to take a hasty leave. With the compliance of a courtier, he genuflected his way out the door and had formed his letter of apology ere the footman called for his coach. A letter would be accepted. However, there was little chance that Feakes would insult propriety at Pemberley again. (There was little chance any persons witnessing Mr. Darcy unhappiness upon such a transgression would either.)

As the instigator, Bingley assumed an ingenuous—even beatific— expression and betook Jane's hand. Thereupon, he led her and her poor, delicate ears from such unseemliness. Abruptly, Lady Howgrave found herself offended by the language and subject that she had listened to a hundred times over during her husband's political campaigns. With a hint of distaste and upraised hand, she made it apparent that she was to be led away as well. Howgrave was busy haranguing another guest, punctuating his remarks by poking his finger in a man's chest. There were any number of other gentlemen who would have climbed the Austrian Alps to take that delectable hand, but she eschewed them. With a glissade of one velvet slipper (and the agility of a cat), she moved in such a way that only Mr. Darcy had that honour. Neither delight nor abhorrence was betrayed by his countenance as he allowed her to place her hand upon his.

Because Mr. Darcy and Lady Howgrave took their leave, the other guests disbanded that corner of the ballroom as well. That entertainment having dissolved did not mean there was nothing left to amuse them. This dispersal was accompanied by the synchronous opening of a dozen fans. The ladies who owned these fluttering accoutrements floated away, kept aloft by raised eyebrows and wagging tongues. Their husbands did not follow their wives in any haste. Lady Howgrave looked to great advantage when she walked. Indeed, not an eye was spared from ogling her. She had honed that walk over years of practise. It was said that she had more swing to her undercarriage than a well-oiled barouche.

If Darcy believed himself to have been manipulated, it was unapparent. Those who knew him did not expect otherwise. The more inquiring his company, the more impenetrable was his countenance. Perchance he might reflect disapproval, but never would he display any hint that he was the victim of a manoeuvre. Upon this occasion, his noble mien remained fixed—albeit as if he had smelled something a tad... fetid. It might have been concluded that he was simply offended by the company he just quitted, not that of Lady Howgrave.

When the couple did not step onto the dance floor, most onlookers became disinterested.

Darcy's expression altered but little as the good Lady Howgrave gracefully propelled him from thence up a staircase to a vacant hall. She did so by admiring each the vast number of paintings that lined the wall. Juliette appraised a fine Dutch painting and the parquet floor with a long look of approval. She only stopped her consideration to gaze at the ballroom floor below. Dancers awaited the allemande as the orchestra retook their places after an intermission. As if by preordination, they commenced a waltz. It was quite the fashion amongst those who amused themselves by admiring the neoteric.

There were a few gasps and several couples left the floor. Others did not hesitate and began to whirl about. They were either blithely unawares (or quite possibly happily witting) that some believed the piece of music was unseemly. The flash of colour as the gowns twirled grandly around the room was quite exhilarating. All of London was entranced by the dance. With the strong, propulsive rhythm—not to speak of the hold (which was nothing less than an embrace), it was a heady, sensual dance. One could actually detect the outrage of those in the ballroom who kept track of such offences.

Mr. Darcy's usual hauteur was overspread by a rare shade of crimson. Juliette issued a premature smile, believing she was the cause his discomposure. It was not she, however, who held his attention.

Mr. Darcy placed both hands firmly on the balustrade. His expression as he looked down upon his conductor was dour. Mr. Darcy's glare was forbidding. The conductor looked up as if touched by the hand of God. No word passed between them. However, the conductor immediately (and with great fluidity) guided the orchestra into a sedate quadrille. Passably pleased with the hastiness whereof the dance was altered, Mr. Darcy's colour began to return to its customary hue.

Juliette was not one to allow the matter drop.

As if musing, she said, "How far afield from heated passion we have chanced...."

Said he, "I beg your pardon?"

She disliked having to repeat what she believed to be a perfectly delivered bon mot. Nonetheless, she did. The importance of her observation must not be dismissed. Nodding towards the tranquil dance floor, she said, "How far afield from heated passion we have chanced."

In the repeating, her remark had not improved on him. He offered no response. For a man known to own a quick mind, his behaviour was well-nigh hebetudinous. It was quite maddening. She reminded herself of his incomparable self-possession. Had he been untouched, he would have spoken more. Therefore, she took his want of ardency as a compliment and delighted in his silence.

When he did speak, it was a seemingly incongruous remark.

"I here beg to offer my apologies," he said. "I was not informed that particular dance was to be part of tonight's selections."

She found it exceedingly regrettable that he had halted the waltz. It would have been superb ambience for a conversation, perchance a foreshadowing of what was to come. Hence, she pursued the subject.

"I am exceedingly disappointed that you disapprove of the waltz," she said. "I find it quite provocative."

He responded, "I fear not all of my guests agree with you, Lady Howgrave...."

"Juliette," she interrupted.

As if he had not heard, he continued, "It is my obligation as host to entertain everyone, not just ladies and gentlemen of the ton."

That remark could have been ill-taken. His manners had always been high and imposing. He had not the insolence of the English sort, but he often gave offence. She was loath to be offended, proud in the comfort that she knew him well enough not to be.

She replied, "It has been my observation that many critics take far greater relish in censuring others than anyone ever did immersing themselves in sin."

He smiled and she laughed, happy that she finally elicited one from him. And when she did, the lilt of her voice hung in the air like a melody.

With the unerring misfortune that some incidents invite, Elizabeth Darcy happened to hear the echoing laugh and turned her eyes upward at that very moment.

20

$\mathscr{T}$he Retort

It was late and the room was compleatly in shadow. Having flamed out, most of the candles sat in a puddle of wax.

It had been a long evening and Darcy was altogether fordone by feigning felicity. Above an hour with more than a half dozen people tried his patience. Despite the ball being pronounced a resounding success by all, he believed that he had never seen more over-dressed twits and under-hung jaws in one place in all his life.

Moreover, his feet hurt.

He despised dancing slippers. No matter how carefully they were fitted, by the end of the night, his insteps ached. It was further proof that man wasn't meant to dance. It was a wholly unnatural occupation. Women were meant to wear slippers; men were meant to wear boots. Was his opinion on the matter not incontrovertible, he had several blisters in proof of it.

He tossed the despised slippers aside. They landed just outside his door giving Goodwin to understand he was dismissed for the night. Mr. Darcy was in no mood to suffer any other ritual—his nightly ablutions or not. He sought nothing more than the arms of his wife. Was it not for her, he might have become a compleat recluse.

By virtue of his vexation, he did not take notice until then that his wife had preceded him to bed. On an evening so heavy with duty and small consternations, he had little doubt she would be fast asleep. Here, his desire collided unhappily with his conscience. The evening had left him near spent; no doubt she was as well. It would be unthinkable to come to her in service of his own passion for a second time. As much as his heart was in want of possessing her, he feared imposing himself upon her again might do her harm.

As he turned aside all thought of amour, he stopped. Perhaps she was awake, anticipating his disquiet. Such was his history. The larger the gathering (especially one infested with politicians), the longer it would be ere slumber would come to him. In the future, he would be more vigilant about alarming her in that. She needed her rest, not stand guard over his. Heaving a great sigh, he renewed himself to husbanding her and their coming child. From this moment forward, prudence would rule his every thought; caution, his every touch.

But for tonight, to lie next to her—just for a brief while—would console them both.

The balcony doors allowed a shaft of moonlight to illuminate the bed and the ivory curve of his wife's bare back. She was not asleep. She sat in the middle of the bed, perched on her knees. A suspiration of desire all but choked him.

Desiring nothing but to feel her skin against his, he drew his shirt over his head and cast it to the floor. At the sound of his footfalls, her arms crossed her bosom. Momentarily, he thought he had given her a fright. But she did not turn about to see who was there.

He stopped short of the bed, uncertain as to why. Something forbidden was in the air. He could smell it, feel it, sense it. Owing to the power of that sensation, his flagging spirit was reinvigorated. As he stepped closer, he saw that she was in a state of nature—exquisitely so. So fetching was her nakedness, it might well have given him leave to cast all thought of prudence to the wayside. However, he did not think of that. Still resolved to be her guardian, he was struck by two successive thoughts. Firstly, that her nakedness might invite a chill, and secondly, was she cold, he must warm her.

It was then that he saw that she was not compleatly naked. Initially, she looked to have a shawl draped about her hips. But as his eyes adjusted to the darkness, he could see that what clung to her hips was that which he had so vehemently removed earlier that evening. He was aghast (more or less).

"Mrs. *Darcy!*"

He had not truly raised his voice, nor had he actually gasped. But it was near enough to have given her a start. She, however, did not respond as if disturbed. Rather, she very slowly and, admittedly, quite seductively, looked at him over one bare shoulder.

It was both an invitation and a dare.

A pause was needed for him to collect his thoughts. No doubt, she believed him slightly vexed. He was, or at least he knew that was the part he was to play in the performance she had foreordained. Notwithstanding the abhorrence he held for disguise of any sort, he scowled (allowing that to appear vexed was not a compleat perjury). Indeed, when he spoke his voice was a husky mixture of indignation and hunger. Yet, his words were not those of a man who desperately desired to make love. Another man might have been more wise.

"Have we not decided against that indecent garment?"

"This?" she asked innocently, placing two fingers inside the waistband. "Indecent?"

"Perhaps I misspoke. It is merely immodest."

She retorted, "I believe that it not the garment that is indecent or immodest. A garment is but a 'thing' and therefore, cannot be either chaste or debauched.

It can be silk or cotton. It can be plain or ruffled. It can have a pink ribbon drawstring...."

Here she grasped one end of the ribbon and held it daintily in her fingers. "... or not."

She pulled it loose. Therefore the top of her drawers fell just far enough down her hips to reveal the cleft of her derriere. He could not see the dimple in the middle of her soft, round buttock, but he knew it was there.

Not altogether trusting his voice, he nodded. To what he had just acquiesced, he was uncertain.

He gathered his dignity, bowed from the waist, and said, "I would by no means suspend any pleasure of yours."

"I do not take your meaning, sir. Do you, or do you not, approve of my morally ambiguous undergarment?"

With remarkable fluidity, he slid onto the bed behind her, his hands resting lightly at her bare waist.

"On closer inspection, they have improved on me."

These drawers were ruffled, two rows of lace adorned the drawstring. He had not fully appreciated the frills upon the other pair as he had suffered from a severe case of masculine want at that time. Indeed, he had not investigated them in a gentlemanly fashion at all. He had meant to apologise for his fit of pique. But addressing his want of gallantry would come later. Just then, there was a more important mission at hand.

His fingers spread wide, nearly spanning her waist. Skimming beneath her drawstring they slid across her abdomen and down between her legs. Her breath, which had been quite relaxed, increased at his touch. It became even more stirred as his lips found the indention just behind her ear lobe. That kiss begat a frisson of electricity that shuddered down her body and pooled into the deepest reaches of her womanhood. No caress, no endearment could ever surpass that kiss—save for the one to come.

Such was her fervour, she fell to the side, her arms open and inviting. With great economy of movement, he drew himself atop her, his fingers still reconnoitring with tender urgency.

"There is no need...," said she.

She need not fear that he would tear this garment asunder. When he had rent the other, it was simply to make a point. The separation of the leggings was quite impassioning. Within that gap could be found the most bewitching furrow; the great persuader of his flesh. Nothing at all lay between him and his single-minded need to have her. Every sinew—so ungovernable still—very nigh overtook his reason once again. Nothing would have kept his passion in check except for the knowledge that there was found far greater pleasure in removing the offending garment, aided by his every stroke, her every response, the bending knee, and undulating hips.

It was quite unlike him to be moved to whisper a sonnet in her ear. But he did.

"Love is not love," he said. "Which alters when it alteration finds,

"Or bends," she whispered, "With the remover to remove...."

Drawing the last of the lace from her legs, he tossed them over his head and said no more.

"O, no!" she gasped, "It is an ever-fixed *mark*...."

Indeed, it was.

The Daisy is Also a Flower

Although London's citizens were beyond her counting, in many ways its insular neighbourhoods made it as meddlesome and gossipy as the quaintest village in Sussex. Daisy had learnt of what direction little Miss Arbuthnot had taken before she was a hundred feet down the path.

Sally had always been an odd little chit. Daisy harrumphed at her strange need to return Mr. Darcy's money to him—what with him being richer than Croesus and all. That girl always was in want of some pence in the shilling. Likely she would follow the man all the way to the North Country to repay him. Sally always had a peculiar view of honour. Daisy had learnt from an early age to watch out for her own interests. But then she was the last living issue of her mother's various unions and alone in the world.

Daisy's mother, good Mrs. Mulroney had been a prolific breeder, but only three of her children survived to adulthood. That was not unusual; only the strongest lived to see their majority in the Dials. If they did, they were hardened by meanness and pinched by want. Both her brothers met an inglorious fate. Frank had managed to find a good situation, but allowed Tommy to lead him astray. Tom Reed spent time on the Newgate treadmill. Folks said he was rotten before he got there. He should have hanged for murder, but escaped by garrotting a guard.

Daisy had not been the poorest naïf in London. In the warren of rooms crowding every festering street, the hungriest begged from open windows and bawled in doorways. Some of them were able-bodied; some of them were not. There were plenty of peg-legged men, one-eyed women, and toothless oldsters of both sexes. Children went barefoot in all seasons and babies often had long-standing coughs (severe enough to influence their parents not to form a deep attachment for them).

Daisy counted herself amongst the fortunate of her neighbours. She was not mad, sick, nor otherwise impaired. Being a bit stunted never held her back. Some called her a dwarf, but she was something far rarer than that. (Yea, had she been a dwarf, she would have been turning summersaults for the Crown in the corridors of St. James Palace.) She grew no taller than fifty inches, forever a child—at least in body. In spirit and understanding she was a woman.

Early on she displayed an extraordinary head for business. There were not many ways to earn one's keep. With no man to see to her, like most girls she sold what she had—and she had something quite unique. The usual sexual favours were bought and sold in every nook and cranny in the Dials (notwithstanding the breadth and imagination of the possibilities) for what you could get. Attending to carnal perversities paid best. The taking of a young girl's maidenhead was the most rare and therefore, expensive. Daisy sold herself as a virgin over and over again. Executing this farce involved cat guts and the like—quite a messy business. Daisy had engaged in the ruse for years. It paid for her lodgings, two dresses, and an ermine tippet—high-living when it came to her neighbourhood.

Her high commissions did not last forever. Eventually word got around to potential clients that she was no virgin.

A saggy, old street woman (whose only entertainment was to interfere with another's trade) began hooting at likely clients, "Daisy's been 'round the block more times than a hackney coach!"

The exposure of this information did not compleatly put off her clients. There were always the sort who liked to pretend they were docking a maid— and she was happy to oblige. When anyone hollered at her on the street, calling her a loose woman, she was good-humoured.

"I are nothing of the kind!" she liked to whoop. "Tight as the bark on a tree, that's me!"

Opposed to illicit trade in general, her friend Sally Frances Arbuthnot was more appalled by the purchasers of debauchery rather than the purveyors. Daisy sniffed at such pretensions. Hip cocked and a perennial cigar in her hand, Daisy blew one cloud after another.

She asked, "Will fools burn in hell any hotter for one sin more 'n the other?"

Sally knew as much as the next person that Daisy was no more a sinner than half the people in Mayfair. Daisy Mulroney was a survivor.

As the history of her brothers suggested, Daisy had many influences that held sway over her beyond just a premature inauguration into the flesh trade. The money they took off of Wickham meant to her what it would have meant to anyone else. Money meant power—and power meant freedom. Daisy would no longer live by anyone else's leave—and that was a price above rubies.

When Daisy left Wickham's lodgings that night, she was in no particular hurry. Having bid her goodbye to Sally, she was not yet disposed to indulge herself of her new-found wealth. Another might have run up the street offering pints to everyone in sight. Daisy knew that particular move would have aroused the suspicious. Thieves were always on the watch for unusual signs of affluence. However, she did not return to the Gates of Hell brothel. She had other, grander plans.

She took a slow, thoughtful stroll down Gowell Street. Usually she fancied morning walks. But that night the air appealed to her. It had been late enough not to be bothered by street urchins, but too early for blood-leaking corpses to be a threat to one's shoes. The air stank and fog enveloped her. Still, she had wanted to savour her last day as a poor harlot of St Giles.

Several streets over, she took lodgings in a small house, paying for a night. The innkeeper looked at her queerly, haughtily explaining they did not let rooms by the hour. Daisy gave him a sovereign and told him to keep the change. It was a dangerous thing to do, but she could not deny herself the expression that overspread the man's face. The trip from disdain to awe was brief, but profound.

Once locked in her room, she paid a single tribute to the riches she had just gained. Throwing the bank notes in the middle of a tattered counterpane, she tore off her clothes and jumped in the middle of them. Baying like a hound with a cornered fox, she allowed herself to enjoy her very first sexual release of her life. Suddenly, a question that had always troubled her was answered.

Why were men so bewitched by a piece of a woman's snug?

It was quite clear to her then. A man did not ride a woman merely to get his bangles rung. He did it for domination. Nothing was more titillating than power. He who had the funds had it all. Men had always held the legal tender, the guinea, the coin, the gold.

Now, at long last, she had it too.

The Last Word

The night after his wife's bravura argument in favour of the scurrilous breeches, Mr. Darcy (happy to capitulate) fell into a deep, satisfied sleep. Nothing brought rest surer than spent ardour and an untroubled brow. His wife was happy for that. Not withstanding her own satiation, slumber did not come easy for her. She lay quietly by his side waiting to waft off to dream, but her mind did not rest. It revelled in every urgent beat their hearts had taken. Eventually, she was lured to the balcony by the same soft moonlight that had enticed her husband to their bed.

She padded from thence to the doors and opened one. The air was brisk, but she stepped outside. As she gazed upon the glistening lawn, it pleased her to know that their guests would find their way home well lit by the full moon and cloudless sky.

From the darkness behind her, she heard a moan. Startled, she was relieved to see that it was only Cressida. The dog had managed to insinuate herself into the room and was laying in a corner thrashing her legs—most likely chasing a rabbit in her sleep.

Perchance that was why Elizabeth did not desire sleep just then. She had no influence over her own dreams. Awake, she held sway over where'er her thoughts took her. They went no further than the hour past.

Leaning against the door post, she closed her eyes, recalling her husband's every touch, his every murmur. Their blood had been so stirred; she wanted not to forget a moment of it.

As her pregnancy progressed, they would continue to enjoy carnal embraces, but not with the same abandon. He (a master of *coitus reservatus*) would become increasingly cautious, daring not to plumb the depth of her womanhood. Their pleasure would be undiminished, but less wanton, more tender. Her own passion, however, was not as disciplined. In recent weeks she had become evermore eagre to lay with him.

One would think that maternal serenity and libidinous inclinations would be at odds. Once a woman was with child, nature's wisdom should have convinced her that further ministrations to that end should have been superfluous. It was quite the reverse. Her erotic desires, which were usually quite... sedulous, had become even more ardent. The merest flick of his finger sent her writhing with orgiastic spasms—the sort that threatened to never to end. Yet riding the crest of exhilaration a half-dozen times, she remained aroused.

Perhaps it was nature's plan—to inspire a husband to keep league and truce through the long winter of gestation. That thought amused her. Granted, alterations would have to be made were they to continue such excitations. Nature's glory could be incommodious to her vessel's wants.

But she did not receive pleasure from her satisfaction alone. Her excitation had always been furthered by his achievement. She had once confided in him that she could discern when he pulsated his seed into her—and that the sensation inflamed her passion. Had they not been lying hot and depleted, she might not have been so forthcoming. The moment she said it, she wished she had not been so frank. She had dared not gauge his response. God save a husband from a candid wife

Looking back through the doors, she could see the bed and his outline. His chest rose and fell in deep, even respirations. One arm was flung out to his side as if reaching for her. His hair was tousled, begging her to return and run her fingers through it. His dishevelment always pleased her. Only when he slept did he fully divest himself of lordly pride. Their bed and his warmth beckoned her.

The urge for sleep overcame her ruminations at the precise moment that it should—ere her thoughts became caught up in a labyrinth of the night's intrigues and scandal. There would be time enough to consider those vexations in the cold light of day. One more glance at the moonlit lawn, however, and any chance for brooding was compleately lost.

A caped figure caught her eye as it swept like a bat across the grass.

It ran to the edge of the drive where a carriage sat, its door open wide. No footman stood by to hand the lady into the coach—if it was indeed a woman. Nonetheless, the figure leapt into the coach and the door slammed shut. Elizabeth fancied that the door shut on a corner of the cape, but she could not be certain. The coachman cracked his whip and the horses lunged in response, with the coach lumbering on its way. She did not watch as thither it went up the road.

For some reason, her eyes darted to her husband still fast asleep.

As to why the fleeting vignette left her with a queer feeling in the pit of her stomach, she could not say. The livery was familiar, but its colour unclear in the darkness. Was it Beecher? And if it was Caroline, why did she steal away. The scene left Elizabeth so unsettled that she well-nigh tempted to awaken her husband to tell him of it. She should have told him. Furtiveness was reason enough to believe something was amiss. For some nebulous reason, she chose not wake him.

It was easier not to tell him at all than to explain to herself why she needed reassurance that her beloved Darcy was, indeed, in his own bed.

The Shadow

It was the year '16 when Sally Frances Arbuthnot took the long walk back across Goodman's Field and stood before the huge, grey charnel house, praying she was not too late.

Matron did not even blink when she came to collect Nell.

Giving a wet snort, she said, "Happy to be rid of the old cow."

Sally held her temper and followed the jangle of her keys up the corridor to the lunatic ward. At least it was not Bedlam. That place harboured naked inmates whose toes were chewed on my rats. Nell's brain had gone soft long before, so it was not the hurt it might have been that she no longer knew Sally's name. She came along quite peaceably, but coughed and wheezed so much Sally knew she was not long for the world. Her disorder also meant that the coachman had to be paid extra to open his door to the old woman.

Locating a small house near Bishopsgate, Sally had a rocking chair sitting by the front window and had thrown all frugality to the wayside with the purchase of a feather mattress for Nell's bed. Sally slept on a straw pallet (which was made all the more uncomfortable by the canvas bag and the bank notes she hid inside). Once settled, she fed Nell draughts and explained to her uncomprehending countenance why she had run away from the workhouse and left Nell there all alone.

"You know I had to see to John, grannum," she whispered. "Someone had to answer for what happened to him. I got more to do yet...."

That was all she said. John was her brother and no kin to Nell. Knowing that she rescued her grannum first chance she had was all the salve Sally had for her conscience. She brushed Nell's hair and watched over her until the old woman passed from this life to the next. Sally cried for her when she did. Her tears were more of relief than sadness, knowing that Nell's suffering had finally ceased.

Sally had her laid to rest in a small, but kempt cemetery. Obtaining her sister's coffin from a Potter's Field and relocating it next to Nell's ate into the funds, but it soothed Sally's mind to know that they lay together for eternity.

After doing what she could for her kin, Sally had not taken so much as a shilling more of the money in that canvas bag, save to buy her fare for a seat atop a post-chaise to Derbyshire.

Had the Darcys remained at their London House, she would have been saved a great deal of bother. But they had not. Upon learning they had hied to Pemberley forthwith of the great altercation, she had to stifle a turn of vexation. As much as she wanted to give him his money, she would have been far happier to have made her way no farther than across town to do it. It was a constant worry that the bank notes would be stolen. Travelling the length of England meant she had to leave the draconian slums of London and submit her welfare to the scurrilous louts who bedevilled the roads of the outer counties.

A sensible girl, before embarking upon her journey, Sally prepared herself for the possibility of road brigands by donning her most threadbare garb. (Mr. Gardiner would have been pleased to know they were of like minds on that matter.) Admittedly, her worst dress was not a fair leap from her everyday one. She knew it was unlikely that she would be a target of thieves. Still, she did not want to risk that—or to be otherwise interfered with. (She had lived long enough on the streets to know that bad men wanted to do bad things to good girls.)

She had sat next to the coachman the length of Derbyshire and, as he knew of her destination, she had been a captive to his extensive colloquies of Pemberley and its inhabitants. He said that Mr. Darcy was known as compunctious and intractable.

"But I hear the lady is kind," he added.

Her relentless silence in the face of his unending yammering finally convinced him that she was uninterested in his tales. In truth, she was worried. Mr. Darcy had treated her well, but Sally knew he thought himself rid of her. She did not hold that against him—he appeared to be a sight better principled than what she imagined the average rich man. It was clear to her that his confrontation with that rat, Wickham was not one he relished. Her sudden appearance would beg no glad tidings.

Fortune saw the money and her honour still intact as she descended the coach onto the Lambton green. From there, she walked the remaining distance to Pemberley. She meant to toss the canvas bag into the hand of the first liveried person she spied and give up asking Mrs. Darcy the favour, but the footman looked inside it and insisted upon announcing her. Whilst he made inquiries within, she was left standing by the Weeping Ash that stood in the courtyard. She watched it sway as she steeled herself for her meeting with Mr. Darcy by reminding herself that was he not happy to see her, he would at least be glad to see his money.

When she was led into a morning-parlour, it was Mrs. Darcy who greeted her. On the night of Wickham's reckoning, the lady had conversed quite freely with her. Not withstanding those circumstances, Mrs. Darcy was still quite welcoming. She even smiled. Then again Sally had determined that lady's kindness was not the sort to be withdrawn once it had been extended. She admired Mrs. Darcy almost as much as Mrs. Gardiner (and Mrs. Gardiner had once given her a shawl—one she wore even then).

Mr. Darcy stood just behind Mrs. Darcy. He and his wife were as alike as chalk and cheese. His expression was just as inscrutable as his wife's was open. But then that was an observation she had come to on their previous undertakings. Nobody much knew what that man was thinking—although the night they ventured down Gowell Street, he had exhibited a bit of hardness about the eyes. When that doxie at Daisy's brothel went up and cupped his family jewels, the man was mortally offended but he barely turned a hair. That is true nobility for you. Because of their shared tribulations, Sally fancied she could decipher Mr. Darcy's thoughts a sight better than others could.

Upon seeing her, Sally saw a bit of wariness in him even then. He most probably thought she had come to extort money from him. That, of course, was downright ridiculous. She already had more of his money than she could count. She tried not to take any disfavour to heart. It was likely she had been right—to him, she was the personification of a very untidy problem that he had believed to have been reconciled. Never the timorous sort, she quickly came to the matter at hand.

"I brung yer money."

With that revelation, a wave of incredulity flickered across his countenance. Sally did not disagree with his low opinion of the general populace, but she could not help but be affronted by his presumption that she was as avaricious as others. Indeed, she was quite miffed. If Mr. Darcy was so dead-set on Wickham getting his comeuppance, he certainly knew to what depths some so-called gentlemen sunk. It then occurred to her that Mrs. Darcy may not have known about any of this money and mayhem business. If Mr. Darcy was acting in defence of his wife, Sally thought she might just overlook his ill expression.

Still, she said defensively, "We ain't all thieves and the like."

Mrs. Darcy interjected, "Ill-character is hardly singular to any one society."

With a slight toss of her head, Sally allowed any insult to be fully appeased.

Mrs. Darcy fell quiet, but Mr. Darcy looked upon her with a keen eye. Although Sally and Mr. Darcy shared a common enemy, he appeared not disposed to speak freely with her. Clearly Mr. Darcy had not told Mrs. Darcy of all their doings that night. That was unsurprising. After all, Sally had not only escorted him to Gowell Street, she introduced him to a notoriously lewd woman, seen his privates fondled, and led him through several rooms of the Gates of Hell brothel (whilst the couples therein were still engaged in illicit companionship) to point him towards George Wickham—a man both he and Mrs. Darcy sought with exceeding vigour. Unknowing though she was of marital disclosures, even she knew that might be a pesky conversation.

If that little adventure was not behind his reticence, certainly their class, sex, age, and disposition were. She broke the impasse by setting the canvas bag containing the bank notes on the floor in front of her. Mr. Darcy seemed to recognize the bag, but he did not move to retrieve it. Untaught in the ways of the rich (and with an inward shrug), Sally supposed gentlemen were not disposed to take something from the hand of the likes of her. (Although that night on Gowell Street he was happy enough for her to grab his hand to and pull him out of harm's way.) She clasped the bag and tossed it to a place upon the carpet roughly halfway between them. He nodded his head in acceptance of her relinquishment, but remained silent. Mrs. Darcy gazed up at him with an odd expression. It was a mixture of love and exasperation.

In return, Mr. Darcy nodded to a footman. That man took hold the bag, set it next to a straight-backed chair, and then retook his place next to the door. Darcy waved him from the room

To Sally, he said, "I thank you."

Sally said, "Sorry to say that it's only 'bout half of it. My associate was disposed to keep her share."

Mr. Darcy's composed hauteur altered. Gradually, an expression of pleased purpose overspread his countenance.

Said he with no small gravity, "You have gone to great lengths to bring this to me. I believe a fair recovery fee for such measures to be ten per-cent. Would that be acceptable to you?"

Her sums were not so good as to know precisely what that figure was, but Sally knew any portion of it would be more than she had before. Flushing with pleasure, Sally ducked her head and nodded.

"Yes sir. That would be very, very acceptable."

Mr. Darcy took the canvas bag with his own hand and began putting notes into a leather case. Sally said, "If you please, the canvas bag'd do me. No one knows what kind of robbers and such are on these roads. A body can't be overly cautious. And leave out a crown, if you please, sir. I had to use that for my fare and other business...."

"For services rendered," he said, returning the bag.

As he handed it to her, he bid, "Am I to understand that you have relinquished your position with Mrs. Kneebone?"

Sally nodded, "I guess you could say that."

"Have you yet found another situation?"

"No sir," Sally replied.

He continued, "Might I offer...."

Understanding this inquiry foretold a suggestion of charity, her chin instinctively jutted in defiance.

She said, "I don't need no alms. I make do just fine even without your money."

Hereupon she regretted her gust of recalcitrance—not only because at present she had no prospects, but behind Mr. Darcy's usual reserve she detected the barest flicker of injury.

Mrs. Darcy had remained quiet whilst these negotiations were in progress. Only upon this lack of agreement, did she stand. She walked to Sally Frances and stood facing her. When Sally did not look up, Mrs. Darcy cupped her chin in her hand and bade her return her gaze.

"Dearest girl," said Mrs. Darcy, "I wish you not to return to London. If you have family there, then you must. But I bid you stay."

Sally's seldom used tears appeared. Angrily, she wiped her eyes with the backs of her hands.

"I truly thank you, Milady," said Sally. "But I have other business."

Her resolve wavering, Sally turned to take her leave before it was lost altogether. Before she could, she was stopped by an awkwardly constructed inquiry by Mr. Darcy.

"Did you," he asked carefully, "Bring with you intelligence as to our mutual acquaintance?"

With a level gaze, Sally replied, "No."

It was a decision that she had come to prior to embarking upon her journey to Pemberley. What occurred within the walls of George Wickham's lodgings would remain confidential. Outwardly, she attributed having made this resolution to the avoidance of any chance of prosecution. But she had a deeper reason, one she could not account for or really explain. She felt the need not only to protect her own culpability, but that of Mr. Darcy too. Indeed, she could not explain wanting to be custodian of that man's sensibilities. It was clear he would abhor any hint of care from her. She had begun to suspect, however, that the reason Mr. Darcy was so guarded was not his lack of heart, but just the opposite.

If that was so, she was happy to be the keeper of Wickham's fate whether it was hell or halfway there. In that moment she decided not to allow her pride to make her ultimate goal that much more difficult.

"I thank ye most kindly," said Sally, "In truth, I come to ask a favour too."

Mrs. Darcy nodded.

"I come to find a lady—a neighbour of yours. She's a lady of condition, but I donno her name."

Mrs. Darcy expression altered slightly. It betokened her puzzlement. Understanding that she must employ all her powers of description, Sally was at a loss to do so without giving offence to a woman who had hardly a good feature upon her face.

"She's fleshy—looks to be a bit over-fed," Sally mused. "Mulish teeth too. I'd say a bit of a magpie."

"I cannot imagine who you mean," stuttered Mrs. Darcy, clearly loath to identify any friend upon the basis of that description. Seeing no flicker of recognition, Sally was frustrated, but was willing to give it another go.

"She looks a bit like them horses she was always talking about."

Eureka! Identification at last.

"Lady Millhouse," Mrs. Darcy told her. Relief bathed her countenance, but she was still bewildered, "May I inquire why you seek this lady?"

"I hear she went to the Low Countries and brought her boy home. True?"

"Tis true," Mrs. Darcy agreed, "It was not her son, but her nephew—she loved him as if a son. She wanted to bury him in Derbyshire."

"I aim to do the same for my brother," Sally announced, "He was born between near Wapping, but I hoped to find a vicar kind enough to let him lie beside a church. I need her to direct me as to how she went about it."

They both looked at her quite oddly.

Holding tighter to it, Sally asked, "Do I still get the money?"

That was spoken a bit defensively. Sally appreciated the audacity of her plan and anticipated opposition. She had not really meant to share her intentions, but she knew it reasonable of Mrs. Darcy to inquire.

"One has no bearing upon the other," Mrs. Darcy replied. "I commend your ambition and shall do all in my power to assist you."

With that, she beckoned the housekeeper.

"Please see to this young lady, she must be famished."

Admitting to being a bit peckish, Sally was happy to be offered a meal. As she quitted the room fast behind the steps of the housekeeper, she came to a skidding stop.

"I almost fergot this," she said.

Digging beneath her bodice, she produced a scroll. It was besmudged and a bit crunched, but she tried her best to straighten it. This time, Mr. Darcy took the vellum forthwith. Indeed, the gentleman nearly snatched from her hands. Notwithstanding the time that had passed since it was last seen, it was obvious he recognised it as the one Mrs. Darcy had meant for Wickham's signature.

He nodded. Sally went on to the kitchen.

A Note Too Late

Due to a throbbing headache, Lady Howgrave had her husband summon their coach not long after she spoke to Mr. Darcy the night of the Pemberley ball. Except for her sudden bout of ill-health, she appeared quite pleased with herself and the evening.

She was not.

When Elizabeth Darcy chanced to see them standing on the gallery above her that night, Juliette had been utterly delighted. Darcy's smile was as rare as it was fleeting, therefore all the more propitious that it occurred when his wife looked up at them. Juliette had kept her countenance however. It would have been imprudent to reveal her pleasure to either of them. It was enough to know that Darcy's wife had espied them together—in what looked to be nothing less than a stolen moment.

Was fate not grand?

No woman was immune to jealousy's cruel barb—that was a certainty. Creating marital disorder was not Juliette's true calling, just an amusing consequence. In deliberately gazing up at Darcy when (and how) Mrs. Darcy did, Juliette was not only aware that she might vex his wife, she gloried in that possibility. It had long been decreed that all is fair in love and war—although generals bow to ladies when scruples do account. Surely, Miss Bennet did not marry Mr. Darcy without understanding those rules of engagement.

There was a time when she might have liked Elizabeth Darcy, but once Juliette embarked on securing Darcy for herself, she was deemed a mortal enemy. A successful courtesan employed her conscience only marginally more frequently than her heart. That was the way of the world—her world, the demimonde.

Knowing full well that Darcy would tarry with her for but a moment, it was imperative that she put what time he allowed her to good use. Yet hurry could cause the most well-plotted seduction to go awry. It had only been through considerable guile that she had managed time alone with him at all.

Mr. Darcy was unlike other men. He did not come when she beckoned. (She had only to curl a finger and a College of Cardinals would be veritably panting at her slippered feet.) He was haughty and terse; passionate and particular—and he alone seemed immune to her charms.

If he was arrogant, she knew he had good reason to be so.

He had spent his life thwarting unwanted female flirtations and in doing so, become almost legendary for his refusals. One story had a lady passing Darcy a note asking him to meet her in her carriage. Somehow that note was secreted into the coat pocket of the lady's own husband. When he, rather than Darcy, climbed into her coach, the man's wife was called upon to perform more improvisations than a Piccadilly puppeteer.

Had Juliette not known Darcy so well, she could have expected to fail the way countless others had. Libidinous women forgot to take into account his immoveable pride. He did not dally with inferiors. He held his family name above all else. As all rich men, however, he enjoyed the power of doing as he liked. It was unlikely time had mellowed that inclination.

Although she would have rather died than admit it, Darcy's long-past visits to her had always been perfunctory. He had come irregularly and no exclusivity had been implied. Yet, her ever-faithful spies told her that he did not spend time with any other. She would have agreed to a more formal arrangement in a trice, but she dared not suggest it. To him, theirs was a business arrangement—incurring no more sentiment than had she laundered his shirts. Truth be told, she would have seen him without pecuniary inducement whatsoever. He recompensed her to befit his sensibilities, not hers. Hence, his loins had been consoled at no expense to his heart.

Although it had been some time since they had lain together, the recollection of the *générosité* of his manhood and the vigour wherewith he employed it was not easily forgotten. A night with young Mr. Darcy did not pass without numerous achievements. Her mettle could not afford to think of it often, but when she did, the memory gave her pause. His fierce ardour always left her breathless; his inexplicable nature kept her perpetually perplexed.

Seeing him again at Pemberley, she had to remind herself that she was in want of Mr. Darcy's seed, not an *amour*. (But then there was absolutely nothing to forbid enjoying the delivery of either.)

In the brief moment that Darcy's hands had rested upon the balustrade, Juliette was able to sketch more than merely the shades of his mind. She saw implicitly what was at stake. He was still the man of imperious bearing and exceptional leg. If she was any judge of a man (and she believed she was), he had not lost his admirable potency. She had not scrupled against taking a furtive glance at the crotch of his trousers. She made a mental note to send her compliments to his tailor.

Before he could bow and take his leave, she quickly made the observation, "You do not come to London as you once did."

By invoking London and it vaunted milieu, she begged the memory of their once-intimate association.

"No, I do not," he explained.

It was urgent that she hasten their discourse, but he was maddeningly uncooperative. His wife could intrude at any moment. Moreover, Darcy's wavering gaze implied he was readying his escape and she had yet to draw him out. Juliette, however, was nothing if not light on her feet when forces united against her.

She said, "When Sir Howgrave and I are more settled into Kirkland Hall, we shall send round invitations. It shall not, of course, rival your gala, but then the house is much in need of repair. To be frank, the place is in ruin." She checked herself, or pretended to, "Oh, do forgive me. I meant no offence to the Bingleys, they are a charming couple. Their children are quite enlivened."

At the mention of the abominable condition of the Bingleys' house, Darcy seemed amused.

Juliette was encouraged. Her mental machinations were much in use, so she did not listen closely to what he said. Later, she chastised herself for not taking greater note of that.

As a rule, Juliette had cordial feelings for children so long as they remained in their place. The Bingleys' brood was cherubic, but hardly angelic. She had seen that when Jane attempted to stand them in line to make introductions the day she visited them. They stayed still for nigh a quarter of a minute and then ran off on some sort of loud, running game. With more good intentions than success, Jane shushed them and led Juliette into a quiet afternoon parlour. Juliette was offered a seat, but when she took it, she was stabbed by a toy sword. She hoped it was not a bad omen.

"Yes," Darcy was saying, "Bingley's children are quite ungovernable. Happy lot though."

Juliette made a show of agreeing, "Mrs. Bingley is quite handsome. That she has remained so after the birth of so many children is a great wonder."

To this observation, he remained silent.

"Children are both a blessing and bother in equal measure, are they not?" she continued.

His eyes barely fluttered. His nostrils flared imperceptibly. She mistook his agitation. He bestowed her a cursory bow. It was most certainly not one of submission.

He said curtly. "I can no longer trespass upon your time."

"Are we doomed to meet amongst the tedium of country manners?"

Juliette thought she took the sting out of such impudence with a spectacular smile. Her smile had rarely failed her. With just the right tilt of her head and an expression that promised everything, she had obtained her two houses, dozens of lovers, and an adorable white bichon named Tout.

"Shall we meet in London next season?"

"No," he said firmly.

As dispassionately as she could manage, she said, "A pity."

Juliette was not heavily powdered—only a light dusting across her bosom. Hence, the colour that crept from thenceforth to her neck was unnoticeable. She had realised that her lack of subtlety had offended him—possibly a fatal blunder.

With his usual grace, he clasped his hands behind his back and moved to a group of party-goers who had gathered a few feet away. They might have seen the beautiful Lady Howgrave—few did not. But they had little time to conjecture what, if any, conversation passed between her and Mr. Darcy. By no means would they have detected it from her ladyship. Her countenance was hidden behind her fan.

As Darcy stepped away from her, his scent remained—if only for the smallest moment. Yet, it was so familiar to her that a tear troubled the corner of her eye. Or at least it did until her delicate nose whiffed out a second scent intermingled with his. It was not perfume, but a musky combination of aromas. A lifetime dedicated to men and amour meant that she had recognized the scent. It was the odour of requited passion.

With the lightness of the wind, Lady Howgrave descended the staircase. As she did, her countenance did not reflect her acute vexation.

Why, Darcy had come to the ball fresh from his wife's embrace!

How many times did that seductress have him take her? Two? Three? He had to be compleatly fordone by the exertion. Certainly he had been left in no condition to take another woman that night. What devious wiles that wife of his had.

Bloody hell.

For all her recollections, Juliette forgot the specific circumstances of how her acquaintanceship with Darcy had come to an end. In the lonely shadow of lost opportunity, she thought of it only at her leisure.

At the time she believed that Darcy had quit her bed in honour of his wedding vows. But he had forsworn her acquaintance before his marriage. Indeed, once he had fancied himself in love with Miss Bennet, he refused her.

There was another, more difficult truth she had to address.

Mentally stamping her foot, Juliette recalled that Elizabeth Darcy's figure had been exceedingly voluptuous. No doubt she was again with child. The night of the Pemberley ball, something else was quite evident besides his wife's blossoming waistline. The bulge in Darcy's breeches (that she so surreptitiously admired) had not shrivelled from disuse.

Was she to gain Darcy's cooperation, in her quest for his seed, she would have to appeal to his chivalry, not his cock.

It was much engaged with his damnable wife.

oldier On

Before Sally had gone on her way that day, Mr. Darcy found her.
It was unusual for a man of his eminence to seek someone sitting
in the kitchen. Hence, when they saw Mr. Darcy he did not ask the servants
to take their leave. Indeed, the cook and her scullery maids scattered. When
Sally spied him, she knew instinctively that he meant to ask her of the event of
mutual interest. She hoped that he would not ask if she plugged that bastard,
Wickham, for she did not want to have to lie. In fortune, he did not. He held
the piece of vellum she had brought with her. Perhaps he wanted her to retain
it herself. No accounting for rich men's motives.

But, he did not want her to take it. He had a question—indeed, several
questions.

"I recognise Wickham's hand. Tell me why did he sign *this* name?"

One long, aristocratic finger pointed to the signature.

"If he was to vow Wickham was dead, we figured that he needed another
name. 'Thomas Reed' was one Daisy thought up."

A quizzical expression passed over his countenance, "Beg pardon?"

"Daisy Mulroney," she said, then explained further, "My partner—the wee
brothel-keeper."

Recognition lit his eye, but that was not the end of it.

"Can you tell me why she advocated this particular name?"

Sally had not thought of it over-much. At the time, she believed that it had
just been a caprice. Tapping her finger upon her chin, she did what she could
to recall precisely what Daisy had said about it.

"It was her half-brother's name. She said he'd escaped from Newgate and
if Wickham was to try to use it he might get pinched. Still, when we left him,
Wickham wasn't goin' no where...."

Mr. Darcy's face lost a bit of its colour, giving Sally to recall the rest of the
story. She did not know if she should expound on the subject or not.

Before she could, Mr. Darcy said, "Is Miss Mulroney witting of the fact that
her brother is dead and that he died at the point of my sword?"

His gaze was keen. So was Sally's.

She said, "Yea, both of 'em."

Again, he asked, "Beg pardon?"

"She knows that Tom's dead and that you kilt 'em—both of 'em. She had two bothers, you kilt 'em both."

Not one to shrink from possible reckoning, Mr. Darcy stood a little taller. He said, "I see."

Sally would have liked to hear the hows and the whys of that story, but he did not offer them.

What he said next was not exactly a question.

"And she aided me nonetheless?"

"She didn't know her kin well—they were older'n her and didn't share the same father. She said that Tom was no good and that he probably duped poor Frank into some bad business."

All Mr. Darcy had to say was, "It was a bad business, indeed."

More to herself than to him, Sally said, "Maybe that's why she kept her share of the money. Due compensation."

When she looked up, Mr. Darcy was gone.

There is little doubt that, left to his own devices, Mr. Darcy would have taken the scroll little Miss Arbuthnot brought to him and hidden it away—never to be looked upon or thought of ever again. His wife was not disposed to allow him that just then.

Sally had just withdrawn from the room when Elizabeth turned to her husband and extended her hand.

"Pray, may I?"

Tucking an expression of amused trepidation in the corner of his mouth, he responded mildly, "I am quite sure I have no idea to what you refer."

"Do not be mischievous when I am in such a state of curiosity. Pray, is it signed?"

"His signing this document means nothing," Darcy reminded her. "It alters nothing."

Upon speaking those words, any hint of frivolity evaporated. Try as she would to check any recognizable vexation from his expression, she was reminded of the full measure of grief he had suffered—and suffered yet at Wickham's hand. Injury to her husband was injury to herself. That was as it always would be.

"Indeed, what does it matter? George Wickham is dead," she said softly. "It is done."

He repeated firmly, "It is done."

In fortune, the foremost chin-waggers in service at Pemberley were not privy to Mr. Darcy's conversation with the little girl from London. The walls of Pemberley were thick, but not impenetrable. Mr. Darcy was aware of this above anyone else. Little went on in any room of such a vast house that was not overheard, glimpsed, or eventually sniffed out. He chose his moment for conversing with Sally with great care.

Sally was known to most in service at Pemberley as the girl who served as Mrs. Major Kneebone's nursemaid. Other, more senior servants knew of her connection to the boy, John Christie who had once been a stable-hand. There were other, darker tales passed round.

In the year '16, they were considered by most as just talk—Sally kept what she knew to herself.

Heart & Hearth

Two years after Sally's call on the Darcys, little had altered within Pemberley's august halls when it came to gossipry.

Those who served within were free to discuss more urgent matters—like whether or not Mr. Darcy did or did not rip Mrs. Darcy's fancy new drawers to shreds. For society had it on good word and general observation that Mr. Darcy's directive on any matter within his manor was inviolate.

No member of his household argued this presumption. Yet it was not entirely true. Upon occasion, Mr. Darcy's opinion was countered. When it was, his wife was the violator. Had society presumed to know of what passed between Mr. and Mrs. Darcy in their most intimate moments, they might have thereby believed that Mr. Darcy's word on the matter of her undergarments was infrangible too. That would beckon a misapprehension. By his own words, one might have understood Mr. Darcy did not favour his wife's wearing such an indelicate garment. No one, save her maid, knew this for certain.

Although the tattered lady-breeches had been stashed away, word of their condition soon escaped by way of a nosy upstairs maid. Back-stairs tongues wagged. It might have been said then that the newest in fashion was all for nought. It might have been said, but that would have been wrong—quite wrong. As it happened, Mrs. Darcy continued to wear her drawers—and not just when a chill was in the air.

As a woman who had been taken to the straw three times and had two children live beyond infancy, Elizabeth Darcy was much more fortunate than many mothers. That did not mean she was not wary. She saw it her duty, however, not to allow her own apprehension to be apparent to her husband. Indeed, when the coming event entered their conversation, she invoked an expression of false gaiety that elicited more trepidation than any other she could have invented. Darcy was uncertain whether to allow her to think her disguise was successful or not. In the end, he permitted her that.

They soldiered on their usual fashion, each of the opinion they were a balm to the other. In a roundabout way they were counterirritants. Her determination to commit a ruse and his indecision upon whether to expose said ruse successfully diverted much of their attention—time that might otherwise been spent fretting over the outcome of her pregnancy.

There was no possible circumstance that would have influenced him to leave his wife's side during her confinement. Indeed, he kept to her side so diligently that she had to shoo him away to tend to her indisposition. For each morn inevitably brought a bout of sickness with it. The only food she could keep down was a broth that Georgiana concocted. It was vile-tasting, but it kept nausea at bay.

Although Georgiana had two small children to see to of her own, she brought them and their nurse with her to Pemberley for Elizabeth's laying-in. The children played happily, and Geoff was pleased to have other little girls to tease than just his sister.

It was known to everyone that Georgiana and Elizabeth loved each other as sisters. Because it was never alluded to in company, few people knew that Darcy's sister was in want of repaying an enormous debt to his wife. The weight of Georgiana's duty became even greater upon the birth of her own child. She fully understood what Elizabeth must have suffered whilst her brother was off trying to recover her from her own impetuosity. She had been so determined to reach her love, Colonel Fitzwilliam, she thought of nothing—and no one—else.

Guilt plagued Georgiana. She could not repair the past, but she meant to do all she could to see to the future. Once Elizabeth's morning sickness had subsided, it took all of her powers of persuasion to convince Georgiana that nothing would be more pleasing than to have her retire to Whitemore and return for her labour. Pleased with the arrangement, Georgiana did.

As dear as she held Georgiana, it was Elizabeth's fervent wish, for the time leading up to her delivery, to be one of solitude. (Such a sequestration suited propriety quite well.) Privacy was needed for her to indulge herself in ways that others might find odd. Her husband certainly did.

Although they both knew her pregnancy had not yet outgrown her own dressing gowns, she drew her husband's enormous robe about her. When he questioned it, she explained that it alone was commodious enough to encase her growing belly. As a gift, he had a blue velvet robe made up just for her, lined with satin and bedizened with gold braid. She told him that she loved it and he believed that she did, but she eschewed it for his day after day.

"Pray have more dressing gowns made, have a dozen. I believe we can bear the expense."

That was hardly the point. Some caprices men did not comprehend. With a merry tone to her voice, she said, "Whilst you were detained upon the Continent, your wife cared not to employ a seamstress. She was far too enormous for a bolt of patterned fabric to cover."

"You were not," he said mildly.

"I beg otherwise. There was a fine bolt of Madras, but we had to save it for the draperies. My amplitude was enough to tempt an eastern potentate. I am astonished one did not hear of me and arrive at the gates of Pemberley atop his elephant."

"I am not at all certain potentates ride elephants," he said dryly.

She ignored him, claiming, "Thereinafter, I was as large as a wash tub—or perchance yon dresser. I told Jane to throw a table scarf across me and be done with it."

"I am sorry in all ways I was not here to witness that," he replied.

"There would not be enough room in this bed for the both of us."

"No?"

He had always been entertained by her wit. It was appreciated then more than before, for it was a far greater pleasure to think upon that perilous time with humour than the alternative. He spied a silver box in her hands.

"What have you there?"

"This contains my dearest treasures."

When she opened it, he observed that it held several cuttings of hair. All three were different shades of brown and tied with different coloured ribbons. He held out his hand and she laid two locks of hair across his palm. Seeing the ribbons, one pink and one blue, he presumed them to be locks of their children's hair. Another lock was still in the box. It had a dark blue ribbon attached.

"What is that one there?"

"That one is yours," she smiled. "I had Goodwin collect your hair trimmings for me."

His brow furrowed.

She held it up admiringly, "It is of uncommon length because it was gathered after your sojourn across the water. Your hair hung below your collar...."

He remarked, "I had no notion...."

"I assure you that you looked quite dashing," she said.

Also in the box was a single ribbon. It was from the first gift he had given her. She had treasured it for one reason alone—the bow was so badly done that she had known that he had tied it himself. She did not show him that. He was gazing upon her and her box with adoration (albeit a trifle indulgently) and he might not be so pleased to be the object of a condescension himself.

When he finally inquired why she kept the box so near, she said simply, "I take comfort in it."

He was happy to look upon her whimsies as just that and ignored her sudden penchant for sleeping with an old shirt of his clasped tightly in her fist. It was still a mystery as to why she clung to that particular shirt. It was spun of the softest gauze, to be sure. But it had been stained with sweat and dirt from a day he spent in the saddle. She was of fastidious habits; therefore the reason for the shirt was just as capricious as the robe. It was not for a husband to wonder what fancy pleases a woman when with child. If such small rebellions provided her comfort, he was happy of it.

Observing Mr. Darcy's quizzical looks and mystified expression over his wife's odd predilections, Hannah was not disposed to intercede. But when a specific opportunity bechanced, she decided to try to tell the master what her mistress could not.

It came about because Mr. Darcy happened to come into the bedchamber as Hannah was rescuing those very garments. She wanted to retrieve them before the chambermaids changed the bedclothes. Hannah heard Mr. Darcy's boots and glanced behind her to make certain it was he who had entered before she spoke. Her manner was light and, at first, Mr. Darcy did not know that the maid spoke to him.

Then he did.

She said, "I fancy it's an odd thing to those who were not here for my lady's last confinement. For me, I was I here and I knew. From the very first, it was. She wore that dirty shirt every night. She found it kicked under the bed the day the master took his leave and put it on. Goodwin wanted it washed, but she wouldn't have it. She wore it every night—for you see, she had only that."

Humming a vaguely familiar tune, Hannah took the treasured shirt and robe to be put away. Mr. Darcy did not turn to observe Hannah take her leave, nor did she dare take measure of his reaction. She knew what she said was for the best and was content to have done it. Her thoughts had already turned to Goodwin, for he disliked Hannah having say over Mr. Darcy's robe. She smiled knowing that until the end of Mrs. Darcy's pregnancy she had the whip hand over Goodwin in at least one matter. That pleased her to no end.

Hannah was on her way to other chores and Darcy stood still as a statue.

He had come thither to the bedchamber looking for... he had forgotten why he had come. Hannah's words hung in air, rung in the air, wrenching his heart.

"She had only that."

$\mathscr{L}$ove's Labour

Jane and Bingley rarely disagreed. The greatest peturbment of Jane's marriage was that her beloved Charles hid his looming financial disaster from her, thereby not allowing her to solace him properly in his many hours of distress.

She would never accuse him of mishandling his fortune, for she loved him far too much.

Happy once again, Georgiana, Jane, and Elizabeth were pleased to share companionship. They chirped of their children's newest feats, knitted stockings, and ruched little bonnets whilst commiserating Elizabeth's pregnancy. They were not dunces, however, and upon occasion they spoke of what went on beyond the parameters of their own contented households. No one actually recalled how it came into the conversation, but it was Elizabeth's particular recollection that it was all Georgiana's doing.

Bingley had gradually gathered himself from financial reverses, in part by retaining interest in a number of coal mines. During Georgiana's time spent bringing remedies to the ill and foodstuffs to the poor, she saw a great deal more of the land and its inhabitants than most gentlewomen. She had travelled to Matlock and the coal and limestone mines beyond. With two small girls, she still no longer went thither regularly, but was kept apprised of the doings of those families who had enjoyed her assistance. She was alarmed by what she had learnt.

"The most distressing information has come to me," Georgiana said. "In our very county of Derbyshire, heartless mine owners employ poor, pitiful ponies to haul the coal. They are kept in stables beneath the ground. They never see the light of day and often go blind."

"How ghastly!" said Jane.

"Pray tell, are you not pleased that my brother has closed what mines existed upon Pemberley?" Georgiana asked Elizabeth.

The closures had occurred prior to their marriage. Therefore, Elizabeth had no comment. She knew, however, in all things he did as at his own character demanded.

Jane said, "Charles has maintained his mines. He says that in these hard times he must, for every mine supports a hundred families."

Georgiana responded, "Herein lies the issue. The men are there by choice—not a handsome choice, I agree—but of their own volition. These pit-ponies have no say in their fate."

"It could not be," insisted Jane. "Certainly not at Stavely. Charles would not stand for such cruelty. He is far too kind."

Indeed, Bingley was a kind man. However, against Darcy's advice, he continued to lease his mines through partnerships of mineral agents. Bingley's land was not family land and he was far happier seeing to his race horses than those poor animals labouring beyond his seeing. Jane promised to speak to Bingley of it, knowing he would see that misuse was stopped. When she did, Bingley patted her hand and said he would look into it when next he went to Stavely. As he had never been to Stavely, his pledge remained unfulfilled.

Although Fitzwilliam was aware of his wife's abhorrence of the plight of the ponies, he owned no mines and was therefore in no position to aid them. Georgiana had proven herself to be a young woman of considerable self-will (some accused wilful). Hence, she went to her brother with a proposal—one that left Darcy aghast. He flatly refused her request.

He blustered, "I shall not pledge your inheritance towards freeing these horses...."

"Ponies," she interrupted.

"Be they ponies or horses, their ill-treatment would be as abominable. I shall do nothing that would endanger your daughter's legacy."

Unused to her brother denying her, Georgiana blinked several times. Darcy knew that was not a good sign. It was imperative that he step in lest she do something rash. Through the travails of war he had come to understand that she was not to be easily thwarted.

"I shall buy the ponies from the mines," she announced.

"They shall only be replaced. If you shall allow me, I shall make inquiries as to what might be done to improve matters."

His pledge was far more reliable than was Bingley's.

Whilst having his solicitor look into the situation, Darcy saw to his wife and their coming child. Elizabeth's ever-increasing girth was becoming unmanageable.

Indeed, with every passing month, Elizabeth was less and less certain her pregnancy would be single birth. (That concern she kept to herself.) Because she regaled him with jollities about her bulk, he knew that he must laugh with her. Her belly had been a goodly size with the child they lost; thus it was difficult for him to imagine how she could have possibly carried two. Their first child had been breech—and large as well. That still plagued his mind unremittingly.

He saw that as his fault alone. The sire was more important when it came to conformation. He was tall and broad shouldered. It was he who had the length of leg; Elizabeth was surprisingly small-boned. After the stillbirth, he had castigated himself relentlessly for impregnating her with a child too large for her to deliver safely. He did not see himself as he was—a finely-chiselled patrician, but a brute of a man whose wife suffered bearing his issue. Try as he might, he could not keep those thoughts from invading his mind again.

Or worse—what if she was to have three babes? He had heard of it. Good God in heaven, say not.

Elizabeth alone recognised the subtle signs announcing that his apprehensions ran amok. Rather than unrestrained, he became just a little more reserved, his features more composed, and his posture more in check. He smiled but little and every time he looked at her, a crease furrowed his brow. She did what she could to divert him by jesting again over her size.

"I could not see my feet and dared not take the stairs without a hand to guide me," she laughed. "When I walked in the garden, I waddled so convincingly that a trail of ducklings followed behind."

He smiled dutifully, but remained discomposed. She had expected that he would worry. She had been right to delay as long as possible informing him of the coming blessed event. Nonetheless, she was quite content for him to guide her down the stairs when she became unsteady and was beside herself with gratitude when he rubbed her feet.

"My toes are the size of sausages. How can you even want me again?" she moaned. "In your minds eye I shall forever be a snuffling pig...."

"On this, you must trust me, my love. I shall always want you."

As they took their tea before the fire, Darcy's attention was upon his paper. Elizabeth sighed. The sigh was such that he continued to read the same line again and again.

"This child is likely to be a bit of a rogue," she said. "He is putting up quite a fuss."

Glancing at her, he could not disguise his concern. Seeing that, she hastily altered the conversation.

"Of course it is entirely possible that I suffer doubly. Four feet may be vexing me, not two."

He sniffed, "Do not imagine for a moment I find such talk amusing, Mrs. Darcy."

"Imagine, sir, what acclaim you shall have. Two sets of twins—or perhaps a set of three! The king may give you a knighthood and the scholars shall insist you pen a book."

"I do not have the pleasure of hearing a word you say," he said placidly.

"Neither of us have any say in it now," she reminded him. "The seed, so to speak, has been sown."

Putting down his paper, he turned to offer a drollery when he saw that she had lost her colour. He was at her side ere she could assure him all was well.

"Just a twinge," she insisted.

The Politics of the Blind

When the invitation arrived announcing the ball at Pemberley, Henry Howgrave had been exceedingly delighted to accept. It would be the perfect opportunity to make a grand return to those hallowed halls (the scene of his most ignominious humiliation) as the conquering hero, sporting a knighthood, a considerable fortune, unrivalled fame, and an exquisitely handsome wife (the finest his money could buy him). Everyone in the county would envy him for it all.

The embarrassment he had suffered at Darcy's hands so long ago had been nurtured into a certain kind of hate. Howgrave had partially revenged himself when Darcy came to him (came to *him*) in London for assistance with his friend Bingley's financial reverses.

Of course Howgrave had acquiesced. He was happy to have Mr. Darcy indebted to him. Such a man would be a valuable associate (and source of funding) in his political pursuits.

Howgrave's return to Pemberley had been as triumphant as it was short-lived. Ere the month was out, he was once again desperate for additional backers and their money. It was necessary for him to pad his corner. One could not stand on one's honours. A man of vision had to hold to one's guns, eagre for the next battle before the fires from the first one had yet been put out. With talk of insurgency, those in power were desperate to stay there. In his heart, Howgrave did not give a flea's ass about mechanisation and job loss. The necessitous charity children were the worry of privately funded almshouses. His interest lay in the men who could ensure that he keep his dominance.

Certain smoke-filled dens were alive with political upheaval. The smallest wrong word and a gentleman would be labelled a revolutionary. That equalled political catastrophe. It should have been no surprise that to relieve the anxiety consequential to such havoc, he had no choice but to debase himself sexually with his wife.

Whilst enduring the whip, his dear wife continued to be an asset to his office. The ball at Pemberley had proved her worth in the hinterlands. He had befriended a dozen men that night, landed gentlemen who would be of good cheer when it came to financial support.

Sides were easily identified. Reactionaries bought good wine. Civil libertarians bought ale. Of the two, the radicals certainly sold more newsprint. Rabble-rousers inciting riots stirred blood on both sides. They were often of the Methodist persuasion. A courtesan of the highest order, Juliette was witting of the prevailing politics. She haughtily foretold that Utilitarianism would not become law—for it did not side against man's vices.

Of late, his dear wife had begun to drag her tiny slippers when it came to accompanying him to his speeches. When Howgrave announced that he was to speak once again at The Marylebone Reading Society, she begged another engagement.

"Heaven forbid! They discuss political pamphlets!" she complained.

Once his office was secured, her distaste for politics had waned in direct proportion with the press's interest in her. This displeased him. His hand circled her arm just above the elbow firmly enough to convince her that she was happy to join him. She might have objected further, but he had lured her felicity by promising Rowlandson would be there taking likenesses for his popular caricatures. They were particularly cutting to Howgrave, but one could not ignore publicity no matter how denigrating.

Once again, Juliette did her part (indeed, Rowlandson's likeness of her was quite complimentary), but Howgrave was not above reminding his dear wife of what they both knew—her bargain was not compleat until she produced an heir.

When he acquired her, there had been whispers that she was older than she had admitted. But Howgrave did not doubt his own eye. Her skin was dewy as the morn. He had no illusions in regards to his wife's honour, she was a courtesan. Every man of station in London knew of her, she was possibly the most singular woman in England. That was her cachet. She was a woman of accommodating morals, but an excellent one.

If he found out that she had lied to him in relation to something of such great importance as her childbearing capacity, a carriage whip was not the only thing he would administer against her lovely, white flesh. (Just thinking of it, a small bit of spit accumulated in the corner of his mouth.) He did not need to remind her of her duty. She knew it inherently. Her unhappiness was disguised as indifference, which was exhibited repeatedly by a stifled yawn. When her husband orated, however, all demeaning gestures were kept hidden behind her heavily-decorated fan.

Even Howgrave became bored by such meetings. Most groups were dry as toast until they were supplied with gunpowder. The few sparks that were ignited that night were overruled by cooler heads. It was remarkable how excruciatingly monotonous the oratory of rioters could otherwise be.

The mile between Tyburn and Piccadilly was strewn with broken waggons, crushed vegetables, and fractured hopes. Whilst the poor ran rampant in the streets, the fashionable dined with Coleridge and Byron, nodding their heads at the mellifluence of the poetic words. Given a choice, Juliette was happy to be amused by stargazing poets. Moreover, there was a good bit of tittering over Byron's alleged liaison with his sister—any party was improved by lascivious gossip. Howgrave sniffed at such light amusements.

The political pot was stirred as it boiled by other speechmakers, both caustic and appealing. Their words disturbed the masses upon both sides. Amongst them slunk spies and counter-spies. It was one great cacophony of bedlam. Desperate for an influx of new blood in his camp, Howgrave continued to coax Alistair Thomas to his speeches. The man seemed resistant. Slipping away for days at a time, Howgrave's friends questioned where he went and thus his loyalty. Lord Orloff defended him.

"A gentleman such as he must weigh all his options before making his commitment."

Howgrave nodded in agreement and his friends acquiesced.

"When you know the gentleman better, you shall think better of him," he assured them.

Uninterested in political winds that did not affect her, Juliette grew increasingly wan. She began to anticipate public disturbances just to have an excuse to get her slippers muddy.

All the while Mr. Darcy kept to the north.

The Third Rose

With a history of beforehand labours, Jane had meant to be by her sister's side when such time was upon them. Unfortunately, two of her children were ill with scarlet fever. (Elizabeth would no more allow her take leave of her children than she would have chanced bringing contagion with her to Pemberley.) Hence, Georgiana became the chief architect of the birth. Her soft voice and calm air was always a great reassurance during such times. Also on hand was the physician, Mr. Upchurch. However, Georgiana dismissed the pair of midwives he brought with him.

Once her labour commenced in earnest, Elizabeth was torn whether to bid her children to her or not. She feared that if she did, her words might be given too much weight. She most certainly did not want them to take an audience as some sort of farewell. In the end, she called for them. As she kissed their foreheads, both were more solemn than she would have liked. Geoff held his sister's hand as they were led away. However, once beyond the door; they ran to play without a backwards look.

As soon as they were out of hearing, Elizabeth emitted a deep groan. When she did, Darcy abruptly stood, looking as if he had been hit in the stomach. In a moment, the pain subsided. Seeing his deep apprehension (and knowing the next contraction would not be less painful than the last), she insisted that he must go too.

"All shall be well," she reassured him.

Although he took her hand gently in his and kissed it, his voice was unusually taut.

"Of course," he said.

With a forced smile, she reminded him, "This is the one thing that I must do all on my own." Thereupon, she announced, "I shall be done with this business in a trice. All *shall* be well. This I promise you."

Without releasing her hand, he nodded.

"I *promise*," she repeated. Then girding herself for another contraction, she bid, "Go now. You must."

He nodded once more, very nearly bowed, and walked quietly away. He stopped at the door. Pressing his forehead against the frame, he grimaced.

"I shall see to her, brother," Georgiana said.

Without responding, Darcy stepped outside the room. He did not trust his voice. Indeed, helplessness overwhelmed him. It was a sensation he held in great abhorrence. Mr. Upchurch stood a few feet away and Darcy was most pleased to vent his vexation upon him.

In what could only be described as a bark, he told him, "You shall apprise me should Mrs. Darcy become unduly distressed."

"Yes, Mr. Darcy," the doctor answered.

As Mr. Darcy strode away, the doctor called after him, "I presume you mean other than that which is required?"

The good doctor regretted his question almost as soon as he uttered it. Both were well-acquainted with "that which was required." Mr. Upchurch had not attended Mrs. Darcy upon her first, tragic confinement. He most certainly had heard of it. Having brought many a baby into the world, he understood what had gone amiss then. As Mr. Darcy waited at the far end of the corridor, the doctor ducked into Mrs. Darcy's room for his initial assessment. He knew what her husband was most in want of knowing.

It was Georgiana who brought the pertinent information. Her brother stood looking out a window, his hands clasped behind his back. She called to him. As he walked to her, she saw him square his shoulders.

She announced, "The baby is in the correct position."

If Darcy found comfort in that news, he did not betray it. Once again, he nodded. In truth, his mouth was dry from trepidation. Had that not rendered him speechless, he might have inquired as to the size of the child.

Thenceforth, he remained in his library, the door ajar. That set the tenor for the house. It was as if all of Pemberley was carpeted with eggs. Everyone was quiet as mice and frightened as rabbits. The servants did their duties calmly, but would stop in seeming unison and put a hand to one ear. Not that they expected the baby would come directly. They settled in for a long wait and steeled themselves for the outcome.

It was all for naught. The birth of the newest Darcy was notable for nothing except a compleat want of folderol. Elizabeth was taken to her bed at four and gave birth by half-past seven. Mr. Darcy had not time enough to generate much angst whatsoever.

Both were relieved for the other.

Word had been sent to Darcy as soon as the birth was imminent. He heard the first mewling cries of the babe from outside the birthing room. Bathed with relief for that, he knew, of course, was not the end of it. An hour crept by before the doctor felt it was safe to announce all was well.

When he came out, he speculated, "I'd say the child is above eight pounds. A good size, indeed."

In want of a bit of drama, Elizabeth bid no one tell Darcy the gender the baby. She also made him wait whilst Hannah tied a ribbon around her hair. He paced until he was at last given leave to enter.

At the door, he hesitated. Elizabeth's smile was weak, but reassuring. Only then did he allow himself to take a deep breath of relief and turn his thoughts to the child. Wrapped in the gossamer shawl (one notable by reason that Hannah knitted it herself) and tucked into the curve of her arm, the baby opened large, sleepy eyes and let out an unexpected yowl. Thither Darcy went to inspect his newest offspring.

As he reached his wife's side, Hannah burst out the news.

"I knew it was a boy! I knew it!" she blurted forth.

Mortified, Hannah clamped her hand over her mouth. (She had overstepped her station and her duty to a grievous degree.) Quite hastily, she withdrew. Georgiana followed her out of the room.

The delight that overspread Darcy's face kept Elizabeth from being too exasperated at Hannah. Still, she was a bit miffed to have done all the work and then been denied the glory. Unwitting of his wife's designs, Darcy was actually too pleased by the outcome to think of anything else—at least at first.

He sat carefully on the edge of the bed and put a protective arm around his wife's shoulders. It was important to her not to look as exhausted as she felt. That was not pride alone. Her dearest desire had been to be the one to introduce him to his latest progeny.

Turning back the corner of the shawl, Elizabeth allowed her husband his first look upon his son's face.

"Mr. Darcy," she said, "May I present your son?"

Peering cautiously at the bundle she held, he marvelled, "A boy, you say?"

"Proof that you are not deceived is as quick as this."

She withdrew the shawl. The baby indeed owned male credentials and directly put them into use. An arc of urine spewed in the direction of his father's waistcoat. Both parents anticipated the fountain. With remarkable aplomb, Mr. Darcy placed a pocket square atop the geyser, saying, "Actually, my love, I was quite willing to take you at your word."

She smiled contentedly as the baby began to squirm.

"He is strong, like his father."

His father begged to differ.

"He is strong, like his mother."

Now that all seemed well, he gave himself leave to jest.

"You are the most economical mother of my recollection," said he. "Your efficiency wastes no one's time at all. Why I shall be able to compleat several letters before supper and take an early night...."

"There are matters to attend to before you take your rest," she pointed out. "Pray, what are we to call him?"

"We must call him William," he said with finality. Then, he asked, "There is but one? I find myself a bit disappointed."

Happy he could be droll, she answered, "I may live to vex you yet. For now, we have but one baby and must be happy in a humbler way."

A smile tugged at the corner of his mouth. He then kissed her forehead.

She laughed, "For now, I dislike you seeing me so indisposed. My hair is compleatly out of curl and what am I to do?"

In time, nurse carried the baby away. Darcy sat upon the side of her bed until sleep overtook her. When she awoke, he was gone. A silk pillow lay just beyond her hand. Upon it lay three red roses.

The House That Daisy Built

Once in a while Blind Fortune bestows her gifts on such as can use them. That was Daisy's justification for becoming so rich, so fast. After taking an exhilarating roll in her share of the money, she went on holiday to Brighton.

It did not suit her.

She hied back to London and immediately returned to her previous haunts. Against all good judgement, she did not hide her new found riches, she flaunted them. If pushed as to how she came in possession of such a fortune, her answer was always the same.

"Me auntie died."

Faster than that, everybody in the Dials knew Daisy had enough money to live anywhere she wanted, in any manner she chose. All the money, in all the banks in London, could not, however, make her a lady (at least as defined by nobs of the West End). She had no delusions about that. Her precipitous rise was not in class—she was who she was and always would be. Her elevation was one of situation.

Daisy's mother had always held that there was no making a silk purse out of a sow's ear and Daisy figured she was right. Money allowed her within elbow-rubbing distance of quality folks and she did not much like what she saw. Before riches befell her, she had taken quite a gander at them as they scurried up Drury Lane, handkerchiefs covering their noses lest they be offended by her foul approach. When it came to sows, the fancy folk with their fart-catching footmen following fast behind were pure pork. There were whores aplenty walking the streets of the Mayfair. Their game was as fine as any strumpet in St. Giles Parish.

Caught between these two reprehensible worlds, Daisy decided to build her own social order.

She bought a decaying old mansion house a block away from Regent Street and had it pulled down. In its place she erected a house to match any other. (This action sent the surrounding property values into a stunning state of flux.) The bricks were painted white, the pillars black, and the fence surrounding the place, red. No blowsy women screeched ribald repartees at passing men as they had on Gowell Street. Daisy thought that a pity.

Once the cashmere drapes were up and the Smyrna carpets down, she hired a quartet of footmen to stand by the door. Just to agitate the ladies of the ton, she sometimes ambled into stores where they shopped. Soon she had enough trappings of the rich that she could pass for a lady of society—so long as she did not open her mouth. It was merry work indeed to watch the shopkeeper's expression alter when she flashed her money and then told them where to send her purchases. In the end, money always over-ruled discrimination.

She then set about filling her house with her own special sort of servants. They were more like guests who worked for their keep. As she was not exacting when it came to letters of recommendation, she had her pick of maids and footmen from a host of origins. (Many were suspected of having lodged within hollering distance of Old Bailey.) Due to Daisy's relaxed standards, her residence soon became a haven for indigent whores, wayward thieves, and motherless urchins. So long as they did not bring the law to her door, she let them be.

In her house, all of her maids seemed to be unmarried wenches in a family way. Every room in her house became so thick with fallen sisters that it looked as if Daisy was into missionary work. She was not. It mattered little to her what arrangements her girls had made for their ever-lasting souls. She asked nothing of them so long as they did not try to sell it to her. Daisy still harboured an abhorrence of religiosity. From what she'd seen, nothing was so cold as Christian charity.

Her penchant for rescuing damsels with a bean up the spout meant that she curried a more than passing relationship with a doctor up the street. He was a sot, but better than no help at all when a baby came due. He had been a surgeon until his hands grew too shaky to hold a knife. His coat was that of the butcher trade, stiff from blood, it boasted his years of practise. It stank like a slaughterhouse.

Daisy demanded "Why don't you wash that blessed coat?"

The man was haughtily self-righteous, retorting, "Would you have an executioner pare his fingernails before chopping off somebody's head?"

She did not ascertain exactly how one had anything to do with the other and kept a keen eye on his doings. With time and repetition, she became a fair midwife herself. Sometimes, however, all did not go well. Despite due care, mothers died. More often, babes were stillborn. At times, both were called. Whatever the tragedy, Daisy upped for the burial and paid for a grave-watcher to boot. Those hastened to the grave through misfortune or chance became known within the household as Daisy's Dear Departed. To be recognised for something other than being a carnal oddity was fine with her. She guessed that she had truly found her calling—she who God had made barren—was the womb and the way of babes of the left hand.

It was easy to see how her house came to be overrun with rag-tags and riff-raff, outlaws and working class agitators. Its corner lot was well-situated; she had an empty great room and an open-door policy. So long as they paid for the ale they drank and did not tear the drapes, they could make free with their speeches all the night long. She had always been a late-riser anyhow.

By virtue of the size of her house, she had more trouble from the righteous looking for a handout than from starving beggars. Panderers for the Lord and crammer-weaving politicians came by daily in want of a donation. No matter their cause, her response was all-inclusive.

"Piss off!"

She knew trouble was bound to find her. Ill-will from do-gooders and fifty-odd men gathering each night was certain to alert the wrong sort.

As seditious meetings were prohibited, those within her walls claimed to be simply a reading society. Unfortunately, they did more arguing than perusing literature. Defying the law did not bother her conscience, but Daisy knew any minute torch-bearing reactionaries could set fire to her rafters. It was worry enough that she began to have a look at the newspapers. She was not untaught, but words above two syllables gave her trouble. As part of her refashioning programme for her wayward wards, she vowed to improve on that. Disinclined to invite a tutor into her house, she looked amongst her own maids and found one who had been convent-raised (an education considered good as gold to Daisy).

Mary Catherine Patrick was a day maid with a perpetually runny nose and a penchant for sad tales of woe. Daisy spent part of every day at the cook's table, reading books of varying lengths and difficulty to Mary Catherine. Although she could be talked into lifting her skirts for a kind word or a piece of hard candy, Mary Catherine soon became a bit of a pet. It did not escape Daisy's notice when one of the firebrands of the society began to sweet talk the girl. Not unlike the others of his ilk, his orotundity included healthy doses of what he called "the working man's plight."

"I'll wager he'll stand for Parliament one day," said Mary Catherine.

Disdainful of men in general and politicians specifically, Daisy said, "Yea, he's given yer a poke and told yer he's doing yer the favour, now hasn't he?"

As Mary Catherine's apron was tied under her armpits to cover her belly, she had no riposte. In truth, her new man-friend was not her baby's father, but she did not have the heart to tell Daisy (or her man-friend) that. Belly or not, every night she was in the middle of the raucous speechmaking in the downstairs hall. She saw that as entertaining as any man's kisses.

"Cash, Corn and Catholics" was their rallying cry, but the dearth of jobs was the real issue. Once the Lords Lieutenant was given leave to apprehend all printers, writers and demagogues responsible for seditious and blasphemous material, even Daisy was outraged. Whatever Habeas Corpus was, it had been suspended. That meant she had to close her doors to their meetings lest she be drug off to Old Bailey herself.

Thereafter, the only men who came to Daisy's house came to visit with her already fiddled-with maids. Peace seemed to have been restored, but unrest simmered near the boiling point.

Daisy's foremost concern was the neediness under her own roof. At the rate babies were dropping, she knew time would come to improve her accommodations. A dormitory would be nice. Perhaps after that, a school. Or at least that was how she saw it play out in her mind's eye. She was no longer known as Daisy Mulroney, but The Marmot Mother of Method Street.

All in all, she was rather pleased with herself.

Once in a while she thought of little Sally Frances. If asked, she would have said that she hoped never to see the girl again.

She meant no ill will.

Sally gone meant Sally was free. She had escaped St. Giles Parish and all that came with it.

 lysium Fields

The Darcys had forsworn inviting their children to perform for the delectation of captured guests. However, even the most reluctant parent cannot refuse when the audience is much in want of being amused.

Young Anne, Cathy, and Janie sat together on the piano bench, each ready to take their turn at the keys. After several months of practise at the pianoforte, Georgiana believed that her young students were prepared to play for a receptive audience.

She announced, "Lady Catherine admires proficiency upon the instrument. But as she no longer finds herself a good traveller, we shall take Anne and Cathy to Kent week next to exhibit their progress."

To this, Fitzwilliam made the aside, "When the bell heralds a caller at Whitemore, there is no longer cause for alarm."

Looking all round, Georgiana continued, "Pray, allow us a rehearsal for my aunt."

Consent was cheerfully given.

The little girls were far too young to be truly accomplished, but their enthusiasm was well-represented. Moreover, everyone enjoyed the sight of their tiny slippers dangling from the piano stool as they plunked on the keys. When they compleated the piece (as it was), Georgiana helped them down and they curtsied.

Before the last notes were wrenched from the instrument, Fitzwilliam had called, "Huzzah! Huzzah, I say!"

His daughter, Anne was clearly the superior of the three, but he applauded them all equally. Georgiana beamed proudly, insisting that the girls were true musical prodigies.

Elizabeth whispered to her, "It is clear that Anne has inherited her mother's talent."

Georgiana blushed, clearly pleased by the observation. When the exhibition was concluded, little William was then brought centre stage. The other children were then allowed to trot back upstairs to the nursery.

The Gardiners had come thither from London just to admire the newest

Darcy. All admired his healthy cheeks, strong legs, and happy disposition. He had large eyes surrounded by a tangle of lashes, but William's hair was a lighter shade of brown than his siblings. Their hair was thick, his was surprisingly wispy. In the sunlight, it was almost gold. Elizabeth held him in her lap for all to admire. By clasping each of his mother's forefingers for leverage, he tightened his podgy knees and drew himself upon his feet. His legs wobbled like a new calf's, but he managed to maintain his foothold. His father looked upon the struggle with great paternal pride. Mr. Darcy was not one to crow, but his wife was happy to do so for them both.

"Look there! Is he not the strongest boy in the county?" she exclaimed. "You are as sturdy as you are handsome, Willy!"

For a countenance that was so recently overspread with pride, Mr. Darcy's expression hastily altered. Such a suggestion left him keenly displeased.

He said to his wife, "I beg your pardon?"

As it happened, Mr. Darcy had a particular dislike of nicknames.

The single sobriquet his wife had ever heard him invoke was the diminutive of her name. (When he whispered "Lizzy" against her ear, the susurration caused her heart to leap and her womanhood to tremble.) Therefore, it was Elizabeth Darcy who called his son Geoff, his daughter, Janie. As Darcy had been unaware of her confinement (and she much overtaken by apprehension whilst he was away), their choice of names for their first-borns were not made at leisure. They were chosen in a hasty haze of sentimentality and relief. It was not that Darcy disliked the appellations assigned, to his mind they were just not well-considered. It was also an unspoken agreement that they did not employ shortened names in company.

They selected the name for their second son whilst at their ease. Darcy had liked William rather than Fitzwilliam only for simplicity's sake. His wife agreed.

"If we do not," she said, "We shall be annotating our conversation evermore with 'the father' or 'the son' or 'the Colonel.'"

As only family was there to hear her, Elizabeth believed she had not erred in calling her youngest "Willy." She saw the name as an endearment. Mr. Darcy did not.

Mr. Darcy's disfavour was well-apparent. As if in the hushed presence of some deity, they fell silent—save for baby William. His chubby face turned red and he directly expelled a rather noisy movement of gas. As Mr. Darcy always avoided that which exposed a strong understanding to ridicule, no one dared laugh. If no one else dared, however, Darcy could, upon occasion, laugh at himself.

"I fear I have just been countermanded," said he.

Made free to give way to merriment, they all did—as did his son. William laughed aloud for the first time.

"Look, Darcy," Elizabeth exclaimed, "you have given William his first laugh!"

Not yet through diverting everyone, William continued to gurgle. Grabbing at his feet, he managed to pull one of his knitted bootees from his foot. It came off with such force that it landed on his head. When Elizabeth held him aloft, he giggled and wriggled like a puppy.

"It is clear that your son shall add a great deal of dignity to the name of Darcy," Elizabeth observed. "We must reengage Morland directly. I want him to take a likeness of the children."

Darcy had been very nearly beaming, but at the mention of Morland's name, his countenance altered. He had no regard at all for Morland as a gentleman. However, as a portraitist, he was unrivalled. Hence, in this matter, Darcy acquiesced to his wife's wishes and nodded his agreement.

Georgiana said, "It is my understanding that the painter is much engaged at Carlton House."

Relieved that the royal commission would put off the visit, Darcy kept his pleasure from being obvious.

With unabashed facetiousness, he said, "We must, of course, wait our turn."

Elizabeth arched an eyebrow in his direction. With the smallest shake of her head, she told her husband that she was not deceived by his feigned regret. His gaze was unequivocally unrepentant. Her eyelids fluttered, an indication that their exchanges would be resumed in the privacy of their chambers. Having made that silent promise, the Darcys returned their attention to their guests.

Two weddings had taken place. Both were of great interest to them all, but for different reasons.

To Jane, Elizabeth said, "What are your thoughts on dear Charlotte's marriage to Mr. Pratt?"

"I am happy as can be for them."

Indeed she was. But then Jane loved everyone and wished them to have the bliss she and Charles shared. Jane looked lovingly upon her husband's handsome countenance as he stood semi-majestically by the mantel. Now nearly thirty, Bingley had kept his boyish good-looks and near child-like ebullience. (His extensive enjoyment of the dining table, however, had thickened his waist.)

Upon learning that Charlotte had remarried, Jane and Elizabeth were genuinely happy for her. Yet Elizabeth suffered an unyielding ache when she pondered the union. Mr. Pratt was an odd man. Together, they made an oddly constructed couple. Elizabeth had never heard Charlotte jest in such a manner as she had with Mr. Pratt at the Pemberley ball. Granted, they seemed equally matched (Charlotte had revealed a stinging wit; one to which Elizabeth had never been privy.) A sensible, deserving woman of steady age and character, Charlotte had been left a handsome living. She had no financial need of a second marriage. One Mr. Collins in a lifetime seemed more than enough. Another might be thought of as inviting misery. However, more than one woman enjoyed verbal frays.

"And you, Mr. Darcy," Elizabeth inquired. "What say you of Charlotte's choice of husband?"

"I have no opinion upon a matter wholly unconnected with me. I offer Mr. and Mrs. Pratt my best wishes."

A smile tempted the corners of Darcy's mouth when he spoke. Elizabeth knew better than to ask him to speak candidly in the presence of others.

However, she did not quit the subject, musing, "Once again Charlotte has been wed, despite a compleat absence of esteem for both men and marriage."

Startled at her own frankness, Elizabeth apologized. Whereas Darcy kept his countenance, Charles Bingley laughed and took no pains to pretend otherwise.

Without a single measure of reproach to her sister, Jane reminded Charles, "Charlotte has not our sensibilities, dearest. She has remarked that she was not a romantic."

"In Mr. Pratt's defence," Elizabeth added, "He does seem quite able to laugh at himself. Many of us are in want of that meritorious trait."

Bingley said glumly, "Mrs. Collins marriage to Mr. Pratt was far more fortunate than some."

Jane and Bingley had come from London having attended to financial matters in regards to his sister Caroline's marriage to Sir Beecher. Although pleased that Caroline had finally wed, Bingley could not pretend he was happy with the match. Accompanied by the Hursts, Caroline and Beecher were enjoying an extended honeymoon on the Continent. All wished them well and enjoyed their absence whilst they could.

Aunt and Uncle Gardiner sat upon a satin settee. The fabric of Mr. Gardiner's breeches kept him making continual adjustments lest he slide off his seat entirely. Mrs. Gardiner placed a pillow behind him for support. As that redistributed his weight, he was able to allow their conversation his full attention. Elizabeth looked in Darcy's direction, wondering if he noticed this small, but telling kindness. But he had not. Instead, he reached out his arms to William, for the baby had begun to struggle in her lap. With him in his arms, Darcy walked over to a Bingley, who then began to make silly faces for William.

Although they understood all implications and nuances of the discourse surrounding them, the Gardiners had the good manners to keep silent. (The Gardiners had had the dubious honour of meeting Mr. Collins.) Mr. Gardiner was Mrs. Bennet's brother, hence they were not disposed to criticise Mr. Bennet's relations. Their Aunt Gardiner, however, was a lady her nieces' heads naturally turned to when in want of a sensible opinion.

Elizabeth bid, "What say you, Aunt, of Charlotte's match?"

Mrs. Gardiner had made Charlotte's acquaintance prior to her understanding with Mr. Collins. She did not know Charlotte so well as her nieces, but they had shared a cup of tea more than once. It was enough time for Mrs. Gardiner to deduce that, although Charlotte Lucas had appeared accepting of spinsterhood, she was not. Her deduction was proven true when Charlotte accepted Mr. Collins's proposal on the heels of his rejection by Elizabeth.

Mrs. Gardiner said, "It has been my observation that, just as some ladies find the company of anyone is preferable to no one, others admire the familiar above any other evil."

No one could argue that postulation.

Piercing a brief silence, young William shrieked in the inexplicable way that only a baby can. As if on cue, Margaret and Franny came with the twins. Geoffrey held Mrs. Heff's hand, Franny held Janie's. This was not by assignment, but by chance. Margaret was more tolerant of boyishness and Franny loved tying bows (that never seemed to stay put) in Janie's hair. Upon their reentrance into the parlour, the twins were all sweet-smelling and sleepy-eyed. However, they were not altogether willing to go upstairs to bed without a fuss. Hence, Elizabeth handed William to Margaret and took a small hand in each of hers and led them away.

As soon as William began to walk, Mr. Darcy believed they would need to begin interviews for another nurse. Elizabeth might well oppose that. She liked to keep the nursery help to a minimum.

Darcy would just as soon not again be caught "looking for shoes" under the bed.

$\mathcal{T}$he Fortune of War

A ll things have their season.

The Newgate scaffold was erected directly across from the Debtors' Door. *The Fortune of War Inn* stood at the intersection of both, making it a prime location to watch public hangings. Because it also sat on a busy corner situated midmost between Guys Hospital and Kings Bench Prison, the place was a handy cabstand. The regulars lived down near Naps Head Court.

With the decline of public executions, the simple inn had disintegrated into nothing but a slag hole—one thick with the purveyors of a spanking new, and very noxious trade. Its propinquity to the teaching hospital made it a haven for body-snatchers.

By the ghoulishness of their business, one might expect these grave-robbers to be yellow-eyed, fang-toothed demons. Those who dared cross the walk in front of *The Fortune of War* knew that they were vastly more frightening than that. Men such as they wore the same thick features, dirty coat, and waistcoats of the average tradesmen. That was not to say they were indiscernible. Their one commonality was a penchant for furtive glances and low conversation. Tips on where fresh corpses could be found came from both sides of the street—sextons, gravediggers, undertakers, and local officials. As they passed on their information, all of them took a cut of the sales price of a cadaver. (There was a long tradition of subornation in all business dealings, not just those of the left hand.)

Indeed, money for the taking tickled the fancies of men of all levels.

Anatomist liked older children. They labelled them by size—smalls and big smalls they called them. It was the bodies of young men who fetched the highest dollar—something about their tendons lent them better to dissect. A good solid fourteen-year-old was worth eight pounds, if a shilling. As always, times were hard and money was difficult to come by. A good resurrectionist could dig up a corpse in half an hour. A night's work would feed a family of five and have enough left over to drink away the thought of what he had done to earn it.

More than one housebreaker turned to body-snatching to make ends meet.

If caught, burglary got you a long stretch picking oakum at Newgate. The law called stealing children from their graves "Unlawful Disinterment." So long as the coffin was not marred or stone busted, grave-robbing cost a man only a fine.

If they were lucky, a snatcher could avoid the night work by claiming an unidentified accident victim or a dead pauper as a relative. Sometimes the snatcher's wife would rent out their services to tend a sick bed. Once the "subject" expired, they tied their bounty up in a blanket and threw it in hamper. To cart him away took only minutes. Even if they were caught in possession of a dead body, the charge was only "Improper Possession of a Subject" and the penalty was as lax as disturbing a grave.

No one was better acquainted with the lower echelons of alehouses than Daisy Mulroney. In her previous office of harlot, Daisy happily brokered the sale of teeth—a full set of snappers or a single tooth. Teeth were easy to come by for plenty of folks would willingly have their choppers knocked out for the price of a drink or two. Daisy, however, had her limits. The abomination of a corpse to obtain teeth was not well-looked upon by the public at large either. Therefore, when young boys began to be throttled to feed the anatomy seminars, outrage grew. Something had to be done to stop it. But the end was not in sight. More and more doctors attended these anatomical lectures, observing autopsies of three corpses a day.

Now ensconced in her elegant townhouse, Daisy did not care to think of such baseness. However, it was a hard truth and no one dared chance an unwatched grave. That meant that grief-stricken mourners had to lay out good money to hire someone to see that their loved one was not dragged from their final resting place and sold to the highest bidder. There was but one blessing to the victims of this trade. The window of opportunity was small. Unlike some crimes, time was of the essence. Depending on the weather, in a day or so the body would be too putrid to be saleable.

As watch and ward over a certain sickly arm of society, Daisy had paid her own money to watchers when one of her girls died. When poor Mary Catherine was brought to the straw and bled out in an hour. Daisy was particularly saddened. Labour had come early, hence the baby did not live much longer than its mother. (Mary Catherine's liberal-minded boyfriend made himself scarce lest he be looked to for any outstanding bill.) Daisy had the young mother and babe placed in a carved mahogany coffin with the baby wrapped snugly at its mother's bosom. Daisy then paid the yellow-skinned old man who emptied her chamber pots an extra shilling to stay with the body and laid out two more to the caretaker at Moorfields Roman Catholic Chapel to see that Mary Catherine's remains were not thereafter stolen.

Daisy knew that it was heedless to have trusted the old man. She had dismissed him once for filching silverware. Second-chancers were never a good risk. He and his obligations never made it to the cemetery.

The poor little maid was likely wrapped in a shroud, sitting somewhere ready to be loaded for her trip to King's College Anatomical Department. The most shameful part of the crime was that the baby had been stolen along with its mother's corpse. Anatomists did not pay well for infants. (In their part of London, foetuses were too easy to come by.) No doubt it had been discarded like so much rubbish.

"If a man would put a spade in a grave, they would not scruple against anything else!" Daisy exclaimed.

Not a soul took exception to that statement.

What the old man was paid for selling the girl's corpse would likely keep him insensible of his betrayal for weeks. Daisy Mulroney, however, would not stand for such business. The old man could go hang himself, but she knew where to go to get the body back and she meant to do just that.

It was common knowledge that bodies were hauled through the streets concealed in hampers of certain straw and weight. Unafraid of any man (and damn few dogs), Daisy knew the most likely culprits and headed directly to the *Fortune of War* to demand Mary Catherine's return.

With cigar in the corner of her mouth, and her new fox tippet thrown over her shoulder, she stood in the middle of the *Fortune*'s floor and bellowed, "What've ye done with her? I know ye got 'er back 'ere behind the bar. Tag on her toe, no doubt. She ain't fresh no more, by gawd, and I'll have her back now or know who says otherwise."

After that ejaculation, she withdrew her trusty pistol and clapped it down on the bar. Anyone who thought to ignore her took notice of that. From thence furtive glances flickered to a partially concealed alcove behind the bar. It was covered by nothing but a tatty curtain. Replacing her gun in her waistband, Daisy walked across the floorboards. The place went silent and each step she took echoed a bit. With great care, she drew the curtain aside. Sure as the sunrise, two hampers lay side by side. Her hope that both mother and child might be recovered was for nought. In one basket was a boy, no older than sixteen. Opening the lid to the other, Daisy recognised the quickly-decaying remains of Mary Catherine. Mid-day heat meant the resurrectionists had to move fast else their bounty would go bad on them. A fresh gash on the girl's forehead had not bled. Daisy noted that it must have chanced when her body was off-loaded. The baby was gone—Daisy could not let herself think of that. It was most likely thrown in a ditch.

She shook her head. A feeling came over her that was new to her. In time, she would recognise it as despair.

It was undeniable that she had become a bit of a gull for a sad story. Not only was she taking in every female with a bad chest, a bad leg, or bung up her pipe six months gone, she was paying known thieves good money to do honest work. Disgusted, Daisy slammed the lid shut and stomped out of the alcove and into the room of drinkers.

Angry at... the loss... the insensitivity... the bloody, worthless men who traded in such horrors, she pushed her way back through the crowd. Several well-muscled, small-headed men had lined up as if to intimidate her. The publican waved them off. He was a smart man. Bloodshed would bring the law and they didn't much want the law eyeing what was laying in the back room. They might be accused of murder. As a woman of property, Daisy knew her word on it would have some weight.

"Out of here!" she told them all. "Scat or I'll give yer a topper!"

The men separated, several leapt out the door. Daisy stepped briskly towards the same door, waving her gun and barking orders as she did.

"Get that hamper with the girl. I'm taking her to Moorsfield cemetery now. And if you know what's good for yer, find that *baby* and bring it or I'll come lookin' for yer!"

Her toe caught the corner of a box lying at her feet. It capsized, sending twenty or so teeth scattering across the floor. Daisy picked one of them in her hand and eyed it.

"How much you get for a full set of these?" she asked holding up a tooth.

Reluctant to be seen making arrangements with someone out of the trade, the publican stood mute. So did his patrons.

"The Guild of Cadavers," she sniffed at the bunch of them.

Apathetic and callous, their hands flopped loosely at their sides. Ashes to ashes, stripped bloody bare. Daisy saw theirs was just an extension of her former trade. Dead flesh, however, brought a better price.

Two men lugged the hamper behind her as she stomped out. The footman she had purposely left to guard her carriage leapt down and scurried to help. With surly gazes at the wretched alehouse, they tied the hamper onto the back. Still furiously puffing on her cigar, Daisy eschewed help and climbed into her carriage by herself. She ordered her driver to walk on, but a sedan chair blocked their way. Ready to issue all manner of curses to make it move, something made her hold her tongue.

From the chair, a well-shod gentleman stepped onto the walkboards. He paid her no mind whatsoever. As befitting a gentleman entering such a place, he wore his hat low, his countenance partially hidden behind his collar. He was well-tailored in a nut green coat with white piping and did not look as if he belonged amongst these squat working men.

She knew the type. No doubt he was fresh with tips of new "subjects" and warnings of the law. Certain professions often overlapped. No doubt this man took his share off the top and bugger the rest. When he was not rousting the dead, he was most likely rousing the irate in the street.

The *Fortune of War* pub-keeper did not see the gentleman as he alit. He was too busy crawling about the doorway collecting the scattered teeth. Pivoting on his walking stick, the gentleman gingerly stepped around him. As he did, his limp was pronounced.

Pearls Have Their Place

With candle in hand, Darcy crept down the steps from the nursery.

The Master of Pemberley was not obliged to see that his children were fast asleep in their beds. It was a duty he chose to undertake nonetheless. The peace therein was a reassurance. To have spent his day in the saddle and an evening with family and friends suited his notion of true contentment. Once he fell into his wife's arms and reminded her of the many ways he loved her, his day would be deemed perfect, indeed.

As he entered their bedchamber to attend to that obligation, his nostrils flickered. The scent of his wife's favourite perfume meant that she had preceded him. Yet, it was unusual for her to bedew herself with scents at bedtime. That alerted him to the possibility that something unusual was afoot. His interest piqued and his ardour kindled, he looked about the darkened room to ascertain what libidinous delights she might have conjured. Had she donned his breeches? A French corset?

He espied a large lump beneath the bedclothes. Was he prepared himself to be sent reeling with lust when he threw the covers back, he was to be disappointed. Truth be told, he was even a bit befuddled.

His wife lay beneath the counterpane with her knees drawn to her chin. Not only was she not in a French corset, she wore a plain, high-necked nightdress, last seen when she had taken to her bed with a nasty cold. Not an hour ago, she was quite well—and looked to be in an amatory mood.

Any distaste he had for her night dress could be dealt with by claiming a pre-emptive right to dispose of it. However, her expression did not invite familiarities. She appeared to have been affrighted. Her eyes were wide as dinner platters—but not with fear. Taking her trembling hands in his, he realised that they were cold as ice and rubbed them briskly. Her alarm was genuine.

Ere he had leave to inquire, she burst forth, "You shall never believe... I cannot believe... I am mortified beyond all reclamation!"

Despite being pleased that she was merely embarrassed and nothing sinister was involved, her disconcertion disconcerted him.

"Pray, tell me—what can be the matter?"

"I am such a blunderer! I made a ghastly error! I am humiliated beyond measure!"

"If you cannot gather yourself.... Wine! I shall get you a glass of wine!"

"I need no wine!" she moaned. "I need only to become a mouse. A mouse, I say... to hide in a little, tiny mouse-hole for the rest of my days."

Given of her last remark, Mr. Darcy understood that if his wife's life had been threatened, it was through mortification. Yet, he could not coax her into telling him what befell her. When he asked again, she fell back upon the mattress and, groaning, drew the counterpane back over her head.

With an expression that suggested extreme impatience, he awaited.

Reluctantly, she tossed back the bedclothes. Taking a moment to speak, she groped to think of a way to describe what occurred without her humiliation of her own making.

She said, "I did not give instructions for my Aunt and Uncle Gardiner to be put in the Blue Room."

Darcy returned her gaze, but did not speak, for he could not disagree with that assertion.

She continued, "I gave particular instructions that they were to be in the Gold Room! When they are here, pray tell, are they not always taken to the Gold Room?"

"Indeed, they are."

At that moment, she held up a crumpled note.

She said, "This was for you."

Unfolding the missive with all due diligence, he read it aloud. It was quite economical.

It read, "D, Pray come to the Blue Room, love E."

His brow furrowed when he looked at her. She widened her eyes, twice for emphasis. For a man of quick wit and exceptional understanding, it took him far longer than it should have to comprehend what had come to pass—or at least that was what he pretended.

She said, "I repaired to the Blue Room to await you, *dearest!*"

He was silent.

"Regrettably," she explained. "I was preceded."

"By the Gardiners?" he said finally. "I am sure they can forgive so small an intrusion...."

"When I entered, they were in bed," she said

As he did not respond, she emphasised the specifics of the encounter.

"They were—*in flagrante!*" cried she.

Said he, "Forsooth."

As his rejoinder was not issued in the exclamatory form, she was miffed. To her great vexation, he remained collected. There was but the barest flicker of amusement in his gaze. Clearly, he did not understand the full nature of the event.

"In flagrante, Darcy! *In flagrante!*"

He announced, "It has long been my ambition to have no part of those situations which offend dignity."

Such a remark was unhelpful.

She explained further, saying, "They were not in the bed, but on it. He was in *her* nightdress; she in his *nightcap*—!"

Rare are there visions of such humour as try the countenance of a man of Mr. Darcy's taciturnity. Yet the image as described by his wife did just that. He had to smoother a laugh. Drawing herself to her knees, she slapped at his hand.

Despite all proof otherwise, she insisted, "This is in no way diverting!"

He overcame his mirth long enough to ask, "However indelicate, I must inquire—were you observed?"

"I cannot say," she answered.

That was understandable. The Gardiners may well have been otherwise occupied.

She said earnestly, "I pray not."

"I then pronounce that you were not seen. If you were not seen, it did not happen."

Thinking about it logically, Elizabeth believed her husband had made a good case for how such an embarrassment, for all parties, should be dealt with.

Darcy wondered, "Why, pray tell, did you want to meet in the Blue Room?"

She sighed, "I had amorous leanings myself."

He raised one eyebrow, "These leanings could not be consoled in our own chambers?"

Raising her own eyebrow in return, she said, "Is it not said that variety is the very spice of life?"

"This is quite true," he answered. "Albeit, I bend to your will in all matters, in this I one I shall have my say—you may wear a nightcap to your heart's content, dearest. However, I absolutely refuse to wear your nightdress."

Voice lowered, she said, "It was my fervent hope that you should wear nothing at all."

Kicking off his boots, Darcy proved he was not a man to over-think a point, especially when they were so obviously of like minds. That was one accommodation that she was more than happy to make.

His wife lay upon her stomach, happy to watch him as he removed each piece of clothing. He had always been remarkably untroubled to be observed in such a fashion. (Under his scrutiny, her colour always rose.) His insouciance was not guileless. It was visceral—even primitive.

When he joined her upon the bed, he stretched out beside her, settling on his side. He did not speak. His expression alone explained that he awaited her to rid herself of her fustian nightdress. Her buttons were many and she undid but a few ere she slid into his arms. She meant only to linger long enough for a single kiss—for she did not want to be lured from a well-planned scheme (one she meant to implement in the Blue Room).

At one time, they took love in the oddest of locations—the stairwell, the larder, even the scullery. Upon this occasion she had desired variety, but also was in want of privacy. Theirs would not be a hasty lifting of skirts and a fare-thee-well. She meant to have a lengthy (and circuitous) engagement. The Blue Room would have been superb. It had a lovely little alcove with a cushioned chimney corner. It was fortunate that the Gardiners had retired first. Otherwise, it might have been the Darcys who had been found *in flagrante*—bechancing another mortification altogether.

Although thwarted in her initial design, another portion of her scheme had not been ruined. As her husband was unmindful of her true intentions, she had to struggle to disengage herself from his arms.

Abruptly, she sat upright.

"Pray, a moment," she said.

He, a bit miffed, returned to his side and made himself comfortable by propping himself upon an elbow. Smiling impishly, she slipped her hand beneath the pillow case. With great delicacy, she withdrew a string of pearls. It was as long as a man's arm—her husband's arm. The clasp was of diamonds. The necklace was quite precious.

"I found this trifle in my sewing box. Pray, did an elf leave it there?"

It did not occur often enough for it to be called a habit (perhaps just a whim), but her husband liked to leave exquisite gifts for her to find quite by chance. His gallantry was incomparable. He gave extraordinary gifts with the same casual grace that he gave of himself. Whilst it was possible that he overheard Caroline Bingley's snide comment about the lack of fashionableness of certain pearls, it was exceedingly unlikely that he paid her heed. If her husband gave her pearls, it was from his heart, not at another's instruction.

He made it quite obvious that he cared not to engage in discourse about the necklace. He did not speak of this preference. Rather, he drew her near and began to kiss her neck.

As his tongue flicked around her earlobe, her eyelashes fluttering wildly and her eyes began to roll upwards. The pearls almost slipped from her fingers. It was only then that she caught sight of another, far more estimable endowment. (One she had admired and enjoyed many times lo these many years.) Despite how often she had witnessed it, she never tired of watching his manhood tumefy from somnolent suzerain to impatient warrior. At times, merely the promise of what it would become arrested her breath. As it lay just then half-erect against his thigh, she was reminded of the plan she had conceived to show him her gratitude for the necklace.

However, the pearls had slid beneath her hip and it took great care to retrieve them without suspension of the favours he was paying to her ear.

132 ᪥ LINDA BERDOLL

Only when she had them again did she redirect his attention.

Cupping the pearls in her hands, she gently rubbed them together. Then, she gifted them a great exhalation.

"They must be warm," she explained.

Sitting before him cross-legged, her gaze was exceedingly persuasive. (He looked at her as expectantly as she looked at his virile sceptre.)

"I rarely question your methods...," said he.

"Shush," she whispered. "I shall beguile it."

Holding the pearls above him, she slowly allowed them to undulate around his ever-engorging member. As she was intent upon watching his burgeoning erection, she did not see that his eyes were trained upon the edge of her nightdress. (It crept higher upon her thighs with every twirl she made with the pearls.) With his wife's pearls decorating him as if a... er... maypole, his manhood was quickly at full attention.

Pleased with herself, she threw back her head in triumph, crowing, "My adornment is compleat!"

Ignoring what delighted her, he reached for the sentient seat of his own desire. As his hand moved up her thigh, she capitulated compleatly. In a fit of exultation, she whipped her hair across his chest and fell back in compleat surrender.

Clutching her hip, he drew her leg about his. The pearls did then begin to unravel. Neither noticed. Having encouraged a tumescence of exceeding magnificence, it was only right and good that she should enjoy it as much as did he.

"Darcy," she cried.

"Lizzy," he gasped.

It was an acknowledged fact that the fire that burns most fiercely, flames out first. It does not necessary follow that it remains doused. Given time and attention, love at leisure is just as fulfilling.

And pearls can be restrung.

Lady Millhouse's Confidant

A carriage betook Sally Frances Arbuthnot from Pemberley to Pennyswope Manor that very day.

Once there, Sally's plan took a surprising spin. Indeed, what had been a bold but simple scheme, wholly unconnected with the Darcys. altered rather hastily. In the end, Sally was beside herself with anticipation—and Lady Millhouse was tickled to her toes to have part in a new adventure.

Surprising no one except Sally, Lady Millhouse had been quite delighted to aide in an endeavour that she herself had inspired.

"Dearest child!" said she, her trumpustuous voice reverberating throughout the house. "You are courageous and good!"

The lady had florid cheeks and a clumsy wrist, making it quite obvious that she was far happier on horseback than serving tea. In her enthusiasm, her ladyship reached out and engulfed Sally in her considerable bosom. Sally grimaced (for she was unused to affection), but not noticeably. Poverty was a keen teacher and through its agency, Sally was quite precocious when it came to adapting to her circumstances. She yielded to the stronger force, knowing it was to her benefit to do so.

"I see a girl before me with my pluck, Lord Millhouse!" Lady Millhouse exclaimed.

Holding the office of his wife's foremost approver, he nodded his agreement. Sally admired the praise—such as it was.

Lord and Lady Millhouse resided at Pennyswope; they lived for the hunt. It was months before the season would commence. When not on horseback, Lord Millhouse was happy in his library. Lady Millhouse, however, had little to occupy her time except to complain how long it would be until the kits would be weaned. With no daughters to marry off or sons to badger, it pleased her to bring the sad little urchin from town into her sitting room— particularly one who bid her retell the rapturous story of retrieving her dear nephew's bones from across the water. In each successive telling, the bribes they paid to sentries were bigger, the boat they made off with was smaller, and the daring altogether greater. As she spoke, she became more enlivened. She was so taken with her own adventure, she was in want of a part in young Sally's too. Rather than be her advisor, she decided that she must escort the girl instead. As Lord Millhouse was not disposed to tell his wife what not to do, she went merrily on her way—and he with them. All her ladyship asked of Darcy was a letter of introduction to his uncle in whose family plot John Christie was laid to rest.

The burial of John Christie (and all that it encompassed) was an episode Darcy was most desirous of putting behind him. Time did not improve the notion of digging up the evidence of a history of troubling family events. Elizabeth patted his hand, for she knew that his compliance came at great cost to his sensibilities. As Lady Millhouse was a friend of longstanding, Darcy wrote the letter. He did not want to write it, but he was disinclined to give a reason why he should not.

The Millhouses and their young consort set out for Dover with surprising haste.

Sally had never set foot on a boat. She had watched many a ship dock up the Thames. The wharves were thick with stories about shipwrecks and lives lost. Hence, Sally looked at the channel crossing with trepidation. Once they set sail, she stood on the balls of her feet and looked down at the swells of the sea as they churned beneath her. Directly, she made herself sick. Thenafter, Lord Millhouse joined her at the rail and both of them emptied their stomachs over the side. Neither could bear look at Lady Millhouse as she clung to the bowsprit, glorying in the stinging spray. After they moored, it took Sally and Lord Millhouse half a day to be fit to climb into a carriage. When they were, Lady Millhouse had already commandeered a coach and a coachman.

"Make haste you silly geese!" she called.

They were a merry band until they arrived at the little cemetery where John Christie had been laid to rest. Sally had not thought of flowers and began to pick some running wild amongst the grass. When she knelt next to her brother's grave sniffling, Lady Millhouse would not have her give way to sentiment, at least not yet.

"That is a waste of good flowers, girl," she said. "For they shall die and we must take your brother's humble remains with us."

"Well," thought Sally. "The lady was right about that. It was a rare gentlewoman who was both plain spoken and sensible."

Sally nodded her agreement and stood aside as a half-dozen men bearing shovels went to work. For some, the exhumation would have been too gruesome to watch. Lord Millhouse walked back to the coach holding a handkerchief to his face (one not meant for tears). Sally Frances and Lady Millhouse were too engaged in overseeing that the task was done right to be off-put by the earthiness of the activity. Lady Millhouse disliked how the men were doing the job and was in a pother because of it.

"Stop you fuddle-headed oaf!" Lady Millhouse boomed as a shovel hit the crumbling wooden coffin. "Shall I do it for you?"

The diggers spoke French and the string of oaths they issued was uncomplimentary to the English race in general and to the English lady in particular. Sally knew enough French (at least of the sort she just heard) to know her ladyship had been deeply maligned.

To her, Sally said, "I think they just said you got brass whennymegs, m'am."

Lady Millhouse sniffed, "I dare say I have more stones than the lot of them together."

With no blows thrown or shots exchanged, John Christie's bones were extricated and brought home. Although Sally Frances knew the intimate connection her brother had to the Darcy family, she kept that confidence. (She had a notion that Lady Millhouse knew something about it anyway.) Despite his qualms, Mr. Darcy had been kind enough to let it be known that because her brother had once been employed there, he would not oppose the boy's remains be committed to the Pemberley cemetery.

That, however, was not Sally's intention. She wanted all her loved ones together. How to go about it was a conundrum. John was no kin to her Grannum and having him interred in the little churchyard cemetery in London did not seem right. The closest connection he had was to the Pemberley horses he so loved. Lady Millhouse understood. Herself a horse-lover, she could think of no finer place than to share the earth with those magnificent beasts. So she insisted that there was but one place for John—on the hillside where Pemberley's finely-bred animals were laid to rest.

Mr. Darcy was initially opposed to it, pronouncing it unseemly. But in time, he relented. After all, John Christie was not only sired at Pemberley, he was a heroic grenadier of The Wars. Sally, so difficult to please in many ways, was satisfied with that. Her kin might not be together, but they would lie where their souls would be content.

Lady Millhouse had looked with a keen eye as Sally Frances dutifully counted out repayment for all the expenses she had incurred along their journey. Her ladyship was taken with the girl's singular pride and diligence. Impetuously, her ladyship said that she was much in want of taking her home that minute.

"You shall have a bath and I will call the seamstress...."

Sally was grossly insulted.

"I ain't like no dog to come lay by your fire."

Seeing she had overstepped, Lady Millhouse bethought her design. Sally was wilful; Lady Millhouse more so.

"Do not be obstinate. I have need of your assistance. It is an employment that your brother would particularly approve."

Lifting her chin, Sally was all ears.

What Duty Demands

W hen she had learnt of the turn Sally Frances and Lady Millhouse's scheme took, Elizabeth had been quite happy with her portion in it all. She had been so pleased that she veritably beamed when she had told her husband of it. Mr. Darcy, however, was a good deal less pleased than everyone else. Indeed, he was quite vexed when his wife told him.

"Is she mad?" he spat out before he caught himself.

He had not designated which female's sanity he questioned, hence; his wife raised an inquiring eyebrow and waited patiently for him to do so. With one flick of his head in her direction, he both apologised for his curtness and told her his pique was directed elsewhere. His vexation should have been anticipated. Although he had not shared the particulars of the many tribulations he suffered to save John Christie's body from being committed to a mass grave after the great Battle of Waterloo, she knew enough of them to see that his fit of temper was understandable. Before she could offer him her commiseration, he attempted to voice his reservations more succinctly. (In truth, it was more of a complaint.)

"I went to a great deal of bother to see to it that the boy was buried properly. I am not altogether happy to learn all my trouble was for naught."

Suddenly, Elizabeth was not half so pleased with herself. Not only had she erred in encouraging the venture, the whole plan had stirred her husband's recollections of exceedingly dreadful days. She did not speak in self-rebuke. That would imply justification and possibly beg further gentlemanly apologies. Rather, she went to him and pressed her forehead against his breast. This expression of regret meant far more to him than mere words.

His enfolded her in his arms, saying, "Once our Miss Arbuthnot and good Lady Millhouse put their heads together, no mere mortal has any say in the matter."

In truth, the introductions may have been made, but a word from Darcy and Lady Millhouse would have abandoned the business altogether. They did not believe that it was theirs to thwart a sister on such quest—or a brother on his either. He withdrew his objections.

"We must bear that which is inescapable," he said.

∽

That past bid for shouldering one's own travails became quite well-used.

After the unexpected (and altogether) unnerving interruption of her Aunt and Uncle Gardiner's connubial exchanges, Elizabeth feared facing them again. The first moments of breakfast were exceedingly uncomfortable. Her husband (as was his nature), remained entirely composed. Unknowing of the incident, the Bingleys and the Colonel Fitzwilliams conversed with ease and amiability. Elizabeth was pleased to believe that the Gardiners were unaware of her intrusion, just as they were pleased to believe she did not intrude.

It was a great consolation to know that passion, as the Darcys knew and enjoyed it, could endure even after twenty years of marriage. That tenet was one she reminded herself of with regularity—and Darcy as well.

Before, during, and after that visit, young Geoffrey Darcy had his own tribulations. They were small, but insistent, and he did not bear them well.

As it happened, he had meant for his baby brother to be his (if not literal, at least spiritual) second when he lorded over his sister Janie. Regrettably, Janie claimed William as her own particular ally. She solicitously combed what there was of William's honey coloured curls, oversaw his meals, wiped his chin, and generally hovered over him, whispering conspiratorially as she did. As he could not yet speak (but jabbered quite well), she usurped his will whenever she needed furtherance in her schemes to thwart Geoff's increasing dictatorial behaviour.

Somewhere, somehow, he had come by the information that he would one day (and forever more) hold the whip-hand over his sister.

"You must do as I say, sister," Geoff announced. "One day I shall be your master."

Flipping her hair defiantly, Janie refused him with one single, disobedient word.

"No!"

"You must do as I say!" demanded Geoff.

"No." she said.

Witting that he should never hit his sister, he pulled a ribbon from her hair.

"You *must*," he pronounced evermore adamantly.

"I shall not! I shall do as I want!"

"You shall do as I say," he said stiffly, his demeanour strikingly similar to his father's own. "I am to inherit. You must do as I say or you shall be cast out."

Putting her ear to William's jabbering little mouth, Janie pretended to interpret.

She replied just as curtly, "Willy says that you are not anything unless Papa says so."

Geoff sputtered, "I heard William! He did not tell you that...."

Airily, she replied, "You cannot hear him, for he speaks only to me."

"That is not so." Geoff countered.

His voice did not rise, but the colour in his cheeks did. William babbled happily.

Wearing stately hauteur, Geoffrey Darcy claimed the office of William's interpreter.

Bowing next to the baby's ear, Geoff said, "See there, he told me I am to be the master."

As Mr. Darcy overheard this conversation, he was of two minds upon it. He admired his oldest son in all ways (for he was, in all ways, quite like his father). He was also quite impressed with his daughter's ingenuity. Quite probably this discourse was a precursor to many more arguments to come. He was also quite astonished that young Geoffrey, not only knew that he was to inherit, but that he had an elementary understanding of what that meant.

Darcy intended to lead his son by example. However, he saw that an instructional talk was necessary. The Master of Pemberley was required to exhibit unfailing decorum and a certain level of humility. (If he was of true Darcy strain, decorum should come far more easily for him than reining in his pride.) To converse with his son it was necessary for Darcy to recall another conversation between a boy and his father—the circumstances whereof he would have liked to forget.

Darcy had been considerably older when his father instructed him upon what it meant to be master of such a vast estate as Pemberley. He had been remonstrated only after he had engaged in a serious affront to his station with a very willing upstairs maid. (As the upshot of that seemingly innocent tryst was reverberating about the great halls of Pemberley still yet, he did not try to justify that youthful indiscretion.) He had admired his father above all other men. Therefore, that verbal switching stayed with him always. When he learnt that his father was just a man and not a god, he loved him no less. He could only hope that he inspired the same loyalty in his own son.

Calling to Geoff, Darcy drew him to his knee. It was a test not to tousle the boy's head, but the solemn expression upon his small countenance begged otherwise. It was evident that he knew his father meant to engage him in manly conversation for he stood with his hands folded behind his back.

"Begone, sister," Geoff said over his shoulder, lest she interrupt them.

Had her father looked in his daughter's direction, he might have observed the rude gesticulation she gifted her brother. He would not have approved. (It would remain for her mother to explain to her what was expected of a gentlewoman.) Her gesture did not escape Mrs. Heff's notice—nor Franny's (whose look of disapproval was ignored by her young ward). Both the nurses scurried to Janie's side and Franny took her by the hand.

Margaret mumbled, "Law, where do these babes learn such foul business?"

Darcy disregarded that small contretemps and recollected the very words his own father employed in elucidating how he must never be ruled by anything other than the highest of motives and the worthiest of principles.

His son was but four, so he paraphrased.

"You are a Darcy, a gentleman of honour. You must never use your place unkindly."

Putting a hand on each of his shoulders, he said, "You are to be your sister's protector."

Geoff's large eyes grew ever bigger as his father spoke. With those last words, they filled with tears. He refused to blink, perhaps knowing that should he, his tears would fall upon his cheeks and trail down his face. They pooled in his eyes in such a way they were highly injurious to his father's reserve.

Had it been *his* tears, Darcy knew that his own father would have done him the favour of ignoring them. Upon this occasion, however, he was quite torn whether kindness lay in turning a blind eye or possibly offending his burgeoning dignity by addressing it. Although he was sorely tempted, he decided that wiping away tears was a mother's occupation. It was his to offer affectionate benevolence.

Softening his voice, he said, "Go now. Be good to your sister for she loves you—as do I."

With a swipe of his index finger across his nose, Geoff nodded his head and turned to go. Before he made for the door, there was a significant straightening of his shoulders.

Outside the door, Darcy heard his daughter's urgent voice trembling as she inquired, "Was Papa angry at you, brother? Was he?"

Understandably, there was no audible response from her brother. Janie's dismay over her brother, Geoff's distress was heartening. Perchance his children would cease bickering and love each other as did he and Georgiana—and Elizabeth and her sister, Jane.

These felicitous thoughts were interrupted by those less agreeable.

Jane was not Elizabeth's only sister—simply her dearest. Libidinous Lydia and Mary the Reprover were her sisters as well. The long-observed truth that one cannot chose one's relations should be a caution to any persons overly impressed with their lineage—even the Darcys.

When Darcy believed that the twins behaved more kindly to each other that day, he was quite pleased with himself for handling their squabbling so easily. He had little time to sit in self-congratulation. Indeed, that very afternoon an invitation had arrived by post.

It was from Howgrave Hall.

The Devil's Trade

It is said that when a man must choose between good and evil, most lean towards good—except when his own interests would be best served by evil.

Alistair R. Thomas was not really a veteran of Wellington's staff. He was a gentleman down on his luck, banished from good society for a triviality. The Beau Monde was heartless. Expulsion is all the worse for a gentleman who knows his rightful place and is denied it. (This is most especially true when one fancies himself a part of the coterie that never quite recognised him as one of their own.)

There was but one way to regain one's status. One must marry well (royalty would be nice), or obtain a great deal of money. (England was fast becoming an island where all things were attainable—be it land, title, or respectability.) As the first was incumbent upon the second, he set out to earn if not a fortune, at least a living. With nothing to promote himself but a quick tongue and an honest, open face, he put these attributes to their best use. He entered into the web of criminality that encircled the town's various courts and scrambled for cash. As he had a willingness to engage in the basest of employments, he was hereupon largely successful.

The streets were writhing with chicanery and his introduction to underhandedness (as seen in a legal sense) involved informing on criminals to the parish constables. The magistrates were notoriously slow in recompensing their informers, so he eventually decided to take his game to the other side and defend the accused in court. The law became his constant study. He offered his services as a witness or furnished an alibi as needed. (He also became adept at employing whatever coarse inflection his cultured voice needed at the time.) More than once he stood as a fictitious lover in a divorce. Wise in the ways of the proceedings, he made his way from court to court and judge to judge, never staying in front of any one bench long lest he come to be recognized.

His most prized possession became his greatest liability, forcing him to cover his silver mane with bootblack. Even then his countenance was quite remarkable, particularly when opposite the vilest wenches and most depraved chaps that ever visited His Majesty's courtrooms. The whole place was a disgrace to refined society. The jurists' wigs were in want of powder and the solicitors' handkerchiefs looked beneath that of a White Chapel fellmonger. His own collar was sullied just being in their company. As he was making money hand over fist, he managed to overlook the grubbiness. He would have been happy to continue servicing His Majesty's courts, but his face eventually became too familiar to keep up his facade.

He had always been a bit of a spendthrift, but he put away enough money and influence to buy out a carting enterprise (the owner, lately battered, was quite willing to sell for a good price). Very soon he amassed a dozen drays without sullying his own soft hands. Its corner position gave him an office whereupon he could watch over the politics of the street. His pursuits soon became far-reaching. Not a single baker's waggon passed by that he did not have a finger in each of their meat pies. And a trio of harlots stood on the street corners, all paying him a gratuity to keep from being thumped, bagged, or snatched.

The shops sold nothing but brummagem as the street was inhabited by guttersnipes and people of poor circumstances. From this it might be presumed that there would be no money for low entertainment. The habitués of White Chapel and the like were often invaded by gentlemen and ladies of quality in want of being diverted by the poverty they saw. People of all nationalities and class occasioned to prance down the walkboards, finding themselves delighted by the miasma. They were known to rent rooms above Newgate when hangings took place. (The renowned caricaturist, George Yancy Parr once travelled a hundred miles to see a triple hanging, but then it was said that he was given to necrophilia.) Drury Lane theatres fought for a share of the merry-making coinage with makeshift penny-gaffs and horse drawn caravans featuring midgets, two-headed goats, and people with hideous deformities— all which could be gawked at for half-penny a look.

For every exotic fruit that arrived in a Covent Garden market, a gratuity was paid to someone. No one questioned that. Alistair realised that there were a dozen ways to make money without leaving his chair. Every other man, woman, and child would play another false without a moment's hesitation— and he took his share. Even street entertainers paid him an honorarium. If they were reluctant, he had a bevy of embittered, disbanded soldiers ready to be hired to convince them otherwise.

The one nod to propriety was to influence thieves and prostitutes to keep off the thoroughfares. Their business was better suited down side streets where, it was generally agreed, a gentleman taking a risky piss deserved an ambuscade. Beggars who wandered off Carnaby Street got worse.

It was to be expected then that a man who was so happy to take from the living would not give a damn about the dead.

The resurrectionist trade was one particular to Alistair's needs. It was infested with rats who were disorganised and stupid. All that was needed to turn a team of them into a thriving concern was a firm hand and quick mind. Anatomists wanted newly dead cadavers—the fresher the better. Because he was in possession of a carting business, Alistair was able to have bodies trotted about in daylight hours whilst their competition had to do business by moonlight.

Moreover, the other gangs engaging in these nocturnal digging expeditions did not wait for the nicety of death to deprive the dead of its earthly vessel. Alistair cautioned his men to be certain the deceased had breathed his last (or mash a pillow over his face until he did) before offloading at one of his preferred locations. The constabulary frowned upon death occurring too hastily of the dissection. It begged investigation.

Most of Alistair's snatchers had been released from the worst prisons. Clerkenwell New Prison and Coldbath were dreadful, but paled when compared to those prisons made from decommissioned warships moored along the Thames. Alistair did not care how horrific their punishment had been. Whatever they endured whilst trying to survive on a floating prison ship made them ideal for digging up corpses. Such was their pride that they sported primitive gun-powder tattoos. Between each finger was carved a figure noting their level in their gang's hierarchy. They were tenacious, heartless, and brutal. They were also desperate and that served Alistair's ambition.

As grave-robbing became more prevalent, however, the newspapers got wind of it. Such bestial doings touched on the fears of decent folk, thereby selling tons of newsprint. It also made Londoners evermore vigilant over their loved ones' graves. Hence, the body-snatchers had begun to strike out unto the surrounding countryside to keep up with demand.

It had been a keen temptation to have the bloody mark of Cain between his fingers to warn his enemies of his daring, but Alistair was too clever to mar his body with indelible proof of being a resurrectionist. That cesspool of a profession was a mere way-station upon his climb to a higher level of society. He had proudly come to the realisation that he had the gift of adaptability. Once he decided that the time had come for him to rejoin the ranks of gentlefolk, he knew just how to go about it.

Within one year of his reappearance in Southwark he had begun attending meetings of the Marylebone Reading Society. There were a number of such groups throughout town. Marylebone was the most respected. To Alistair it was a place where the bored read boring political pamphlets. However, he learnt from the bores that the authorities employed spies and agents to agitate and inform upon anyone suspected of liberal tendencies. He soon learnt that within Marylebone lurked a radical plot—one he had little interest in until he saw that he could make money on both sides. By stealing gunpowder from the dock and reselling it to the radicals, he was happy to appear a man of their cause.

It was whilst he straddled the line between the indecent and the bold that he washed the bootblack from his hair. If he was to be accepted by the ton, he had to look the part. He also began to introduce himself as a retired officer and attaché to Wellington. Every time he made the declaration, and it was not impugned, he became more smug. After all, it took a magnificent liar to make such an easily disproved statement.

That was its brilliance.

*U*ntil the Morrow

It did not trouble her countenance, yet Elizabeth was not at all welcoming of a card from the Howgraves inviting them to a ball. This was not owing to any fear for her husband or his affection. The Howgraves' company was simply unappealing. Moreover, she despised the notion of embarking upon a sojourn to seek other company when she was quite happy where she was. Had she needed one, young William supplied the perfect reason to send her regrets. He had not yet been weaned (Mrs. Littlepage notwithstanding).

The one knot in the rug was that the Bingleys were much in want of the Darcys to accompanying them. (They had little choice but to go as the ball was in their honour.) Jane was exceedingly sympathetic to her sister's desire to remain with her baby. Disinclined to spend an evening with what passed for friends to politicians, Darcy believed his wife's excuse should exempt his as well.

He said, "If Elizabeth cannot attend, then I shall send my regrets as well."

Charles Bingley, however, very nearly sulked. Rarely could Darcy be cajoled, but Bingley knew that small chance was better than none whatsoever.

"I have been most anxious to have this outing, Darcy. I shan't enjoy myself at all if you do not attend. I beseech you to accompany us," Bingley said. Then, in a harsh whisper, he added, "If you do not, we shall have to share a carriage with Beecher!"

Unhearing of her brother's disparaging remark, Caroline gushed, "You must add to our merriment!"

In all other ways, the finest of friends, the Bingleys had once again brought his sisters to Pemberley with them. Caroline and Louisa were beside themselves in anticipation of admiring not only Lady Howgrave's ensemble, but her fine house too.

Caroline continued, "There is no handsomer feast, no grander gowns, no more exhilarating conversation than shall be had at the Howgrave's ball! I understand they have renamed the place."

"Yes," replied Elizabeth. She did not want to appear unwilling to speak of the Howgraves. It might cause Caroline to comment. However, before she could compleat her answer, Caroline interrupted.

"*Yes*," repeated Caroline. "They now call it Howgrave Hall."

"How droll!" laughed Bingley. "As we have reclaimed "Deering Lodge," I fancy it would not do for Howgrave not have his name upon an estate somewhere."

The Bingley sisters had come to Pemberley ostensibly to admire the newest Darcy. In truth, Lady Caroline had quickly run out of people to curry favour with in London and had repaired to the country in anticipation of Lady Howgrave's fête. (While her gown was being stitched, she came to visit the Darcys as much to amuse herself as to avoid her brother's children.) Upon taking in Elizabeth's aspect, her usual disdain was set aside. Suddenly, she was taken in paroxysms of true delight.

"Your pearls!" shrieked Caroline. "Your pearls are divine! Where ever did you get them?"

Without a moment's thought, Caroline reached out and took them in her hand. Startled, Elizabeth took a step back, fearing such ungentle behaviour might cause them to need another restringing. Caroline, however, had whipped out her quizzing glasses and peered at them as she rolled several between thumb and forefinger. Abruptly, she ran them across her front teeth.

"Superb," she admitted.

Observing Elizabeth's startled expression, Caroline explained, "The front of the teeth—that it is the surest way to gauge their genuineness."

Stumbling to alter their discourse, Elizabeth bid, "Does your husband stay much to London?"

"Yes," replied Caroline. "Sir Beecher remains dedicated to the card tables. He became reacquainted with them whilst we were abroad."

That information was unheralded by any ovations. Not long before their engagement was formed, Beecher was on the unhappy end of a duel over a gambling debt. Word had it that, whilst professing himself a Christian, Sir Beecher was worshiping other gods. It had long been known that he bowed regularly to the throne of Bacchus. However, whilst recuperating from an acute wound to his posterior (received in the duel over a string of ponies that he had put up against a card debt), he had gained an affection for laudanum. Caroline took it away from him, but he repaid her dedication by attempting to bed every chit who spoke to him. Caroline soothed the deprivation of her husband's constancy by sharing his wine.

Caroline could be obliging when she chose, but over time her heart's generosity continued to decline. Living all her life with a doting brother and enjoying the exceptional kindness of her sister-in-law, she was unprepared to reside with a husband who considered his own wishes well above those of his wife. But then, the gift of marriage rather than that of love had been her design. Her match with Beecher brought her both the title of lady and of wife. Hence Caroline was, largely, happy. If anyone thought otherwise, she attempted to convince them of their marital felicity by reciting how they dined in the first circles.

"We have twice dined at Carlton House and sat within earshot of the Prince Regent and his retinue at the Argyll Rooms. Charles could have come had he wanted, but chose to stay away."

She shook her head at his audacity.

"Charles favours nothing above the race park. As Beecher lost his ponies—he used his prize racing ponies as collateral and lost them—Winton no longer enjoys going there. My husband blames me for his bad luck at cards, so what am I to do with myself but come to Derbyshire with Charles? Whilst in Italy, we came across Winton's friend, Alphonse—you recall, Mr. Darcy, the man who shot Winton in the great duel?"

"I thought he was shot in the hindquarters," interjected Bingley.

Not wanting her aside to Darcy interrupted, Caroline gave her brother an angry glare. She then looked back at Darcy, still awaiting his reply.

Darcy said, "I recall the man."

She continued, "It was right of Beecher to have slapped him across the face with his glove, he is a beast. But he has made a great deal of money in trade. You should do business with him, Charles. You are certain to double your fortune."

Said Charles, "I do not care for Alphonse's business practises for they include evicting old women and sick children from his properties."

"Oh, why care? I see these people in the street. They are simply lazy. Would they just take work, they would be well-fixed."

Bingley opened his mouth as if to reply, but she proceeded on to another subject more appealing to her senses.

"Vauxhall Gardens!" she gushed. "With every visit they have added new entertainments. Concerts, plays and I do not know what all—every night there are fireworks as one has never seen since Madrid. Dirty little place, that. I abhorred every minute of our stay there save for the fireworks. I should have stayed abroad forever had not my dear Winton become homesick for London. He is such a dear. I could not allow him to take his leave alone."

As Caroline continued to prattle, Bingley turned to Darcy. Behind his hand said, "I believe Caroline is a bit in her cups. Ere long she, her husband, and Mr.

Hurst will all snore through dinner."

Darcy smiled his consolation. That was all he could do.

When they retired for the night, Elizabeth felt a great exhaustion envelop her.

"What tires you so?" Darcy bid. "Is it Caroline or the thought of the Howgrave invitation?"

"Both of them—all of it," she sighed. Finally at leisure to talk, she added, "I am surprised Caroline can tolerate our company, she liked her time abroad so very much...."

"'Abroad?" he sniffed. "That fine place where ruined reputations find a home."

She nodded, quite witting of the truth of his observation.

He said, "Beecher came home when Lady Catherine's endowment gave out. They are living solely on Caroline's funds now. At the rate he is gambling, they shall be in the poor house before year's end."

Truly worried, Elizabeth asked, "Who shall see to them? Lady Catherine has washed her hands of them. Jane and Bingley cannot cover his losses. They have not yet recovered from their own reverses."

Darcy replied, "They shall make their way as they always have, sitting open-mouthed as if fledgling sparrows, waiting for someone else to feed them."

"And yet she has the gall to call the poor, lazy."

Slipping beneath the bedclothes, he altered the conversation, saying, "I shall send round our regrets to the Howgraves tomorrow."

Turning to him, she said, "Perhaps, you should go without me. Bingley wants you to so very much."

"I think not," he said, reminding her, "It is thirty miles. I do like the prospect of a night at an inn."

"What would one night matter if Bingley be pleased," she answered (inwardly satisfied that he did not like the prospect of staying the night at Howgrave's house). "Moreover, if you make Bingley happy, so then is Jane."

"I do not live to please Bingley or Jane," he whispered. "I live only to please you."

"And happy you have made me."

Then, smiling impishly, she said, "Did you observe Caroline assessing my pearls?"

"I did."

"I nearly lost my countenance. Had she known their full history, I think she would have not been half so inquisitive."

Although the notion was diverting, he was not amused. His thoughts had turned decidedly amatory. Once upon that road, his will was rarely thwarted.

"Come," he said, drawing her to him.

There was a chill in the air, but she was not disposed to believe that he wanted her warmth alone. Placing her hand upon his cheek, she smiled wickedly and pressed him back against the mattress.

With one swift move, she cast the bedcover off and drew herself upon him.

"I do not believe you have escorted me out for a ride since William was born," she said.

He endeavoured to speak, but placing her forefinger against his lips, she shushed him. Indeed, he did not think he could have commanded his tongue was it necessary. As it was, she held some interest in his tongue, but only to taste, to fight, to accept. There was another outthrust she was keen to enjoy as well. Engirdled and enraptured his flesh responded. He surrendered himself unto her until she cried out in the delicious ache of requitement.

Lost in desire, they did not hear the long off sound of Cressida, howling in unison to their love.

*S*olitary Soldier

"**A**nd I said, 'You cannot attend as your child is not weaned?' What lady is this that does not have a wet-nurse?"

In Sir Henry Howgrave's house, upon the occasion of the ball held in her brother's honour, Caroline and her group had a good laugh at Mrs. Darcy's expense. None were so clumsy as to be in earshot of Mr. Darcy excepting Caroline. She often pointed out that her brother was that fine gentleman's dearest friend. Her implication, of course, was that she was as well. Any member of her circle who had even a nodding acquaintance with the actors who moved about their particular stage remained unconvinced. Few were of true rank, the others jockeyed constantly for better position. Caroline had gambled when she allied herself with Beecher.

As her marriage was as desperate as it was perceived, she liked to relate how at one time she and Mr. Darcy might have come to an understanding had he not come under the sway of some sort of country incantation. Most were quite witting that Caroline's recollection was unreliable. They laughed and swatted their fans at each other (much entertained by the absurdity of Mr. Darcy making an offer to Caroline).

The ladies were divided into two camps that evening—those who thought it was a fine treat to have the handsome Mr. Darcy attending without the accompaniment of his wife, and those who knew he kept his reserve in company or not. A few ladies attempted to breach the conversational gap and were thwarted. Licking their wounds, they became a source of jest that they had made such a futile attempt. A saucy girl with dewy lips, short nose, and bumptious bosom was not dissuaded.

Fortified by libations and a distaste for her own escort, she cooed, "There is no man I cannot tempt."

A friend of Juliette's thought differently, tugging at the girl's skirt, she said, "Trust me, my dear, the man would not deign to speak to a woman not of his acquaintance except, possibly, to apprise her that her hair was on fire. He is quite implacable. Spare your vanity."

The girl shook her away and flounced up to Mr. Darcy. In a moment, he looked down at her and she smiled dazzlingly up at him. Having perfected it over years of practise, he gazed upon her as if a bug had just landed upon his sleeve. He then bowed slightly and walked away. As this entire vignette was watched by a coterie of ladies spanning several social levels and three separate age groups, the girl was mortified.

Her colour reddened with humiliation, the girl could only complain, "He is exceedingly dour."

Caroline overlooked the exchange. In addition to tending to an increasingly rancorous opinion of Elizabeth and her country ways, she was also hiding two injurious habits. Whilst she took wine in company, she swigged regularly from a flask of whiskey hidden in the folds of her gown. She also harboured a fondness for snuff, but was most attentive to propriety which forbade partaking of the substance whilst engaged in conversation. Scurrying away from her lady-friends, she stopped behind a portiere. Taking out a handsome inlaid box, she consumed a dollop through the agency of a well-filed fingernail. Thereupon, she re-entered the ballroom with a ready supply of quips, gossip, and outright calumny.

Already in his cups, Beecher avoided his wife. Rather, he attempted to gather himself enough to present his person to Sir Henry Howgrave. He hoped to have a private audience with the man. For synchronous to his mounting debts, Beecher had taken a liking to the idea of public office (whereby piles of cash were to be made beyond the report of the tax-collector). Preferably, his appointment would be one befitting his station (and come with a house, he was much in want of a house in town, his apartments were intolerable.)

Sir Howgrave's propensity for hobnobbing with the debauched and the self-important had thrown him more and more frequently into Beecher's path. Beecher had noted that Sir Howgrave craved Mr. Darcy's ear and spoke to him every time the opportunity came round. Well-respected in all circles, Darcy's support would be a feather in his political cap. Was he to deliver Darcy unto Howgrave, Beecher might well be fixed for the foreseeable future. It was quite possible. Darcy was, after all, his illustrious relation.

Beecher's illustrious relation, however, wanted little to do with Beecher (or for that matter, Howgrave either).

That did not keep Beecher from pursuing Mr. Darcy about the edge of the grand ballroom. When at last he found him, Darcy clasped a glass of wine as he conversed with Bingley and Jane. Now an intimate member of Bingley's family, Beecher did not hesitate to join them. Not even a little "hail-fellow-well-met" blood stirred in Beecher's veins. Even if it had, he would not have dared to slap Mr. Darcy upon the back. His very carriage forbade it. Beecher gave a small tug upon Mr. Darcy's sleeve, very nearly causing his wine glass to slosh. Still, that man did not extend him a greeting beyond the slightest flick of his head. Beecher was deflated. Clearly, in marrying Bingley's sister, Bingley's friend was not part of the bargain. Beecher prayed Howgrave was unwitting of this small snag.

As Beecher rarely lifted his head from the trough of gambling and excess, there was a hard truth he had yet to uncover—one particularly prevalent since Napoleon's defeat. In London-town one's place eventually came down to one thing. It mattered not who were one's people, but how much one was worth. Howgrave did not care a fig about Sir Winton Beecher now that Sir Winton Beecher had not a pot in which to piss.

Leaving Beecher to Bingley, Darcy bid Jane for the honour of the next dance. She accepted forthwith and he extended his hand. As they gained the dance floor, Jane offered her dear Bingley a glance of commiseration (for she knew he did not care to be left to Beecher). Just as they danced away, Caroline whirled up. The feathers adorning her headdress were so bounteous that they bounced long after she stopped. Her headdress was a monument of architectural wonder. Jane had already waded through the treacherous waters of politesse by sounding as if she admired Caroline's head garb without actually lying. Halfway through his second glass of wine, Bingley admired every gown he saw. His sisters, he knew, were always well-presented.

"What a fine adornment, Caroline," Bingley gushed. "Do those feathers come from the West Indies?"

"Nearer than that," smirked Beecher.

Directly, a look of abhorrence (one of the rarest sort) overspread Bingley's usually happy countenance. The feathers looked remarkably similar to some he admired at Rosings Park in another capacity altogether.

"Surely...," he insisted.

"Why not?" sniffed Beecher. "That bloody bird dare not peck me...."

Fortunately, Darcy did not learn of the fate of Lady Catherine's macaw. His dance with Jane, however, was but a passing escape. The orchestra was pleased to play a waltz every other dance all evening. That affront meant that he had long been decrying his decision to come to the ball at Howgrave's without Elizabeth. It was as if he were once again alone in the world, ladies circling him as if he were the evening's main dish, obsequious gentlemen vying for his time. He had vowed to never to be caught in such a position again. He was quite out of spirits.

He suspected that his wife's design was more than merely to serve Bingley's desire for his friend's company. It was entirely possible that in encouraging him to go without her that she wanted to make a sort of statement. Whilst pondering that possibility, he joined Bingley at a side table. There Bingley filled his plate to the brim with turtle, oysters, crab, and lobster. Darcy's appetite was not whetted by the sight of such a repast. He picked up a peach and made do with that. Determined not to be ill-tempered, he teased Bingley about his diet.

He said, "Your big toe shall swell the size of your fist if you do not stop eating such rich food."

Bingley was indignant, "That is just an old wives' tale."

"I see no old wives with gout," Darcy retorted.

As Darcy took a generous bite of the peach, a bit of juice dribbled down his chin. Had not fastidiousness been one of his core traits, he would have wiped the juice away with the inside finger of his glove. Rather, he discretely reached for a napkin. Before he could secure it, he was anticipated.

Another gloved hand, this one bedizened by a diamond bracelet, held a napkin before him. Before he could take it from her, she took the unprecedented liberty of daubing it against his chin. The hand moved with haste and discretion, still it was an inexcusable breech of his person. In the moment it took for him to decide whether to take note of the culprit or simply ignore her, his consideration of possible redress was interrupted. When he realised just who had taken the familiarity, he was most displeased. Of all the affronts, that he allowed Lady Howgrave to agitate him was the greater vexation.

She teased, "The *élégant* Mr. Darcy's hauteur conquered by a mere peach! *Tres scandale!*"

Without thought, his hand went to his chin. Lest his disconcertion be betrayed, he hastily disposed of the remainder of the peach and clasped both his hands behind his back.

Darcy bowed gracefully, "Your fruit put up quite a struggle, but I subdued it."

"My fruit is quite desirable, is it not?"

She smiled fetchingly, keeping her gaze just long enough for him to recognize the double entendre of his jest. He behaved in no way that betrayed he understood her meaning. He spoke of the roads and the weather, nothing else.

When the subject was exhausted and she could see the beginnings of his retreat, Juliette queried, "You have not seen the house since it has been redone. May I show you our renovations?"

He nodded curtly, saying, "My wife bid me particularly to take note of your decorations for she was much in want of hearing of them."

This was entirely true. Elizabeth had employed a specific tone that allowed him to know she would like him to say exactly those words. He suspected that she wanted Lady Howgrave to be certain that she was not seen, in any way, as a threat. Darcy admired his wife for that. Any other wife whose husband was in Juliette's cross-hairs would not allow him out of her sight. It was testimony to their marriage, and her trust in him, that she did. Therefore, however reluctantly, he allowed Lady Howgrave to guide him through the finer rooms of Howgrave Hall. They had barely gained the gallery when a breathless footman found him and thrust a missive in his hand.

Whatever was so dire as to come by courier at ten-o-clock at night could not be felicitous. He inquired where he might go to read it.

Juliette did not give him that information. Rather, she reached out and placed her hand on his forearm. Her fingers dug into the fabric of his coat. He looked upon her as if she had taken leave of her mind. He did not have the opportunity to determine that, however. She spoke to him first.

"He beats me," said she.

Whereupon, she put her face in her hands and began to weep.

Of the Clouds

Juliette unbosomed herself unto unlistening ears. Once Darcy had been given the missive, he recognised the hand as his wife's. All other cares evaporated. The message itself could not have been more terse.

Come.

With great care he folded the note and placed it in his waistcoat. As he betook himself down the steps, his eyes swept the ballroom for Bingley. He caught his eye directly and met him as he gained the doorway. With great economy and almost unnerving calm, Darcy explained to him that he must make his away. Fortune saw that he would not have to avail himself of their coach when he did. Having travelled to the Howgrave's with the Bingleys, he had tied his saddle horse to the back for the journey. Hence, he was excused from having to beg an unfamiliar mount from Howgrave's stable or unharness one of Bingley's.

Bingley followed him outside. Whilst Darcy drew on his riding boots, Bingley held his horse's reins and beseeched him to take a footman.

"These roads are thick with highwaymen," he reasoned.

"I shall not stay to the road," Darcy said.

His point was not a comfort to Bingley—nor to Jane who had just learnt of the message. Bidding them both a brief good-bye, Darcy turned his horse for home. In times of alarm, he preferred his own company. He knew his way well—where to stop, what lanes were safe, what houses to avoid. He allowed himself to think of that and nothing else. One word was his siren call—*Come*. It told him nothing, yet everything. The circumstances that demanded such measures had to be dire indeed. Anything less and Elizabeth would not have written at all.

The closer he got to Pemberley, the more he allowed reminisces to urge his way. He reminded himself of another bold ride for home—the one he had taken upon his return from the Continent. That journey had ended exceedingly well. It was quite probably the happiest reunion of his life. Then he had been wearing his travelling clothes. Had he not brought his boots this time, he would have had to come by coach. A coach would have slowed him by half. (The vicissitudes of life had taught him well.)

Yes, all ended well last time. Perchance this time would be the same. He would arrive at Pemberley greeted by his laughing family. Whatever evil was afoot would be overcome. He prayed that happiness would greet him with every bone-jarring mile.

When at last he arrived at Pemberley's door, dawn was breaking. A lookout had been posted at the lodge-post. He swung a lantern to announce the master's arrival. That did not bode all was well. At the portico, a footman stood by to take his horse. He was both grateful and alarmed to see his wife standing in the doorframe. Her face was drawn with worry and she wrung her hands despairingly. Deep circles were imbedded below her eyes. If she was not ill, she had been hovering at the bedside of someone who was.

The minute he stepped from his horse, she was in his arms.

"It is William!" she exclaimed.

He had been away but two days. Illness had struck within hours ere he left. There was nothing he could have done had he been there, all the same he could not help being unhappy to have been gone.

Elizabeth told him, "I sent word to you as soon as I saw we had need of a doctor. Georgiana is here, thank the heavens above...."

She struggled not to weep, covering her face with her hands. It was useless.

He drew her to him, soothing, "I am here now."

In a moment, she gathered herself and they both went to William's bedside. On the way up the staircase, Darcy asked of Janie and Geoff.

"They are well and are kept to the nursery," she explained. "William's illness may have begun as quinsy. Then fever, followed by chills."

Darcy took her elbow as they entered the room. (She did not for a minute believe it was to steady her alone.) William's small countenance was splotched red with fever, but he did not cry. Darcy did not believe that to be a good sign. It meant that the illness had sapped his strength. The baby's aspect was at great variance to the laughing boy he had seen just two days before. Unknowingly, he put his hand to his mouth, his thumb digging into his cheek so deeply that it left an impression.

Although few were witting of it, Mr. Darcy was well-acquainted with trepidation. Upon more than one occasion he had been in the clutches of outright fear. Whilst gazing upon his son, their son, his heart was gripped by the cold, black hand of terror.

A chair was next to the bed. He sat and began to stroke William's brow with the back of his fingers.

Whispering, he said, "Papa is here, Willy. Papa is here."

The candlelight caught William's eyelashes as they fluttered in recognition. Still labouring to breathe, he turned his head towards his father. Darcy smiled at him and for the sparest moment, the baby smiled in return.

Placing the back of his fingers upon his son's pink cheeks, Darcy then looked at Elizabeth. Their gazes were briefly locked. In that moment, they united in both desperation and dread. Darcy longed to see reason for encouragement, but she seemed to have none. Every breath little William made was a struggle.

"We should have taken him to Brighton as we did the twins...," she fretted.

"I shall never forgive myself for not being here...," he said, as if he could forestall illness by his very bearing.

It was not to be.

The Beauty of Ice

In the first salvo, Juliette realised that she had made a serious misstep. At the Pemberley ball, she had vowed not to speak ill of Darcy's wife, but desperation had moved her to make a generalisation that did not suit him. Juliette learnt from her mistakes. At Pemberley, she had been too forward. Was she to have him, he must come to her.

Unfortunately, her husband had forced her to hie to London immediately after the ball to attend more bloody political meetings. In the field of amour, it was the woman who should have had the upper hand in some fashion. It was difficult to have a hold over a man who spent much of his time upon the other side of the country. She fretted that Darcy was, quite literally, beyond her reach.

Months upon months of her fertility had been usurped with her husband's concerns. She had to engage him connubially often enough to maintain the ruse that he would father her child. Whilst enduring that chore, her time had been employed overseeing the repairs and refurbishment of their country estate. As she seemingly committed herself to these projects, her scheme *la manifique* had improved until it was nothing less than an obsession. She no longer meant to escape her marriage via Mr. Darcy's seed, but that their child would keep them connected evermore. Perchance, they might even resume their previous association.

Then, abruptly, it seemed to have utterly fallen to pieces.

Initially, she had been gleeful that his wife had birthed a son—*another* son. It was further validation that he would gift her a male child. However, her mind on the subject had suddenly altered. It had seized on the notion that the child he begat was not hers. It *should* have been hers. Had she had her way, it *would* have been hers. She could not think of it without near suicidal regret.

So close, dear Darcy, yet so far.

Desperate to regain his good graces, it was by her design that she and her husband would host a ball honouring the Bingleys. Her husband adored the notion, for he would have say over the guest list. Howgrave had been unable to work on Mr. Darcy at Pemberley as he had hoped. He was much in want of another go at him and others like him. As if a school girl, Juliette awaited their next engagement with bated breath.

She had not been disappointed.

When she saw that he had come without his wife, she had been faint with anticipation. She had no doubt that he had come alone in want of her. The only astonishment was that his wife had relinquished him. Her belief that even the greatest of romances eventually cooled under the constancy of a nagging wife and bawling children was borne out. Mr. Darcy did not move upon the whims of his wife. He followed nothing but his own wishes. He wanted her.

Unsurprisingly, his arrival at newly deemed Howgrave Hall caused a great commotion amongst the ladies. Not unexpectedly, he was reticent, speaking to only Bingley and Jane. Even when that little toad, Beecher attempted to have his ear, he was rebuffed. Whilst the Bingleys danced, Darcy prowled the edge of the room with his hands folded behind his back. He struck a fine figure, tall and aloof. Granted, he was a handsome man. Other men were far more handsome; almost all of them more charming. *Riche*, he was too. That was not his allurement. It was less tangible. His was an enrapturing combination of arrogance and *étalege*.

When he bit into the succulent peach, it was as if it had been her flesh he had pierced. He was but a half-step from her arms when that bloody billet arrived. Had she thought of it, she would have given her footmen instructions against such an intrusion. It was disastrous. The expression upon his countenance barely altered as he read it. Yet she knew, the moment he took the note in his hand, that all was lost. Some yawing panic authored her words just then.

"He beats me!" she had declared.

It was all she could think of to keep him by her side. It did not appear that he had heard, or that he had comprehended what she had said. Had she just had more time, he would have been hers.

Rather, he evaporated like the mist.

It left her longing for him ever more urgently. Her only hope was that, in time, he would recollect her words. Perchance he did even then. He was in no way an impetuous man. Now he would need additional time to gauge what she told him and decide upon a course of action. It was not the guarded Darcy she hoped to engage. It was the unconsidered act, the improvident response that she was in want of inspiring.

It was a great pity about the child.

But, no misfortune came without compensation. It had been her experience that when faced with such tragedies, men often sought solace from others than those closest to them. They would rather forget than wallow in grief. It was that sort of succour she furnished to many gentlemen over the years. If Darcy had come to her when all was well, he was ever more apt to seek her out to escape the weepers and forlorn countenances at home.

She would be there with open arms, an alluring smile, and her own sad tale of woe. In his heart, he was a rescuer and she most certainly was a damsel in distress.

4I

The Whistle

When death did arrive, it did not come roaring, but on little mouse feet, silent in the night.

Each breath William took was a struggle. Was prayer enough; was love enough; he would not have died.

But he did.

His last breath left him with a low, soft hiss. The little chest, which had quivered so valiantly to breathe, ceased.

A sob hung in the air. Unclaimed, communal, it lasted a lifetime.

Slowly, William's eyes became sunken and still, as if the angels lifted his soul and with it, the reflection that had so often danced in them. As one of her last motherly chores, Elizabeth closed her son's eyelids.

Unable to stop herself, she continued to tend him, smoothing his hair, straightening his gown, folding his blanket....

Darcy stood next to her, his hands clasped behind his back. When he saw that she was consumed with a task that had no end, he took one of her hands in his. She dared not take measure of his countenance as much for his sake as for hers. (Desolation had not yet set in, but it was on yon horizon.)

Darcy's expression could not be called grim, for that would ascribe an emotion to that which was truly ineffable. His aspect was at once stoic, resigned, forbidding, and, above all else, near compleat disintegration. After a moment, his mind stumbled from the twilight of inertia. He cleared his throat. What he said was a denouement. It came out as a command.

"Bring the children, for they must say their goodbyes."

Elizabeth did not hear his order as such, but as he meant to speak—kindly. His words were a part of an unleashing of sorrow. Indeed, only through vehemence could he manage to speak at all. There was nothing else to be done, but wait for their two living issue to assemble. As they stood, the tick of the large clock that stood on the first landing infiltrated their sorrow. Mr. Howard sent a maid scurrying to stop the pendulum.

Knowing that her sorrow would try her husband's composure, Elizabeth still could not stop herself from turning to Darcy then. She hid her face against his chest, curling her arms within his.

He patted her awkwardly, saying, "William joins his brother. We must think of them hand in hand, waiting and watching over our days left on earth."

"Yes," she said, endeavouring to keep that image in her mind. "They are together."

It had been oft said that men, by reason of their sex, avoided life's disagreeableness. Elizabeth did not subscribe to that rule. If her husband did not weep, it was not because he cared so little. It was his duty to stand erect and endure. Women were given leave to mourn, despair, and wail all they wished. A man was not to expose his sensibilities. He must be strong when the world about him has been rent into tiny pieces.

Pressing the back of her hands to her eyes, Elizabeth reclaimed her composure. That was imperative, for within his embrace she had felt a faint quiver and knew his resolve was weakened by her tears. All about them, Georgiana, Jane, servants cried openly. (Easily stirred, Bingley fled to the parlour when he saw the end drew near.) Only the curate was dry-eyed.

The arrival of Janie and Geoff galvanized the others. The twins had been awakened from their sleep and slightly puzzled as to what had come to pass. Elizabeth took each one in hand and led them to William's bedside. She whispered to them that they must say their goodbyes to their brother. Both looked stricken. Geoff did not gaze into the crib, but Janie came forward.

"Is Willy still sick?" she asked.

It was her fervent wish to tell Janie that her little brother no longer suffered, that he was in heaven looking down upon them all. In time, Elizabeth would relate those and other, more eloquent, sentiments to her children. Just then, she was struck silent.

Standing very straight, Mr. Darcy announced, "We had him with us for eight months, seven days, and a bit more. William Darcy now abides in God's loving arms."

When the time came, the little coffin was to be carried to the cemetery in a small waggon. Before the lid was closed, Janie tugged at her mother's sleeve. In the girl's hand was a whistle. It had not William's favourite toy, but hers. Elizabeth understood.

"Yes, my sweet," she said softly.

She did not dare look at Darcy, sensing that their daughter's gesture bid him turn away. (Just then, accepting condolences was a welcome escape for him.) Taking the whistle in her hand, Elizabeth tucked it beneath the shawl swaddling William's body. Elizabeth could not bring herself to look at her youngest now that his body had gone grey and cold. She wanted to recall him pink and healthy, bubbling with laughter.

Geoff stood next to his sister, wounded by the same stoicism as his father.

When Janie began to cry, Elizabeth knelt to comfort her. As she did, her brother took Janie's hand in his and led her away. In an hour foreshadowing life's bold inexactitude, that was a great comfort for their mother. She meant to tell Darcy of it in their next private moment. Perchance it would sooth him as well.

Their procession was orderly, well-used emotions finally tethered. It was only after prayers were recited and they turned to go that it all became too much for Elizabeth. Her knees buckling, she wanted to cry out. She kept her silence, but placed her hand atop the coffin.

Whispering only to her husband, she said, "How can we abandon him to this desperate corner?"

"We must," he answered.

She steadied herself for him and for the two little faces that remained.

Remembrance

The house did not clear of guests with great rapidity. Family and true friends lingered. Those who had suffered losses themselves understood the curative effect of remaining after the official rites had been carried out. Were Pemberley's hallowed halls not kept awake with children's footfalls, every creak the house made would be heard as a cry; its groaning floorboards; lamentations. For the mother of a dead child, it was an eventuality Elizabeth hoped to suspend for as long as possible.

It was quite late when they finally lay their heads on their pillows, but even in their exhaustion, neither she nor Darcy expected to sleep.

As if the sky was commiserating, a storm threatened, leaving the air unpardonably heavy. They lay abed, together in silence, listening to nothing but the clock that did not tick. There was nothing more to say, nothing to do to comfort each other. No doubt they might have laid there in that manner until the dawn (of a day they dreaded to face), when a sudden thought came to Elizabeth.

She sat up.

"I have forgotten!" she announced. "How could I have *forgotten*?"

Reaching for her, Darcy's first thought was that she suffered a nightmare. She had not. Corporeality was troubling enough.

"How could I? What sort of mother am I? How could I? How could I?" she repeated again and again.

Leaping from the bed, she clawed wildly at her neck and nightdress. Her husband leapt up with her, but knew not how to comfort her.

He drew her to him, asking, "What is it? What is the matter?"

A more stupid question he had never uttered, but assumed she would understand the inquiry if not the way of it.

Her eyes turned to him as if suddenly aware he was there and, gripping his night shirt, she said, "I have no lock of his hair! Do you not understand? I have nothing of him! These hands, what are they to hold?"

She began to weep in deep gulping sobs.

"I have nothing of him," she cried again.

Sweeping her into his arms, he placed her upon the bed. She struggled against all his attempts to calm her. Knowing Hannah was just beyond the door, Darcy called for her to come. Together they tucked Elizabeth beneath the bedclothes, Hannah sat next to her.

Darcy told Hannah, "Stay here. Do not leave Mistress for a moment. I shall return directly."

It was not his nature to explain himself and he offered no hint of what he meant to do. Simply put, if it was within his power to make something right for his wife when all else was so terribly wrong, he would do it.

Goodwin was asleep sitting in a chair. When Mr. Darcy burst into the dressing-room, he stood before he was fully awake. As Mr. Darcy drew on his breeches and his boots, Goodwin fussed about trying to assist him. He was brushed away without a word. Mr. Darcy grabbed a coat and made for the door. By the time he was down the staircase and to the back steps, he had issued orders for two men to follow him. Head down against the threat of rain, Darcy trod with great deliberation towards the cemetery. There, an ageing man and his adolescent grandson stood watch—not to fend off grave-robbers, but a sentry of a gentler sort.

The old man had a lantern in his hand and held it high. When the light lit Mr. Darcy's portentous countenance, the man's hand flew up to shield his face from whatever fury was invading him.

"Get shovels," Mr. Darcy demanded.

The man and the boy looked at him with gaping jaws and eyes wide with apprehension.

"*Do it now!*" he scolded.

The old man knew what Mr. Darcy meant to do and took issue with it.

"Ye can't be disturbing the dead," he wailed. "God has taken the soul and once committed to the earth 'tis not to be bothered."

Mr. Darcy placed the flat of his large hand against the man's chest. He meant to push him out of the way, but could feel the poor man's heart racing with indignation and fear.

Rather, he said, "Step aside."

Unused to being challenged, Mr. Darcy would not brook it then. The man did as he was told, less inclined to incur Mr. Darcy's wrath in this life than the Lord's in the next.

The men Darcy had bid follow him knew what they were to do and needed no explanation. It was what Mr. Darcy wanted. The boy was faster witted than his grandfather, for he had claimed the lantern and held it over the grave. The men began to dig. As they did, gusts of wind swept whorls of dirt back into their faces. When they had cleared the top of the little coffin, Darcy waved them away. He would open it himself. As he did, he steeled himself for what he had to do.

Bracing one leg against the edge of the grave, he reached out a trembling hand and touched the edge of the scarf Elizabeth had so lovingly placed about her son. With a great intake of breath, he drew it back just far enough to expose William's hair. He recalled that it was longest just behind his ears. Tenderly, he took a lock between his fingers and clipped it from the others. He had enough wherewithal to bring a pair of embroidery scissors, but had nothing wherein to put the strands of hair. He looked up at the men standing above him. All had their hats in their hands save one. He withdrew a handkerchief.

"It's good and clean, sir," he assured him.

Uncertain of his voice, Darcy nodded his approval. It was all he could do to enclose the lock of hair in the handkerchief without the whipping wind stealing it from his fingers. When it was at last safe, he tucked the handkerchief and its precious contents into his waistcoat—next to his heart.

One might have thought that deed was the most eviscerating task a father might be called on to do. But that would be wrong. Replacing the scarf and closing the casket one again was an excruciation above all others. After it was done, Darcy sat down hard on the mound of exhumed dirt. The men around him were weeping. Above them all, he heard the young boy cry.

With an inward groan, he drew himself to his feet and, placing a reassuring hand over his waistcoat pocket, said, "Do it."

His greatest desire just then had been to leave. But he knew it was his duty to see the grave re-covered. Turning his face away, he dropped to one knee as if in prayer. He could hear the shovels as they dug into the dirt, and the dirt as it fell onto the top of the casket. When the shovels ceased, he stood. He did not look at the men. He turned and walked quickly away.

It was a great temptation to run with his treasure back to the house, he did not. His pace was brisk, but measured. His countenance was exceedingly composed. He returned to their bedchamber by the postern steps so as to be certain he would not happen upon anyone who might expect him to speak to them. When at last he was back with Elizabeth, he saw that she had fallen asleep. That was well and good. Hannah sat next to her.

Hannah whispered, "I give her some of my special tea. She cried herself out."

He nodded. Hannah withdrew.

Elizabeth's breath was not deep, but it was steady. He went directly to the side table and found her treasured silver box. Opening it carefully, he saw the coarse handkerchief would not fit inside. Had he smaller, more nimble fingers he might have endeavoured to tie a ribbon around William's lock of hair himself, but he feared he would make a mess of it. It was best to leave such dainty work to his wife. Rather, he closed the lid to the box and laid the handkerchief beside it.

Once that duty had been done, exhaustion overwhelmed him. Elizabeth lay asleep in satin bedclothes and he wanted nothing more than to lay with her. His coat and breeches, however, were coated with a mixture of dust and mud. He sat heavily in a side chair and rubbed his face in his hands.

It was done. He could do no more.

Rain began to fall.

Behind the door, Hannah could not keep her countenance. Mr. Darcy so proper, it was peculiar to see him besoiled that way. Although she knew not what he had done, she knew where he had been. A thick layer of Pemberley's dust covered his face liked a mask. The dirt was quite solid save for the track the tears had traced down his cheeks.

Ever Wicked This Way Goes

To be robbed by children! To have mere street urchins cause emasculation to an officer of the Royal Grenadiers, a veteran of three of the largest and cruellest battles in the history of mankind, was unspeakable. Not only had he been forced to fight off vicious attacks to his person, he was also robbed of his fortune! What was this world coming to when chits carrying pistols do not mind shooting a man in his vitals?

With the last shot in *his* locker, he would hunt the pair down and avenge himself!

Wickham's many vows of reprisal were often made late at night with a half-empty bottle by his side and, therefore, had to be taken with a grain of salt. Generally speaking, when it came to employing brute force, George Wickham was all talk. (To him, discretion was not only the greater part of valour—it was very nearly his creed.) Even he understood that his survival that night had been only due to a whim of his attackers. The smaller of the duo had drawn a bead on his forehead.

There had been grave doubt whether he would survive his wounds at all. The apothecary claimed that most groin injuries took lives through haemorrhage. Poisoning of the blood took the rest. Neither of those facts were a comfort. However, death was not his gravest fear. If emasculated, he would not have had the will to live. (Although he held himself far and above the unkempt masses, his opinion on this was not any different from most men.) The apothecary had done what he could through digging around in his scrotum with a stick. Not unexpectedly, Wickham had howled in protest.

"You bloody fiend! You'll leave me a castrato! Never, do you hear? Never! You must let me die, do you hear me? *Die!*"

Impassive, the apothecary replied, "They all say that."

Wickham's continual pleadings had eventually convinced Mrs. Younge to send for an actual surgeon. (He promised to pay her back for the expenses she incurred, but even *her* loyalty was tried at this lie.) When the surgeon did arrive, he disliked the look and the smell of Wickham's wound.

Sniffing the bandages, he said, "It looks to have festered beyond saving. I'll have them out forthwith of payment." (Medical circles concurred that dead patients were notoriously poor financial risks.)

Well-fortified by rum and laudanum, Wickham had disliked the man immediately.

"You sir, are full young to be a man of any skill."

Now, with the man demanding money, Wickham became combative.

"Are you a qualified surgeon or a tonsorial student?"

"I am a member of the Royal College, sir," Alfred Chubbe said airily.

"I fancy the last person you attended was in want of a tooth removed."

Mrs. Younge interrupted, pleading, "He's a good one, Georgie. Look here at the man's coat."

No evidence of proficiency was higher than a blood-caked frockcoat.

Chubbe, replied, "It would be my recommendation that a man not give insult to he who is charged with saving his balls."

Few things were to penetrate Wickham's fog of pain and outrage as did that bit of logic. As if to emphasise the point, Chubbe held up his scalpel. It was an ambiguous gesture, one that might have been taken as a threat. Lest he be remanded to the apothecary once more, Wickham altered his voice appreciably.

This time, hubris was forgotten. In its place, was a very sincere plea.

He cried, "Pray, use all your skills, but save what you can of my manhood."

Mrs. Younge placed a sovereign and a few pence on the table. Chubbe was well-satisfied that she had the means to pay him and proceeded to reorganise Wickham's genitals. Mrs. Younge clung to the periphery of the procedure, not daring to take a closer look.

"More rum!" Wickham called out to her. "And see that he takes but one ball, Henrietta! Dare not take them both! I would rather die!"

"They all say that," remarked Chubbe dryly (having similar experience as the apothecary).

Mrs. Younge had pressed her apron to her lips, took her money, and fled the room. Witnessing her poor George writhe with pain was more than she could bear. Taking the bottle of rum that dear Wickham had been nursing, she upended it. When the surgeon finished his handiwork, he found Henrietta Younge's head resting on the kitchen table, a pool of drool beneath her chin. Carefully and quietly, Chubbe slid the coins from the table (lest the patient take a turn for the worse). He stopped long enough to ascertain if any rum was left. Seeing that it was empty, he took his leave.

When Mrs. Younge awoke, Wickham was stirring from the mixture of opium and alcohol he had ingested. When it wore off, George Wickham was, that month and many more thereafter, afflicted with every suffering he had lied of enduring in France. Such irony was lost on him. It, along with contrition, was adrift in a sea of narcissism and drugs.

When he finally emerged from benumbment, trusty Chubbe announced him a fortunate man, indeed.

"The 'whiffles,'" the surgeon said enigmatically.

"The *what*? I do not take your bloody meaning!" Wickham cried.

The effort to speak tore at his vitals. Knees up, he rolled upon his side and howled like a hound in heat. Chubbe felt obligated to sit beside him in a straight-backed chair until the groaning subsided. Whilst he did, he crossed his legs and took a deep inhalation from his cigar. When Wickham ceased his lamentations, Chubbe repeated his diagnosis.

"You were saved by a propitious case of the whiffles."

Chubbe explained that the whiffles was an instinctual reflex of the scrotum. When under attack—be it by cold air or, as in Wickham's situation, gunfire—the scrotum contracts. Wickham recognised the condition immediately and wondered if that filthy case of undescended testicles he had braved as a youth had played a part,

"You lost a ball," opined Chubbe. "But the whiffles and my superior skill has saved the other."

Wickham thanked Chubbe with the finest grandiosities that it was within his power to offer.

The medical field had a second axiom when it came to speculating the probable remuneration of a patient. Dead patients were the worst credit risk, but those who waxed most eloquently about a physician's expertise came in a close second. Mrs. Younge had paid him for his proficiency. Chubbe hoped, however, the propitious outcome brought about by his skills might influence added remuneration. He turned to her again, as she was hovering just beyond the door. She gave him a couple of pence more and he left his patient to reflect upon the mutability of life.

Awaiting repair, Wickham had a great deal of time for reflection—had he been disposed to introspection. As he was not, he spent two months in bed with his remaining testis swollen the size of a muskmelon (gladly accepting leeches in places he cared not to recall) and plotting his own sort of revenge. The unlikelihood that he survived at all, much less that he kept one good ball meant that he was a walking (or rather, limping) miracle.

However, he spent little time pondering how, or whether, the supernatural intervened upon his behalf. He knew good works or godliness had little to do with life or death. As a man of cards, he believed in luck above all else. And if one believed in the God of Chance, it must be premised that one had to play the hand one was dealt—for better or for worse.

As months turned into a year, he tallied his injuries. The large contusion marring his forehead had faded. The small bones of his right foot that had

been splintered by a small bore pistol still caused him a tender foot. The gunshot wound to his privates had left him half a eunuch, but had not rendered him dead.

Along with a few truly monstrous memories, he had a renewed sense of purpose and reminded himself of a long adored adage.

"One must seize the moment else another shall rule the day."

Opportunities came about when one least expected them. What was important was that one recognised the bloody buggers when they came round. (As they were often disguised as labour, he did not always take heed.) Whether he was even half a man was yet to be learnt.

There was his greatest concern. That a man without vitals, and all the privileges to be annexed thereof, was truly no man at all.

Music for the Dead

The forenoon after William had been laid to rest, Elizabeth had awakened with the dawn. Her first thought was to reach out for the reassurance of her husband's warmth, but he was not there. She presumed he had arisen before her.

But he had not.

Still dressed in his boots, Darcy sat slumped in a side chair fast asleep. Elizabeth was pondering awaking him when she noticed his dusty boots and begrimed coat. As he had fallen asleep in such a state, he must have been overtaken by exhaustion. She did not know where he had gone the night before. Nothing else could account for the state of him save taking a ride on Blackjack. The chance of him taking such a perilous, night-time ride affrighted her. Yet, she knew that if he had, his motive was understandable. To run free of their grief, for but a few moments, would be a godsend.

It was a temptation to try to move him to the bed, but that might wake him. Allowing him a bit of sleep was the only solace she could fathom for him then. His hair had fallen upon his forehead and she would have liked to brush it back from his brow, but dared not chance disturbing him. Rather, she repaired to the nursery to give her children what she could of herself before she had to be strong for others.

Elizabeth spent most of the morning in a bit of a daze, hence, it was her sister, Jane, who took her hand and led her to the stairs. It was Jane who called for Hannah. It was Hannah who tried not to gasp. Together, Jane and Hannah went about removing Elizabeth's gown. They were halfway through the process of removing her soiled dress when Elizabeth finally realised what was amiss. Looking into her glass, she saw milk stains on her bodice.

It was afternoon before Elizabeth realised that her husband was nowhere to be found. He was the port she turned to in any storm and her last vestige of fortitude was fast dwindling away. So in his absence, she fled for the stairs and the solace of their chamber.

Having held out hope that he might be hiding from visitors too, she was doubly disappointed not to find him there. No doubt, he had gone out on Blackjack again. She forgave him that. (Indeed, given the opportunity, she would have encouraged him to take an hour in the saddle.) His riding boots, however, still sat where he removed them, untouched by Goodwin, and reminding her of his begrimed state that morning.

Suddenly feeling both bereft and forsaken, she fell to the chair that her husband had recently occupied. Face in her hands, she was overcome. It was as if the levee of her soul burst, tears began to pour from her eyes. Mortified by her compleat want of restraint, she mopped at them with the hem of her skirt before fumbling for a handkerchief from the table. When she had it in her hand, she saw that it was folded squarely. However, it was of coarse cotton, not delicate lawn. Indeed, it was so out of place that she was in want of looking at it more carefully.

Her weeping arrested, she wiped at her eyes with the back of her hands.

Placing the cloth in her lap, she knew not what to make of it and glanced to the table from whence it came for clues. To her, it looked to have been placed thusly for some particular reason. Initially, she did not see that it had been positioned next to her beloved silver box. When she did, a chill ran the length of her spine. Settling herself, she carefully took a corner of the handkerchief and turned it back. The chill then turned to a shiver and the shiver became a shudder. It travelled from her back, down her arms, and thence to her hands. Her fingers trembled so relentlessly that she feared that she might spill the treasure within the muslin.

His hair—Willy's lovely silken curl!

She covered her mouth with both her hands lest she cry out. She had something of him above memories after all!

Only when she dared take the cloth in her hand and unwrap it fully did she wonder by whose hands it was brought. The answer to that came to her immediately. She also understood what her beloved husband had done to obtain this, her most treasured gift.

The magnitude of his sacrifice brought her to her knees.

"Oh, my dearest love! When I am lost, you find me; when my soul is rent, you are my balm."

Although she wanted most desperately to say these words to him, she could not. She must forego such sentiments. Her husband would not want his gallantry acknowledged. After placing a ribbon around the precious lock of hair, she laid it on top of the cotton handkerchief next to the silver box. He would see it and understand. The colour of the ribbon about William's lock of hair was white.

That night, she watched from the bed as Darcy went to douse the light. He stopped when he saw the lock of hair. He said nothing, but touched it tenderly with the back of his forefinger.

She said, "Just when I think I cannot love you more, I am astonished once again."

Opening her arms, she bid him come. They did not make love, nor even whisper sweet tidings. They held one to the other and took whatever restive sleep they could.

The Key

The Darcys did not soon find comfort within the walls of Pemberley. For as others took their leave, another relation this way did come.

Not without ado, Mrs. Bennet hurried from Hertfordshire to shine her light of comfort upon the aggrieved family. As she was the grandmother of the dead child, she knew her place was at the forefront of such rituals. She scurried to Pemberley as fast as she could gather the proper wardrobe. She arrived two days after the burial.

The good lady could have salved her grief at home, but hers was the sort that liked to be fully admired. Having missed the interment, she did not sit in a window seat and daub at her tears. In truth, Mrs. Bennet disliked any event wherein her nerves and fits were not prominently featured. Therefore, as a rule, she suffered funerals of the immediate family better than those of mere friends. She wept copiously, lamented loudly, and beckoned for her salts whenever there was a lull in the wretchedness.

After accepting his mother-in-law's effusive condolences, Darcy bid Georgiana to play the pianoforte, specifying her selections not be melancholy. Elizabeth withstood Mrs. Bennet's company more than an hour ere she was overtaken by a headache.

Mrs. Bennet did not concede the advantage all that easily. Although Jane did her best, no one could stop her from what would be the apex of her exhibition. It was supper before there was a decent enough audience for her to threaten a swoon. She held it at bay until in the parlour that evening. When she finally did faint, it was no small back-of-the-hand-to-the-forehead capsizal. She keeled over with such élan as to twirl a full revolution before she upended herself into the arms of a burly footman. With all due respect (and gritted teeth), Mr. Darcy requested she keep to her chambers lest she make herself ill. Oftentimes sad tidings were too much for such fragile sensibilities as hers.

When she protested such measures, he said, "As it is my duty to see to your well-being, Mrs. Bennet, I fear I must insist."

Snapping his fingers, two maids escorted her up the steps and stood monitor over her every need. Indeed, Mr. Darcy's fear for her health was so great that he stationed a footman next to her chamber door to accompany her should she happen to wander about. Consigned out of sight, it was not long ere Mrs. Bennet bid farewell.

Daintily daubing a tear from the corner of her eye, she said, "I hope you forgive my taking leave so soon, but I cannot bear umberous occasions for they remind me of your poor father's passing."

Here she beckoned Hill to bring her salts and, prostrate with grief, she was carried up the steps of the coach and hoisted inside. Standing in the cloud of dust left by her mother's departing equipage, Elizabeth managed to hide her dismay. Indeed, she bore the deprivation of her mother's comfort exceedingly well.

It was then that Elizabeth vowed to stanch her own weeping for good.

If she did not, they might all run mad. For Elizabeth saw herself as the captain of a listing ship. If she lost her balance, everyone aboard would perish from sadness. As the last of their guests departed, she bid loving good-byes and told them their words were a comfort. Much of her time thenceforward was spent in the company of the twins.

As he always did, Darcy found solace at the stables. When he went there, it was often to speak with the stableman, Edward Hardin. Sore hocks and brood mares occupied their conversation—a relief for both of them. In the succeeding days, Geoff gave up the nursery to follow his father. Indeed,

Geoff's mimicked his father's every step. He especially liked to follow him to see the horses. The older he was, the more his carriage mocked Darcy's. As she watched them stride down the path (Darcy taking shorter paces to allow for his son), Elizabeth felt the leadenness in her heart a bit relieved.

It was Janie who seemed to suffer most for her brother's death. This took Elizabeth by surprise. Of the twins, Janie was the happy-natured one. After his death she often crept up to little William's bed, to suck her thumb and stroke his pillowcase.

Each time Elizabeth discovered her there, she drew her on her lap and cooed, "We miss him too, my sweet."

Margaret queried, "Shall I keep her away, mistress, or leave her be?"

"Allow her what consolation she needs," Elizabeth said.

She finally told Darcy whereby his daughter sought refuge.

"Would that we all could do the same," said he.

Until then, their commiserations had been largely silent. Time had come for them to speak of their heretofore unspeakable sorrow. If she believed that she would be the agency whereby he would find sympathy, she was mistaken. Indeed, it was not Darcy's tender feelings that remained unexplored, but hers.

"I have not seen you weep since Mrs. Bennet took her leave, Lizzy," he whispered in her ear. "I daresay you are not all that recovered."

If it was an accusation, it was kindly meant. Still, she demurred. His quiet insistence finally broke through the wall she had begun to construct about her.

Pressing her fingertips to her forehead, she finally said, "I vowed not weep. Indeed, I shall not weep... for if I do, I fear I shall never stop."

In a single stroke, he cupped her chin and brought her head to his chest. She could hear his heart. It beat as did hers—the same wounded rhythm.

She said, "Are we selfish to have wanted him longer?"

Extending a forefinger, he waited for the tear that formed to drop so he could wipe it away. However, it did not fall.

"We shall struggle onward," said she.

In the distance, the pianoforte erupted. It was not Georgiana's melodious playing. There were but two notes. Black, white, black, white, black, white, over and over and over.

Janie had found another way to express her grief.

The notes were the sound of absent footfalls.

Black, white, black, white, black, white. Plunk, plunk, plunk, plunk, plunk...

Knowing that the child must be contained lest she drive everyone mad, Elizabeth reluctantly withdrew from her husband's embrace. At the door, she tarried.

Looking back, she asked quite earnestly, "If death has a thousand doors, when our time is come, how shall we ever find him?"

Plunk, plunk, plunk, plunk....

$\mathcal{U}$nwound

Friends, servants, cottagers, and kin were united in one belief. Happiness would once again reign in the House of Pemberley would the Darcys just conceive another child. Simple as that. Adieu to melancholy forever.

The Master and Mistress, a couple of exceptional handsomeness and understanding, would have liked nothing more than to once again enjoy the delectation of three children capering before them and thereby insure the felicity of local bystanders and passing tourists. They were far too sensible to believe it would be that simple.

In the same way their stillborn was not replaced by William, another baby could not replace him.

The general populace were inclined to look to the bright side of misfortune. The Darcys may have lost a child, but two were alive. That was, on average, a tolerable ratio—even for persons of station. Mr. Darcy was quite fertile and his wife had proven herself to be an excellent brooder. She would soon be with child again.

Even good Lady Millhouse had her own opinion upon the matter. She believed all injuries were best healed by exercise. She insisted to Elizabeth that only through long rides upon the surrounding park and rededication of conjugal exertions would the Darcys repair.

"You must fight any tendency to lowness! Melancholy does not make a fertile bed," she boomed. "Go now on a hunt, for nothing is better for one's constitution than fresh air and exercise."

Jane would give up her life before injuring her sister, but she offered advice as well.

"Yes, dear Lizzy," she insisted. "Another babe to hold in your arms shall help you mend, of this I am certain."

As if to cement that recommendation as right and true, Mrs. Bennet opposed such a notion out of hand. She submitted her admonition by post, for travel no longer agreed with her. (The four and twenty families of her acquaintance were much in need of hearing of her recent sojourn and

Pemberley's many additions and alterations). Her letters were many and their subject was always the same. She insisted that Elizabeth had done her duty. She could desist with further affection.

"You have given Mr. Darcy a son. That is all that is required of you. If you continue to bear his children you shall lose what little is left of your bloom! I should not like to have a daughter looking old before her time. I must insist. You shall not have another child. Close your door to Mr. Darcy. He has his son and cannot complain."

The only bug in the honey pot of good will was the distant blat from a certain lady in Kent. Holding forth to a retinue of sycophants, Lady Catherine DeBourgh had what she believed was the last word on the matter. She concluded that the Darcy children were naturally doomed—tiny victims of the pollution of the Darcy line through the auspices of an unfortunate marriage.

Whilst they encouraged the Darcys to produce another offspring, their friends dealt with another vexation on their behalf. It was a great perplexity for them to determine how best to provide succour to the Darcys' wounded breasts in the meantime. Therefore, everyone avoided the subject of William. This arrangement was instituted without delay (or without the nicety of apprising the Darcys of it).

As it was, Mr. Darcy's reticence made him quite amenable to this policy of silence. Mrs. Darcy, however, was not like-minded. It would have been her particular pleasure to be able to speak of her dear William and delight in his memory. When she did, she was met with well-intentioned (and uncomfortable) silence. As she did not want to discomfit her acquaintances, she quieted herself of such reminisces.

That allowed everyone to be of the uncomplicated view that the Darcys' hearts were well on the mend. It was the general custom not to sacrifice present happy thoughts to a distant sorrow. It was only in the privacy of their chambers that Elizabeth dared venture a complaint.

She told Darcy, "We did our friends an unnecessary evil when we erected a headstone for William's grave. His memory is a great bother to them."

"Their intentions are well-meant," said he.

"Does it follow that they must be well-taken? I should not want our dear child to be a ghost, never spoken of again,"

"Our minds are alike. Given that it would be impolitic to force this sort of discourse upon others, we must accept it."

The lack of conversation regarding her lost child was a regret second only to one other. Their procrastination meant that they had not engaged Moreland to take William's likeness. Their family portrait was incomplete without him. Admittedly, it was a bit like picking at the scab on a wound, but not a day passed that Elizabeth did not stand before that once beloved portrait and decry it for what it lacked. Not a day passed that Darcy did not see her standing there. If she saw that she had been spied, she offered a cheery little smile, one meant to reassure him that all was well.

That smile was of no such comfort. It was only one of many such mannerisms that were so fictitious that he was given to shiver. In company, when in every other way his lovely wife was the epitome of grace and charm, her countenance was chillingly placid. Behind her smile, her expression was wan. If he inquired if she were ill, she begged indigestion. It was all disturbingly false.

Desperate to disrupt her alarming composure, he said, "Perchance, another child...."

She turned away and he did not compleat his thought. He believed that the moment had slipped from his grasp. And along with it, was their chance to reconcile the point.

In consequence of that conversation, Elizabeth realised that it would be best for everyone that she bore another child. Her husband, family, and friends would no longer be burdened by her gloom. Moreover, a new baby would divert Janie and Geoff (who often stood about as if they had been slapped by angels) and she would be much engaged with nurturing a new life. Her husband could abide in his study, wise in the knowledge that their happiness would never be torn asunder again.

Had she conceived again directly, she might have taken her husband's arm and gone thither into the future as it shone like a beacon before them. As it was, she did not. Her ability to look ahead with dispassion was lost.

Therefore, beneath the connubial covers, apprehension took its toll.

Lying with her husband had always been a singular pleasure, improved only by the knowledge that when he cast his seed within her, that a child might come of their union. What had once been a splendid apogee, she began to see as an act of ultimate violence. If a child was begat, the child may well die. The risk of conception was too dear. Still, she could not turn her husband away. Her love for him had not wavered.

But, imbedded in a muddle of fear and grief, she did not allow herself to take pleasure in their amorous inclinations. She clasped his nightshirt and buried her face against his neck as he took her.

Thus to her mind she did it for his sake. For her sake, and for the sake of a child she dared not to have, she urgently uttered one word to him as he crescendoed.

"Withdraw! Pray, withdraw!"

An Inconvenient Request

It was late evening. The sun struck a crease across the opposing wall. Within that shaft of light stood his wife's escritoire. It was of delicate design, quite suitable for a lady. That day its outline loomed ominously as it was heaped with several stacks of bereavement cards yet waiting to be read. The missives would no doubt contain sentiments that touched that part of their hearts that were still raw with grief. Nonetheless, Mr. Darcy felt it a duty to read each and every condolence. It was a small facilitation, one chore he was happy to spare Elizabeth.

Setting aside her chair, he drew a taller one to her desk and began to sort through them. He opened those from friends; those from mere acquaintances he set aside. (It was difficult enough to read genuine words of sympathy; he refused to spend emotion upon those written by rote.) As he took each in hand, one arrested his attention. It was from the pen of the mistress of Howgrave Hall. He recognised Juliette's hand immediately. At first he set it aside. Then, he retrieved it, but did not open it.

Pensively, he flicked the card with the fingernail of his middle finger.

Understandably, he had eschewed all thought of the ball at Howgrave Hall for it did nothing but remind him that he had not been home when the calamitous event beset them. However, the card stirred his memory. Those recollections came to him, not hastily, but as if waves lapping at the shore, one over the other. In his mind, what occurred that night at Howgrave Hall all moved as if in half-time.

As he recalled it, he and Lady Howgrave stood at the top of the staircase. A footman bearing a note ascended. There was nothing particular about the footman. Perchance it was in the way the man walked, or the expression upon his countenance, Darcy could not say why, but he knew that the man bore a missive from Elizabeth. His own thoughts were lost to him. As the man handed him the letter, Lady Howgrave continued to speak. Darcy did not hear a word she said. Once he had the note and read it, he folded it neatly in half and placed it in a pocket in his waistcoat. He recalled little else between that moment and when he arrived at Pemberley.

The odd sense of something left undone influenced him to open Juliette's card. It contained nothing of note. Lady Howgrave extended sympathy upon their loss. Despite such brevity, it was enough to prod him into recalling the specific words she had uttered to him that night.

She had said, "He beats me."

How could he have forgotten such an admission? As he bethought it, more than just her words came to mind. He also recalled her gaze. It was peculiar. Although she bore the same expression of barely contained ennui that she always had, something was amiss. Behind her impeccably powdered countenance lay something unrecognizable to him. As it came to him then, he determined that it looked remarkably akin to fear.

The flood of tears that erupted from her that night had been forgotten. In Darcy's mind, he had already made his away. It was possible that she had wept, but as that was uncertain to him, it did complicate his belief in her sincerity.

Her embarrassing disclosure seemed to have been borne of desperation. Had she reached out to him seeking his aide in escaping her husband? Why she approached him rather than her many paramours, lady-friends, and benefactors he could not imagine. Allowing a moment for reflection, he reasoned it out. No doubt their prior intimacy gave her leave to confide in him. Howgrave meant to stand for re-election. If such information became public, an unholy scandal would ensue.

At one time Howgrave had his sights upon becoming the Prime Minister. Of late, just keeping his seat in Parliament was a trial. With anarchy at hand, a great deal of power and money flew about. There was chaos enough in England. Voters would be difficult to lure even without the stench of marital disgrace.

Juliette's overture left Darcy in a very precarious position. Law and society were at odds. It was a matter of class. Whereas a poor man would be gaoled for beating a horse, a gentleman could take a stick to his wife with compleat impunity. It had been his observation that if a man would take a cane to his wife, his scruples were compleatly compromised. Other malfeasances were certainly at work. Power was a true pestilence in the hands of those disposed to abuse it. He had seen that in his own home. Indeed, Smeads looked to have crowned himself feudal lord of his own little Pemberley fiefdom.

It was a quandary. Lady Howgrave had not asked for his service in furtherance of any design. She had issued a statement.

Their conversation the night of the Pemberley ball had left him annoyed. Unwittingly or not, her intimations had offended him. At the time he had set her remarks aside, attributing them to the worst sort of oblivion. She had led a pampered and narcissistic existence. In her vaunted circles, those who bore children hardly delighted in them. Juliette's life had been dedicated to entertaining men who held no respect for their wives. What did she know of marital devotion or filial pride?

At this turn of self-righteousness, his conscience did not remain unbothered. He did not like to recall their connection, Granted, when he came to her, he was unmarried and unattached (and his loins ached with all the considerable heat of youth). She had been charming as well as beautiful, yet he did not seek her companionship. In truth, she had been no more than a receptacle to him. He sought only to soothe his fevered blood. It was never an *affaire'd amour*. And if it was not, it was to be despised as unbefitting a gentleman—whatever his justification was at the time.

Such reminisces were abhorrent. He quitted thoughts of the impertinent past for those of the pertinent present.

He wanted to believe that Juliette's sudden eruption over her husband's misuse was but a ruse, born of the wiles of a woman bored by her husband and the shallowness that surrounded them. But he could not. Her disconsolation appeared to be quite genuine.

Regardless, if he was to trouble himself by a lady's unhappiness, he would see to his wife first. Her dispiritness was far more alarming.

"*Withdraw*," Elizabeth had urged.

He had been most unnerved by his wife's sudden request. (As much as he wanted to oblige her in all ways, at that particular moment her wants were unattainable.) Their unions had always been anointed by compleat achievement. He had no greater pleasure than when they reached fulfilment together. However difficult, he would honour her wishes, mollified by the notion that given time, her opinion would alter. If she was too discomfited to chance another child just then, he understood compleatly. How best to go about it was not a conundrum.

The ways of love were many—and their union had always been a collaborative one.

Her desire to satisfy him had remained as it always had been. She stroked, nuzzled and drew from him his very marrow. Her methods left him compleatly fulfilled. (Indeed, there were sonnets devoted to such raptures.) What astonished him of late was that she did not care to be pleasured in return. His delectation had always been improved by bringing her to achievement (again and again and again, and, sometimes, again). Would she allow him to attend her properly, she could be brought to exquisite triumph without fear of falling with child.

Indeed, it was his particular gratification to stroke her to submission.

Closing his eyes, he imagined the journey his tongue would take, snaking down between her breasts, across her belly....

He sat up. Only then did he become witting that he had not only slipped halfway down his chair, he had a conspicuous bulge in the crotch of his breeches. In fortune, there was no one about to witness his embarrassment, for the impromptu reveille of his nether-regions was not easily conquered. As he struggled to do so, the possibility that Elizabeth faced a similar dilemma struck him. To be taken partially down the road to ultimate rapture only to be diverted onto another path might be unduly demanding upon her sensibilities as well. Perhaps she feared throwing all caution to the wind as did he. Concluding that she dared not trust her own passion was a more palatable thought than others, but not a true consolation. Yet, he would protect her from that which she abhorred. That was his duty.

Heaving himself upon her only to spill his seed into a lace handkerchief was an indignity he preferred not to endure. If Elizabeth did not care to give of herself wholly to him, he would just as well do without too.

Having sunk into what might have been accused of being a bout of self-pity; his unhappy thoughts were broken by the arrival of a servant carrying a tray. Upon it lay a letter. It had come by courier. This missive was also in Lady Henry Howgrave's hand. It was not, however, further condolences. It's message was implicit.

It read, "I must see you at your earliest possible convenience."

48

$\mathcal{U}$nstrung

Physical congress and under what auspices they would take it did not burden Elizabeth Darcy just then. Her thoughts commanded her deeds, and her thoughts were unhelpful.

Having concluded that Darcy was witting that she stood in the Portrait Hall gazing longingly at their family's likenesses and that such behaviour troubled him, Elizabeth ceased. Nonetheless, her most profound fear had not altered. She was transfixed with the notion that her memory of William's happy face was fading. The more she endeavoured to imagine him, the hazier his countenance became to her. Of the mind that no one was aware of it, she silently, but persistently, fretted that she had not had his likeness committed to paint.

She had kept to one vow. Other than one tremulous moment, she had not wept, nor by any other means, appeared unduly bereaved in front of her family. Indeed, she continued to be uncommonly collected. She also began to spend an inordinate amount of time in her bath. There, she could lose herself in her dearest recollections without fear of observation. It was of the utmost importance that her continuing misery would not disturb others.

That recent predilection had come to Mr. Darcy's attention. (Granted, he used the deplorable tactic of spying on her to obtain this information—he believed the ends justified the means.) It was urgent that her melancholy be addressed. However, he did not want to appear accusatory. They each had their way of contending with misfortune. (He took to the downs on Blackjack—which could be accused as simply avoidance.) To him, her method seemed to be harbouring the hurt, rather than conquering it.

When she had fallen into a black abyss of despair after the stillbirth, she had found solace in her bath. Consequently, he was not surprised that she did so once again. He had come into the bathing room and joined her then. Upon that occasion, as this, he did not mean to take liberties or to commiserate. In naked recumbence, he hoped they could share an intimacy of the heart; one that would contain certain filaments—mad and despairing thoughts—that threatened them both.

Now lost to an internal call, she did not hear him come in or his dressing gown drop to the floor. Startled, she did take notice when he slipped in behind her. She neither spoke nor looked upon him. However, she allowed herself to be engulfed by the length of his legs. The considerable displacement of water his body did disturb, sloshed onto the floor.

She leaned back against his bare chest. Her soaked chemise lay flattened against her as if a second skin. The only thing dividing them was that—and a thousand sorrows.

She spoke, not mournfully, but something far worse. Without inflection, she said, "There are times that my very flesh aches."

Determined to speak of what she dared not, he whispered in her ear, "It is a time-worn question—is it not? That it is it better to have loved and lost than never to have loved at all?"

As if she had not heard his words, she suddenly sat up, again losing water over the side of the tub.

"My children! Do I hear them?"

His arms hugged her to him as he soothed, "Hush, my love. They are safe. Listen, you can hear their laughter."

Her body, which had tensed, gradually settled. He kissed her on her neck and ear. Then as he had done before, he took a sponge, dipped it in the water and drew it across her shoulders, squeezing water from it as he did. She neither revelled in, nor recoiled against, his ministrations. It was a submission. In time, she nestled against him and sighed. The sound was intoxicating. Ere he had a chance to improve on that, once again her attention was stolen by her imagination.

"Yes," she called out. "Children, I shall come directly."

She betook her robe about her and rose from their bath, thinking of nothing but her motherly urges. Indeed, as she left the room, the saturated tail of her robe drug behind her like a wet mop.

Darcy slid down into the water until it lapped at his chin; a small whiff of her scent was all she left him. It was just as well. Her body lying wet and slippery against his had inspirited him. Had they lingered together longer, the gods of lust might have overtaken him. His loins tingled even then. After a moment, he realised that the half-open door did not suggest her imminent return. So he stood, pausing only long enough for the excess water to cascade down his body ere he stepped from the copper tub himself.

Hannah observed her mistress leave her bath and quickly gave her a dry robe. Although Mrs. Darcy waved her away then, it piqued the maid's pride to be privy to her lady's privacy. Hannah gathered a chambermaid and hastened to the bathing-room to see to their duties. Hannah was rarely taken unawares by Mr. Darcy in Mrs. Darcy's chambers, for he was often there. Therefore, when they gained the room just as Mr. Darcy stepped from the tub, it was not Hannah who shrieked.

In a trice, Hannah clamped a hand over the young chambermaid's eyes lest the sight of Mr. Darcy in all his naked glory compromise the poor girl's expectations in any of her future copulatory endeavours. Both of the women hastily turned their faces to the wall. Unperturbed by the encounter, Mr. Darcy was in his robe and on to his own dressing-room in less than a blink. The maids remained in place long after he had gone on his way.

Hannah had brothers and assured herself that she had been more startled than shocked. Still, she trembled as she went about wiping the wet floor and draining the bath water. She noticed the chambermaid stood yet with her face to the wall.

"Make haste, you hear me!" she told her urgently.

The young maid turned first one foot and then the other as if sneaking upon the tub and its water. When she finally reached the edge, she peered over the side.

Hannah hissed, "Get with it now. The gentleman has gone. Do you think he'll rise again like Lazareth?"

"No'm," said the maid, who was slow to retrench her thoughts. She marvelled, "Such a sword I have never imagined! If a lady canna' be happy with that what is there for the rest of us?"

"Hush up!" Hannah insisted.

The door had not closed all the way behind the maids and Cressida crept into room for its warmth. First, however, the dog trotted to the water on the floor and began to drink. Hannah grabbed the dog and scooted her out the door before returning to her chores.

As they worked, Hannah said, "Everyone must learn for themselves that we have but today and must live for it or be lost forever. The master and mistress shall recall that when their sorrow is finally wore out."

epair

The next morning, mist clung to the oaks and the eerie shrieks of peafowl could be heard in the distance. A lone figure moved stealthily between trees beside the path that wend its way down to the stables.

A way up the road stood a boy of perhaps fourteen, his face was quite solemn. He was Edward Hardin's oldest son and newly promoted to stable duty. He nervously scratched his upper lip with his lower teeth. The expression he bore announced that he knew well that the office he held was of great import. He clutched the reins of a bay mare with both hands. The horse was saddled; its head hung low as it nipped at a tuffet of grass. When the figure approached, he recognised her. The horse nickered softly and the boy gave an awkward bow. Without a word spoken between them, the boy legged the rider onto the steed. Then with nary a heel to its flanks, the horse and rider cantered away. The boy watched as they crossed the bridge and headed towards the valley.

Dampness hung in the air, causing him to shudder. A storm loomed. It was good she wore her cape.

With a flick of Elizabeth's crop, Boots began to a canter.

It did not escape her mind that her husband often took to the saddle when he wanted quiet to ponder his cares. That was not her reason, however. She wanted to escape from that which grieved her and was in want of privacy to do so. A wild gallop—the sort that Darcy always cautioned her against—was what she desired.

As her feet were bare, she feared giving a bit of heel to the mare's flanks would be useless. However, with only a nudge, the horse began to run—welcoming a chance to stretch her stride. They raced with unschooled abandon, setting her heart aflutter. For a few moments, she was elated. As the horse began to pant, Elizabeth slowed her to a walk. Just below lay her favourite prospect. Crossing the bridge, she pointed the horse where the valley narrowed into a glen bordered by a rough coppice. She and her husband had spent many an afternoon there languishing in love's embrace. Those carefree hours seemed several lifetimes past.

"Ah, to picnic in Eden once more," she whispered.

In want of reclaiming those long lost days, she urged her horse towards the shelter of those recollections. She and her horse knew the way thither intimately.

The mist increased to a light rainfall. She was well-aware that riding in the rain was dangerous. The leather of the saddle and reins would play tricks on her. However, going where she chose in the manner she so chose, was an impertinent excitation. Whilst Darcy had always ridden wherever he pleased, he had insisted that she kept to the paths. His gentlemanly caution was both charming and an enormous perturbation. This morn, she did not want to be seen or confined. She did not care to meander beneath the tulip trees, but to embark on a mad sprint in the brambles, splash through the brook, and then ride up the hill to the ruins of the hunting tower.

Beneath her cape, Elizabeth wore nothing but her nightdress. Her feet were wet with dew and slipped in the stirrups. She gave them up altogether, the risk of being drug was too great. However, that was the only caution she heeded. Her escapade had suddenly elevated from mere excitation to risking life and limb. She reminded herself that, as a wife and mother, she owed it to her family to be more prudent.

First, she would take yonder hill.

Another flick and Boots began to labour up towards the crest of the rise. When they gained the top, she drew her to a stop and gazed at the mist-laden hillocks. The wind rushed under her sleeves giving her the fleeting sensation she had wings. Feasting upon the thrill, she tossed her cape back over her shoulders and urged Boots to begin their descent.

The reverse side of the hill was steep—far steeper than the incline. Rather than slowing, Boots gathered speed. Elizabeth drew back on the reins, but that only made Boots fling her head wildly about. As the mare plunged downward, her hooves skidded on the wet turf. Elizabeth tried to slow her. It was useless.

By the time they gained the bottom of the hill, Boots was unmanageable. Unused to having her head, the horse bolted forward. It was all Elizabeth could do not to be thrown. As rain began to spatter harder, the horse ran madly towards the wood. Elizabeth's cape twirled as if whirligig, every rotation tightening it about her neck. If her cape caught on a tree limb, she would be dashed to the ground. The more she attempted to restrain the mare, the more violently the horse ran. All she knew of how to gain control of a runaway horse fled her. The instinct to leap from the saddle was strong; however before she could decide to do it, a call rang out.

"Turn her to the side!"

Boots was running full out, but Elizabeth tugged on the right rein, turning her in a wide circle. By then Blackjack's long stride overtook her. Darcy's command notwithstanding, Elizabeth reached out for him. With one swift movement, he plucked her from her horse and onto his.

Clasping him tightly, she was overborne by a frisson of gratitude and—was it ecstasy?

His highest interest lay not in passion, but in scolding her.

Slowing Blackjack, he asked, "Are you mad? Are you *mad*?"

As the question was at that moment rhetorical, she did not feel compelled to answer.

When Blackjack came to a stop, she released her grip and slid to the ground. Her brewing ardour was not suppressed. Panting with excitement, fear, and anger, she attacked the gnarled ties of her cape. Although she dared not look at his reproving countenance, she was well-aware that Darcy had come after her with such haste that he rode bareback. She spied steam rising from Blackjack's withers and immediately quit fussing with her ties and looked about for Boots. The horse had stopped a short distance away, quivering with fright. She called to the mare, but was ignored. Darcy whistled and Boots perked one ear. Unhurt, but a bit unforgiving, the horse walked towards them.

Darcy slid down from his horse and walked purposefully in her direction. His gait was so firm, quite without realising it, she backed up several steps. He was right to be angry. Not only had she endangered the mother of his children, but her horse too. As he neared her, she could see just how unamused he was. Drawing her cape about her, she looked at him defiantly. His eyes softened and he reached out to her palm down, as if to settle an excited filly. Such a gesture did not appease her. She turned on her bare heel and stomped off in the direction of her horse. Hearing Darcy fast behind, she hurried her step. Yet, within three strides he caught up to her.

Catching her shoulder, he said, "Do wait."

"I cannot," she said, shrugging him away.

"You shall."

With a keen eye, she looked back at him. The expression upon his countenance had not the imperiousness of his words. Soft rain dripped from the end of his nose. Without a thought, she used her sleeve of her gown to wipe it and his chin. Catching her hand, he dropped to one knee and bid her sit. Her cape was rapidly becoming soggy, but she wrapped it about them both (for she had no shoes and he had no coat).

In their snug shelter, she put her cheek to his. They kissed.

Within that time, the rain became a mere drizzle. Still, neither was willing to return to the world of restraint (where well-born people do not scamper about half-dressed).

However disinclined Darcy was to quarrel; time had come for them to speak of what they had so scrupulously avoided.

He said, "I truly feared you meant to do yourself harm."

She was aghast at such a notion, retorting, "Sir! It is you who are mad to think such a thing!"

Lowering his chin for a moment, he then looked directly at her, saying, "You have turned me away."

There. He was out with it.

Indignant, she rebutted his accusation, "I have done no such thing!"

"I shall not sit here in this rain and argue the point. You have, in essence, turned me away," he said with finality.

Touching his face tenderly, she said plaintively, "Not in my heart—never in my heart."

Said he, "If you do not want to bear another child, I shall protect you against it in every way possible."

He thought to tell of another time, another decision.

"After our first son was taken, you were near death, Lizzy," he said softly. "I thought you would die. I vowed then that I would do what I must—chamber alone if necessary to keep you safe. I will renew that vow now if you so wish."

She shook her head.

"No, I do not wish that," she insisted. Her voice light, she said, "I am merely in a bit of a muddle."

He spoke not a word, but his expression questioned her assessment of her state of mind.

Seeing that, she reminded him, "I rallied then, did I not?"

"You rallied," he admitted.

"I shall rally again"

Finally, she admitted to herself that she had not yet repaired.

"Can we not stay here...?"

It did not occur to him that she desired him then. He covered her toes with his hand and began scolding her again for her bare feet.

"Never ride out without your boots. Not only shall you catch your death, your foot shall slip through the stirrup and you shall be drug to death. Never ride barefoot. Always wear your riding boots," he lectured. "And if your horse cannot be checked...."

"Yes," she interrupted, for she did know what she should have done.

She nodded like a child, for he was quite right. Indeed, he wore but a shirt and breeches, but he had taken the time to draw on his boots. Always fastidious, always correct. Even when pursuing her, he drew on the proper boots. Were they never to frolic as if lusty young lovers and make love in sunlit fields and golden flowers without a care? That seemed an impossibility.

Without asking, Darcy led her to Boots and legged her onto the horse's saddle. Claiming the stirrups, he drew himself on behind her. He then whistled for Blackjack. The horse trotted along behind them.

By their return, a new day had dawned and men were at their chores. Both Darcys knew that the rear postern was the most discrete entry to the house and would therefore generate the smallest amount of attention. With nary a word, Darcy handed the reins of both horses to the footman. Well-trained by generations of service to Pemberley, the man's countenance did not flicker recognition of their déshabillé. Nay, he did not even appear to look at them. Despite his appearance of discretion, word would reach the furthest echelons of the house that the master and mistress had gone riding in an odd state of undress.

That would be grist for gossip-mongers for some time. At the thought of it, Elizabeth threw her head back and laughed. Darcy did not laugh. Indeed, he cleared his throat and frowned. This was not because he was not glad, for he was—very glad. His countenance rarely betrayed mirth. Indeed, his countenance betrayed few emotions, most especially the one she had just excited.

For the sound of his wife's laugh had entered his ears and settled directly in his loins. They were both mired in desire; just on separate paths.

The Laughter of the Gods

It was an altogether lovely morn. The windows were thrown open and the sun danced a dappled pattern across the tabletop. A soft breeze rippled up from the bottom of the curtains, shook them slightly and then let them go. Blue tits chattered at a cloudless sky. All was not right with the world, but it would do.

Quite witting of the flagitious alterations of life, Mr. Darcy sipped his coffee carefully. Mrs. Darcy put down her cup and turned to her husband, for she had an announcement.

She said, "I wish to visit Longbourne."

Once again the breeze caught the curtains, this time whipping them loose. It was as if a squall had suddenly burst through the balcony doors, threatening the fabric of their easily rent happiness. A servant hurried to secure the drapes. Just as hastily as it had arrived, the gust was contained. During this small drama, Darcy's eyes did not betake themselves from his newspaper. Even careful study would not have revealed that his wife's unexpected fancy to sally forth unto Hertfordshire was remarkable to him in any way.

It was, however. It was not only remarkable, it was alarming. Outwardly, he remained calm. No such thing could be said of his soul.

Every fibre of his being screamed out, "Secure the shutters, lock the doors, drag the dogs inside, and pull the covers over everyone's heads."

As a man of known fortitude, fear rarely troubled him. A cold sensation clamped onto Darcy's spine then. His heart was vulnerable in ways he never thought possible. He would not have it. He would not allow the sorrow they had meticulously tucked into their hearts be ripped asunder by the thoughtless harping of his mother-in-law. Had Elizabeth truly lost her head? Was she seeking penance? They had barely begun to reconstruct some semblance of their former lives. The crises they had suffered bid him keep his family under his protection, and thus under Pemberley's protection as well.

These feelings, so violently felt, remained unexpressed.

He carefully replaced his cup in the saucer. Darcy did not look at his wife. His gaze was purposely transfixed on a point just between two lines of his newspaper. Whilst his eyes remained enthralled by what they did not see, he gathered his thoughts. A query was in order—this he knew. Try as he might, however, he could find no way to couch that inquiry without insulting her sanity. They had both dwelt upon the edges of distraction far too long.

"Your mother would be most happy to see you."

Having conceded that point did not mean he had to approve of her plan.

"A more finely crafted agreement is not to be found in all of Derbyshire," she said.

It took him a moment ere he could determine if she mocked him. As he considered that possibility, his eyes did not flicker in her direction (despite how radiant she looked in the morning light). Rather, he read and reread the same sentence several times in a row. He bethought the matter and admitted that she had never been known to mock him. That would be an unforgivable trespass against his dignity. Their situation had not altered to that degree.

Having worn out that page, he carefully turned his paper to the next. He gave the next one all the attention of the last. It was his distinct hope that his apprehension was unapparent. At one time he was the master of his countenance. It had not reflected any emotion he did not choose to expose. Of late, inscrutability had become his greatest struggle.

He felt the weight of her gaze upon him. He dared not look at her lest she see his displeasure. He wanted to be her champion, not her disapprover. Still, her plan seemed nonsensical. Some might even call it a reckless endangerment of one's being. Mrs. Bennet was a callous goose. Her thoughtlessness was of legend. Why would Elizabeth seek her mother's consolation above his?

Just when he decided that she had lost her wits, he recalled her exact words.

She had not said that she wanted to see her mother.

She said that she wished to go to Longbourne. For whatever reason, she sought comfort in her childhood home. Just as he found solace in Pemberley's quiet beauty, Longbourne and the recollections of a more innocent time beckoned her.

Of the need to explain herself, Elizabeth said, "I know I shall not find him there, but I do miss my father."

Standing, Darcy pushed back his chair and walked to her.

With a low bow, he said, "It would be my great honour to accompany you."

Knowing the cost to his sensibilities each time he was in her mother's company, Elizabeth was exceedingly grateful. In want of displaying her gratitude, she stood so hastily that she bumped the table leg, overturning her tea. A young footman made a move to clean up the spill; another waved him away. Both of the men withdrew from the room, and it—the morning breeze, the chirping birds, the sun-kissed tabletop, all of it—was left to the Darcys. Elizabeth did not observe the aesthetics of their situation. All she knew was that her husband had wrapped his long arms about her and rested his chin upon the top of her head. She closed her eyes.

She said, "My affection for my father did not blind me to the occasional impropriety of his behaviour...."

"There are none amongst us who can say we have not exposed ourselves to ridicule. If that was the standard of love, I fear you would never have accepted me."

She said, "You and my father are so unalike. I cannot imagine two men with so little in common."

Tears, sweet tears, filled her eyes. His arms tightened about her.

Speaking of her father brought a particular recollection to Darcy's mind.

He had stood beside a tiny baby's coffin more than once. Their first child, a stillborn son, was buried whilst Elizabeth lay abed, lost of her senses. No one believed that she would survive. She lay all but motionless, in the pit of her own special hell, for a week. Her husband left her side only to mark the burial of their son. Grief-stricken for their dead baby, he was cold with dread that she might die as well. No one spoke to him; no one dared.

Darcy had lingered by the gravesite long after others had repaired to their own houses and loved ones. It was bitterly cold. Years later, a grey, blustery day would gift him a chill particular to that recollection. Less frequently, he remembered that Mr. Bennet had stood shivering as he waited for his son-in-law to quit the grave. Darcy did not recall Mr. Bennet's words, but the warmth of them solaced him through the difficult days to come.

For years, Darcy had been troubled by nightmares of those events. Only the continued happiness of their situation and the faces of his children had finally allowed the pain in his heart to ease. His only consolation then was that Elizabeth was spared the full horror of that day. Her suffering had been deep enough. Eventually, Jane had told her of the baby's burial, the bleak truth of it all shined up nice and pretty for her consumption. He did not want to open old wounds. Those more recent were test enough.

Rather, he told her, "You are wrong, my love. Your father and I had something very great in common."

She looked up at him quizzically.

"We shared a love for a particular lady."

She smiled at the thought of her father, droll and crusty, full of affection.

"Perchance," she mused, "Papa is in heaven now, hand in hand with our lost sons."

$\mathscr{A}$listair Steps Up

Having cast caution (and a good bit of her pride) to the wayside, Juliette had nothing to do but to wait and see if Darcy would come to her rescue. Howgrave still insisted she accompany him to his political rallies and, as she was beside herself with apprehension and anticipation, they became evermore unbearable.

When she was the darling of the political ring, she found it all quite diverting. Now, the tedious arguments over the gold standard and ecclesiastical appointments left her bored senseless. It was her dearest hope that one disputant would slap the other's face and demand a duel. Any violence would be preferable to her than the endless rhetoric. As malcontents became more frustrated, their speeches inflamed others. At last, fomentation was at hand.

"Our voices must be reinstated!" screamed one red-faced man.

His eyes bulged dangerously and Juliette silently prayed apoplexy would strike him—and all his political cronies—dead. That was not to be. Someone insisted that calm be restored and she was once again desperate to escape the tedium.

Smoke choked the air and made her eyes red. When she dared, she fled the dais holding her handkerchief to her lips. The small antechamber behind the hall was bathed in a haze of smoke, but it was not half as stifling as in front. Only a few men stood about. All, save one, wore work caps. The man in the silk hat was tall and quite distinguished-looking. He was well-dressed by most standards, but stood toe to toe and mired in conversation with the others. After a moment, the gaggle of what looked to be jobbers and packmen, left. They paused by the door only long enough for each to pick up a club from the dozen or so standing against the wall.

The man wearing the tall hat was puffing hard on his cigar. In a lady's presence, that was uncivil. It would be a test of his manners whether or not he disposed of it when he saw her (as she knew he would). As soon as the door closed behind the others, he threw his cigar on the floor and then mashed it out with the toe his boot. She was both surprised and delighted that a man within the boundaries of political doings subscribed to any part of gallantry.

Her husband's associates were heathens.

The gentleman spoke first, observing, "I see you could no longer listen to the oration of that boss-eyed nincompoop, Mr. Harvey."

As they had not been introduced, she turned her head haughtily in the opposite direction. Behind her, the gentleman bowed low.

"I do beg your pardon," he said, doffing his hat. "I am your husband's secretary, Mr. Alistair Thomas. We met but three days ago... in the vestibule of your home."

Had she been any other lady, she might have been a bit embarrassed to have mistakenly issued a cut. As the gentleman before her was far superior to any other in Howgrave's enclave, she decided to be amused.

"Of course," she chirped.

With singular agility, she altered the conversation. "I fear that these subjects do not excite me as they should."

He smiled in return, saying, "Economic issues are not for the faint of heart. As many lives have been lost as murders below Bethnal Green, over the Gag Act."

She held little more interest in murders than she did the Gag Act. If this gentleman could not improve his conversational topics, she meant to leave his company. Desperate for lively talk, she gave him another opportunity to entertain her.

Dipping her chin, she replied, "*Pas possible.*"

Her French accent was always more marked when speaking to a gentleman she cared to charm. From the cut of his coat, he was a gentleman of discernment. (He was either well-born or well-fixed.) His hair was white as snow, yet his skin was not weathered whatsoever. He leaned heavily upon his cane and as they walked the length of the room, he told her candidly that he had taken his wound as a British officer.

"*Outre mer,*" she whispered. "How *courageux*! You must have many medals!"

Men loved to be complimented—most especially in regards to their courage. This man was no exception, but he had sense enough not to preen.

"I would trade all my medals for two good legs any day," he replied. "Only a lord can make a limp *distingué.*"

His French was imperfect. But as he was the only marginally interesting gentleman she had found in the political milieu, she endeavoured to look pleased. A lifetime of convincing men that they were irresistible made that easy.

He said, "You are quite used to men losing their hearts to you, are you not?"

She slapped him lightly on the forearm with her fan and said, "*Quelle impertinence!*"

He smiled. His witty retort, however, was drowned out as the crowd on the other side of the wall exploded into wild applause.

Mr. Thomas bowed, saying, "Your husband takes the podium."

Looking towards the cheers, she observed, "The people seem to admire him."

"And you, do you admire him as do they?" asked Alistair.

His question was brazen. She answered it in a tone that begged neither tidings nor commiseration. Pausing briefly, she looked coyly at him over her shoulder.

"My husband brings me great joy...." said she. "Every time he leaves the room."

Mr. Thomas, limp and all, reached the door before her. He opened it for her with a fascinating combination of obsequious ticks and sexual gravitas. That pleased her.

Just as the applause quieted and Howgrave took his place before the crowd, he turned towards his wife's empty chair. As always, her timing was superb. With the assistance of Mr. Alistair Thomas, she ascended the steps of the dais as if a grand duchess. Raising one hand, she extended two fingers and accepted a second, even greater ovation. Thus introduced, she reclaimed her chair and looked lovingly at her husband. She did not see, but knew regardless, that Alistair's eyes were not on the prestigious man of Parliament speaking. His unabashed admiration was directed at his wife.

She did not reproach him. It was but a harmless flirtation.

He was beneath her, but still a man.

With liberties forsaken and sedition at hand, Lady Howgrave was happy to have a gentleman's undivided attention. As she looked out onto the shrieking mob, she was quite unruffled. It would take far more than a torch-bearing, rock-throwing melee to discompose her. The English were so... uninspired. When they began to chop heads off on the steps of St. James palace, she would make note. Until then, she would sit and smile in public—and in private long for her husband's castration. All was not lost.

"*Vouloir, c'est pouvoir.*" Where there's a will, they say, there's a way.

Darcy would come. He was the way, the light, the beginning, and the end. And if he did not come, she would go to him.

The Great Beyond

The sad business of commemorating death had given Elizabeth Darcy ample excuse to keep from travelling anywhere.

In the dreadful days following their loss, Elizabeth had begun to admire the simplicity of the past. When Hertfordshire was mentioned, Mrs. Bennet's quarrelsome nature came to Darcy's mind. However, her mother had no part in Elizabeth's reminisces. She recalled nothing but her father's warmth and Jane's companionship. The thought of the twins playing in the same park she had as a child cheered her.

Their conversation of that sunny morn was furthered that eve.

"The children are old enough to enjoy humbler surroundings," Elizabeth told her husband.

His silence in no way implied acquiescence. Indeed, Mr. Darcy was aghast. He saw no reason under the sun for his children to enjoy beggarly environs. They would live their lives under the auspices of Pemberley and its largess. Those of lower station who bid audience would come to them.

He checked those thoughts.

It was surprisingly easy to regain his contemptuous leanings. He reminded himself that the doltish inhabited all rungs of society. Nobility was not assignable. If it would improve Elizabeth's spirits to take their children to Longbourne, he would not object—so long as he was the overseer of the journey.

Although Darcy would not think of his family travelling all the way to Hertfordshire without him, he did not plan to tarry at Longbourne the length of their stay. Once they were settled in with maids and footmen, he knew he must take that time to attend to certain affairs in London. He had been long from town and certain business could not be seen to from Derbyshire.

He announced, "I shall accompany you to Meryton and thither I shall go to London. I have business in town."

She raised her eyebrow, inquiring, "Shall you be much engaged with Bingley's affairs?"

"I shall see to no one's business but my own," said he.

They seldom spoke of what had occurred the last time he went to town without her. It was an escapade filled with menace and unseemly doings. They had attended locales where good intentions meant little and life was cheap. Extortion and bribery ruled the day. Indeed, they were fortunate to have escaped with their lives. London had not improved in recent years.

"The Prince Regent's carriage was not immune to rioters," Elizabeth said quietly.

She was in want—nay, in need—of reassurance.

He reminded her, "That was well above a year ago...."

"Calm has hardly been restored. If anything, violence has increased," she said.

He assured her, "I shall keep to the West End."

"Your coach... it shall announce your class."

"I shall not be alone."

"Four footmen," she said firmly.

"Two," he countered.

"Four," she insisted.

He placed his hand atop hers. As it dwarfed hers twice over, it was a comfort. Indeed, he struck a commanding figure. Few men dared challenge him. Although he was not by nature confrontational, his personal rectitude often led him unaccompanied into battles that were not his alone to fight. Her worry was not compleatly assuaged.

To her even greater relief, he acquiesced to the four footmen, saying, "As you wish."

With well-practised precision, she spread her fingers. Clasping hands, they were bound together.

He whispered, "I promise I shall stay safe."

Although it was often said that children are equal parts boon and bother, the Darcys were not of that mind even before their great misfortune. Mrs. Darcy came under particular scrutiny by certain ladies of condition for what they saw as an unnatural indulgence in her young ones. This accusation remained unchallenged. Although dutiful to her position in society, Elizabeth Darcy believed that the manner wherein she chose to nurture her children was of no concern to anyone else.

As she had not relegated her babies to a wet-nurse's care, it should have come to no one's surprise that when embarking upon a journey of some distance, she would not consign them to ride in the luggage coach. Indeed, it was her particular wish that she have her share in their excitement upon encountering every new vista. She bid Darcy's opinion and his approval as well, for it would mean a concession for them both.

He said, "In this, as in all things, I trust your judgement, Mrs. Darcy."

In his youth, Darcy abhorred taking a coach. When he travelled, it was by horseback, unless the weather insisted otherwise. When all of society adored prancing about in a barouche, he despised it. (To him such an equipage meant being forced into a sort of indentured servitude to the other travellers—knee to knee with silly ladies or pedantic gentlemen.) Such reservations all changed upon his first journey together with his new wife.

Their nuptial night was taken in London. It had been exquisite—a triumph of his stamina and her very willing lucubration. However, it was upon the journey from thence that their love was solidified. No pleasure they enjoyed in his sumptuous bed surpassed those they partook on the road north to Derbyshire as a married couple. Theirs were two parts of one heart—and it beat with love, loyalty, and unrelenting lust.

With the children in tow, passionate liaisons within the plush coach were out of the question. In designing their upcoming journey, the romanticism of those past would have to be set aside. Not only would it be a relinquishment of some magnitude, no doubt nerves would be tried as well. She would not allow him to escape the finger of blame simply by capitulating in favour of her judgement.

Her voice was teasing, she said, "If our children misbehave, you must have your share in it."

Turning her head slightly askew, her eyes did not quit him. He glanced at her and hastily looked away.

"I have no idea to what you refer," he said stiffly.

"I suppose not. I am the indulgent parent. Perhaps, I ask too much of you...."

Before she realised it, he had come behind her and slid his arms beneath hers.

Whispering in her ear, he said, "We do not indulge our children, we love them."

"You do not mind them intruding upon our privacy? At one time, we enjoyed nothing above a cloistered ride in the coach. "

"If we cannot outfox children not five years old, we do not deserve time alone."

"How long, pray, do you think they will believe we have yet to find my shoes?"

Despite their banter, Mr. Darcy's reminisces of pleasures past were no consolation when their upcoming sojourn promised none whatsoever. Yet, his forbearance was not over-worked. He also looked forward to their children's excitement, even at the cost of reining in his own. (His hand would not have leave to wander.) He had to suppress a slight pout over his desires being controverted, but was not altogether successful. He busied himself out of his pique by attending to the many chores attached it their journey.

Such a trip was a large undertaking, requiring the assembly of three coaches and their drivers, twelve horses and six footmen. Darcy's inspection of each was meticulous. No pin, rod, or bolt was left to chance. Every button on the footmen and fetlock on each horse was scrutinized. The duteousness wherewith Mr. Darcy addressed all of these endeavours was of legend. (Behind such care was a recollection of another trip, quite the opposite in all ways of their first—that ordeal was so unendurable they rarely spoke of it.)

Elizabeth watched these preparations from a window above. She had seen him make the same verifications, examinations, and confirmations a dozen times. Fastidious in all things, Mr. Darcy was most mindful of his horses. Stamina was essential in the planning of each journey. Of primary importance was that the trip was broken in a propitious fashion. Common thought was that the horses' exertions should be rewarded every fifteen miles. Darcy spoke to Edward Hardin and lectured the coachmen. No stone was left unturned in assuring a safe trip.

Darcy was not the only one who had looked upon their travels with near-wanton expectation. Elizabeth had enjoyed the privacy of their coach as much as her husband. Indeed, upon their first journey to Pemberley, she had been altogether astonished what a churched couple could engage in so long as windows were covered. Gazing down upon her husband, she gave a sigh of regret for what once was.

From afar she heard the excited exchanges of Janie and Geoff. Darcy and Elizabeth found ample recompense in their children's delight.

When at last they were on their way, the children were again cautioned to mind their behaviour. Both crossed their ankles and folded their hands in their lap. Mr. and Mrs. Darcy exchanged glances. Elizabeth set a penny upon the seat between them.

She told her husband, "I wager this quiet does not last until the lodge post."

Of a mind that a word from him was all that was required to keep his children in check, Darcy took the penny and placed it in the pocket inside his waistcoat

"I spoke to them most firmly," he replied. "They have promised to be good."

Elizabeth smiled sweetly. "Good" meant many things to many people. She hoped that his confidence would be well-rewarded.

It was not.

The twins began to bicker as they crossed the bridge a half mile from the portico. This disagreement came about because each believed the other had a better view out the window. With only a glare from their father they desisted.

Darcy told Elizabeth, "The reverberation of their voices inside this coach makes me long for deafness."

She smiled; happy that was merely a jest. Darcy was quite pleased that he could rein in his children so easily. He saw disciplining their children as a simple task. One only needed to speak to them firmly.

However, once his father looked away, Geoff made faces at Janie. She glowered. Emboldened, he withdrew previously hidden paper from his waistband. Then, quite surreptitiously, tore small pieces from it and tucked them into his cheek. One by one, he began to spit them at his sister. Janie seemingly ignored him. Indeed, she said nothing. Behind her, however, she made a surprisingly solid fist.

Because he gained no reaction from her, Geoff moved closer to his sister. Placing an even larger wad of paper in his mouth, he readied to spit it at her. His face inches away from her; he was blissfully unaware of his peril.

Just as Janie brought her fist back as far as it could go, Elizabeth caught her daughter's hand. Only then was Mr. Darcy witting that his darling daughter meant to deliver unto her brother a rather powerful roundhouse punch. However much he would have liked for his countenance not to register his horror, an expression of appalled incredulity overspread his face. (Then, he decided it was best for all concerned that he ignore the entire fracas.) The mother of his darling daughter had not that election. Catching Janie under her armpits, Elizabeth swung her up on her lap. It took the offering of several dolls and a great deal of soothing before Geoff was safe.

"Do not be mean to your sister, Geoffrey," his mother warned.

Although he blinked more than usual, Mr. Darcy's gaze remained upon the countryside. On the apposing seat, Geoff looked at his sister with great unease. He looked as if he was in want of making amends, but did not quite trust her not to bash him.

Elizabeth whispered to Darcy, "Did you happen to see your daughter? I fear it might have knocked her brother senseless."

"Yes," said he.

Elizabeth inquired, "You have no other comment?"

He answered, "I cannot imagine where she inherited such behaviour."

Initially, Elizabeth's eyes sparked, but she saw quite hastily that it was a jest.

Darcy continued, "I understand her mother is a bit saucy."

There was no time to retort. Janie still needed tending. In an hour her anger was finally worn out and motion of the coach lulled her fast asleep. With his sister no longer a mortal danger to him, Geoff became engrossed in every animal, shed, and stream he saw. He was so excited that his father had to hang onto his coattails to keep him from falling out of the window.

"Geoff must be driving you to distraction," Elizabeth said. "As soon as Janie awakes, she shall be the one full of questions and you shall have no peace. Truly, they are the most inquisitive children in all of England."

Neither of them spoke for a moment, perchance awaiting the other to make what to them was an obvious conclusion.

She said, "I have heard it said that inquisitiveness is the surest sign of an intelligent child."

"Second only to pluck," he agreed.

Before either could continue admiring the many ways of their children, Geoff saw another bird. Once again, the boy lunged as he pointed out the window. This time, much to his son's unhappiness, his father closed the window altogether. Geoff did not cry. Rather, he frowned, crossed his arms, and stuck out his lower lip. Clearly not only were his wants denied him, his dignity was offended as well.

Looking at Janie sleeping contentedly, Darcy said, "Your daughter is a beauty—just like her mother."

He took his wife's hand and kissed it. Longing looks, however, were not to rule the day.

𝓑efouled

"What is that Papa? What is it?" Geoff said, beating on the window. Their coach was the first of their party. So when an enormous dray came to grief trying to allow them to pass, it blocked their way.

The dray was stacked with cages, each filled with chickens. The noise was apparent, even from inside their coach. The waggon driver hollered at his oxen and slapped his reins across their backs, but the wide wheels would not budge. Geoff bounced up and down on the seat in excitement. Darcy had less success at quieting him than the driver had moving his oxen.

The commotion awoke Janie, her pique forgot, she said, "What is it, Mama? Are there chickens?"

Initially, their coachman attempted to go around the waggon, but to no avail. Several footmen leapt from the Darcy coach to assist the dray, one grabbed the reins and began to tug, the others pushing from the rear.

Mr. Darcy opened his window to allow a footman's report, "The driver's pissed as a newt—'scuse me sir—what shall you have us do?"

"As you were," Darcy said.

He closed his window and Elizabeth opened hers for some air. She fanned both Janie and herself in relief of the sun which was beating down on their side of the coach.

As the footman tugged on his oxen, the soused driver searched for further libations beneath the seat. As he did, his cargo began to lean ominously. It was only a matter of time before the entire load collapsed in the dirt. Several of the top cages broke loose and slid to the ground. They splintered when they hit, causing a dozen pullets and a very vocal rooster to escape.

The prospect of losing his whole load brought the man to his senses. He scrambled after the birds. Fortunately, most of the fat pullets settled back on the rail of the dray and were easily caught. But a number of others and the cock scattered. The commotion caused the horses to prance a bit, causing Mr. Darcy some alarm. He cracked his window to better observe the doings. His footmen were chasing the loose chickens and soon had them in hand. (It was quite a sight, even for those not easily amused.) Unfortunately the rooster was less tame than the chickens and it continued to elude its pursuers.

When it finally lit, it was upon Mrs. Darcy's open window. The bird sat there eyeing them whilst Janie shrieked with laughter.

Elizabeth cried, "Shoo!" *Shoo!*"

Her intention was for the cock to take its leave out the window from whence it came, but she only succeeded in exciting it. It flapped its wings wildly and, seeing the other window, attempted to make its escape through it. Darcy encouraged it back out with a swipe with his newspaper, but it made another circle of the coach. On the second attempt, it hit the closed window and knocked itself senseless. It fell to the floor of the coach with a dull thud.

Janie said, "Oh, no! Poor bird. Is it dead?"

The fear that the cock was indeed dead at their feet, Mrs. Darcy endeavoured to shield poor Janie from the scene by means of a motherly hand over her eyes. Janie squealed her indignation and Geoff leapt from the seat and began to poke at the bird.

"Poor, poor rooster...."

Grabbing his son about his waist, Mr. Darcy opened the door and beckoned his man.

"Have this unfortunate fowl removed."

A footman let down the steps. Before Mr. Darcy stepped a foot out the door, the bird awoke and hopped to his feet. Settling his feathers like a lord, he preceded Mr. Darcy, hopping down each step until he reached the ground. There, he flapped his wings, gave a small, gurgling crow and walked towards the dray. By then, the driver caught up to his rooster. Removing his cap, he nodded to Mr. Darcy.

"Beg pardon, sire," he slurred.

Then he tucked the bird under his arm and slunk away.

With the aide of more footmen, the dray was pulled out of roadway, allowing them all to go on their way. The Darcy coaches' stately pace was barely injured by the passing interlude. Elizabeth straightened Janie's bonnet and retied the ribbon under her own chin. Feathers were everywhere, but that would be attended to when they stopped to rest the horses. Darcy repositioned his hat and gathered himself.

Elizabeth marvelled at her husband's ability to remain composed when suffering the most unnerving events. Granted, their lives were hardly in danger, but his expression barely altered during the entire fracas. (He displayed more excitation over his daughter's near basting of her brother.) Elizabeth's heart had not quite settled. A cock scratching about the yard was benign enough. When caught with one desperate to escape, its claws could do damage. She had feared for everyone's eyes. Impulsively, she took her husband's arm and rested her head against his shoulder. He patted her hand. All was well.

"Papa, what is that?" Geoff queried.

Elizabeth smiled wanly at her husband. There had been but a small respite from her son's questions.

With kind condescension, Darcy bid, "What do you see?"

"There," Geoff pointed. "Upon your hat."

Darcy dared not look at what was upon his favourite hat, but at times it was necessary to do distasteful duties. Without looking, he knew that when the rooster had been excited into flight, it had done so with a fit of incontinence.

"Janie! Janie, look here," cried Geoff. "The bird has done something very bad upon Papa's hat!"

Jane pointed at her father's hat, saying, "What a bad bird, Papa!"

Mr. Darcy's expression remained fixed. (Perhaps his hauteur intensified ever so slightly.) He rapped upon the roof with his walking still. The coach came to a halt. With grace and semi-good humour, he instructed his man to exchange his hat for another.

Sitting back with a clean hat upon his head, he said, "There."

Between them on the seat he laid a penny. She smiled, but chose not to crow.

$\mathcal{N}$o Going Home

A second disconcerting event came about not long after the rooster attack. This (like most) came about from good intentions. Elizabeth was simply in want of keeping the children settled and entertained. She noticed that they were just up the road from Fleckney and pointed to a large tree next to the road.

"Look, see there? You were born just there."

"But where, Mama? Where?" begged Janie.

Unwilling to go into the untoward details of their birth, her mother told a fib.

"The place is gone now."

"We were born in a coach, Janie," said Geoff. "Mama meant to go to Pemberley, but...."

Astonished at his store of information, Elizabeth playfully caught the end of his nose and said, "You and your sister were too impatient to wait."

With an expression of amused chagrin, Darcy looked out the window. As he did, Elizabeth made an admirable (but ultimately unsuccessful) attempt at altering their discourse.

She said, "To our great fortune, Aunt and Uncle Bingley were there to catch you both."

"Where were you, Papa?" Geoff asked suddenly.

Just as hastily, Elizabeth replied, "Papa had business."

Mr. Darcy continued to distance himself from this conversation. His son, however, was not easily satisfied by silence. He turned to his mother who was always more forthcoming. He asked another, even more difficult question.

"Why was I born with a sister, Mama? Did you find her next to the road?"

"Yes," interrupted Mr. Darcy. "We discovered you both in a cabbage patch."

Adding misinformation to generalities did not improve the situation. Indeed, this bit of news disturbed Geoff further. It only incited more questions from his sister.

Janie queried, "Where is the cabbage patch? Did Aunt and Uncle Bingley help find us there? What if a fox had found us first?"

Ruefully, Geoff whispered to his sister, "The cabbage patch is just a story people tell."

Their son's precociousness, as a point of pride for the Darcys, was waning precipitously. Whilst this conversation droned on, Mr. Darcy was becoming evermore apprehensive over what indecorous tidings the loquacious Mrs. Bennet might introduce to them. (Her discourse could often be as indelicate and uncensored as Lydia's.) Mr. and Mrs. Darcy exchanged glances that suggested they both feared the same evil.

"Whatever shall come from the mouths of your children next?" asked he.

Noting that she was now the sole parent of the inquisitive duo, Elizabeth said stiffly (whilst hiding a smile), "I am sure I have no idea to what you refer."

"I am certain you are aware that discretion is a stranger to your mother," he replied.

"I agree, she is most indiscrete."

To be reminded of her mother's tactlessness, Elizabeth had only to recall her mother's response upon learning that the Darcys would visit.

"Does Mr. Darcy come?" she wrote. "That man's elegance of manner honours my home when he is so generous as to come here. Do not think of coming here, Lizzy, if he does not accompany you."

By his own design Darcy rarely came to Longbourne. (He did not admit to any disdain for the house or its surroundings, but any affection he had for it was because it had once been Elizabeth's home.) As he seldom came, having the grand man for even so small a time was quite a coup for his mother-in-law. Once the visit had been decided upon, she would have reason to boast about her daughter's fortunate marriage to every neighbour who was not hasty enough to avoid her.

Elizabeth could imagine her Meryton neighbours fleeing her mother's approach even then.

Of Elizabeth's sisters, only Mary had not married. She remained at Longbourne as her mother's companion. Mary had neither genius nor taste—and her pedantic opinions did nothing to improve Mrs. Bennet's disposition. That meant Longbourne was no longer a particularly hospitable place. Given that, Elizabeth did not wonder that Darcy was astonished by her sudden desire to return. Indeed, she had begun to question her own decision. When someone as immovable and unalterable as Mrs. Bennet stood between them, and peace and decorum, it was unlikely decorum would will out. Elizabeth vowed to be a bastion of civility—and dearly hoped it would last the duration of her visit.

When their coach at last arrived at Longbourne, they gratefully descended. Their happiness to escape further interrogation by their children was mitigated by the excited welcome given to them by Mrs. Bennet. Although she was all but prostrate in deference to Mr. Darcy, she greeted Elizabeth fretfully. Before the children were allowed past the doorway, she urgently questioned Elizabeth as to their health.

"Are you certain there is no chance you have brought illness here with you? Your children look peaked. Do they cough?"

They were perfectly well. Nonetheless, Mrs. Bennet could not help but worry. Her health was dearly guarded and children were notorious carriers of disease and caused household disorder. She was often heard to admonish against forming early attachments for the little tykes. Keeping them at arms length avoided the inconvenience of being out of sorts should the little ones up and die on you.

Despite her denials of happiness, Mrs. Bennet did look remarkably well. Her hair did not yet have a single strand of silver. Once assured that there was no threat of communicable ailments, a flood of affection erupted. Mrs. Bennet gifted them all big hugs and wet kisses. She did her best to bestow a motherly buss upon Mr. Darcy as well, but he was tall and she was not, he stayed out of reach.

"Still proud, I see," she whispered to Elizabeth as they came inside.

In the vestibule to greet them stood Elizabeth's sister, Kitty. That was a happy surprise. Kitty and her husband were visiting Longbourne and extended their stay to visit with the Darcys. Seeing Kitty was a pleasure for Elizabeth and made her homecoming all the more promising. The youngest Bennet sister, but one, Kitty had settled in Shropshire and Elizabeth did not see her as often as she would have liked. Once out from under Lydia's influence, her notorious contentiousness was much improved and her marriage to a young vicar had prospered.

Although John Malcolm Finch did not strike a particularly handsome figure, he was of an affable nature and read aloud well. He was also suitably modest in his ways. Unlike poor Mr. Collins, Mr. Finch was not the sort to flatter himself nor was he immoderately obsequious to those above his station. Mr. Darcy was quite pleased to meet him.

Kitty boasted on behalf of her husband.

In rapid succession she said, "Mr. Finch delivers two sermons a week. This year we shall have two students. They shall read both Latin and Greek, for they are to take their degrees from Oxford. Everyone says that Mr. Finch's sermons have improved society in the village. The last curate there was enfeebled by age and drink and he could scarce be counted upon to come to church. More than once the bells called whilst he was found beneath the gooseberry bushes drunk as a lord!"

With a quiet shushing from her husband, Kitty remembered herself. When she spoke again, it was not of what she heard, but only of what she knew.

"It is a handsome living we have. The glebe itself is so large that we rent it out to several households. Even if we did not, the tithes alone would allow us to keep a carriage."

Mr. Finch interrupted again, reminding Kitty, "It is but a curricle—and one ten years on the road, Mrs. Finch."

Curling her nose, Kitty added, "It is a buckish parish, what with all the grouse and streams for fishing and I know not what. Despite that, the congregation is thick with old people. There is little need for his services for marriages and baptisms, but the aged drop faster than autumn leaves, so he is amply rewarded then."

"I understand, Mr. Finch," said Elizabeth, "that you have an interest in globes."

Indeed, Kitty was a far better correspondent than any of her sisters and had related that information to her. Elizabeth was most pleased to have something to ask him.

Before Mr. Finch could do more than nod, Mary interrupted.

"My father kept an atlas, but Lydia's boys were very violent with it and it has gone by the way."

This gave Mrs. Bennet a chance to shush her middle daughter and begin her own recitation of the many vexatious encounters she suffered at the hands of her neighbours in Meryton. Although they had all dutifully come to Longbourne to meet Morland and admire her compleated portrait, to her mind they had never forgiven her for all her many blessings.

Indeed, after Mr. Bennet's demise, some believed that she would live out her days with the Darcys—for who would deign to reside in so humble an abode as Longbourne after enjoying such splendours was had for her at Pemberley. After all, Mr. Darcy had a portion of the house decorated especially to her particular taste (which ran to Spanish shawls and winged cherubs).

Some said that Mrs. Bennet favoured residing at Longbourne owing to that handsome portrait now hanging above her fireplace. Regardless, no other house had handsomer furniture or a prettier park in all of Hertfordshire (this, through the auspices of her generous sons-in-law). Those neighbours who tired of hearing Mrs. Bennet boast of her daughters' well-fixed marriages were disposed to remark a bit spitefully of her sudden regard for her old home. They said it had less to do with the size of the homes than the size of their ponds—and the fish in them.

Mrs. Bennet concluded, "If it was not for Mrs. Phillips, there would be no good society in Meryton at all."

An hour with Mrs. Bennet's incessant chatter, Mary's posturing, and Kitty's boasts, Mr. Finch's company alone was not enough to keep Mr. Darcy's sensibilities soothed. Soon, he turned his back and walked to a window. There, he gazed out upon the grounds. What he observed was of such interest to him that he stood looking at it for some time. (It must have been quite an oddity of some sort that kept the great man's attention, for if it was not, he might have been accused of regret in having come.)

An hour more, he was quite ready to make his away to London. His announcement of his imminent leave-taking did not please Mrs. Bennet.

She beseeched him, "No, no, Mr. Darcy, we cannot have it! You must stay and begin anew in the morning!"

His decision was not to be overturned.

"The sooner I make my away, the sooner I shall return," he said with finality.

Before he bid her adieu, Elizabeth had already begun to regret the visit as well. She walked with him to the coach, but did not share her qualms.

"What is your hurry, sir? I miss you and you have not yet taken your leave."

Her attempt to speak light-heartedly was all for naught.

"I would not go if it was not necessary," said he.

Forthwith, he kissed her full on the mouth. She was both pleased and astonished. In the broad day's light, on her father's doorstep, her breath was stolen.

He whispered to her, "It is my fervent hope that you find what you seek here."

In a trice he was in the coach and on his way. His scent was all that was left.

He was a loving husband, but a perplexing man. Their parting words were not a comfort.

ℐrksome Company

Elizabeth's despondency upon her husband's hasty leave-taking was not improved by her mother's ways. Her partiality to Geoff above his sister irked her to no end.

When introducing the twins to Mr. Finch, she had gushed, "He is to inherit!"

To Elizabeth, she said, "Handsome boy, Lizzy!"

Mrs. Bennet seemed to have no kind words for Janie. Indeed, she took Janie's chin in her hand and appraised her as if she was judging a prize lamb.

Her head slightly askew, she tsked, "It is fortunate that she shall have a handsome dowry. We must be happy with that."

Born second to her beautiful sister, Jane (upon whom Mrs. Bennet had staked all her financial hopes), Elizabeth was well-acquainted with her mother's favouritism. Fortunately, Janie was too young to notice (or at least she seemed oblivious to the meaning of her grandmother's commentary). Elizabeth was indignant on her behalf. Her cheeks flushed with outrage. Knowing full well the uselessness of speaking, she still could not hold her tongue.

"Mama! Our Janie is beautiful!"

"Yes, yes," Mrs. Bennet said absently. "She is pretty enough."

A sudden notion struck Elizabeth.

She inquired, "Do you observe a likeness between us? I mean to ask, do you believe that Janie's countenance favours mine?"

Asked a direct question, Mrs. Bennet looked at Janie closely and then answered, "I fancy... yes, I would say she does. She does not have your chin, but her hair is as tangled as was yours. It has no rule to it. Why, never was a lock of hair more tedious to comb...."

"Yes, Mama," Elizabeth interrupted.

Her mother's mind had always been somewhat fallow. She was prone to repeating that wherein she found solace. Elizabeth had been her father's favourite; Jane the most beautiful. Mrs. Bennet had always favoured Lydia above her other daughters.

Indeed, Lydia's boys were Mrs. Bennet's particular delight. Lydia's oldest son brought her great joy (as he already showed signs of his father's smarmy charm). Whilst enumerating young George's many dubious achievements, Mrs. Bennet often misspoke the other grandchildren's names. Some she could not recall at all.

"There are far too many...," she explained to Mr. Finch.

He recoiled in horror at her thoughtlessness.

"My condolences," he said to Elizabeth helplessly.

Elizabeth patted his arm, grateful for his kindness.

Mrs. Bennet chastised Mary for pointing out that Lydia's children were not remarkable for good behaviour. Mary, however, refused to be checked and gave all her attention to Mr. Finch's every utterance. Kitty did not much like what, she considered, all the untoward attention that Mary paid her husband. (At one time, Kitty had tangled with Maria Lucas for Mr. Finch's affection.) Now a vicar's wife, Kitty was of the opinion that slapping her sister six ways to Sunday would be unChristian (but she could imagine it and that gave her great joy).

Kitty's recitation of the many gratuities her husband had earned through death, marriage, and births left Mary truly miffed. Initially, she had believed Kitty's match was highly advantageous—that she married far better than Jane or Elizabeth. Their husbands were rich and that was tantamount to being the devil's disciples. Now Kitty, the vicar's wife, was under money's evil spell.

"Kitty, you speak of nothing but money. I dare say you should hold your tongue. For does the bible not say 'money is the root of all evil?'"

"I believe, my dear sister," Mr. Finch corrected, "that 1 Timothy 6:10 reads 'The *love* of money is the root of all evil.'"

Mr. Finch was a man of good enough sense not to insult the one who holds the strings to the money purse—or his in-laws. His correction had been kindly meant. Regrettably, that forever lost him Mary's admiration. Vexed, she suffered his presence no better than her other brothers-in-law. Mr. Finch was a tad wiser than some men of the cloth in that he realised he had transgressed upon poor Mary's one proficiency. He scurried to make it up to her, but could not.

Elizabeth was moved to remark, "Some believe there is but one conclusion when it comes to wealth. An income of fifty a year is a happy situation so long as one's expenses are forty-nine and six."

Suddenly, Elizabeth felt silly to be proffering opinions upon frugality whilst being married to one of the richest men in England. However, Mr. Finch took her part in the discussion. Kitty did too, but only because her husband did. Mary frowned at them all. She began to admire the Methodist movement evermore strongly.

"You are all doomed," she snorted so vociferously that it sounded as if she did not much mind if they were.

Mrs. Bennet snapped, "Be still, Mary, lest I shall run mad!"

Her mother's nerves and Sister Mary's sullen proverbs were distracting, but not fatal. By closing her ears to them Elizabeth might have tarried semi-contentedly at Longbourne until her husband returned. However, when at last the bell heralded a caller, it was not Mr. Darcy come back.

He was preceded.

"Lizzy!" erupted Lydia from Longbourne's vestibule.

Lydia Bennet-Wickham-Kneebone had arrived upon Longbourne's doorstep. Accompanying her were her four children, two nurses, lady maid, and one increasingly put-upon husband.

Elizabeth had promised her mother they would stay a week. With Lydia's unexpected arrival, after several days of strained cordiality, she feared she would be unable to spare that. Pemberley loomed evermore inviting. Inwardly, Elizabeth cringed. Outwardly, she was all graciousness.

Elizabeth raised her arms to bid a kiss, but Lydia went to Mrs. Bennet first. That was to be forgiven. After hugs, squeals, and kisses, Lydia returned her attention to her bereaved sister.

"Lizzy dear, it has been far too long. I am so sorry to hear of your loss! A little boy was it not?"

"William," Elizabeth interjected.

"We would have come to Pemberley, but I could not bear to make another requisition upon Hughie's aunt's purse to hire a coach. We cannot keep a carriage of our own. If you could see to give me a small loan, I might pay a bit on my accounts at the dress shops. I use your name liberally, yet they have cut me off compleatly. Chelsea is such a bore! I would much rather live nearer to the park. Had we a carriage, we could take a turn there every afternoon. But here I am, speaking of my own troubles when you and Darcy are grieving so. You did get my note? Hughie! Mind your hair!"

The single accusation that could not be hurled at Lydia was the she had a slow mind. Indeed, she could flit from one subject to another within the course of a single sentence.

Hat in the crook of his elbow, Major Kneebone stood still as a soldier at post. Lydia then spat in her glove and wiped it across his errant cowlick as if he were a child. Elizabeth waited for her to compleat his mortification before she replied to any of Lydia's inquiries. In not deigning to come to Pemberley when little William died, Lydia did them all a very large favour. Indeed, her absence was weathered with gratitude all around.

Without any inflection to her voice, Elizabeth said, "Your note was one of great economy. We all admired it a great deal."

Elizabeth's refusal to lie with any real conviction had long vexed Lydia. Any lady knew that distortion, equivocation, exaggeration, and outright fabrication were social requirements. Therefore, the ability to prevaricate was a quality admired above all others and proved a lady's worth in good society. Lydia ignored Elizabeth's remark and gave up begging for money.

Lydia told her, "I would have come, I assure you. But I was once again without a nurse—I am positive that I told you of that misfortune. We are always in want of a nurse."

The nursemaid with her was but a girl (not all that taller than Lydia's daughter, Susanna). Her hair was uncombed and she looked as if she had been abducted from the street. She wore a dress of coarse fabric which looked too tatty to be one of Lydia's cast-offs. It was chilly and she had no coat. At Kneebone's insistence, Lydia did try to economize (in so far as it did not intrude upon her own wants and needs). Instead of wages, she paid her help in old clothes.

Elizabeth smiled at the girl, took off her shawl and draped it over her shoulders. At this act of kindness, a ripple of excitation overspread the girl's face. It was doubtful she was above fourteen years old. The boots she wore were too big for her as well. They looked to have come from a pile of refuse.

To Lydia, Elizabeth said, "I see that if you cannot offer alms, you do your part for the poor. You invite them into your home to do your bidding

"I pay them!" Lydia insisted.

This was an ongoing dispute. Elizabeth accused Lydia of mistreating her help and Lydia denied it. Elizabeth believed it was a compleat waste of time to do so again. There was a pair of boots in her own trunk that would fit the girl better than the ones she wore. She would see that she received them (and hoped that Lydia would not take them from her).

"Where are your boys?" Elizabeth queried. "I do hope they are well."

"Oh, they have run off to play," Lydia replied nonchalantly. "They are such hellions, I cannot make them mind. They have cost us nothing but grief all this long journey. They keep stones in their pockets to toss at horses and the like. They find great humour in causing a spill. One would think that Hugh could have them behave, but he has no more luck with them than do I!"

Suddenly, a happy thought leapt from the inner workings of Lydia's mind (which was dedicated to the betterment of Lydia Kneebone).

"Soon the boys shall be back at school and they shall not bother me a whit until next year!"

In attempting to converse with her sister regarding where they would attend school, Elizabeth was unsuccessful. Her lips no more than formed the question ere she was interrupted by Lydia's interminable yammering. Time and experience had done nothing to calm her conversational indiscretions. This day was not an exception.

"Is not Mr. Darcy to dine with us? I dare say I have not once seen you apart since that little affray we had at Limehouse Public House with Wickham."

At Wickham's name, Mrs. Bennet's eyes rolled back in her head and she began to swoon, saying, "Poor, poor Major Wickham. Killed in the wars, poor man!"

Her mother's fit of nerves told Elizabeth that she had not comprehended fully what Lydia had said. She was greatly relieved—doubly so. She was most happy that Darcy had taken his leave when he had. Inflicting Lydia on him and the memories of the affair with Wickham would have been unpardonable.

To Lydia, she hissed, "Lydia, hush yourself."

"What?" Lydia quacked.

More and more frequently, Lydia's interjections mimicked farm animals (they wavered between a duck and a gander). When Lydia laughed, she brayed. Elizabeth was sorely tempted to tell her that.

Rather, she reminded her, "Did we not agree to not speak of that to *Mama*?"

"But how can I not? Everyone knew it. And what does it matter now? He is good as dead. He will stay away if he knows what is good for him. My Hughie will run him through it he tries to regain me!"

In fortune, Kitty arrived in the foyer just then to greet Lydia. (Kitty was exhilarated by the opportunity of visiting with Lydia and besting her in situations.) Kisses and laughter improved the noise until such time as Elizabeth's head began to throb. It occurred to her that if not for the lack of Jane, their family would be reunited for the first time since Mr. Bennet's death. However, Jane's agreeableness was what made the tentacles of her family circle escapable—or at the very least, bearable. Every family has its knaves and fools. All one can do is not to contribute to the inanity. With that thought, she slipped away. If Lydia's boys were on the loose, their stones might make targets of her own children.

Her motherly instincts were correct.

Just beyond the paling, Lydia's oldest son, a tall gangly sly-boots with a quick tongue, had Janie by her sashes. He was threatening to tie her up and throw her down the well. Janie flailed at the boy, but without success. From Geoff's expression, he looked as if he wanted to intercede, but did not know how to go about it.

"Stop it!" he demanded, but the bigger boy laughed.

When Geoff did react, it was not indecisively. He ran full force towards the bigger boy, swinging his fists wildly. Wickham's son stuck out a foot and tripped him. Geoff struggled to his feet and looked to make another run. However, Elizabeth caught him by the back of the collar and swung him around behind her. Still flailing, he did his best to wriggle free. Elizabeth hollered at the boy to let go of Janie.

Georgie Wickham dropped Janie abruptly and sauntered away. He did not go quietly. Indeed, the curses to which he gave low utterances astounded her. For one who was not yet ten years old, he had a surprising vocabulary.

"You are in compleat want of manners! I shall not have it! Do you hear?" she called after him.

Janie ran to her mother. She looked back at Georgie's retreating figure and stuck out her tongue. Then, she took refuge in the folds of her mother's skirts. Only when Janie had been rescued did Geoff quit squirming. He did not speak, but Elizabeth could see the tips of his ears were as red as his face. The lady in her knew that she should discourage such behaviour, but a tingle of motherly pride stopped her. It was good to know that when the time came, they would stand up for themselves—and each other.

Kneeling, she encircled both children in her arms.

"You should come to your Mama if other children misbehave," she cooed.

Geoff shook his head solemnly, saying, "Papa says it is my duty."

His voice was that of a child, but his manner was that of a gentleman. In the distance, the bell announced dinner. Elizabeth was not yet ready to subject her children to her family's questionable embrace.

Taking each by the hand, she said, "Let us strike out on another path, shall we?"

As they walked, neither child spoke. She did not want to end their visit to Longbourne unhappily, but Wickham's son reminded her far too much of his father. That similarity recalled other, more disquieting events. She could barely look upon the boy without repugnance. Still, Georgie Wickham was but a boy. There was time for his manners to improve. Not wanting to fall prey to the same sort of biases as her mother, Elizabeth decided it might be best to take their leave.

In fortune, Mrs. Bennet was too much engaged with her other daughters to care if they did.

Needing no more provocation, Mrs. Darcy, Mrs. Darcy's children, nurses, and Hannah were on the road with great haste. Elizabeth, however, had to overcome a bout of melancholy. As her coach passed by, her gaze was arrested by the sight of a familiar oak. Under its spreading limbs, she and Darcy enjoyed their first kiss (and where their passion near ran amuck, leaving her far better informed of the anatomical disparity of the sexes). It was also against that ancestral tree she wept for her husband's safe return after burying her father. As they left Longbourne behind, she had to bite the inside of her lip to keep it from quivering with an overflow of her emotions.

Before they had departed, Elizabeth had sent a rider to inform Darcy of their altered plans. He would be displeased that they traveled without him or, to his mind, enough footmen. (To her mind, he had the greater need of footmen in London.) She held no doubt, however, the circumstances would beg his understanding. Had she dared, she did not care to journey all the way to Derbyshire without her husband. They would stop at Chiltern.

The inn was quite tolerable—even for the family of Mr. Darcy. There they would forgather for a short stay. It was likely that he would make his away from London more hastily knowing that they were from under her mother's roof.

Her thoughts were interrupted by Janie, who laid her head against her and asked, "Mama, are you sad? Is it for Willy?"

Elizabeth was suddenly aware that a tear was making its way down her cheek. Hastily, she wiped it away with the back of her glove and consoled her daughter.

"Just now I miss your Papa. I shall be quite happy to see him."

As a cloud burst opened up in the sky, she felt a renewal of spirits, happy in the knowledge that Longbourne was no longer her home.

It was where she became a woman, not lived as one.

*V*ouloir, c'est pouvoir

It might be presumed that whilst struggling to convalesce from a near-mortal wound that a looking-glass would not be the item most wanted within reach of the patient's sickbed. This particular bed, however, was inhabited by a man of peculiar merit. George Wickham had several good traits, modesty was not amongst them. He admired all of his God-given endowments—his pleasing expression, handsome countenance, and winning ways. Like most men, he was particularly fond of his masculine basket of fancies. Consequently, he was most impatient to learn whether his recent misfortune would disfigure them or create any hindrance in their workings.

It was months before Wickham could manage to stand alone, even with the help of a crutch. Had it not been for Mrs. Younge, there was little doubt he would have bled out. He owed that good woman his life several times over. He did not tell her this. Once assured that he would survive, he could afford to be less generous. (A clearer head reminded him that one must never allow another to believe a debt was owed.) His next undertaking was to determine whether his proud, purple-helmeted warrior of love could still "rise to the occasion." Second to that, he needed to learn if his remaining whirligig would function as nature intended.

This was vital information.

George Wickham agreed with general thought—that the primary purpose of these organs were not evacuation or procreation. It was recreation. His body served only one god and that was Eros. Strictly speaking, he was uninterested in fertility. He had offspring scattered across several countries. (They had a perverse penchant for lurching into his life at the oddest moments.) His masculinity had been assured through spawning several sons.

Still, he liked to leave his lovers well-lathered. It was a matter of aesthetics. When it came to the art of love, the lack of manly cream might compromise a lady's opinion of his performance. A dry bob was to be avoided—it could be confused with a lack of vigour. Therefore, he needed to determine if his one remaining doodad had been decommissioned or not.

In the quest of learning the answer to both those looming matters,

Wickham once again inveigled the faithful Mrs. Younge. Cooperative upon all other occasions, she was not an altogether willing partner in this specific investigation. She was well-aware that due to his wound, the avenue to discovery was limited. He could not mount her nor could she ride him. There was little recourse save hand or oral gratification. She harboured a reluctance to engage in oral stimulation. It was time-consuming, awkward, and unpalatable. She knew full well if one acquiesced to such a procedure once, it would become a constant demand.

"Can you not just... you know... see to yourself?" she asked.

It was a reasonable question, one for which he had a ready answer.

"I look upon committing self-pollution much the same way as two women kissing—it is a misapplication of God's greatest gifts."

Cornered, she was forced to agree. However, since she was to be the ungratified party in this act, she preferred employing her hand. She could twizzle his cock until the cows came home and still stir the dinner pot—so to speak. He insisted upon fellatio. Of the two, it was far more pleasurable.

To Wickham's mind, hers was hardly the greater sacrifice. After all, his very manhood hung on the precipice of rediscovery. Applying ample doses of kissing and tickling, he gained her consent. At least she consented in theory. She continued to protest. Her complaints were so loud that he had to grab her by her topknot and mash her face against his genitals to stop her squawking. Then as he petted her like a setter, she did as he wished.

"Oh, yes my love-y," he crooned, allowing sweet ecstasy to overtake him.

As Mrs. Younge diligently worked, perspiration dripped down her forehead and onto his belly. Fear at clutched at him, clawing at his very vitals (which, it could be acknowledged, is not the most advantageous manner whereby one is brought to orgasm) as she valiantly, if methodically, brought him to arousal and then—dare he hope—ejaculation? In a near frenzy, he clasped her by the ears lest she escape before his last quiver of satisfaction.

"Bleech!" she retched, trying to elude his grasp. "The deed is done! Now I'm through with you!"

Indeed she was.

"But did I spend? Did I *spend*?"

Wiping her face with the hem of her apron, she gave him his answer (and with it came a glance of repugnance). There had not been a great deal of ejaculate, but with time and practise he would surely improve his output.

Chortling happily to himself, he pointed to the hand-glass, "Let us have a look."

Feeling quite ill-used, Mrs. Younge employed her most abused expression (although she would obtain no sympathy from him), but did as he bid. As she extended it to him, he veritably snatched it from her grasp. Turning the hand-glass first one way and then the other, he inspected himself. She was too busy rolling her eyes to care what he saw. Appetence now was just a memory, his virile member was not admirable to anyone but him. It had functioned to its full capacity and he gazed upon it with something akin to love.

Waving her away, he lay back on the bed and sighed.

He had not truly deliberated on a design for his future. Now that he knew he could perform the act of amour, his mind was free to be transported. Overcome by anticipatory glee, he pondered what measures he might take to regain all that he lost.

There were many considerations.

Although he was a known fugitive from justice, he did not deliberate what he might have to do to save his soul or skin. His most pressing concern was that of personal beauty. Before anything else was addressed, he set about concealing that he was one testicle short of a pair by fluffing his under-hair. As he did, he concluded that future amatory congress would require certain concessions. Mutual fondling would have to be avoided at all costs. Pity that. Even worse, fellatio with anyone other than Mrs. Younge would be out of the question. Indeed, was he to keep his semi-emasculation hidden, all future coition would be highly improvisational. But then, he was nothing if not a master of invention. He would have to make do with what was left to him.

Resignation was not familiar to him and he knew not what to make of it.

Hence, he dedicated his next considerations to his identity. George Wickham was believed dead. Was he alive, he was charged with murder.

Quite a little quagmire in which he found himself.

The murder accusation, of course, was compleat rot! He had merely done what was necessary to save his skin. Most of his fellow grenadiers had been killed in battle. He had shot that young private through no ill-will. One could even premise that it was an accident—the bloody smoke from gunfire was dense enough. Of course, there was the matter of those witnesses. Bad luck all round that the young grenadier had been his bastard son—but that was not his fault. What was one to do, inquire the parentage of every man under one's command?

Every time he managed to be on the brink of elevating himself to the rank due him, his hopes were dashed.

It was Darcy's fault. From their youngest years Darcy had envied him old Mr. Darcy's love. Now he understood why. (Wickham had always suspected that he was of aristocratic blood.) Any chance to claim his rightful place had been ripped from him. Regrettably, George Wickham had never been acknowledged as a Darcy. If George Wickham was said to be a murderer and now lying dead, he had no lawful means by which to claim a portion of the Darcy fortune.

Extortion had been highly lucrative, but was no longer feasible. Indeed, Darcy had paid him a fortune to say he was dead and give Lydia up as a wife. Why, he had a fortune in bank notes in his hands—only to have the money stolen by those two little harlots. Shot and robbed! What was there left to him?

Just thinking of the extent of that loss was enough to make him take to his bed like a woman. He wept for his fate, he wept for his defiled name, and he wept for the money he did not have. George Wickham had a remarkable capacity for holding on to hurts, real or imagined. It took some time for him to compleat his mourning for what was not to be (and the washing down of a good bit of bad whiskey) ere he gathered himself and took stock of his options.

Whilst he abided in whimpering abeyance, his aspect had altered. Initially, he was quite alarmed. Then he saw no reason to fear recognition.

At last the Gods smiled upon their most hapless son.

To London Town He Went

Whilst Elizabeth basked in the pleasure of (or at least tolerated) her family's company, Mr. Darcy hied to town with singular determination. When he arrived at their Park Lane manse, his butler stood in wait.

Mr. Hastings had been in service with the Darcys in the London house for twenty years. He had taken Smeads' position as steward when that man took his late mother's place at Pemberley. (The alteration had gone more smoothly in London than in Derbyshire.) Darcy had always approved of Hastings. Unlike Smeads, he had the direct gaze and straight back of a man not given to looking in keyholes. In recent years, the Darcys were rarely in town. Therefore Hastings's dedication was not regularly admired. To assure that all did their duty in his absence, it was of the greatest importance for Mr. Darcy to make unannounced appearances.

He did not warn his people in London when he would arrive, only that he would come that week. Therefore, he was pleased to be met at the stable yard by Hastings. To no one's surprise, Mr. Darcy looked first to see how his horses fared before entering his house.

"Have these horses exercised with regularity?"

Hastings was joined by the stableman who assured him, "Of course, sir. They are taken out every day—depending upon the vagaries of the weather, of course."

Slapping the hindquarters of one of a pair of cherry-coloured geldings, Mr. Darcy was well-satisfied with their fitness.

It had fallen to Hastings, rather than the stableman, to retrieve the horses from a public horse stable near Chelsea after Mrs. Darcy had been forced to sell them. In the letter charging him with this duty post-haste, Mr. Darcy had not explained the mysterious circumstances surrounding their relinquishment. He had made it clear the importance of their return. (Any such reminder was unnecessary as any utterance by Mr. Darcy was looked upon by Hastings as no less than a communication from God above.) Mr. Darcy directed him to employ all due effort to recover the carriage, livery, and harnesses. In retrieving the horses, however, Mr. Darcy was even more succinct. No expense was to be spared to reclaim them.

As discretion was one of his finest attributes, Hastings made a fine steward. Despite great prudence on his part, the household had been witting of the brouhaha. The Darcy servants gained their information from the footmen who had been given fare and hied home after the strange incident took place. The men spent the remainder of the evening sitting in the kitchen drinking coffee with the cook and scullery maids, all pondering the odd occurrence. Although the footmen knew that the mistress had been under some financial duress that evening, they knew not why she would have been forced to relinquish the horses and livery. The Darcy name was good as gold.

"Mrs. Darcy was in great haste, she was! Sold them fine horses for a pittance! That carriage—nary a finer coach in all of town! If I'd any money on me I'd bought it myself and made a fine return on it."

The other footman was of another mind.

"If I'd any money I'd gave it to Mrs. Darcy, I would. She's a real lady. You may like her coach—I'd say a finer lady could not be found in town."

Word of the event made its way through the various stories of townhouses by way of chatty house maids and even chattier ladies of condition. (Indeed, a good portion of Mayfair had been sent into a pother about it.) No one could quite determine just why Mrs. Darcy was in such need of ready money. After all, Mr. Darcy had a balance with his banker that lent him admirations from all quarters. Such mysterious doings were fodder for tongue-waggers for as long as it took for the news of Mr. Bingley's retrenchment to make its rounds. Indeed, Mrs. Darcy's desperate need for cash coincided precisely with Mr. Bingley's. Not only was Mr. Bingley a good friend to Mr. Darcy, the gentlemen's wives were sisters. That seemed to squelch the most unseemly of various speculations.

The story was too good to end there. Prattle continued about Mr. Bingley being attacked on the Ratliff Highway Wharves by creditors demanding payment. They raided his ships and appropriated his merchandise—but not before turning their wrath on poor Mr. Bingley. They relieved him of his inexpressibles (and a good portion of his dignity). Poor Mr. Bingley might have been left for dead had not someone rescued him and taken him away. Such violence was a precursor to the chaos that was taking over the streets of London even then.

Some said that Mr. Darcy himself was the man who came to Bingley's aid. Others said such doings were far beneath a man of Mr. Darcy's standing— even if Mr. Bingley was his good friend. A man as wealthy as Mr. Darcy would have sent underlings to see to his purposes, but would never have gone himself. Then again, rumours of dark deeds and vengeance were recalled and spoken of when Mr. Darcy was not there to hear them.

Whatever came to pass, Mr. Bingley paid his debts and Mr. Darcy had his coach and horses retrieved.

Having them returned to him did not mean that that Mr. Darcy was no longer annoyed over the time they were missing. He was quite piqued about that. He was most precise in regards to his horses' care. Had someone raised a hand to them whilst they were not under his protection, he would have been most unhappy.

The talk was inevitable. However, insofar as Darcy knew, in the midst of all the hubbub with Bingley being chased naked by an angry mob, the name of Wickham was never spoken.

For that, he was exceedingly grateful.

Testifying to Hastings good stewardship, all which remained to be done upon Mr. Darcy's arrival this day was to call for a few items to replenish the larder. Whereas Mrs. Darcy had not accompanied Mr. Darcy, Hastings knew not to bother with fresh flowers in their bed chamber. Mr. Darcy could be quite extravagant, however he abhorred wastefulness.

Not all of the aristocracy admired a turn towards frugality. Indeed, in certain households (some royal, some not), dining rooms were dressed and the meals served every day as if the lord of the house had not been dead a dozen years. In reverence to that lord, the dead man's footmen stood around his dining table each evening and servants filled his plates for all eleven courses. And when they withdrew, each bowed to his empty chair. One could suggest that it was a waste of flowers, food, and servants' time. Others would insist it was tradition and tradition should be upheld at all cost. Mr. Darcy was not the sort to turn a blind eye to such idiosyncrasies and call it charming. He saw such outlandish dissipation as nothing less than buffoonery.

At his leisure in his townhouse for the first time in years, Darcy walked through the garden briskly, only taking time for his gaze to sweep across it. As it met with his approval, he gave Hastings a small nod.

Once inside, he walked through the rooms of the fine house with an altered mood. In allowing his fingers to pass across table tops, he was not checking his

THE RULING PASSION   215

fingertips for dust. His hand slid across the wood in silent query of the future, imagining the rooms as they would be in years to come. Opening the doors of the ballroom, he saw it standing vacant. The chandeliers were covered with muslin, but the floor was well-polished. In his mind's eye he could see couples as they swirled majestically beneath the gilded ceiling. Amidst them all, he conjured the image of his son and his daughter as they swept about the floor in the arms of dance partners.

With time and practise such imaginings might one day be a comfort.

It was his desire for his daughter to find an excellent match forthwith of her eighteenth year. Janie looked remarkably like her mother. Hence, gentlemen would be buzzing about her the moment she was out. Suitors beware. Fie unto the fool who dared to meddle with his daughter's affections. There would be no dallying around with it. The sooner Janie was happily wedded, the better. The vicissitudes of romance would be far too trying upon her father's nerves. Marriage for Geoffrey, however, would wait. He would first take a degree at Cambridge. Perchance, was peace at hand, he would tour the Continent. He would be accompanied by a reliable relative. As his cousin, Colonel Fitzwilliam had accompanied him; some equally estimable gentleman would be called upon for his son.

Satisfied that his will would be done, he closed the doors to the ballroom and went up the staircase. He countenance was unaccompanied by noticeable anticipatory cheer. His reserve was well in place. (Of late, he needed to practise that.)

In coming to London, he had no intention of making social calls. Time would come soon enough when that would be necessary on behalf of his children's connections. Even if he had planned upon making calls, it would be unnecessary for him to send out his cards. Local wags would see to it that every lady, gentleman, footman, tailor, and dustman in the West End knew he was in town before his coach had been unhitched.

He certainly had not sent Lady Howgrave his card. Such a move would invite insidious gossip. (He would not entrust his good name, his children's name, unto the hands of London's scandalmongers.) If they met, it would fall to chance. Indeed, he did not leave his house that evening.

When he took his rest, it was not in the bedroom he and Elizabeth had chambered upon their wedding night. At times those recollections were kind. Just then he could not trust them. Lost as he was between current melancholy and future dread, he feared that his present mood would be at a variance with those happier memories. Rather, he chose to sleep in a narrow bed in a small room just up the hall. It was a comfortable bed, but the air felt stale. He opened the nearest window. Unused to the noxious fumes emanating from London's offensive trades, he coughed. His lingering in the country made him quite unused to the foul air. It was an ill-beginning to a restless night.

The following morn, he called directly for his horse.

It was a well-built gelding of handsome gait, but not his favourite. Not wanting to overuse Blackjack, he had left the horse at Pemberley. Nonetheless, that was the reason he would give should anyone ask. Truth was, he did not want to be seen on an easily identifiable steed. He could not keep his presence a secret, but he meant to be discrete. His mission was one that he would keep close to his breast. He hoped to avoid society altogether, so he set out early.

Midday was when the most ardent of the haut ton betook themselves to the streets to be observed strolling the length of Bond. When visiting shops, ladies of the aristocracy could espy unaccompanied gentlemen quicker and more accurately than the finest sight hound could their prey. He had seen such ladies knock small children to the ground and lose shoes in order to cross the path of a gentleman who would then be obliged to offer them his arm. He did not care to suffer inquiries as to his health, sympathies for his loss, or be asked the whereabouts of his wife. He most certainly did not care to be accompanied.

The Mall and St. James St. had the finest shops and were the smartest streets wherein to stroll. That was not his reason for taking that way. His powers of recollection had been keen at one time. He was uncertain that they were yet. The studio he sought had been in Pall Mall, but much had altered there in the past ten years. Facades had been painted, some replaced altogether.

As before, he simply chanced on the place. It was nothing but luck that he had—or propitious fortune.

He must have it in his hand so she would know he had not forgotten.

$\mathcal{M}$issed Missive

M r. Darcy did not receive the missive sent from his wife. The letter was delivered to his house, but not with the urgency that it deserved. Ultimately, that was unimportant. He was well on his way to fetch his family and, as his wife expected he would, he came by the Chiltern road. Weather was favourable until well out of London. Eventually, the roads became so boggy as to be barely passable. Soon his coach came to a stop due to an overturned stage.

Luggage in the basket at the rear of a coach often rearranged itself travelling uphill and down. Indeed, cresting any steep grade was done gingerly. As it was not unusual for commercial coaches to have passengers clinging to the roof in addition to those riding inside, injuries were quite possible.

Never particularly complaisant to be held back once he was set upon a certain journey; Mr. Darcy was exceedingly vexed to be halted under such circumstances. All roads leading to London had been increasingly congested. With more conveyances over-laden with products, travellers, and trunks: accidents were becoming evermore common. Unsurprisingly, a large crowd had heard of the accident and gathered to enjoy the prospect of observing a death or dismemberment. By the number of people gawking, Darcy determined that the road had been blocked by this particular mishap for some time.

Indeed, two of four horses had become mired pulling a load. One had lain down in the mud and refused to budge one way or the other. Two husky farm-boys were jumping up and down on the shaft whilst one of the coachmen tugged on the downed horse's halter. Another man had uncurled his whip and began laying it across the horse's back. It was obvious that beating the horse would do no good. Parish men were already standing by with pick-axes and shovels to repair the damage to the road, but none of them moved to help clear it.

Rapping his stick on the roof, Darcy caught his driver's attention. A footman hastily opened the door and let down the steps. As he alit, Darcy instructed two of his men to see to the removal of some of the parcels on the disabled stage to lighten the load.

Then, pointing to the man with the whip, Darcy told his largest footman, "Have that man desist with the whip. It serves no purpose here."

To another, he said, "See if there are any injuries."

Simultaneous to these instructions, Darcy spied a small bevy of passengers enveloped by gawking onlookers. From midmost of the group, came a familiar voice.

"Papa!"

Breaking Margaret Heff's handhold, Geoff ran to his father and leapt excitedly into his arms. Mr. Darcy was altogether uncertain why his son and heir stood upon the side of a muddy toll road watching a man flail a horse. His son, however, was breathless with outrage.

"Papa, that man is whipping the poor horse! You must make him stop!"

"He will stop," Darcy said, standing the boy down. Clasping his son's hand firmly in his, he demanded, "Where is Mama?"

Dutifully, Geoff pointed to the crowd of people. To his great relief, he spied Elizabeth and Janie. Next to them stood Franny Tupin; her eye was on Janie. Hannah had turned a basket upon its side and was surreptitiously eating a muffin. Having caught up with Geoff, Margaret breathlessly followed behind Mr. Darcy. Only when Geoff beckoned her did Elizabeth see that her husband chanced upon them. She smiled a greeting.

Janie called joyfully to her father, "Papa!"

Confounded, his expression begged an explanation as his daughter ran to him.

The smile that had overspread Elizabeth's countenance withered slightly. Obviously, the doings were beneath her station, but she saw little else she could do. Indeed, she shrugged. Suddenly aware that her skirt was six inches deep with mud (not unlike the day she hiked to Netherfield when Jane fell ill), she lifted the edge of it and shook her head in dismay. Her slippers were ruined and she wished she had had the good sense to travel in her other pair of boots. It was an awkward beginning to what she had hoped would be a happy adventure. Still, she was determined not to be ill-tempered about any of it. When one bechanced the unalterable, one must bear it with good humour.

She feared, however, her husband did not share that philosophy.

When he arrived at her side, he held Janie protectively in his arms. Franny Tupin punched Hannah on the shoulder to alert her to Mr. Darcy's arrival. When Hannah stood, crumbs fell from her skirt.

Elizabeth said, "Well, there you have it. Your wife needs rescuing once again. I fear I cannot be left to my own devices for a moment without finding calamity and bedlam."

Her cheerfulness in the face of such upheaval was a reassurance for her husband. He hoped that she was on the way to recovering her spirits. He displayed his joy by wiping a spatter of mud from her chin with his thumb.

Looking back at him with saucy eyes, she said, "I must look a fright."

"Upon the contrary...," he replied.

Hastily reclaiming himself, he asked, "Were you and our children aboard this public coach? Pray, tell me not."

With a determined smile, she said, "No, our coach is over there. Our way was impeded, as was yours."

He looked up the lane and saw their livery. His expression told her he had not received her missive.

"We took leave from my mother's house. Do you contend that we should have stayed?"

The question did not deserve an answer and she was chagrined to have introduced it.

"What could have possibly influenced you to remove yourself with such haste?"

One raised eyebrow reminded him that, although he had asked a simple question, it was almost too complicated to answer. She had held out hope that if all went well, she would not have to speak the name so often abhorrent to them both. When she spoke, it was through gritted teeth.

"Lydia arrived at Longbourne one day ago."

That told all. Bearing an expression of both defeat and commiseration, he nodded his head curtly. Janie clasped her father's cheeks in her hands, begging him to speak to her.

She said, "Papa, those horses are stuck fast in the mud and one cannot stand up."

"Our footmen will help them," he replied.

Then he turned his attention to Geoff who had been yanking upon his father's coattails.

"That man is still whipping the horse, Papa!"

Mrs. Heff held Geoff by one hand as he tried to wrest himself from her grip.

"Yes, son," Darcy said evenly. "See there, now he has stopped."

Then he handed Janie over to Franny, saying, "Take the children immediately to my coach."

Although it silenced upon his approach, talk began to buzz again of how the accident came about.

Darcy turned to Elizabeth and asked, "What is this I am hearing? Was this coach deliberately run off the road?"

Not in a position to see oncoming wayfarers, she replied, "I cannot say. Perchance the driver can give you an accounting...."

Darcy took her elbow with insistence, saying, "Nonetheless, you and the children should not have taken leave of your coach."

He escorted her directly to his coach. As he handed her in, she endeavoured to explain that they had been stranded for hours. She would have stayed in the coach, but the twins had seen the commotion and were wild with curiosity. Mr. Darcy did not hear her. He turned and strode to the group of parish men leaning on their implements—jabbing his walking stick into the muck with irritation as he went. They stood up straight ere he reached them. Thereupon, he gave them several orders. Whatever he demanded, it sent the men nodding with subservience and springing into action to help to put the stage and the horses to right. When he returned to his wife's side, Mrs. Darcy's hasty explanations were not listened to with forbearance. Because of that, she was a bit miffed. When she had his full attention, her words were clipped.

Indeed, she said defensively, "I did not, sir, take these measures without thought. I betook our coach and footmen to meet you at Chiltern, wherein I have let an apartment of rooms for us to stay at our leisure for the remainder of the week. Did my letter apprising you of this alteration in our lodgings not reach you?"

"No, it did not...."

Darcy did not tell his wife of his present worriment, for he did not want to alarm her unduly.... However, he was not compleatly satisfied that the accident was just that. He had his man make inquiries of the particulars of the encounter and whether something more malevolent was afoot. A man named Duff took it upon himself to approach Darcy's coach to reassure Mr. Darcy personally that no highwaymen were involved. (By the time these exchanges were made, everyone in the parish knew that it was Mr. Darcy—who had ten-thousand a year—and his family who had been entangled in the mayhem on the Chiltern Road.)

"Only resurrection men come here!" said Duff. "Body snatchers they are! Even this far from London, they come looking for fresh dead! If a young lad, they can get nine guineas for 'em at the dissecting room at King's College. Good set of teeth will bring ye another five. If ye die in these parts, ye best hire a watcher...."

Everyone who read a newspaper had heard of this atrocity. However, Darcy discounted Duff's information, if for no other reason than the distance to London. Putrefaction would make transporting a body that far unlikely. Intent as he was upon hearing and gauging this information, Darcy was unaware that Geoff was listening as well.

Elizabeth clapped her hands over the boy's ears and hissed at Darcy, "Pray, take heed!"

Noticing Geoff's wide eyes, Darcy realised his error.

He told his son reassuringly, "Just country nonsense, my son. Pay it no mind."

Geoff turned to Janie and whispered, "Do not listen. It is just twaddle."

Elizabeth almost, but in the end, could not, correct her son for employing such language. Soon enough their children would learn of the horrors society suffered. It was much easier to think of it as twaddle than what it truly was.

It was dusk by the time the stage was drawn upright and the Darcy coaches were on their way to Chiltern. Both the children believed they had quite an adventure. Janie had given her father an explicit accounting of each and every moment of it. As she did, her father tapped his finger impatiently for he was not much of a mind to speak further of it.

Nor did he notice Elizabeth's gaze. That was just as well, for it was a bit unforgiving.

The Mews

When in town, Mr. Darcy had taken care of several pieces of business. Unsure of her feelings on certain matters, he chose not to share all of his intentions with his wife. He felt right about that judgement after his business was done, for that visit to London was at great cost to his sensibilities. Indeed, it looked to be quite a task to raise his spirits, for they had plummeted to near maudlinness. The only remedy at hand had been to cast out those relentlessly unhappy thoughts through that well-proven destroyer of sentiment—financial affairs.

Mr. Darcy's money drew a solid five percent—hardly enough to pay the many newly-assessed taxes. With all the rancour against those who sat in power, he was much in want of reassurance that the liquid portion of the family fortune was not in jeopardy. To do so, he reluctantly betook himself to the blessed 'Change.

When his business was compleat, his solicitor bade him listen to what was perilously close to a lecture upon which streets were safe and which were not. In the midst of this recitation, Darcy replaced his hat, touched the brim, bid him good day, and took his leave. His solicitor followed fast on his heels, offering a plethora of apologies for possibly overstepping his place. Darcy waved him away. He could see the mayhem lapping at the periphery of Mayfair for himself.

Relieved to be free of his solicitor's vexatious interference, Darcy inspected his watch to see if he still had time to visit the Bingleys. They had been in town a fortnight whilst Bingley visited several physicians seeking just the right potion to cure his long-predicated case of gout. He promised Elizabeth that he would pay them a visit whilst in town. When he was announced, Jane met him on the landing and led him directly to Bingley's sickbed.

Charles was a sorry sight indeed. It was difficult not feel sorry for him and his misery, whether it was all his fault or not. Propped in bed, he wore a puce chamber robe that was bespattered with wine. One foot was propped up on a pillow. His big toe was wrapped with so much gauze it was the size of a fist. Initially, unwitting that Darcy was there, he continued to moan and, betimes, he swore.

It was poor Jane, however, who was most distressed. She had dithered herself into a rash that swathed her décolletage and ran up the length of her neck. It was swathed with dried lotion and she had a difficult time keeping her nervous hands from worrying it. Still, all Jane's sympathy was with dear Bingley. Such was her disconcertion, Darcy undertook the office of her consoler.

"There, there," was all he could say.

With that small an act of sympathy, Jane burst into tears. Bingley moaned.

"My poor Charles," Jane fretted. "What is there to do? Where is there to go?"

Upon seeing Darcy, Bingley cried out, "My toe! My poor toe! I feel as if I am walking on my eyeballs!"

At this, Jane ran from the room, her face in her hands. (Fortunately, a maid was there to guide her lest she knock herself senseless on the doorpost.) Bingley spied her and held out one helpless hand.

"Poor Jane," Bingley cried out again. "She cannot bear my suffering."

"Have pity on your poor wife, Bingley," Darcy scolded.

Brought to his senses, Bingley begged his apologies. His sincerity was somewhat in question. It was clear he believed himself to be supremely wounded and entirely unaccountable for it. Darcy's compassion was compromised. He restrained himself from gloating over having forecast the impairment. Bingley was far too wretched. As he continued to howl, Darcy's vow against rebuking him was strained by Bingley's self-pity and a strong desire that Jane not be further injured by her husband's indulgences.

"You have only yourself to blame, Bingley," Darcy told him at last.

Bingley grimaced.

Dolefully, Darcy asked, "Do you know what physicians call gout?"

Bingley shook his head.

"Rheumatism of a rich man's toe."

Miffed, Bingley said, "I am told that only men of pre-eminent intellectual ability contract it."

Darcy allowed him that fantasy and spoke of it no more. Bingley, however, wanted Darcy's advice on matters of business, not recuperation.

"Your mines, Darcy," he gasped. "Whereby did you divest yourself of your mines? What agent did you employ?"

Surprised at Bingley's sudden lucidity (and unusual interest in his own business affairs), Darcy took a moment before answering. He had not sold his mines. Unwilling to bear the blight on his land and its general inhumanity at large, Darcy had simply closed them down. He told Bingley that.

"I did not sell them, I had them closed. It was my duty to find work elsewhere for the miners."

Having had high hopes for a profitable way to dispose of the mines and their blessed ponies (and thereby restore his wife's happiness on their behalf), this was not good news—especially for a man already taken down by a very painful toe.

Said he, "My present agent says that they are quite profitable and I should keep them. Perhaps goats could pull the coal waggons."

"I would rather do with a thousand less a year, Bingley," Darcy said.

"Well, you can say that as you have many more thousands a year than do I."

Darcy understood Bingley's finances better than he did and was not taken in by his uncharacteristic fit of petulance. Bingley was not the richest man in England, but he was solvent. That was more than many a gentleman could say.

"Be well, my friend," Darcy said as he rose to go. "I suggest you sell the mines. Have a clear conscience and an appeased wife. You owe her that."

"I must have you stay for supper...." Bingley said.

Darcy advised, "You best take your rest whilst your children are not here to play on your bed."

Seeing the wisdom of that, Bingley offered himself up to sleep. Darcy crept from the room and met Jane, now composed.

"He shall recover soon," Darcy assured her. For Jane's sake, he was much in want of believing it.

Few men weather infirmity with any part of good humour. When his hearing had been all but absent, Darcy knew that he had been unforgivably petulant. He could not think of his misbehaviour without abhorrence.

He asked, "What does the physician claim will cure gout other than time itself?"

Jane said, "He told Charles that no one who lived upon sixpence a day ever contracted gout."

"That is an easy remedy," he assured her. "Deny him wine and meat."

She promised, "He shall live on bread and tea until his toe improves."

It occurred to Darcy that Jane might be in want Elizabeth's assistance with Bingley.

As if reading his thoughts, Jane placed a restraining hand on his forearm, saying, "Do not speak of this to Lizzy. I shan't want her to see Charles in his unfortunate condition."

He agreed to her wishes.

Then she said, "Charles must get well. We must return to the country. Town is becoming untenable. Mrs. Aubrey lives just across the way. Her servants were attacked merely because they were situated with someone of station. It is said that no one is safe. I believe it is so. It is almost dark, Mr. Darcy. You must be wary."

This time, words of warning were accepted with the same generosity that they were given. They were not necessarily well-taken. Darcy was more concerned over what would befall them down the road, not around the corner. Moreover, if Bingley could not be a good owner, Darcy hoped that he would sell his mines to someone who would. Bingley was a good man, but simply too hasty to be a good overseer.

Another fear bothered Darcy. Had he his wishes, Bingley would be lucid enough to be cautioned about his loose tongue. Bingley was given to conversing with strangers with compleat abandon. Jane was correct. Contingents of finger-pointers filled the streets seeking an excuse to accuse someone of treason. Even soft-spoken Georgiana was at risk. She was far too vocal in criticising the mines and the ponies. When he returned, he would speak to her about her openness. There was insurrection about and the streets abounded with louts who would not think twice about assailing a lady (and the horse drawing her carriage).

There was no doubt that gangs of men wandered the streets just looking to throttle a gentleman or two (some for the principle of it, others for the valuables they carried). By the time he left the Bingleys, the streets were fast becoming deserted by coaches bearing crests and carriages carrying persons of rank. Used to going where he liked, he did not exercise caution himself. Fortunately, he travelled from Bingley's house in Belgrave to his own house in Mayfair without incident. When he reached his stables, he might have given a small sigh of relief. If he did, it was inaudible to the stable boy who took his reins. For the boy took the horse and disappeared with great dispatch into the stable. The mount was in need of a good rubdown. Thinking that was an admirable end of the day for man or beast, Darcy walked towards his house.

It was upon the approach through the garden that he noticed someone stood just inside the property fence. He had a choice to either to face the intruder or make for the back steps. It was not in his nature to run—even when it might be prudent. An improvident act or not, he knew no other way to respond than to confront that which threatened him.

As he waited for the figure to make a move, he stood his full height.

A voice range out. In the night air, sound carried quite clearly.

"*Mon cheri*, I have waited for hours."

*D*isharmony All Around

When the Darcys at last reached Chiltern, darkness had fallen. The conversation in the coach thither from the site of the mishap had been stilted. That lack of cordiality did not influence him to renege on his promise to Jane that he would not tell Elizabeth of her situation. In all good conscience, he could not keep such information to himself. He told her of the severity of Bingley's gout and Jane's insistence that Elizabeth not come. Still, Elizabeth agreed that he had been right to tell her—even if it was against Jane's wishes.

Said she, "After all, one must weigh the importance of the information. One has a duty to honesty. Although Jane does not want to trouble me, I can at the very least offer them my prayers—and be prepared should the situation alter."

The coach then drew to a stop, thus disallowing Darcy the opportunity to be as forthcoming about the rest of his time in town. He peered out the window. Even in the gloom of night he was not happy with what he saw (as he had decided to despise the lodgings sight unseen, this was of no great surprise). Looking about, he very-nearly sneered.

His voice pinched with hauteur, he asked his wife, "What, pray, is the name of this inn you have taken? Is it not the 'Gutted Goat' or some sort?"

Quite witting of his impertinent tone, she answered him with exaggerated pleasantness.

"There is indeed an inn nearby called the 'The Drunken Goose.' Our lodgings, however, are at the Chiltern Inn."

The establishments were quit dissimilar. The 'Goose' was no more than a haven for inebriates. The Chiltern Inn was quite respectable. The distinction of hosting such illustrious personages had left the innkeeper breathless with anticipation. Knowing of the many needs of the rich, he had cleared the place of other guests and meant to glean the surrounding countryside for a bevy of milkmaids and farm hands to serve them. As it happened, whatever extra help the innkeeper might have forgathered had been at the site of the overturned coach. Their absence was well and good. The Darcys own servants took over the place with great efficiency.

After town, Darcy enjoyed the quiet, but at times the country was not always amenable to his desire for tranquillity. Oftentimes small hamlets were short on amusements. He had known cottagers to quit their ovens and fields to come to the village for no other reason than to admire his livery. Moreover, many common folk displayed all manner of servile tics and peculiarly reverential bows when they saw him. Darcy was quite used to the absurdities of obsequiousness, but never enjoyed them. He would have paid the publican an extra sovereign to keep word of the stay from being known. (Elizabeth would not know to do so.) Unfortunately, the melee on the road had precluded anonymity.

Whilst Darcy fretted about their privacy, Elizabeth instructed Hannah to see if the inn had such a thing as a large wash tub.

Her husband inquired, "For you or the children?"

She looked at the offending hem of her skirt and was unperturbed.

"If my sloth offends, sir, I shall put my own toilette above that of your children."

The Darcys' exchanges had become disharmonious. Elizabeth endeavoured to quell her growing irritation lest it was overheard.

After the baskets, satchels, and trunks were unloaded, Hannah bid a footman to see that water was drawn. In the kitchen, a pot of stew was warming over the fireplace. Even for a man whose taste in all things was discriminating, it looked rather good to Darcy. The serving wench, however, was not. Standing guard over the stew was a toothless woman in a begrimed apron. The publican's stout wife shooed her away and scurried to serve Mr. Darcy a large pewter bowl of stew. Beside it, she laid a half loaf of bread. He tore off a piece of bread, stuck a corner of it in the stew and popped it into his mouth. As it was still hot from the pot, he had to resort to some unflattering facial contortions to keep his tongue from being scalded.

Notwithstanding the irregularities of his countenance and the stew's origin, he found it uncommonly delicious. It was good, wholesome fare. To admire rusticity simply because it was fashionable to do so was unacceptable. Nonetheless, it was exceedingly good ragout—good enough for his children. He motioned for Mrs. Heff to have a tray carried up to them.

Despite Darcy's implied aspersions, he conceded that the inn was clean and tidy. It was, however, little more than serviceable. There was an inn of estimable merit at Meryton. He surmised that Elizabeth had good reason to let apartments twenty miles away. That was not a subject he chose to broach (as he was of the opinion that their distance from Longbourne was a gift he was not in want of questioning). Once their coaches had crossed paths, he expected to stay no more than the night in Chiltern. The ledger showed that Elizabeth had taken their rooms for a week. Her design, had she one, was obscure to him.

Darcy took the stairs to their room in hope of finding some privacy therein to make peace with his good wife. His son, however, awaited him. His eyes looked troubled. This time, Geoff had not escaped from Margaret. She had brought him to his father.

"Beg your pardon, sire," said Margaret. "The boy seemed so worried I knew you would want to talk to him."

Darcy nodded to her and waved her on her way. She did leave, but waited just beyond the doorway. Darcy bent down upon on one knee and drew his son to him.

"What troubles you?"

The boy inquired, "Is it true, Papa?"

"Is what true?"

Geoff's voice trembled.

"Body-nappers—do they steal our teeth?"

In the past months, two of their cousins had lost their baby teeth. That had made the talk of grave-robbers all the more real to Geoff. His father firmly believed that the horrors of stealing corpses should not plague one so young. The very thought angered him. Drawing the boy tightly against his breast, Darcy patted his small back. There was no such talk at Pemberley. The boy was clearly too young to be trotted about the country subjected to morbid talk and rooster attacks. Thank God above that Janie had not been struck by the same fear. Of the two, Geoff was the worrier. His place was already weighing upon his shoulders.

"Do not fear, son," he crooned. "You are safe. I am here."

Not entirely placated, Geoff's voice quavered as he asked, "What of William? Did the body-nappers steal him?"

He did not want to place undue importance on it lest the child's fears be multiplied.

He stood him down, saying, "No, they did not. Fear not, for I am here and I shall protect you always."

Vowing it would be so, he beckoned Margaret Heff.

"Sleep well, son. Papa is right here all night."

To Margaret, he said, "Should the boy...."

She nodded. Taking Geoff's hand, they walked across the hallway.

From beyond the doorway, Elizabeth watched the tender scene with a divided heart. Her husband's quiet reassurance of his son was touching. Although she was not surprised, she was still pleased that a man as proud and reticent as Mr. Darcy did not hold himself above issuing such comfort. Yet, she could not help but feel that in doing so, her husband censured her as a mother. He had, after all, believed her wrong in taking to the road without him—and was most displeased that she had then allowed the children to leave the safety of their coach to observe what excitement had transpired.

No doubt he thought that she had behaved unwisely—even rashly. (If she was at fault for any of it, she had to admit that she was curious about the overturned coach herself.) The incident was unremarkable. They had not sustained any injury. Until Duff's wild stories, it had been a bit of an adventure. Accidents befall the best laid plans.

As she bethought the matter, she became evermore indignant.

Clearly, Darcy exaggerated the entire event. After inflating the danger, he accused her of placing her children in harm's way. Indeed, his words came perilously close to a reproach. He could not injure her more grievously than to criticise her as a mother. Just thinking of it left her all but quivering with outrage.

Taken as a whole, she believed he had treated her with utmost disrespect. The only repair for such an indignity was for him to withdraw his accusations (falling on his knees and beg her forgiveness would be helpful, but highly unlikely). In order to obtain his apology, fractious words might be exchanged. Unlike Pemberley's vast rooms, the walls of the Chiltern Inn were not impenetrable. If they were to speak contentiously, she did not want to be overheard.

She meant to betake herself from their room altogether, but before she could pass him by, he caught her hand.

He said, "Allow Hannah to see to your needs...."

With a near-violent twist of her wrist, she wrung her hand from his.

"I want," she said, "A pint of ale."

Her request astonished him. He caught himself before he laughed. Hers was not a jest.

"My love...."

She whirled and in a harsh whisper, said, "You use me cruelly to improve yourself."

An expression of injured incredulity overspread his countenance.

He said curtly, "I here beg leave to apologise if I have, in word or deed, wounded you in any fashion."

That was apology by rote, not one truly meant. Did he think her a simpleton?

She whispered urgently, "You accuse me, not in word or deed, but in your thoughts—with your eyes."

"Of what do I accuse you?'

When she spoke, it was not what she meant to say. Nonetheless, she believed it true.

"I am condemned for my vulgar relations."

Her recent visit to Longbourne and the ill-behaviour it harboured was very much with her. Unfortunately, it did not occur to her that she was the author of this accusation, not her husband.

He responded, "I am quite certain that none of us can best the other when it comes to ill-mannered kin. This, I have admitted freely. Surely, you suffer from a higher injury than that."

Her chin quivered, but she did not weep—despite how deeply she was offended. When she spoke, she still did not tell him what she had inferred from his talk with their son. Perchance that was best. Rather, she spoke of another grievance, one that festered in her breast long before they came to Chiltern Inn.

"We shall not be happy unless I am enslaved by our designing friends—to sacrifice what we have to the caprice of their inclinations."

Still confounded, said, "I do not take your meaning."

He truly did not.

"Am I to have a child to please others? Shall that please you? Is that what you want of me?"

He was rendered speechless. She was not.

"I am in want a pint of ale and I shall have it."

61

$\mathscr{P}$urgatory Holds On

It fell apparent with great haste that Chiltern was not to be the idyll that Elizabeth had hoped—or the night of rest that Darcy had supposed. If he was confused by his wife's anomalous actions, she was in a spin of her own.

As she made for the door, Darcy called to her.

"Lizzy!" said he. "Where shall you go?"

Upon occasion, Mr. Darcy spoke firmly, but he rarely raised his voice. Hence, she paused. She did not, however, gaze in his direction. Nor did she answer. In truth, she was much in need of finding a place where she could sit and think with pleasure of her own ill-use. The drinking establishment below their rooms looked quite acceptable to engage in a bout of self-pity.

"I shall accompany you," he said, claiming his coat.

She knew that she was nearing compleat want of conduct. Marching into a public room of a public house in any manner was exceedingly ill-advised under any condition—certainly not alone.

She was not so foolish as to refuse his offer—nay, his insistence—upon escorting her. Still, she did not wait for him. She hurried on her way, but by employing two long, purposeful steps, he caught up with her. Although she hastened her pace, she could not stay ahead of him. Indeed, he was all but stepping upon the back of her mud-caked slippers as she walked.

Darcy, of course, was horrified. (He recognised that she meant to injure decorum, but he was uncertain if she was witting of it.) He did not believe that she understood the full nature of his discomposure. True, if they were to quarrel, he wanted to do so in private and not a common alehouse. His very being was repulsed at the thought of entering such a place. The smell, the sounds, indeed, the very bowels of such a place not only insulted his dignity, they fostered another, higher abhorrence. It was a recollection that would haunt him all of his days—one that had not yet come to her.

The other public house had been a far more disreputable place, stinking of vomit and urine. Its habitués turned a blind eye to the indecencies that took place within its walls. He had left its floor stained with the blood of three men. Infuriated beyond any imagining, he had smite them with gun and sword. If any man dared do Elizabeth harm, he would not hesitate to murder again.

His breath grew heavy just recalling that long-past night and he did his best to calm himself. Elizabeth, oblivious to his temper, gaily made her way to a table. As the establishment was empty save for the publican and a lone confrere, she claimed a table in the corner near the fireplace. The earlier rain had brought a brisk, clear night and a draft seeped into the room making the warmth of the fire evermore desirable.

The place was clean, but obviously unused to anyone of higher station that a local squire. Whilst it in no way favoured the other festering canker of a hellhole, Darcy endeavoured to curb his growing pique. By the time they sat, he believed that his dear wife had begun to have a few misgivings about her sudden want of a pint. Neither of them was the sort to concede. The innkeeper hastily came to them, asking Mr. Darcy if they cared for a cut of meat. Darcy shook his head. He motioned for two pints of ale instead.

They waited silently as the publican returned and set their drinks on the table. He stood with a rag over his arm awaiting further instructions. Darcy took a sip, found it satisfactory, and thus waved him away.

Whilst they waited, Darcy had watched Elizabeth carefully. She twitched like a jumpy cat, causing him to conclude her state of mind had been too delicate to weather Mrs. Bennet. Her mother's nerves, fits, and endless prattle had driven his poor wife from the brink of madness into the abyss.

Elizabeth sipped daintily from her mug.

He asked her, "Have you partaken of ale ere this night?"

"Certainly."

She then made a grand display of taking several gulps of the brew. Just as grandly, she set the cup back upon the table. However, when she opened her mouth to speak, not a word came out.

Rather, she belched.

Placing a hand daintily across her lips, she said, "Dear me."

Darcy did his best not to laugh, but was unsuccessful. He suspected is wife's insistence that she had drank ale before to be a small prevarication. Her alteration in colour was obvious as the warmth of the liquor took hold. At it did, she also became talkative—often repeating herself.

"I think you are in your cups, Lizzy," he told her.

"How many alehouses have you visited?" she asked merrily.

He shook his head, not trusting where the conversation might take them. He downed his own drink. The publican hastily replaced it.

She teased, "Is Mr. Darcy above such establishments?"

"As it happens, I have been in the public houses at Lambton and Kympton. I believe that one is called 'The Fox and Hogget, Phineus Turnpenny, proprietor."

(Due to certain improprieties exhibited there during the festivities surrounding their marriage, Darcy was quite displeased with the "Fox and Hogget" and it owner.)

His disclosure was meant to conclude that path of inquiry. Her discourse reminded him of another, similar interrogation years past. In that one she also asked him to put a number to certain acts (those not of drinks he had taken, but of women he had... occupied). If memory served, she was specific, "Less than five, more than ten?" He did not care to pursue unhelpful investigations. His alarm was well-timed.

"Oh, certainly sir you have a more checkered past than that," she urged. "Pray share your wayward conduct."

It was not in his nature to talk openly when he might be overheard, but her question troubled him. Time was for them to be frank. He bit his lower lip once before he spoke. Both were lulled by the warmth and the liquor, but he did not want to vex her unnecessarily. As he formed the words in his mind to answer, her eyes suddenly opened wide and she gasped.

"Oh, my darling! How thoughtless! Can you forgive me?"

He reached across the broad table and pressed a finger against her lips. She shook him off.

"I am a wretch! I am a worthless wife and a senseless mother...."

He hushed her again, fearing that her agitation might cause her to discharge other than an eructation.

Reaching for her hand, he urged, "Let us take our leave."

Of like minds, she hastily agreed. Although Mrs. Darcy had to take careful steps as she held tightly to Mr. Darcy's arm, they managed the stairs without incident. For this she was quite relieved. The misdirection of her ire had finally struck her and she was highly contrite. To bestow even more grief upon his already sullied dignity would have been indefensible.

It was not late when they returned upstairs, but all seemed to be asleep. That was a further relief.

"We must speak," she urged.

He ignored her appeal, "*You* must sleep. Shall I call Hannah?'

"I am not so befuddled as all that. We must speak. I beg to apologise for my behaviour."

"You have been with your mother long enough to try anyone's sanity, the blame is not yours."

"I would be most happy to fault my mother. But it is not hers. It is mine alone."

Her words were sober. He gazed into her eyes to determine if she was impaired. Her eyes were clear—and a sea of pain.

He reassured her, "Time, so often a friend, is also a fleeting thief. Every hour we spend weltering at the very nadir of despair is a day lost to us forever."

She blinked and then nodded.

"I shall not have it," he said. Then softening his voice, he repeated, "*We* must not have it."

By engaging his will (his most admired and feared trait), he managed to put those long past remembrances so abhorrent to him and his inward tranquillity aside. Addressing very present maelstroms was troubling enough. It would serve no good purpose to revisit old ones. He called for Hannah. Elizabeth did not demur.

Whilst Hannah brushed out Mrs. Darcy's hair, Mr. Darcy seated himself on a small wooden chair outside the door. Given that her condition might make her uncertain on her feet, he did not choose to leave her to the servants. The corridor was narrow and dark. Its intimacy gave him leave to loosen his tie. As he sat, he also unbuttoned his waistcoat, placed his face in his hands, and (as he often did when collecting himself) rubbed it several times.

He could hear murmuring from behind the door. He recognised his wife's voice. That soothed him. Tipping his chair onto the back two legs until the back of it touched the wall; he rested his head against the wallboard and closed his eyes.

Whatever he had done to engage his wife's wrath would have to be sorted out in the morning. She was not of splenetic nature. Whatever her injury, it had been deeply felt. Whilst the children slept, they must speak of the more pressing issue (Mr. Darcy compleatly unwitting that the two disconcertions were one and the same). Her recklessness that night recalled to him her heedless ride upon the Pemberley down. His apprehension over her despondency had been assuaged. Upon their visit to the Chiltern Inn, it was reinstated. Although he no longer believed that she had run mad, his concern was keen. Her behaviour remained... changeable.

Whether or not they would regain all that they had once shared tormented him. Her words had been plain enough. She believed herself bullied into bearing another child. If she truly abhorred the prospect, he would acquiesce to her wishes. He would sacrifice intimacy if it would salvage her heart. His only hope was that time might not be feckless in its consolation. Perhaps it would heal those feelings so keenly injured in them both.

When Hannah withdrew, he sat up straight in the chair. Once she cleared the hallway, he stood. Placing his hand on the doorknob, he resolved that sequestered in this plain little inn, he would tell her that the love they shared was far too precious to fritter away through petty quarrels. Her getting pissed as a newt notwithstanding, he would try to reason with her once more.

If reason failed, perhaps passion would prevail. Would she but agree, he would solace them both by sacrificing his love upon her womanly altar and converse about the relinquishment of that gratification in the glow of sated desire. He opened the door and closed it behind him.

His chosen path was fraught with disturbances.

First amongst them was that the room was dark—too dark. All the candles had been doused (dare he hope by her design?). In the dimness, her outline was barely discernible. Making his way was particularly vexing in an unusually small room stuffed with unfamiliar furniture. His legs encountered several unexpected objects and he was tempted to beshrew his displeasure each time he bumped his shin.

When finally he made it to her bedside, he spoke not. Rather, he slid from his clothing with great dispatch. She had been laying upon her side with her back to him when he slipped beneath the bedclothes. Naked and highly aroused, he whispered her name.

"Lizzy. *Lizzy*...."

She turned to him—and, he thought, into his arms. However, when she rolled onto her back, her jaw fell open. From the back of her throat came a most unladylike snore.

There are times when a gentleman's mettle is tested. Upon this occasion, Mr. Darcy was conflicted. With a great deal of self-cajolement, his resolve remained—if not firm, at least, strong.

All was for the best. In the morning light, they would converse without his arousal disturbing the outcome.

$\mathcal{P}$itiful Ponies

With Sally Frances Arbuthnot's helpful inquiries, Lady Millhouse embarked on what she would call her great scheme. (Her schemes were becoming so many; Lord Millhouse was tempted to number them.) This one came about by reason of Mr. Darcy's promise to his sister.

The pit ponies were less a nuisance than a scandal, and by speaking to Lady Millhouse of them, Darcy knew it would be addressed with due diligence. It was well known that no one (even he) had a greater love of horses than did she. He surmised correctly. Indeed, she was appalled over the plight of the ponies as any upstanding horsewoman would be.

She boomed, "Pray tell, how this outrage could occur beneath our very noses, Darcy? Georgiana is quite right; we must save these ponies from the mines!"

He hoped her ladyship's interest in the business was not too eagre, as he did not mean to protect his sister only to jeopardise his good friend in her stead. Although he did not hesitate to caution Lady Millhouse, unsurprisingly, she did not take heed.

She said, "Pish, Darcy, I shall be quite wary."

That was not a reassurance.

In fortune, Lady Millhouse had seen young Sally Frances as not only a consort, but a cohort too. Whilst Lord Millhouse stood in his usual posture (looking lovingly upon her doings), his wife had inveigled the young girl to join her upon her next adventure.

"Dear girl, do you ride?" she demanded.

Sally had seen all manner of horses in town, none finer than those of the West End, and none so humble as the carthorses plodding up the narrow streets of the Dials. Those were wretched creatures, with coarse coats and sad eyes. Before Sally and her family had been consigned to the workhouse, they had lodged across the street from a shop where an ancient white horse, laden with wares, was often seen. Whilst the driver stopped to tend to business,

Sally combed the old horse's mane with her fingers and scratched it between the ears. That horse was the nearest she had come to having a pet.

In response to Sally's admittance that she did not ride, could not ride, and cared not to ride, Lady Millhouse was undeterred. Indeed, she was enervated.

"I have an undertaking for which I ask your aide," she announced. "As you do not ride, we shall take the gig."

More than happy to have the opportunity to repay Lady Millhouse's generosity, Sally nodded her head. She did so with more than a little apprehension. After all, she was but a hapless girl of the notorious slums of London. What could a country lady want of her? No doubt, she was wanted to engage in some malfeasance on the Millhouse's behalf. London bred or not, Sally was no thief.

"You don't want me to filch anything for ye, do ye?"

Lady Millhouse guffawed, "No, no, dear one, I do not. Ours is a far nobler pursuit."

Sally's expression was one of profound relief.

Lady Millhouse went on, "It has come to my attention that ponies labour in the mines just beyond Chesterfield. They are dear, pitiable ponies and they work in compleat darkness. So seldom do they see the light of day, they often become blind!"

Puzzled, Sally nodded as if she understood what had irked Lady Millhouse about that.

"I have been charged with engaging in whatever tomfoolery I care to in regards to the ponies, so long as we cause no delays in securing the coal. We dare not chance any more of this silly rioting now do we?"

As Lady Millhouse spoke, Sally could not help but interrupt, asking, "Why ponies?"

"How do mean, 'why ponies?'" Lady Millhouse asked.

Sally explained, "I mean 'why ponies' and why do oxen not pull these coal waggons? They're big, strong animals. Why don't these folks use oxen in the mines?"

Here Lord Millhouse interjected, "The mine shaft is overly narrow for oxen. Soon the mines shall be overtaken by mechanisation, but Lady Millhouse favours improving the lot of the ponies now in use."

Bombastic she may have been, however her ladyship was not foolish. She understood that in order to save any ponies, they must begin their rescue with one mine and a single pony.

"It shall be a great relief to have all animals out of the mines. Poor, poor ponies," Lady Millhouse said.

Sally was not especially like-minded.

"I guess them folks workin' those mines want to keep earnin' a wage too."

Lord and Lady Millhouse each stood looking at Sally with an air of confused condescension.

A thought struck Lord Millhouse, "Indeed, we should not favour falling victim to a revolutionary outrage as did France,"

This was a point they all agreed upon. And *upon* that agreement, Sally at last understood what Lady Millhouse wanted of her. Sally was to be her emissary.

"A diplomat, if you will, dear girl. As has been proven here today, you can speak more plainly than can I. We must assure the workmen that we do not care to cause bother to their business. We only wish to have those ponies now kept below ground to be stabled above and allowed to graze."

It was her plan to see to, and fund, the building of stables and obtaining ample pasture.

"To implement the plan properly, I am aware that it shall be necessary for me to purchase additional stock so they can be alternated—one day at work, the next to graze," she explained. "It is not an ideal, but an improvement. The ponies would be engaged—and not abused to blindness—not so long as this lady has a breath left in her body!"

Practical-minded Sally saw the sense in the plan. The plight of little blind ponies labouring in the mines indeed plucked her heartstrings. However, she could not help but think of those common folk in England; they who were in want of a piece of bread and a place to sleep. When babes starved and eight-year-olds worked twelve hours a day, it was difficult for her to cough up an over-abundance of sympathy for a pack of horses.

"You know how to speak to these men far better than I," Lady Millhouse said. "I should like you to make these arrangements...."

Sally was not so sure all would go swimmingly. Indeed, she anticipated being beaten from the mine's premises. Hence, Sally protested.

Lady Millhouse put up her hand, "Tut, tut, my dear. You have your brother's blood in you. He was a true cavalier. Fear not, for I shall accompany you."

"Yes'm," said Sally reluctantly.

That day, and the day after, did not improve Sally's enthusiasm for the scheme. Invading another's place and accusing them of having it all wrong might be an idea born of good intentions, but such as that was rarely rewarded. Indeed, the more she thought of it, the more she dug her heels in against it. Lady Millhouse did what she could to influence her opinion otherwise. Sally ate, even relished, all the many cakes and candies with which she was plied, but remained steadfast. In time, Sally not only refused to go, she advised Lady Millhouse not to go either. Unsurprisingly, the lady could not be swayed.

"I promised sweet Georgiana that I would see to this on her behalf," she said with finality.

When Sally finally gave herself over to Lady Millhouse, it was with a shrug of weariness.

Lord Millhouse was a peaceable man. His part was to stay behind, happy that he sent off intercessory letters warning one and all of his wife's approach.

Lady Millhouse seemed quite pleased with her husband's assistance. As Sally did not have the two and twenty years practise in being thwarted in attempting to dissuade Lady Millhouse from her various missions, she did not comprehend why he was so handily overruled when he insisted that they be accompanied by footmen.

Sally fully understood that her ladyship did not enjoy calm pursuits. Still, when she saw they were meant to take to the road in a two-wheeled gig, the girl was well nigh giddy with excitement. Suddenly their mission seemed less a mission than a lark. Her humour was well in place when they were set to scramble into the daring equipage.

Lady Millhouse looked to advantage when in the saddle, but she was a large-boned woman and whilst on her feet, she moved with all the subtlety of a barge. Climbing onto the gig was less a matter of being handed into the seat, but rather lifted. Sally clambered up beside her whilst Lady Millhouse took hold of the reins. With a flick of the good lady's wrists they embarked upon their little jaunt.

Lady Millhouse drove the gig with the same eagerness she took a fence—but not with equal finesse. (As she was thickset and Sally was small, the gig began the trip disadvantaged by a droop to one side.) Lady Millhouse straightened her bonnet and, bound by a long-held affection and keen understanding of the other's nature, the Millhouses bid each other adieu. Lord Millhouse did not abandon his farewell until the huge feather in Lady Millhouse's headdress had disappeared over the horizon. Not unlike a hunt, her ladyship did not hesitate. Every corner was taken too wide and too fast, with young Sally clinging for dear life.

Lord Millhouse saw nothing more of his wife and Miss Arbuthnot until they returned mid-afternoon.

Upon their arrival at Pennyswope's doorstep, it was clear that something was amiss. Her ladyship's hat was askew, Sally's cap gone altogether. When they came to a halt, the girl leapt from the gig, which caused the springs to give her ladyship's descent undue thrust. She landed on a footman, but another drew her to her feet.

Lord Millhouse greeted them just inside the door. Sally stopped before him, her eyes wide enough to suggest she had encountered something... untoward. His wife however did not look his way.

Rather, she dusted her hands and announced to everyone within hearing, "A new plan is now in place! To London we go!"

$\mathscr{C}$hastened

The Darcys' journey, which had begun with equal parts apprehension and anticipation, ended not with a clash, but with a whimper.

As the morning dawned over Chiltern Inn, Mr. Darcy was still unaware of this.

Both he and Elizabeth lay naked as the sunlight crept up their legs, a bedsheet their only modesty. Her hair cascaded across her cheek and he reached out with tender fingers to brush them aside lest he wake her. Nonetheless, her legs moved restlessly. He laid a sheltering arm across her shoulders and pressed against the provocative curve of her supine figure. The scent of her hair in his nostrils, his morning pride soon tautened into a priapism of admirable size.

His desire ever-thickening against her thigh, she responded. A sough escaped the back of her throat and he kissed her beneath her ear.

"Good-day, my love," he whispered.

Abruptly, she sat upright. Just as hastily, she threw herself back on her pillow, the back of her hand across her eyes. She pointed to the drapes, hissing the plea, "The windows! My head! I cannot bear the light!"

With what could have been accused as a reluctance upon his part, he rose and thither he walked to yonder window to draw the blessed drapes. A vision of masculine beauty burdened by concupiscence was ever lost to her—as was the unhappy expression that overspread his countenance upon his return.

"Oooh," she moaned.

He could not remain unsympathetic, despite the fact that her headache was one of self-infliction.

As he drew on his breeches and shirt, he curled his fist and hit the wall several times with the side of it, demanding, "Cold water for Mrs. Darcy."

She half-sat, raising the palm of her hand in his direction, "Desist! I implore you, *desist!*"

As he hastily finished buttoning his breeches, an impish smile attached itself to the corner of his mouth.

He told her, "You, my dearest love, are crapulous."

Narrowing her eyes, she peered at him cautiously, saying, "I am quite certain I am no such thing." She insisted (as much to herself as to her husband), "I have taken sick quite coincidental to... whatever came to pass...."

He queried, "Is your tongue dry?"

"A bit," she admitted.

He would have said more, however she had made a sudden move. Covering her mouth with one hand, she made for the large bowl sitting on the side table. She leaned over it just in time to empty what was left in her stomach.

He reminded her, "As I said, 'crapulous.'"

Upon her second heave, he took pity and sat down next to her. Holding her hair back from her face, he kissed her on top of her head.

"My, poor Lizzy," he cooed.

Before she could respond, another wave of nausea attacked her. Hannah rapped upon the door. Elizabeth cringed at the sound. Taking hold of his coat, he opened the door for the maid. She was carrying a pitcher of water.

"Mistress has partaken of something disagreeable," he lied.

If Elizabeth was grateful, she did not tell him then.

In an hour, he returned to look in on her. The drapes were closed. A folded cloth lay across her eyes. Before he could close the door, she cast her compress aside and sat upright.

He believed that it was not the time to exchange observations or make amends (most particularly when the transgressions were so nebulous). His wife was of another mind. Patting the bed next to her, she bid him come. He rarely refused her, but rather than sit, he walked to the window and peered out. A slice of sunlight pierced the room. He hastily closed the drape and stood before her. He rested his weight on one foot and folded his hands behind him. Recognising his oft-used posture of defence, she closed her eyes as if to rebuff it.

"I beg to apologise...."

"Please. It is nothing. You are unused to spirits...," he interrupted.

She held up her hand.

"Do not," she reproved.

His mask of reserve slipped. He nodded his regret (for whatever injury she believed him to have committed).

She said, "It is said that 'the wicked flee when no man pursueth.'"

He nodded again, but had no notion what she meant.

She endeavoured to explain, "I fled to the inn for there was no park."

Upon this remark, he did not nod. Her meaning was lost to him and he awaited enlightenment.

"Had we been at Pemberley, I should have taken a lovely walk. The brisk air might have spared me the mortification of 'crapulousness.'"

Having taken her meaning at last, he took a step towards her and rested a hand upon the bedpost. She did not notice that, for she was quite intent on what she must explain to him.

"When I spied you becalming our son's fears, though it was not your intention to lay blame, I saw it as an accusation against me, as a mother. However, I *was* at fault. As his mother, I alone am responsible."

He was lost again—for a moment only. Then, as if the heavens opened, he understood. Geoff was not only of whom she spoke.

"Therein lays the problem," said he. "We speak not of fault, for no one is truly to blame. There is but one question. Are you able to forgive yourself for a transgression that does not exist?"

She turned her eyes to him, but was silent.

He took her hand, asking quietly, "Do you have trust in me?"

"Above all others."

"Trust me in this."

Laying her cheek against her his hand, she sighed. For so long a time he had felt as if she were slipping away from him, he chose to take that as a good omen.

$\mathscr{H}$ome and other Disasters

As they rode through Derbyshire and towards home, the hair upon the back of Darcy's neck prickled at what he might find. He feared the brief time he was away that the doors to the hen houses had been left open and that all the foxes were stealing inside.

Therefore, directly upon their return from Chiltern, Mr. Darcy took to the saddle.

It was not unusual for him to do so. Never the sort to leave his vast holdings solely to various overseers, Darcy's time in restive London only strengthened this resolve in that. Shepherding Pemberley and those people who relied upon his land for their livelihood was a duty he held second only to his family. In the past, he and Elizabeth would take to their horses together. However, the fine weather did not influence him to suggest she accompany him just then.

His decision was twofold.

If his wife were to go with him, it would necessitate them engaging in a conversation about the last time that they had been on horseback together (an occasion fraught with disquietude and in déshabillé). Additionally, and more importantly, he feared for her safety. Every protective instinct told him that she must stay within Pemberley and he must get on his horse and survey the lay of the land.

Even on its best days, Pemberley was not without quandaries and disputes. Commonly, these were no more than any other estate through time immemorial. With the country on the brink of anarchy, his rounds were more significant and risky.

Ere he travelled to London, there had been breathy accusations (both high and low) of spies invading the countryside. That was not talk of superstitious bumpkins. Those who kept reasonably abreast of the affairs of Derbyshire knew it was true. The Home Secretary had sent a network of informants into all areas of discontent. Once there, they were to report any hint of political rebellion to the local authorities. Regrettably, these spies were only paid when they had something to recount. That which they could not find, was invented.

No farther than Pentrich, a report had been made to local militia that an armed uprising was to occur. The men involved claimed that they were misled; that an *agent provocateur* had a hand in both the report and any insurrection. Disagreement over the truth of the matter was ongoing. Whatever occurred, what was not in dispute was that six men were hung.

Sorting the political chaff from the factual grain was gaining ever-greater importance. Mr. Rhymes had to take far greater care in all matters of hiring. An otherwise amiable-looking worker might be a true invader of agitation. So far as he had heard, no men of that ilk had been uncovered. That news offered him little comfort. If they were not in their midst, in due course, they would arrive. The surrounding mines invited it.

While wolves passed for men of honour, there were lambs to birth and crops to sow. Political upheaval or not, Pemberley had to forge ahead.

With most of the ruling class in bowel-restricting fear of revolution, Mr. Darcy believed it was his to calm those who laboured on his behalf. Change was afoot. The likelihood that those alterations would suit Mr. Darcy's leanings was remote. He understood that quite well. Nonetheless, he understood the grander design; change was the only constant. The tide would come, one wave at a time.

Leaving Pemberley house that day, he had made an ever-greater circle of his land until he was satisfied that he had done all that he could to see that it was as it should be. Therewith, he turned Blackjack towards home. When he did, his purpose was clear. His most present apprehension had little to do with politics. Indeed, his land was not all that needed cosseting.

The hours he spent solely superintending his vast estate meant that he had ridden out as the cock crows and returned at dusk. During his investigations, it had not been difficult to set aside those conversations with Elizabeth which had been so painful for them both. For the better part of a week, they had done little more than exchange a brief kiss. He knew that he had spent far too much time away from his wife and he meant to repair that injurious wrong.

Riding out again the next day at dawn, he vowed a homecoming by mid-afternoon. Elizabeth would expect him, for he left her a note advising her of his early return. He came not by the road, but a more direct route. And as he rode, he prepared himself not merely to take his wife into his impassioned arms, but first to unkennel certain botherations wholly unconnected with their marriage. One could not patch a ship's sails without seeing to the barnacles clinging to its hull.

A niggling doubt about that presumption began to trouble him. Indeed, a vertical line appeared between his brows announcing that Mr. Darcy believed that whilst in London, he may well have erred.

When last in town, he had spoken to his solicitor, carried out a particular errand, and paid a visit to the Bingleys. Other than Charles Bingley's gout-ridden toe (and Jane's distress because of it), nothing untoward came to pass. Upon his return to his townhouse, he handed his horse's reins over to a footman and walked briskly through the garden to the postern steps. Before he reached them, a lady came out of the dark. The moonlight cast a milky glow across her skin.

Initially, he could not see her eyes for they were cast down. It had been unnecessary to gaze upon her countenance, for he had recognised her voice.

"*Mon Cheri*," she had said.

To have Lady Howgrave step out of the shadows greatly astonished him. Much to his chagrin, his surprise was apparent. Attempting to conquer his expression, he took several deliberate steps in her direction before he spoke. His words were not of a man fully in charge of his thoughts.

"Why, pray tell, why...? Where did you...? You cannot be unaccompanied?"

The last question was one of a consummate gentleman. Upon hearing it, Juliette emitted a soft laugh. In the dark, her eyes glistened like diced plums.

What to do with her posed a problem for him. No good would come from anyone seeing her there... with him. The choices were few. He could escort her into the house or he might speak to her in the privacy of the stables. What he would not do was turn her away in the dark. No gentleman would. The streets were unsafe for men.

Indeed, he did not turn her away.

He took her elbow, leaned next to her ear and said, "Where is your carriage?"

It was obvious that she had not come on foot.

Glancing towards the alleyway, she said simply, "There."

Indeed, an inconspicuous landaulet was in the mews just beyond the stables. He steered her through the garden and to the lane dividing his house from the one behind. As if a virginal maid, she trotted along beside him. Her coachman stood by the head of the horse, his hat low, slapping the reins across his palm. Darcy opened the door for her and held her hand as she ascended the steps. She settled herself inside and looked at him in query.

Grabbing the handgrip, he drew himself in beside her and closed the door behind them.

*R*einvention

Once he was on his feet, Wickham set his considerable imagination upon obtaining a new identity.

Even with Mrs. Younge's help (as a long-time inhabitant of the narrow alleys between lawful and criminal enterprises, Mrs. Younge knew to keep his continued presence in her house a secret), he had been surprised that the army had not winkled out where he was. That piece of vellum those two wee wenches forced him to sign meant nothing that he could see. To them, it was just some farce. He had read it under considerable duress.

It took him a while to work it all out.

First, he had to determine his legal situation. Persuading Mrs. Younge to sally forth to King's Bench on his behalf was the work of a half hour. Once there, she had only to pass a remarkably paltry bribe to learn that several affidavits had been filed regarding Major George Wickham. One attested that he had deserted his post and murdered a private under his command whilst he made his away. The second one was signed by two witnesses who claimed to have seen Major Wickham killed and that his body had been interred in a mass grave. No other details were cited on either count.

After receiving the news that he was a known murderer and deserter, Wickham only laughed. Mrs. Younge was taken aback.

"Did you do murder, George?"

He snorted once before responding, "That other paper said I was dead. Do you believe that as well?"

Shaking her head, she was appeased by his response (that and a slap on her rear end for good measure).

The news dashed any hope that all might be forgiven, thus allowing him to reinstate himself into society as a hero of Waterloo. With Wickham officially dead, so went any chance of obtaining part of the Darcy fortune. He almost took to his bed again. It was Mrs. Younge who brought him to him senses.

"Nobody is looking for you now, Georgie," she told him. "You can walk the streets and answer to any name you please.

That was true. No one cared to look for a dead man. He had no fear of apprehension. He all but whistled with elation. Never was a man better positioned for intrigue than he who cannot be punished.

In inventing his new self, he wanted to keep to the truth as much as possible. He must be wary. Among many other infractions (i.e., sodomy and defacing the Westminster Bridge), impersonating an army veteran was a hanging offence. If he did not play his cards correctly, he might find himself not only semi-deknackered, but gibbeted on the brow of a hill.

His new identity came to him upon an initially disagreeable turn of events.

After he was satisfied that his virile credentials were intact, he quit obsessively admiring them in the abysmally small hand-mirror and turned his attention to his second favourite vision—his own countenance. Laying in supine splendour, having his every desire fulfilled by the ever-loyal Mrs. Younge, he was of a mind that he needed his hair trimmed. It was his habit to keep his hair a bit longer than was the fashion. After his daily shave, he demanded she tend to it.

"My magnificent mane would be excessively unruly for Byron himself...."

The small hand-glass was too small to accommodate his supervision of this undertaking and he bid her bring him the larger one from her dressing table. She dutifully brought it to him. Then she stood back as if in expectation of some sort of explosion.

Upon seeing his own visage and the shock of hair that surrounded it, Wickham erupted, "What is that!"

He grabbed a big hank of his hair and held it up to the gods, demanding, "What the bloody hell is *that*?"

"Your hair," she said excitedly.

For weeks he had done the improbable. He picked at his skin and submitted to having his sideburns trimmed, but he had not once taken a full view of his hair. Now that he had, he was horrified. Mrs. Younge, however, was beside herself with elation. Now that he knew what she knew, she was most anxious to talk to him of the surprising alteration to his aspect.

"It as if you have seen Lucifer himself!" she gushed.

Indeed, in a swath from his forehead to the nape of his neck, his hair had turned white as snow.

He shrieked his disapproval, "It is absurd!"

Indeed, he did look as if he had lately crawled beneath a freshly white-washed fence.

"Go for bootblack! Now, woman, *now!*" he hollered.

"I think not," she said, her lips pursed in a sage pout.

"You must!" he cried, flinging himself upon his cot. "I look like an old man! A very, very strange, old man!"

In a voice one would employ with a child, she soothed, "There, there. All will be well. I have seen it happen upon a fright. One wakes up and the hair has turned white. Yours just hasn't yet compleatly blanched."

"I shan't be seen this way. I demand bootblack!"

She waved off his entreaty. Rather, she pointed to his side whiskers. "See here?"

Grey hair was entwined within them. It was a good sign, said she. Soon they would be as white as the rest of his hair. Hastily (and nonsensically, in that he spent most of his time gazing at his groin), he looked beneath his bedclothes, reassuring himself that his body hair had not turned white as well. (It would not do to look like a blessed albino billy goat). Sighing with that reassurance, he waved her away. Back of his hand to his forehead, he flung himself upon his cot and contemplated living out his life with his beauty disfigured.

As it happened, Mrs. Younge was correct. His hair did turn compleatly white. By the time that came to pass, his opinion on the look had improved. He rather favoured it. Even as he hobbled about his sickroom, he believed that it lent him a distinguished air. It would also serve his new identity. He plucked a new name as if from the air—a name of substance. (When it came to him, he believed that the entire appellation sprang from his fertile imagination alone.)

As for his history, he believed it was best not to claim to be a member of the military. He might be found out. His hand flew reassuringly to his neck. Being hung was a terrible end; the only thing worse was being thrown into prison. England was fast running out of cells for his felons. They were tossing them into decommissioned ships that now lined the Thames. To be consigned to Newgate would have been test enough. To be cast into a flea-ridden, rat-infested, prison ship bobbing on the tide was a fate worse than death. Newspapers claimed that the moans of those consigned there could be heard for miles.

No, he must not chance being found out.

He would not dare impersonate an officer. However, lying about once being an army officer could not possibly be illegal. That way, he would not lose the cachet of service, but would have no fear of a death sentence. Indeed, he was quite pleased with himself, happy in the knowledge that he would never be recognised under his new persona. He was almost silly with anticipation, blowing kisses at Mrs. Younge and vowing this time he would not be outwitted.

Each night Wickham sat locked away in his lodgings (contriving the nuances of his new name), the same call wafted from up the street night after night.

With every watch trudging by his window, lanterns in hand and cutlasses on their sides, they would cry their hourly assessment.

"One o'clock on a rainy night and all's well."

That was what they said; that was not what he heard. It was a taunt that in the county of Derbyshire and in the Manor of Pemberley, all was well.

He would not rest until he put an end to it.

The Conjugal Crop

Mr. Darcy regretted the week's time lost from his wife and children. However, having time in the saddle without those sweet interruptions that a husband and father could not turn away, he had been able to resolve the many hitches, snags, delays and hindrances that regularly hampered the smooth operation of the many ventures taking place upon Pemberley's land. When Mr. Darcy hied for home, he left several servitors and lessees wondering why he had not tarried. The sun was high. When the great man took leave with such haste, they knew he had good reason.

Such was the case.

Whilst addressing the problems presented by anarchists and poachers, he had ample time to contemplate the common belief that a husband should not be altogether forthcoming with his wife. His wife, he knew, was above all others in understanding and compassion. He only withheld information from her when he believed it might cause her harm. After all, it was his duty to protect her.

Hence, he concluded that what had come to pass in London, in Lady Howgrave's carriage, was beyond his control, therefore he could not fault his behaviour. His actions had been forced by circumstances and therefore, unavoidable. If his wife did not agree wholeheartedly, that would be most unfortunate. However, in some fortuities, a gentleman must follow his own conscience. That was his position on the matter.

Unfettered by self-reproach, Darcy dug his heels into Blackjack's flanks and headed for home.

Despite the begrimed state of his boots, he took the main staircase (leaving a bit of Pemberley dust upon each step). It would have been his choice to have passed through the brushing room before seeking his wife, but once the decision was made to go to her, an urgency had overcome him. With ever-increasing haste, he had gone from dining parlour to sitting room in search of her. Servants stood silently awaiting his bidding, but he did not inquire after her. He was on a particular mission and, somehow, that meant finding his wife himself.

Passing mahogany and satinwood wainscoting, walls of stamped and gilded leather, he took the oak staircase two steps at a time until he reached the children's nursery. Drapes of yellow damask bathed the room in sunlight.

Bingley's son played with Geoff, each trying to toot their horn louder than the other. Oblivious to the noise, Janie and Jane's youngest daughter sat before a dollhouse rearranging tiny silver furniture. Sensing Mr. Darcy at the doorway, Margaret Heff looked in his direction. Knowing if his children espied him that their delight would be enjoyed at length, he placed a forefinger to his lips. Margaret nodded.

Mr. Darcy decided to forego looking for Elizabeth in other rooms, holding out hope that she anticipated him in the bedchamber.

When at last he opened that door, his heart was disappointed. The room was awash in shadows. He stood at the doorway momentarily, attempting to decide whether to stay and wait, or continue to seek his wife through the many rooms he had yet to investigate. (There were drawing rooms, dressing-rooms, painted halls, several libraries and a chapel yet to search.) Before he decided to withdraw, some nascent thought bid him stay. As he stepped into the room, he had to allow time for his eyes to become accustomed to the darkness. That did not suit him. Concealment was not part of the setting he had traced in his mind's eye for their conversation. If he was to speak openly, it must be in a well-lit room. He walked to a window, his footfalls echoing in the emptiness as he did.

Drawing back the drape, he gazed onto the lawn. He had hoped to see his wife below, strolling amongst the rose beds. He saw no one, not even a groundsman. His gaze, however, was arrested by the sight of a whorl of dust. It announced a rider coming up the lane. He decided then that the discourse he meant to engage in with his wife must be set momentarily aside. First, he would learn the reason why a rider came with such haste to his door. He dropped the drape. In that new darkness, he became quite conscious that he was not alone.

Indeed, he was not.

A caped figure stepped towards him from the shadows of the opposing wall. So sudden was the movement (and such was the menace of the hood), he looked about for a weapon. A poker stood next to the fireplace and Mr. Darcy strode decisively in that direction. He prepared himself to seize it and bludgeon the intruder. In fortune, he stepped towards the fireplace without taking his eye from the figure approaching him.

A chin was raised beneath the cape and the hood fell back, thus revealing the trespasser to be none other than his wife. He came to an abrupt halt, looking at her with questioning eyes. Recognition at hand, Elizabeth's fingers took the ends of the tie at her neck and pulled them loose. The heavy cape dropped to the floor. Her gaze was coy, a smile beckoned him.

To him, it was as if undraped Venus had risen thither from the sea. She, however, was not naked Venus—or altogether naked. She was nude, save for her feet and calves. They alone were adorned. Indeed, she wore only a well-shined pair of riding boots. They were dark brown—the same colour as her hair.

He lowered his eyes—but only momentarily. He was confounded. He steadied himself for what (and he most certainly knew not what) was to come.

With great deliberation, she placed her hand on one hip. Unbeknownst to her, her movement caused a slow undulation of her right breast. Her husband was so mesmerised by that particular motion, he did not see that her other hand held a crop.

When she slapped it hard against the side of her boot, he dropped to one knee.

The Sins of Gentlemen

Juliette had selected the equipage she would have take her to Darcy's house that night with great care. The laudaulet had a single seat.

When Darcy followed her to the carriage, she settled herself directly in the middle of that seat. Thus he had wedge in next her, leaving them sitting thigh to thigh. She cast off her shawl, exposing bare shoulders and remarkable cleavage. She dipped her chin and turned her head a bit askew (as that was her most fetching pose). Darcy, however, did not remove his hat nor relinquish his walking stick.

Then, she asked him, "You received my missive."

It was not actually a question. When engaged in a seduction, Juliette liked to make statements, rather than inquiries. Darcy gave her a curt nod. He had not appeared especially welcoming, but she knew that hauteur was his general mien. Indeed, the man seemed incapable of effusiveness. However, he had escorted her to her carriage and joined her there. That, above anything else, meant that she had his favour.

Regrettably, she had been unable to provoke him to speak beyond his first floundering questions. His disconcertion was quite unusual—and therefore, all the more enticing.

She said breathlessly, "You came to me!"

"I believe," he said solemnly. "You came to me."

She did not correct him. They both knew that he had been in Derbyshire and was then in town. She had crossed a few streets; he had crossed the country. It pleased her no end to know that he had (whatever moral machinations he had employed to excuse being there). Not attaining his compleat capitulation, she moved flawlessly to her second design. It was called "feint and beg poor English." This, it goes without saying, was accompanied by an avid fluttering of her eyelashes.

"Do forgive my English. I find that when I am distraught, my *grammaire*...."

"Of course," was his reply.

She observed a very familiar expression overspreading his countenance. It was a subtle (and uninviting) shield of reserve. His emotional withdrawal could be followed by his physical disappearance in a trice. If she was to succeed with her seduction, she knew she must move the conversation forward with great haste. Therefore, with unimaginable impertinence, she reached out and clasped the brim of his hat. Before he could stop her, she gracefully removed it from his head and set it upon the seat behind her. Instinctively, he reached out. But she caught his hand in hers. At last they were sequestered and unbothered by the prying eyes of reproof. He was hers.

As she gazed into his eyes, she thought she witnessed the same paroxysm of puissance that had always driven her mad with desire.

"You are here now," she whispered. "That is all that matters."

"I require the immediate return of my hat," he said stiffly.

Wanting to scream at him to forget his bloody hat, she contained her pique. She clasped his hand evermore firmly in hers.

With subdued urgency, she said, "I beg your indulgence, for I could not see yours eyes. To speak as we must—tête-à-tête—I must see your eyes. Forgive me? *Oui?*"

He said, "Am I to deduce that you want to escape your marriage?"

His directness was maddening. Looking away, she touched her cheek with the tips of her fingers.

Wincing, she said, "I fear nothing has changed."

It was not entirely theatrics, just embellishment. She feared subtlety would be for naught.

He reacted with far greater ferocity than she had anticipated. Indeed, his moderately constipated expression turned so angry that it was a test not to flee. Her mistreatment was not a charade, nor was it particularly dire. Above most women, she had the resources to leave Howgrave. What she refused to do was leave him without reimbursement for her time, and most certainly, her use as a whipping post. She wanted Howgrave's money, his home, his dignity. She wanted to exact revenge and she knew just how to get it. Mr. Darcy was one step ahead of her. Regrettably for her, it was down the wrong path.

His ire barely in check, he said, "Under that presumption, I have this day spoken to my solicitor. Should you desire that course of action, I have charged him with taking those measures necessary to see that you are spirited out of England. All that is required is your silence."

Darcy was not one to preen, but he seemed pleased with his efficiency. It would take a great deal of tact to convince him that his diligence was not to be obliged. Her tone was delicate, her accent more distinct.

"*Oui, mon cheri, Merci, merci!* How can I ever thank you!" she gushed.

Before he could bestow assurances that no bother attended his actions (as gentlemen are required to offer), she placed a forefinger against his lips. He stopped speaking directly. It was quite obvious that Mr. Darcy was unused to being shushed.

"My husband has long suspected that I might leave him. This last souvenir," she touched her cheek, "convinced me I dare not try escape."

"He threatened your life?"

"*Non, à vrai dire,* he implied a far worse fate."

Her hands trembled, her chin quivered. A tear stung the corner of her eye, but she daubed it away with her middle finger.

"*Mon cheri*, Darcy, I do not think I can bear it. His threats were vulgar, *tres vulgaire.*"

"If you do not choose to make away, what can be done?"

Her indecision tried his patience, this she knew. He had little time for what some might believe to be a womanly weakness.

"I have but one avenue for escape," she said urgently. "It is why I came to you *en secret*. I have signed a marital agreement with my husband. I cannot leave the marriage unless I give him a son."

"As repellent as that might be for you, I see no other recourse...."

"He is *impuissant*—impotent."

Pulling at his cuffs, Darcy first frowned and then replied, "A conundrum...."

"He can become impassioned only through delivering the whip," With a great shuddering sigh, she said, "I have no more of that to give."

Although it was too dim to see it, she knew Darcy's colour had deepened. Time was at hand for her to put forth her request. In preparation, she flung herself against his chest.

With all due urgency, she repeated, "I have no more to give! I must have a child to end it. I need you! I need you to father my child."

His reply was, in its way, quite succinct.

"Whot?"

⌒he Course of True Love

Darcy had not actually said, "I surrender," to his wife, but it was implied as he fell to one knee before her.

He made no avowals, no utterances of any kind. How ungovernable his desire was implied in all that followed.

That he had not, in fact, fallen prostrate before her, he attributed to his stern self-control (and admittedly, a bit of sheer luck). In a failed attempt to compose himself, he struggled to his feet, placed one hand upon his waist and cleared his throat. He saw her toss the crop aside, but was still too discombobulated to realise or appreciate that she had. Indeed, he was not altogether certain what had come to pass.

As he was much in want of composure, it would not have been to his advantage to allow his gaze to linger upon her naked figure, but he did. Her hair was loose. One long tress fell from her shoulder and, with unstudied grace, circled her breast. With every breath she took (her respirations were deep and many), the one curl promised him untold raptures. Indeed, he stood before her overtaken by unblinking lust. So piercing was his gaze and so obvious his desire, she lowered her eyes under the scrutiny.

When she did return his gaze, he had lowered his chin and began taking slow measured steps in her direction. His was a formidably ardent démarche, but she held her ground. As she was intent on not fleeing, she was quite unwitting that he had begun to shed his coat and waistcoat as he crossed the floor. As thither he came, her early brazenness began to wane. By the time he reached her, she raised a trembling hand as if to fend off the indocile love she had just so unabashedly provoked.

Slowly, he took her hand in his, and placed it against his heart. When he did, their spreading fingers intertwined. Her soul, so injured by loss, surrendered to the incontrovertibility of his love. She did not speak. Her expression went limpid with adoration and abandon. It said all.

Her most fervent desire was to be kissed, but to her great mortification, she began to babble, explaining her scandalous behaviour.

"I feared you might need encouragement for I have given you good cause to doubt me...."

His fingers lightly caressed her ribs then slipped around to her spine, quieting her. She did not alter her position, but beneath his hand her very being emitted a frisson of ignited hunger.

"Whatever you want of me, Lizzy, I am here."

Now that he was there, it was not the time to remind him that of late he had not been.

Wrapping herself in his arms, she bid him only to embrace her. He was not content with that. Hence, with tender purposefulness, he swept her up and betook her and her boots onto the bed. Her passion renewed, she fell back in naked recumbence onto the counterpane. Coquettishly, she pointed a toe of one boot towards her husband. He obliged her by catching the heel of her boot and sliding it from her foot. Whilst he did the same from the other, she teased the front of his shirt with her bare toes until he snared them and playfully pretended to bite them.

"I now understand your admiration for my boots. My mind on the subject has certainly altered...."

As he cast her other boot aside, she continued to trail her toes down his body.

She replied, "Whereas you so seldom err, I take no delight in correcting you. But on this point, I must."

Her toes tickling the front of his breeches, she said, "My fetish is not for your boots. My interest is with the man who wears those boots."

She rose to her knees and whispered into his ear, "I admire how his knees rise from them, sinewy thews surging upwards...."

As her hand slid to his leg, she continued to whisper, but more urgently, "Impenetrable trees, crowned by a stanchion of such measure...."

Never, in all his recollections, had she been so explicit. There was a sudden disinterest in nuzzling and languid strokes. He clasped her thigh, tossed her upon her back, and allowed her to lay there unmolested by thought or deed for the better part of five seconds.

When he lay the flat of his hand against her abdomen, it trembled.

He whispered, "How many ways can I please you?"

With a specific flick of her eyes, a laughing struggle to release his manhood did ensue—that mirth only to be quelled once it was.

Darcy placed one hand against her face, the other gripped her hip. She gasped.

Lost in the sweet cleave of her flesh, a line of perspiration paraded down his breast bone. He reached shuddering conclusion far too quickly.

Spent, but unsated, he rolled onto his back and emitted a small groan of chagrin.

His wife's hair, her breath, her hips bid him. Turning to her, his hands searched her face, her ears, shoulders, the valleys and the knolls, as if a blind man learning a stranger's identity. Her every feature had long been cast in his mind. He pressed his lips against her neck.

No longer a bridegroom, yet still able to arise to engorgement and achievement unstintingly, Mr. Darcy was yet infused with considerable manly vigour.

Her legs claimed his waist, his hand cupped her buttocks. Undulations, slow and seductive, assuring, reminding, ever encouraging, were enjoyed for the better part of an hour.

Their reward was an afternoon of satisfied slumber in the other's arms.

The Gift

When Darcy awoke, the sun was low. Looking upon his wife, he noticed a dampened strand of hair had stuck to her cheek. With delicate care, he tucked it behind her ear. Directly he drew a bed-cloth above her shoulder lest she catch a chill. He looked upon her lovingly and fancied that the smile on her face was in appreciation of their afternoon's amour.

What had begun as a rather lusty prank (suffused with sufficient quantities of unattended passion and suppressed affection) did erupt into passion as fervent as any new love.

It would be understood then why Mr. Darcy left his wife's bed with great reluctance. However, the recollection of a rider come fast upon their door just prior to their extended encounter, bid him do so.

That decision was reinforced when he saw that Mr. Howard himself stood waiting at the base of the staircase. He did not speak until Mr. Darcy's boots reached the bottom step.

"A rider bearing a package has arrived from London. It was to be delivered to your hands alone, sir." Howard added, "The man said that he was expected."

Mr. Darcy nodded.

He met with the man directly. After the courier took his leave, Darcy emerged from his library. In his right hand, he held a package. No one spoke of the visit, at least not openly. He sent for Hannah.

When Hannah curtsied before him, he said, "When Mrs. Darcy awakes, I would like to speak with her."

It was not Mr. Darcy's habit to make a formal request to speak to his wife.

Mrs. Darcy had not tarried in bed once she had detected Mr. Darcy was no longer there. Hence, Hannah did not have to spend many agonising minutes to give her mistress the master's request. Indeed, she told her forthwith. Witting that something of significance was to occur, Elizabeth hastily donned her favourite blue dressing gown (the one adorned with gold braid) and draped herself impatiently in her favourite chair to await an audience with her husband.

Elizabeth was impatient to see her husband. Her regard for him had never been greater. Given a choice, she would have run to find him and leapt into his arms. Instead, she was forced to wait for him to come to her. She did so hope that whatever momentousness should come to pass, that it would not place undue restraint upon her exhilaration.

Placing a book in her lap, she flipped nervously through its pages as she listened for him.

He entered without knocking and she smiled happily. His countenance upon seeing hers did not alter appreciably, but she thought that she discerned a bit of question in his eyes. Perhaps he too feared that the reinvigoration of their union had been fleeting. He drew a chair near her. Unknowing that he was gauging the shades of her mind (and not bearing unhappy news), she grew solemn. A small pang of foreboding made itself known in the pit of her stomach. He noticed the adjustment of her expression, but spoke not of it.

With rare hesitance, he said, "I truly cannot guess your mind upon this matter. Should I wait, or not come to you at all."

With those words, her countenance grew apprehensive. It was clear to him that he should not have been so frank about his trepidations.

To his surprise, she reached out and placed a reassuring hand upon his knee.

Clearly, his countenance was not the mask of impassivity he had believed. Indeed, she appeared quite unnerved. It was important not to allow the quagmire of fear overtake either of them.

Taking her hand in his, he turned it palm up. Onto her out-stretched palm he placed a small package. Her eyelids fluttered in disconcertion, but he still bid her unwrap it herself. For a reason she could not fathom, it was to be opened by her own hand alone.

It was loosely wrapped. Therefore, when she drew the string, the object unrolled easily and fell face up in her lap.

Her hand flew to her mouth, stifling a cry. Whether it was a lamentation or acclamation, he knew not.

He studied every movement of her hand and each expression that touched her countenance. When she began to weep, he knew not whether he had triumphed or failed. His heart had been in his throat for the duration of this presentation, unknowing if she would admire it or despise it as a reminder of what she wanted to forget. In a moment, the truth revealed itself.

Holding the oval ivory against her breast, she turned to him and whispered, "I have never, never had the privilege of receiving such a dear and treasured gift. I shall admire it all my life."

It was a remarkably good likeness. Indeed, the turn of little William's countenance had been captured almost flawlessly. She beheld it as if a precious stone. When at last her eyes were sated, she took it in both hands and pressed it against her heart. Tears tracked down her cheeks.

Fighting against a most indelicate weep, she cleared her throat and said, "The painter has not quite captured his nose...."

Neither believed that was her true opinion at all.

His voice was mild, mimicking hers, "I quite agree. But taken on the whole, I believe it a tolerable likeness."

"Indeed, do I as well. I am all astonishment that such a truthful rendering could be accomplishment without... without...."

Unable to compleat the sentence, she stopped herself.

She said, "I love it dearly."

She would have asked him whereby the miniaturist had managed to catch their son's image so perfectly, but she recalled a time long past when he had a miniature done of her compleatly from his own recollection. Elizabeth marvelled at her husband's powers of description.

"Done when you were last in London?" she asked.

He nodded.

He explained that he chanced again upon the studio where Gainsborough once worked. (The first time he went there, it had been an impulse—indeed, quite rash.) The second time was entirely purposeful. It was difficult to find. However, he recalled the entry was at the back and through a low door. The old painter was still at work. The man recalled Mr. Darcy too. Darcy had commissioned the man immediately. He then spent several hours perched on a stool, looking on as sketches were made to his precise specifications.

"Then it was not Morland?"

"That man was still much engaged with another royal commission. The painter I employed I have used before—on your likeness. Kimble, I believe. He is quite accomplished."

Looking upon the back, indeed she saw Kimble's signature.

She said, "Perchance we might engage him to make miniatures of all of our children. I should favour setting them in a row upon my dressing table next to yours."

"You have no miniature bearing my likeness," said Darcy.

"Do I not?" she replied pertly. "*Au contraire.*"

The only ivory image of his own countenance he recalled was one taken in his youth. At one time, it sat in a case next to Wickham's.

"Yes, I recall it. It was taken above fifteen years ago...." said he.

She replied, "Not that one—a different one entirely."

Now that she admitted that she had it, she knew he would not be satisfied until she produced it for him to criticise. And there was much about it for a gentleman to protest.

She said, "It was done to exceedingly explicit directions."

"I am sure I shall despise it."

"Indeed, you shall," she agreed. "It was done by Morland."

"He, who eschews trivial commissions?"

A smile tugged at the corner of her mouth. To him that signified a furthering of playfulness they had shared just that afternoon. That observation was a great relief. He began to believe that they had truly experienced a renewal of spirits. As she continued to speak of the miniature, he looked upon her with unbridled affection.

She told him, "Morland took it at my particular request. It is quite... dashing. It might even be described as indecorous."

Her expression was a bit mischievous and he was altogether uncertain whether she had such a miniature of him at all—and if she did, just what she had imagined. A frown attached itself to the ridge between his eyebrows as he considered whether or not it was true, and if it was, just how explicit it could be.

He did not like his disconcertion on display. Imagining her describing the contours of any part of his person to Sir Robert Morland was displeasing enough. It occurred to him that he had never actually gazed upon his own reflection. (If they frolicked by the looking glass now hidden beneath their bed, he gazed upon it to admire her form, not his own.)

She laughed and pinched his knee, telling him that hers was a tease. His relief was palpable.

He said, "I knew full well you could not have kept such a work from me."

"Oh my love, it does exist. It simply is not as indecorous as I implied. Indeed, I should like you to see it. I had it painted after your journey across the channel. As much as I love the one in the portrait hall, I longed for an image I could keep near my breast; one to gaze upon at my leisure."

Clasping William's miniature in her hand, she stood, announcing, "I shall no longer test your patience. Come!"

Darcy allowed Elizabeth to lead him towards her dressing room. Hannah was within laying out several combs and brushes side by side, with soldierly precision. She hastily withdrew when she observed that Mr. Darcy was with her mistress. Elizabeth repaired directly to her table. He saw no miniature then, nor had he before. She sat William's likeness carefully on the table top, allowing her to open a small drawer.

She removed a key. With that key, she opened another, hidden drawer. From it, she withdrew a small, paper-wrapped object. Carefully, tenderly, she unfolded the paper. She placed a small, flat piece of ivory in her hand and held her palm in Darcy's direction.

To his great happiness, his face did not adorn some undraped cupid. The image was quite as tradition dictated—except for one thing. He recognised his face, his hair, and even his sideburns. However, his wife had made one, nearly obscene, omission.

It would not do. He looked at her.

"That is not me," he said with finality. "It is an invention."

The visage upon the soft, white surface was as she saw him—without his collar and cravat.

"Indeed, it is your neck. It is particularly strong and muscular," she insisted. "See, I cannot get my two hands about it...."

"You have uncommonly small hands. Besides, are not thick-necked men believed to be stupid?"

Now a bit impatient that he did not see himself as did she, she argued, "That is thick-witted, thick-*witted*."

It was then that she realised he was repaying her tease.

She then said, "Who would know the nature of your neck better than your wife?"

He had no answer. Had he chosen to argue, he might have suggested that Goodwin (who saw to his shave every morn) knew his neck, but he did not care to further the discussion. Elizabeth, however, did want to further the point. Slipping into his lap, she pulled the end of his tie, loosening it. Turning back the collar a bit, she kissed him there.

"The painting caught your image perfectly. Your strong chin, fine nose, beguiling eyes, and yes, your exceedingly handsome neck. It is remarkable for its strength."

Convinced of her sincerity, if not her facts, he whispered against her hair, "As you are disposed to vex your husband, I shall not deny you that pleasure."

"Yes," she said. "You deny me nothing...."

Their discourse that day had served several purposes. William's miniature gave permanence to their lost son. Moreover, they spoke of their tragedy openly. The abyss of melancholy was avoided. Those obstacles, once so heavy with regret and pain, had been leapt passed within the confines of a few brief moments—and went unremarked upon.

The outcome to this conversation followed the path of many before them. Verbal banter often led to more amorous inclinations. He did not, however, take her there in her dressing room. He took her in his arms and carried her to their bed. Pressing her back against the mattress, he interlaced his fingers in hers.

It was not he, but his wife who bid, "Let us make a child tonight."

The afterglow of passion did not wane.

Their steady attachment, of late a bit tremulous, was once again as it should be—solidified by love and consecrated with passion. However, he did not allow smugness to overcome good sense. His Elizabeth had returned to him, but he knew well that there was no armour against fate.

Indeed, Death lays his icy hand on kings.

*W*hot?

*D*arcy's response to Juliette's importunacy that night in London was said as a question, but was offered more in the exclamatory.

"Whot?" he repeated.

Juliette had never seen him quite so ruffled. As expected, his immediate response had been to retreat into conspicuous decorum. It was imperative that she keep him engaged.

"My design is impeccable," she said hurriedly. "I have thought of nothing else."

Thrust and parry was essential in a seduction. Desperate straits demanded desperate moves. After so bold a move, she knew she must reveal acute vulnerability. Placing the back of her hand to her lips, she stifled what was nothing less than a mortified cry.

He seemed unmoved, "Your suggestion is impossible. It is also, I might add, an insult to me as a gentleman."

Placing a restraining hand upon his forearm, she pointed out, "There are few true gentlemen in England."

"Be that as it may...." he replied.

She hurried to coax him lest he withdraw from her compleatly.

"Any number of *noblisse* would be *déliriant* to come to my bed. I ask you for this favour, for you have sired sons. If you open your heart to me in my hour of need, it would be without ensuing connection or regret."

His very masculine presence brought certain reminiscences to mind.

Foremost amongst them was the pleasure by lying with a well-timbered man who knows how to wield his sword. It had been far too long....

However, he did not appear to waver. His quaint notion of honour had always intrigued her.

He sniffed, "Such a suggestion is not only impertinent; I question your sanity in asking it."

Launching her final volley, she said, "I am swept away by confuse and alarm! What am I to do? I must have a child, yet I cannot bear another stranger's hands upon me. I would rather die!"

Whilst she engaged in her entreaty, he leaned towards her. Was it compassion in his eyes? Or, pray, desire? She leaned towards him, her lips but inches from his.

In one last gasp, she whispered, "I implore you. It would mean nothing to you, but everything to me."

Before her lips quite brushed his, he snaked one long arm around her and captured his hat.

"I bid you adieu," he said, opening the door.

She grasped his sleeve, not to restrain, but to say, "Do not say farewell, but *au revoir*—until we meet again."

Then, he was gone.

The brisk night infused with that of her carriage, but did not overwhelm the aroma he had left behind. She waited a moment. When he did not reappear, she told her driver to walk on.

As the carriage lurched forward, she bethought her intrigue's success. She refused to believe that her bid was a failure. To her mind, Darcy's indignation was no higher than that of a virgin whose corset strings were fiddled with. He was in no way an impetuous man. (Was he, she had little doubt they would have consecrated the affair in her carriage.) She knew that he would brood upon the matter before deciding his course of action. She prayed that he would not contemplate the matter for long.

Her great hope had been that she would secure him that very night. Her womb was ripe. It had been her certitude that once alone (truly alone), their prior connection could be reignited. However, were repeated couplings necessary, she would not object.

Although she did not believe all was lost, to come so close to her quarry only have him elude her was a great disappointment. In truth, her pride had been sorely wounded that he had not leapt upon her at the first opportunity. She had been forced to prey upon his honour, their past intimacy, his pride, and promised no future inconvenience. Short of climbing into his bed, she had no notion of what more she could do.

She knew one thing. It was not over.

$\mathcal{C}$loset Canoodle

It was not life as it once was (for that could never be), but it was far better than it had been.

Her husband's gift was far beyond William's remembrance. In its way, it bound them more firmly as a family. Once Elizabeth had made arrangements for Kimble to take likenesses of the twins, she placed William's miniature lovingly away in the drawer next to Darcy's. It was her design that neither be observed or damaged by other parties within their house—for Pemberley was often full of company.

Worst of the lot was Lydia.

Having not compleatly enjoyed Elizabeth's company (nor squeezed a penny from her purse) at Longbourne, Lydia and her brood made a precipitous call on her at Pemberley. Elizabeth refused to be put in a pother, although Lydia did what she could to test her. Indeed, she arrived at the Darcys' door complaining about her children and begging poverty. Even before they sat down to dinner, she began inveigling Mr. Darcy. She was determined to cajole him into loosening his grip on the monies he had set aside for her sons. When he refused her, she turned to Elizabeth. Both Darcys remained amiable, but steadfast, in their contention that the funds would not be touched until each of the boys had attained their majority.

"But I need it now!" she whined.

Elizabeth reminded her, "It is not yours, Lydia."

No matter how much money Elizabeth gave Lydia, it never quite found its way into serving her family's wants and needs. Instead, it was laid out in payment to various dressmakers and corsetieres. Because of that, what Elizabeth did give Lydia was transferred directly to Major Kneebone. Knowing only of her fifty a year from her father, he had been appalled to learn that his wife applied to her more affluent sisters for more money. They could subsist quite handily upon his income. Regrettably, Kneebone seemed altogether lost as to how to please Lydia or bring her to heel. Boyishly earnest in all things, Elizabeth could not help but pity the man. Her own husband was less sympathetic. Seeing a full grown man, an army officer, compleatly emasculated by his wife rendered Mr. Darcy quite without comment.

There had been an unspoken agreement between Elizabeth and Jane to share the joy (and the burden) of family visits. When Jane had the questionable pleasure of a visit from Bingley's sisters and their spouses, they were all invited to stay for a time at Pemberley as well. Lydia was also parcelled out in the same manner. Upon occasion, these visits overlapped. When they did, chaos reigned.

Inevitably, Lydia's sons ran wild. This kept Elizabeth on constant guard over not just the twins, but all of the other children. Lydia's oldest boy, Georgie, had grown taller and meaner. He had been off at school, and his time out from under his mother's ineffectual control merely coarsened his language and taught him crueller tricks. Elizabeth chose not to relate every trespass the boy committed to Darcy, lest her husband's already poor opinion of Lydia's family be forever compromised.

To curtail Georgie's mischief, Elizabeth installed her wiliest footmen in each of the children's rooms. The boy did not hesitate to deliver a severe kick to the odd-man's shin, thereupon running away from him and cackling like the devil's spawn. Through a combination of threats and bribery (and once taking a good hold of the boy's earlobe), Elizabeth managed to contain Georgie and his rampages to Pemberley's top floor and the garden. When she learnt that he pulled up an entire bed of spring bulbs and flung them one by one at the dogs, she went looking for him.

During this rigorous search, Elizabeth chanced upon some strange noises coming from a linen closet. Under the belief that she had found her culprit, she put her ear to the door. The voices within were not those of children. Indeed, it sounded as if something more amorous was at play. There were strict rules forbidding romantic associations between servants. The ash-boy and a young chambermaid had been exchanging glances for a fortnight. It was quite likely they were now exchanging kisses on the sly.

Mrs. Darcy took a moment to decide whether to report the infraction to Mr. Howard. It was he who took care of such matters. Quite probably, the osculating couple would be dismissed. Hence, she decided to intervene instead. Young lovers should not to be immoderately censured. However, any young woman in Pemberley's employ had to be protected. She would remind the two of that.

Rapping lightly upon the door, she hoped not to startle, simply constrain, whatever was under way. Just as she placed her hand upon the doorknob, she recognized a very annoying laugh. In her disgust, Elizabeth flung open the door so soundly that the noise reverberated down the corridor. Astonishment flooded her senses, leaving her in speechless indignation.

Half-dressed and giggling, Lydia and Sir Winton Beecher were in a most compromising position. More specifically, Lydia had a leg around Beecher's bulging corset and his nose had been buried in her bosom. When startled, he looked up, exposing Lydia's breasts (which looked then like two collops of rolled bread ready for the oven). Elizabeth instantly concluded both would do well to leave off desserts for the foreseeable future. When Lydia saw her sister's horrified expression, she was not chastened. Rather, she began to guffaw. Making no attempt to curb her laughter, every peal grew louder and louder.

"Hush yourself, Lydia!" demanded Elizabeth, "You sound like a village Neddy!"

To quiet the duo lest every one in the house learnt of their misconduct, Elizabeth closed the door. Rightfully, she harboured the belief that they would clothe themselves. After all, spouses and children were all about. Indeed, Elizabeth heard rustling of clothing and then, she was quite certain, another round of lurid moans. Affronted, she listened again and heard more kissing. With her ear pressed against the door, an enormous clamour erupted from within. Aghast, she flung open the door only to discover, not only had they not repaired themselves, they had broken a shelf.

Huffy as the second cook at Tuesday lunch, Elizabeth found herself wagging her finger at them.

"I am shocked, Lydia! How dare you defile my home with such indecency?"

A long-held apprehension had suddenly came to Elizabeth. The night of the Pemberley ball—it must have been Lydia! It was Lydia who scurried across the lawn to Beecher's coach that night. Had they been conducting themselves adulterously since then? She dared not imagine. Mrs. Darcy had never been troubled by a tendency to swoon. However, light-headedness overtook her, sending her stumbling backward.

Lydia snorted another laugh, but this time her sister's expression seemed to curb her. She pressed her fist against her lips to stop herself. Regrettably, she did not silence herself before Major Kneebone heard the commotion. He arrived thither, just in time to catch the lovers still engaged within the closet. Seeing his wife in a state of undress, the full brunt of the situation hit Kneebone and he made a grab for where his sword might have hung had he been in full uniform.

Beecher (taking the premise that the best defence was a good offensive strike) roared, "What is this disturbance! Leave us be! I demand it!"

"Unhand her man, lest I run you through," Kneebone demanded impotently.

"Ha!" laughed Beecher.

Lydia sniggered, "Oh, boo, Hughie, you haven't your sword. How shall you run anyone through with your watch?"

Propitiously, Elizabeth had regained her head, for the commotion caused all the children to come running to see what the matter was. With Beecher and Lydia in an undressed state, she knew the older children might deduce the indecorous doings. Moreover, none of the children needed to hear the threats to life and limb.

With Lydia unrepentant, Kneebone saw no course to regain his honour but to call Beecher out.

He said, "I shall see you at dawn. Name your weapon!"

"Hush up, you two," hissed Elizabeth.

Both disgusted beyond measure and determined to keep the children out of it, she put out her hands to corral them and called for help. In consequence, nurses, footmen, and the limping odd-man were right on the children's heels. That was, of course, a double-edged sword. If the children were unmindful of the lascivious juxtaposing of the half-naked bodies within the closet, the servants were not. Elizabeth did her best to curb the madness, nonetheless.

Once maids and offspring were soothed and back up the hallway, Elizabeth turned her wrath upon the adults.

"I am sickened and astonished at you all. Major Kneebone, I understand your outrage, but I cannot condone talk of violent retribution in this house."

Pushing him off down the hall, she turned to Lydia who seemed not quite so amused as she had been.

"Lydia, I wish I could say I am shocked, but indeed, I am hardly so."

Turning to Beecher who was hastily struggling into his breeches, she advised, "You sir, are no gentleman and my husband shall speak to you of it. However, it is my considered opinion that you not engage in another duel. For, if we are to predict the outcome of this one by your last, you have more to lose than your standing."

With stately precision, Elizabeth left them to their folly.

Marching down the hallway, she repaired to her dressing room to collect herself. Directly, Mr. Darcy learnt of the unseemly doings and came to find his wife. She appeared pale. Indeed, she was still trembling with anger.

"Pray, are you unwell?"

She smiled weakly and shook her head. He encouraged her to move aside so he could perch next to her on the chaise. First pressing the back of his fingers to her forehead, he then clasped her hand. Tenderly, he reached out and brushed her hair from her forehead.

She insisted, "I am merely vexed at the unseemliness to which our family has been subjected. No doubt my hair is quite out of curl because of it...."

It was well and good that Mr. Darcy came to his wife's side before addressing those person's responsible for her distress. Had he not, his wrath would have been fully employed (and more than mere recriminations might have been committed by the master of the house). He could barely contain his anger as it was. It was reprehensible to him that his wife was forced to not only witness such a lewd activity, but she also had to intervene. Upon this occasion, his mask of impassiveness forsook him entirely. Although he spoke softly, his ire was quite obvious. She patted his hand.

"I am certain at any moment my sister shall be here to beg my forgiveness," she said—only half in jest.

"Shall you give it?"

"Not until she makes a better show at Sunday services."

If he hoped to ascertain whether her upset had passed by surreptitiously feeling her pulse, she was not fooled.

Said she, "I am quite well. You should know that I am of hardier stock than that."

"I was told that you swooned. You never swoon," he fretted.

"My swoon—had I one—was due only to the vagaries of wretched relations," she assured him.

His displeasure did not ebb.

She reminded him, "I have had the distasteful task of exposing a pair of rutting swine in the second storey linen closet. You, my dearest, have a more daunting obligation."

She then gave him a more explicit account of what came to pass. Repugnance fought anger as his foremost emotion. From his expression, she could not tell whether his thoughts remained upon the event she just described, or that he realised what duty demanded he must do.

Hence, she asked, "Shall you tell Bingley of his brother-in-law's infidelity?"

He said, "I shall speak to Major Kneebone before Bingley. Of the many injured parties, I believe his sensibilities have been wounded far more than Caroline's."

A thought struck him, "Neither of the lovers have serious designs on the other...?"

She shook her head, for she did not know. She then spoke of what she hoped to be true.

"I should think that their affair is nothing but a fancy of convenience."

The adulterers did not even have the excuse of love—Elizabeth was sure of that. Regardless, it was necessary to ask Lydia to leave Pemberley post-haste. Such animalistic behaviour could not be condoned, most especially when the eyes of their children were there to witness it.

When told of her banishment, Lydia pretended great contrition. Clearly, it had come to her that Major Kneebone might not take her back.

She whined, "Where shall I go, Lizzy?"

"If your husband does not cast you out, you have a fine house in Chelsea," Elizabeth told her. "I fear not only for your marriage, Lydia, but your soul as well. You betray your husband with all the insouciance of a harlot. If you do not alter your course...."

Lydia put her hand up, palm out, saying, "Spare me your lectures, Lizzy. What do you know of want, you with your riches? What do you know of unhappiness?"

"Unhappiness is not solely the domain of the poor, if indeed you think yourself poor. We all suffer misfortune and sorrow," Elizabeth reminded her.

Lydia cried, "I have suffered too! You forget that I have lost my dear husband...."

Elizabeth interrupted, "And an admirable one he was. You should now hope that you have not lost your second through your own stupidity."

Having had her fill of reproach, Lydia did not attempt to tarry. In a half day's time, she had laden a coach with her children, nurses, lunch baskets and luggage. Major Kneebone, however, was nowhere to be found. Once she realised that he might truly have left her, remorse had begun to bother Lydia. She waffled over whether she dared face him at home or hie to the safety of Longbourne.

"As you wish," said Elizabeth dispassionately. "When you decide, tell the coachman."

Elizabeth's only true fear was that Major Kneebone might have chased Beecher down. They soon learnt that Beecher had betaken himself back to Bingley's house, no doubt cowering under a bed fearing the Major might to do him mortal harm.

The truth of the affair was not long kept from the Bingleys. It came from Lydia, however, not Elizabeth. She wanted Jane's sympathy before Elizabeth could muddy the way. Finding some good in everyone was Jane's special gift. It was far more difficult to excuse Lydia's impenitence than the adultery. Jane was perplexed.

"If one was denied love, it could be understood. With such a devoted husband as Major Kneebone, we cannot reason why," Jane said. "Lydia is Lydia and we cannot ask more of her than she has to give."

As they waved their youngest sister on her way, Elizabeth told Jane, "I care little of what befalls Sir Beecher, but I do not want Major Kneebone to be hung for it."

It was all quite troubling.

Elizabeth said, "It is as if one sees a monstrous storm upon the horizon and can do nothing to prevent its destruction."

$\mathscr{C}$hatter Amongst the Chaps

As she weighed whether to stay in town and await Darcy, or go to Derbyshire after him, Juliette sought diversion. In her husband's circles, this was difficult.

The single gentleman within his coterie of political cronies who was not entirely in want of wit was Alistair Thomas. It was he who dared tease her about Jacobin leanings when she complained of their tiresome tirades over the national debt.

Walking on the periphery of yet another political meeting, she pouted, "The only wager of any interest is laid upon whether that tiresome Prinny shall be murdered before he can wrench the throne from the mad King's cold, grasping hands."

Looking fretfully about, Alistair attempted to caution her.

With urgency, he said, "I implore you. Your French birth makes you suspect by these madmen. They see inkle-weavers as assassins and old women as spies. Your ladyship must take care upon whose toes she treads."

Certain of her place, she replied haughtily, "I am a French noblewoman who escaped the guillotine. I am much beloved in England and can speak as I want without fear of reproach from peer or ironmonger."

He gave a low bow, apologising, "Of course. I am in want of nothing but your safety. If my remarks were unwelcome, please blame my apprehension on your behalf.

As gallantry was sorely wanting in all quarters just then, Juliette allowed him to grovel a bit and then forgave him. Once again, she took his arm and he escorted her out of earshot of the tedious speeches. As the evening progressed, his limp became more pronounced.

"Your wound must trouble you," she said with unusual forthrightness. "I believe that your sacrifice to your country has not been well-rewarded. We should all be in your debt."

"I allow that fallacy," he said with a laugh. "In truth, mine was a trifle scuffle, nothing more."

"Indeed?"

He nodded, but did not elaborate, only saying, "The telling of it would take longer than the event itself."

In the political sphere, wit and self-deprecation were rarely seen singly, much less inhabiting one being. She was very nearly charmed.

She smiled, "I would believe it far more likely that you were a casualty of a lover's quarrel than a battle."

Feigning great offence, he gasped, "Your Ladyship, how could you believe that of a gentleman?"

Due to rising tensions, Howgrave had banned her from dining with her previous circle of friends. Alistair's company was, indeed, the best she could manage. His rank was several tiers beneath hers and his flattery was hardly ingenious. Her esteem of late had been a bit battered, so his pretty words were well taken. It pleased her most particularly to have a flirtation with him right beneath her husband's nose. Howgrave was easily riled. Any hint of waywardness on her part would have enraged him. She truly doubted her husband had the audacity to draw a weapon on someone. Nonetheless, the prospect of bloodshed had inflamed many an affair. The possibility that her stubby husband might stick a dagger between Alistair's shoulder blades made an intrigue with him all the more titillating.

No doubt Alistair was quite witting of the precariousness of such an infatuation. By speaking to her in such a loose fashion, he could lose more than his situation. Not otherwise occupied, she meant to keep his interest keen. To do so, she employed every device known to her (a considerable arsenal) to keep him at arm's length, but allow him to believe that he might just beguile her yet.

Eyes cast down, fan fluttering, she said, "I understand that my husband is in want of you to go to Derbyshire. I shall miss your company."

"What!" he squawked. Clearly surprised, he hastily becalmed himself, saying, "Have you heard something I have not?"

She replied, "It appears that I have."

She had not meant to discompose him so compleatly.

"Am I to be another 'Oliver the Spy'?" he mumbled.

"Pray, not," said she. "Even I am aware that charade did not go well."

"It was an unmitigated disaster," he said, shaking his head.

The political ramifications of sending a spy northward were still reverberating.

Turning to her with great solemnity, he said, "I must speak to Howgrave, for I truly cannot go there. I shall be recognised."

His alteration from *distingué* to discombobulation was astonishingly abrupt. She was amused.

"Why would you fear being recognised?" she inquired.

"I have relation in Derbyshire. They might guess my mission."

He then altered the discourse with great fluidity.

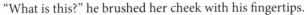

"What is this?" he brushed her cheek with his fingertips.

That was a great impertinence. The sudden tenderness, however, touched her.

She said, "I stumbled gaining the carriage."

"And this?" he pointed to another, less obvious bruise upon her chin.

"I stumbled gaining the carriage."

"What of this lovely purple one just here?"

"I stumbled gaining the carriage."

"I thought perhaps you stumbled against your husband's hand."

With a heavy sigh, she admitted the obvious, "He is a beast."

"How can you stay with him?"

She said with prim cynicism, "I have solaced my wretchedness with a sumptuous new carriage and the promise of a house in Manchester Square."

"Surely, a woman of your *savoir-vivre* would not be without a design of some sort," he cajoled. "You are far too venturesome."

"I am to give him a child and he is to give me a generous allotment and a...."

"A regular beating?" he bid. "Or is that just a tawdry rumour?"

A chill overtook her. Her countenance did not reflect her apprehension. The care she took not to reveal her discomposure included masking a great revelation. Not only had her husband beaten her in the privacy of their chambers, he must have boasted of it to his friends.

No doubt details of their sexual conduct had been tittered about in every gentleman's club in London. The coarse laughter echoed in her ears even then. His was the worst kind of betrayal—far worse than flagellation, or even the back of his hand. She had never believed Howgrave struck a particularly fine figure, but neither did she expect him to be such a dishonourable wretch.

She had little left in the world but her vanity. Now she was robbed of that as well. The world at large was witting, not only of her humiliation, but the worst of his character. Therefore, she would be unable to pillory him herself.

"It was my intention to give my husband a son, take his money, retire to Marseille, and write my memoirs. If he was generous, it would not be necessary to be explicit. If he was not, I was to recall every scandalous detail of his peculiar peccadilloes."

"Extortion," Alistair smiled.

She corrected him, "Not *extorsion*, mon ami, a *roman à clef*. He would be seen as a buffoon—a laughingstock. He would rue the day he raised a hand to me."

Her voice was flat, emotionless.

In an attempt to raise her spirits, he said, "Such a book would still be well-taken. It might not carry the same weight with those who were witting of his perversions, but their wives would certainly be entertained."

She said dejectedly, "I am left with only one way of escape."

He awaited her elucidation.

"I must birth a child."

Alistair furrowed his brow with engaging inauthenticity.

"Despite his proclivities, surely your husband attends your bed properly. No man could withstand your allurement. No one suggests Howgrave buggers boys."

His sentiments were not expressed with great élan. Seldom, however, were words better timed. She staunched any remarks unbeneficial to her very tenuous situation. Alistair was no naïf. Clearly, he knew of flagellation. To Howgrave, the whip only inflamed his desire, not requited it.

"His diligence often goes unrewarded," she said glumly.

Alistair queried, "Have you considered... a proxy?"

She looked upon him coyly, "Are you offering your services?"

"I dare say that it sounds as if her ladyship has no spate of offers. Unless you enlist a draft, gentlemen may not be aware that the post is vacant."

She said, "Your concern does you credit. Nonetheless, I have chosen a surrogate. As you can imagine, it is a matter of some delicacy."

Juliette was even more determined to have her revenge against Howgrave. Nothing would injure that under-hung weasel's self-possession more than being unmanned by the very repository of aristocratic arrogance, Mr. Darcy of Derbyshire. Granted, she had promised Darcy compleat discretion. However much she was in want of keeping her word to him on that, circumstances had altered. Now it was her all-consuming desire to throw it all (the affair with and child by Darcy) in her husband's face. This, of course, would be only after the transfer of funds had been made.

The Dog Will Have Its Day

At one time, Cressida followed her master and mistress from room to room. Of late she had grown too enfeebled. The poor dog had not the strength to climb upon the bed. Rheumy-eyed and half-blind, she thrashed in her sleep, chasing after rabbits only in her dreams. Neither of the Darcys could fathom consigning her to the kennels. That was how it came about that Graeme, a stalwart young man with a kind face and gentle hand, was consigned to be Cressida's sole caretaker. Graeme alone was to see that the dog was carried from one room to the next.

When alone in their bedchamber, however, Elizabeth did not call for Graeme to attend Cressida.

Mrs. Darcy was disinclined to meddle with the operation of a household that had been in place for centuries. It was her particular wish not to be tended by housemaids and footmen once the Darcys had retired for the night. That had been her single request, a preference initiated upon the Darcys first night together. (Her humiliation upon being found naked in the bed with the master of the house was no longer recalled with abhorrence, but it was hardly forgot.) They re-pledged themselves to decorum due to their children's habit of prowling about.

That meant their time-honoured tradition of consigning the dog to the corridor once connubial pleasures had commenced, had remained in place. The only adjustment was that Cressida no longer took leave under her own power. As Cressida had been a great comfort to her in Darcy's great away, she was happy to help the dog. When Cressida clawed at the bed-skirt, she meant to lift her herself. Darcy was quick to stop her.

"Dare not, Elizabeth! She is far too heavy!" Darcy said. "Either allow me, or have a footman collect the dog. Pray, do not exert yourself in such a manner."

She acquiesced, saying, "One day, you may be shoving your wife aboard this bed."

"With more pleasure, I assure you, than I do the dog," said he.

Once ensconced on the bed, Cressida laid her muzzle on the counterpane and dolefully eyed him as Darcy read a letter from Bingley. Brushing her hair,

Elizabeth inquired if there was news.

Glancing up, he said, "Bingley's gout is much improved. He is in great hope of soon wearing his boot."

Cressida's tail whapped mournfully against the bed, her large eyes begging only to be petted. Tossing her brush aside, Elizabeth walked over to the dog and ruffled the soft fur behind her ears. She was rewarded by a contented whine. Seeing his wife unattended, Darcy came to her. He wrapped a shawl about her shoulders, giving her a kiss on the side of her neck for emphasis. Before he could step away, she leaned against him and nestled in his arms.

"I love it here," she said. "A veil dropped over us and we are left with our true selves."

"Are our true selves so different from those we present to the public?"

She placed her hands behind her and, after briefly caressing his thighs, she gifted him a tweak on the buttock. Taken unawares, he flinched. Then, he hastily wrestled her onto the bed.

"You are quite correct," she teased. "We have no public facade."

He kissed her again.

Quite unexpectedly, he released her and sat up. Then, he rose and stood by the bedpost, an expression of unease overspreading his countenance. She gazed at him quizzically. Something was certainly amiss. They had not spoken much of Lydia's most recent (and far greatest ignominy). Elizabeth hoped that Bingley's letter had not reignited those recollections. Scandal followed Lydia constantly. When she did not find shame, she manufactured her own. No amount of money or finery would make a lady of her. She had remained unabashedly and whole-heartedly impenitent. Elizabeth did not want to speak of Lydia just then.

If her relations were vexing him, he did not say so. His expression was unfamiliar to her. Indeed, she knew not what to make of it. He seemed oddly hesitant. When he finally looked as if he was to speak, he appeared to change his mind. Walking to Cressida, he tugged her off of the bed and urged her through the door. Before it was shut, the dog had curled up to sleep.

With Cressida settled for the night, Darcy turned and leaned his back against the door. He stayed there but a moment before returning to his position at the footboard. Elizabeth had seated herself in the middle of the bed with her legs crossed. Something in his manner bid her come to the edge of the bed and place her feet on the floor. It offered her more stability—for what, she was yet to know. She did not speak, but awaited him.

With exceeding formality, he said, "I must share with you tidings of the sort that you may find unsettling. I promise you, there is no call for alarm."

Telling her that there was no reason for alarm, however, was to put all her senses on high alert. He curled a forefinger against his mouth to contain a small cough before continuing.

"As you well know, disguise of any sort is my abhorrence. Nonetheless, I have withheld certain information from you solely for your protection. If I have distressed you in word or action by doing so, I hereby offer my sincerest apologies."

Her countenance betrayed little emotion, save an exceedingly eagre interest in what he was to say. In fortune, her thoughts and concerns were as familiar to him as the subtle nuances wherein they were conveyed. Hence, he perceived that she was unlikely to brook further delay in his narrative.

Choosing his words carefully (but, regrettably, through his own perspective, not his wife's), he said, "Whilst I was in London, I engaged in a private conversation with a lady of our acquaintance. This meeting was in no way by design. The lady was simply in want of my assistance in regards to difficulties of a highly confidential nature."

Anticipating the question, he hurried to say, "Her husband's station is such that she believed that she had no one else to whom she could turn. I know that your trust in me is implicit, therefore, I am free to tell you that due to the intimate character of the information shared in this meeting, I must respect the lady's privacy and make no further elucidation upon the incident."

His position, once so sure, wavered ever so slightly. Somewhere in his recitation, the possibility that he had erred presented itself. Therefore, he felt moved to repeat the pertinent facts.

Taking a deep breath, he said, "To summarise, I am to advise you that whilst in London...."

Here, Elizabeth interrupted. Her voice had a pinched quality, one that did no bode well for the supposition that she would accept his rationale as befitting a man of keen insight and superior judgement. Indeed, she looked at him as if he had gone off his head.

She said, "You are confessing to me that whilst in London you engaged in an assignation with a woman you refuse to name and exchanged confidences of such intimacy that you are unable to repeat them to me?"

Mr. Darcy was unused to being scolded and he thought that he did not like it.

In a voice dripping with condescension, he said, "Allow me to apprise you that the information just related by me, to you, in no way could be described as 'confessional', nor was the meeting an 'assignation.'"

With one eyebrow raised, she disputed that he was, in any manner, the aggrieved party. He pursed his lips, not in agreement, but that she had a point. She made the most of it.

She inquired, "And where, pray tell, did this tryst take place? At your house in town? Or did you go to her? Perchance, you were in a carriage! I understand hired carriages are favoured for clandestinity."

At this last snip, she ceased. Unbeknownst to her, she chanced upon one element of her husband's meeting with Juliette that was undeniable. His disconcertion kept him from immediately realising that his wife had accused him of, not imprudence of conduct, but outright misconduct—of the most egregious sort. When that realisation struck him, he was most unamused.

"If I may interject," he raised a finger. "You have, good lady, used my own words quite handily against me. The meeting whereof you speak was in no way a tryst. I am aggrieved and injured that you would make that accusation."

He bore an expression of such appalled incredulity that she immediately (and admittedly, half-heartedly) regretted her diatribe.

They had been perhaps six feet apart. In order for their minds to be alike, Elizabeth knew that she would have to be the one to go to him. Once they stood toe to toe, it was he who reached out for her.

"I here beg leave to apologise," she said simply. "I spoke of how it seemed, not of what I believed."

It was quite difficult for him to admit to himself, much less to her, that he might have misdeemed another's motives. Elizabeth knew that.

Finally, he said, "I should have spoken to you of this odd incident sooner. I waited for the right moment to present itself, but that moment never quite came about. In the telling of it, my opinion of the circumstances has altered. Now I fear I have unburdened myself at the expense of disturbing you."

As her colour had heightened, she was unable to deny that, indeed, the information he had related did affect her contrarily. Aware all common wisdom advised that one should never dare to presume, she becalmed herself before she spoke.

"I gather that the lady in question is Lady Howgrave?"

If he was surprised at her guess, he did not expose that he was. He nodded once. His gaze held hers and did not waver at the admission. His countenance remained contained, as was the information he chose to recount. Loath as he was to be less than forthcoming, he would not chance just then exposing the entirety of Juliette's request. It was quite difficult for him to admit that he had spoken to her privately; he could not imagine how to tell Elizabeth that he had been importuned without sounding like a prig. That was hardly the point, he knew. Truth be told, he had not yet looked upon the incident with a dispassionate eye.

He said simply, "Lady Howgrave has accused her husband of dire misuse. She hoped to gain my assistance in escaping him."

Raising her chin ever-so slightly, Elizabeth said, "I believe that, as a gentleman, you did what you could...."

He replied evenly, "I fear not all ills are within my reach to cure. I contacted my solicitor on her behalf."

For reasons that were beneath her, Elizabeth was pleased—not that Juliette was abused, no one deserved that—but that Darcy was not to be her rescuer. A beatific expression overspread her countenance, supposing everything was, indeed, now in the past.

Darcy was most happy to have finally told Elizabeth of the incident with Lady Howgrave. His struggle, however, had not been compleatly resolved. He had merely broached the subject, not told the whole of it.

Heaven's Rejoice

"Watch this, Papa!" said Geoff.

A handsome tent had been erected where two foot paths crossed so the family could enjoy the air without the sun. Mr. Darcy turned to his son, expecting to see the boy doing a somersault. (His acrobatics were becoming quite reckless.) Rather, Geoff had two fingers against his teeth and was blowing hard. Nothing, however, came out, save a little spittle. Darcy looked in his wife's direction.

He bid, "Do you see what he is attempting to do?"

She protested, "I had no part in such business."

As Darcy was unable to define his son's attempt with haste, he omitted any qualifying remarks, saying, "Geoff, come and tell me of this... this."

Solemnly, Geoff came to his side side.

"The Colonel has been teaching me to whistle," he replied.

The Darcys exchanged knowing looks. When he was a boy, the good Colonel taught Darcy to whistle. Indeed, Darcy's technique had never altered. Blackjack was well-trained to respond to it when afield.

"Upon what occasion, pray, shall you need to whistle?" Darcy asked his son.

"To call for my pony! For Cressida—or any of the puppies."

It was true, ponies and spaniels abounded. The dogs were often in need of being called to heel. Before Darcy could give him fatherly advice, Janie interjected. She emitted her own whistle. To no one's great surprise, she whistled quite well—far better than her brother (and she was certainly more proficient than her mother).

"That is how to whistle," Janie announced.

As her father's full attention was upon containing his amusement, her mother corrected her.

"Whilst gentlemen may whistle for their horse, ladies do not."

Janie was unconvinced, "What if a lady falls from her horse and the horse runs away?"

"I fancy," Elizabeth debated, "a lady would wait for a gentleman to do it for you...."

Janie interrupted, "If Geoff is the only one there, I best whistle myself."

"Janie!" hushed Elizabeth. "One must never triumph over another, especially a brother."

Quite impudently, Janie had issued a loud whistle directly in Geoff's face and then dashed away. Whilst his parents were intent upon protecting his budding pride, Geoff gave his sister chase. Taking to the nearest path, she alternately ran and skipped as she did.

"Mama says you are not to run!" Geoff hollered as he ran after her.

"And Mama says that neither of you are to bellow!" Elizabeth called after them both.

Miffed, she sighed heavily, understanding that some innate predilections were unalterable.

"Here," said her husband, handing her a book.

"I rather thought you enjoyed Scott. Not this one?" she asked, having determined by his expression that he was unenthused.

"I prefer re-reading Gibbon," he said.

Elizabeth was not surprised. His predilections did not alter much either.

Having learnt of Beecher's latest debauchery, Lady Catherine was much in want of reminding one and all just who held sway over her granddaughter. Hence, she made her way to Derbyshire with increasing frequency. Young Cathy showed an aptitude for the pianoforte and Lady Catherine would not be satisfied until she knew that Cathy was a true proficient. With Georgiana's tutorials, she was well on her way.

As Darcy had never found tangible evidence that his aunt had transgressed their privacy in collusion with their steward, Smeads, they could not, in all god conscience, hold her responsible for it. Hence, when in the distance a small white cloud of dust announced her imminent arrival to Pemberley, Elizabeth made herself not cringe. Indeed, she managed to put on a decent show of welcome. Young Cathy was a sweet, charming little girl—one whom Elizabeth could not find fault with should her son one day find her in particular esteem. She refused any prejudice against Lady Catherine to interfere with that opinion.

Lady Catherine had the good sense to approve of the Fitzwilliams' stewardship of her granddaughter. That judgement bespoke a generosity not usually seen in her. It was enough to hope that her heart, so often vengeful, had improved. She had not altered her opinion of Beecher. It was fortunate that he hied to London when she travelled to Derbyshire. Her granddaughter's father or not, Lady Catherine had good reason to despise him. His moral inadequacies notwithstanding, her ladyship's ancient macaw had gone missing and he was the chief suspect in the theft.

That night, the Darcys entertained only the Fitzwilliams, for Lady Catherine had been bid a semi-fond farewell the day before. Darcy felt free to apprise the Colonel that he was aware of his whistling tutorial, and that it had been only partially successful. The information was received as good-naturedly as it was presented.

Although Darcy was a doting father, Geoff Darcy was his namesake. Therefore, Fitzwilliam's affection for him was understood. He listened raptly as Darcy related the events of that afternoon.

"Yes," Darcy told him. "My daughter has taken your directions quite well. She has taken them so well that she has exceeded her brother. I believe that must be remedied lest he hold that embarrassment the rest of his life."

His tone was one of bemusement, but Elizabeth believed him quite serious. Usually, Georgiana sat quietly embroidering whilst the others bantered. This conversation, she entered.

Without looking up, she said, "The Colonel tells me that my whistle is better than any other he had ever heard. Have you, brother, been wounded by that?"

Raising an eyebrow, Darcy answered, "How could I be put out of countenance by something I was unaware of—if in fact it were true."

"You deny my talent?" she said primly.

Her older brother spoke to her as an older brother would, "I only say that I have not had the pleasure of hearing you whistle."

She replied, "No, you have not, but then that has been by my design. For you would chastise me for doing so, would you not?"

"If I may interrupt," said Colonel Fitzwilliam, "I alone may be the judge for I have heard you both whistle...."

Before he went further, Darcy interrupted him, "Are you saying that you taught my sister to whistle?"

"In that, she did not need my assistance," the Colonel replied. "It must be a family virtue."

Knowing that her own poor attempts at whistling would do her no credit (the occasions upon which she had engaged that questionable skill were not to be discussed in company), Elizabeth was silent.

Seizing the competitive nature of their conversation, Darcy went to his wife's side and whispered for her ear alone, "I say, my wife whistles quite well."

"No, dearest," she whispered in return. "I shall not have a share in this contest."

Darcy looked at her thoughtfully, reminding her, "When you choose, you can be heard."

Anne, Cathy, and Janie played at their feet, seemingly unaware of their conversation. Elizabeth observed that Janie was unusually quiet. That meant she was paying heed to their discourse. She put her finger to her lips, suggesting to the others that they alter their topic, lest it be an encouragement to the children. The jests were set aside. Other subjects were introduced and discussed.

As Georgiana had yet to conceive again, she had confided to Elizabeth that she feared she could not give Fitzwilliam another child. She, of course, was not indebted to do so. Was she to have a son, it would have only been a matter of pride for his father. As brother of the blade, a gentleman of the first order, a hero of the Peninsular and Waterloo engagements (gallantry cited more than once in the Gazette), Fitzwilliam in no way needed a son to prove his manhood. As delicately as possible, she communicated her opinion upon the matter to Georgiana.

Just as delicately, Georgiana replied, "On this, as on many other occasions, are minds are alike." She smiled and then added, "If the Colonel is ever in want of a boy to teach the art of soldiering, a very willing pupil is before him."

There, at Fitzwilliam's knee, stood little Geoff. In his hand was another wooden horse, this one white.

Geoff said, "I shall ride into battle with a horse just like this."

"An officer should not ride a white horse," the Colonel advised. "He would be too easy a shot for his enemies."

"Napoleon's horse, Marengo was an Arabian like this one, but for its mane and tail—they were grey," Geoff answered holding up his wooden horse.

Fitzwilliam countered, "And look what happened to him...."

"Actually," said Geoff. "Napoleon was captured...."

Darcy interrupted, "Do not think to correct the Colonel. He knows Napoleon and his history quite well."

All watched as Geoff nodded, no one quite certain how well he took his father's reproof. Fitzwilliam affectionately ruffled his hair. Without a word, Geoff smoothed his hair back into place. Fitzwilliam did not speak of it, but made note that Geoff was soldierly enough not to be put in disarray. Georgiana smiled, recognising her brother's fastidiousness in her nephew. Hands behind his back, Darcy looked upon his son with approval (for indeed, one must never be mussed, particularly in company).

Elizabeth did not smile.

The very notion that her son might go into battle one day sent a shiver down her spine. She did not often think of Geoff's future as Master of Pemberley, but she hoped he would not be disposed to find distinction in war. It was not unknown for a landowner to fashion their own uniform and trot off to battle.

There were tussles enough with their offspring even then.

The twins were generally well behaved, but when their cousins visited (which was often), they became even more rambunctious. Their antics could not all be assigned to ill influence by their kin. Geoff was caught sliding down the banister in the grand hall more than once and his sister managed to keep a box full of newborn mice under her bed for a week before they were discovered by Franny Tupin. Despite her wrangles with her brother, Janie was usually quite feminine. She was happy to be drawn in a goat cart (but allowed no one else to ever hold the reins). Geoff turned his nose up at the thought of goat carts and ponies. Perhaps because Darcy was wise enough not to insistent upon it, Geoff was never happier than when he was allowed to ride in front of his father whilst he was on Blackjack.

Watching Geoff with his wooden horse, Elizabeth told Georgiana, "Darcy says Geoff shall not be satisfied until he has a horse of his own."

Elizabeth bit her lower lip as she pondered future hurts. Georgiana, however, altered the conversation from their pampered pets to those abused.

She asked her brother, "What do we hear of the pit ponies? Has Lady Millhouse made any progress there?"

Darcy blanched at the question. It reminded him of a story that may well have travelled halfway to London and back—but one he had not encouraged. Indeed, he had spoken of it only to Elizabeth. If Fitzwilliam had heard of the tale, Georgiana's open expression made it obvious that he had not related it to her. Darcy thought it only fair to tell his sister what had come to pass at her behest—intercessory letters notwithstanding.

He said, "Our good friend has made progress, but not without great loss to her dignity."

Georgiana gave a little gasp and placed her fingers against her lips, "Oh, dear!"

He continued, "With only Miss Arbuthnot to accompany her, she took a gig to the nearest mine to negotiate a rearrangement of the workings of their operation. They were loath to take her or her accomplice's advice. It is no surprise that more than a few miners believed them to be rabble-rousers sent there by the government to disrupt their work. Apparently, Lady Millhouse was sent on her way in a hail of coal."

"Yes," added Elizabeth. "Young Sally stood in the gig and threw the coal back at the mob as fast as it was flung."

In the unlikelihood of the Millhouses relating any of the tale to them, Sally had thought it prudent to make a report of it to the Darcys. Sally was most impressed with Lady Millhouse's performance.

Sally told them, "I have never seen man nor beast run quite as fast as her ladyship had that day. She lifted her skirts above her knees and ran like the devil was on her heels!"

Despite Sally's words of praise, Darcy saw it his duty to protect Lady Millhouse's dignity insofar as their present company. He omitted that part of the story and launched directly into a careful admonishment.

He said, "That is why I was so opposed to you taking part in such business,

Georgiana. They could have easily been arrested and tossed in prison for treason. You have children under your care."

That was the only argument she would not debate. Darcy did not want her to believe her good intentions were wholly thwarted.

He told her, "Lady Millhouse has seen the error of her presentation. She will go to town to watch the equestrian performances at Astley's and then visit the horse auction where she means to purchase ponies. The next time she approaches a mine, she shall not go to ask the miners to relinquish their stock, but rather to present them with ponies instead. It is her design to have them rotate these ponies in their work."

Hearing him speak of horses, Geoff leapt up, asking, "Papa! Can you go to Astley's and buy me a bigger horse?"

"And me Papa! If Geoff gets a bigger horse, may I have one as well?" cried Janie.

"Of all the horses we have in our stables...." he began.

Then he stopped. It was far easier to agree, perhaps, than explain why not.

The Rabbit Hole

Truly, Juliette did not want to confide in Alistair Thomas. He was a man she knew not to be trustworthy. (As he was a politician, she believed it was a given that his scruples were malleable.) She certainly would not confide in him of her visit with Darcy.

When Darcy did not come to her before he returned to Derbyshire, time, which had once only been a taunt, had turned lethal. Without word from him, she became evermore anxious and apprehensive. Soon alarm troubled her so gratingly that her fingers shook when she took her tea.

As her constant companion, Alistair could not help but notice. With Juliette's nerves shattered, his repeated entreaties that she share the details of her plan with him were at last met with success. When she spoke, it was with great purposefulness.

"As I have previously advised you, I aspire to have a gentleman of my acquaintance, a former lover, father my child...."

Alistair, possibly lost in his own intrigues, looked away. Taken as she was by her manoeuvring, she did not make note of it.

In a moment, he asked, "Would your husband's suspicion not be aroused?" The query was unworthy of a seductress of her abilities.

She simpered, "You question my powers of persuasion?"

Increasingly thrown into his company, Juliette still did not particularly fancy Alistair. His figure was fit (but unduly narrow-shouldered to tempt her admiration). As time passed, she simply longed for diversion. He remained the least revolting man that had access to her chambers. Moreover, he was greatly interested in her schemes against Howgrave. She knew that Alistair had some motive that would improve his situation (all men did), she simply had not yet winkled his out of him.

Initially, she feared he was merely baiting her—in want of betraying her to her husband. More likely, he meant to extort money from her for his silence. She let it be known that under such circumstances, she would not hesitate to accuse him of being her lover. If she did, Alistair would be in far greater danger than was she. Howgrave would run him through—or at least have one of his minions do it.

Sequestered and lonely, she allowed his company for what it was—preferable to what she had been enduring. His interest was always keenest when their discourse tarried upon her plan to escape and extort her husband. No doubt, he hoped to receive a portion of what she would gain from Howgrave for himself. If her plan was as lucrative as she hoped, she would be happy to allow him a share of the pelf. His talk was always witty and occasionally even helpful. He kept her spirits high when she began to believe that Darcy would not come to her at all.

As she was closely watched by her husband's henchmen, she schemed of ways to make her away. Only Alistair knew how to avoid their sentry. Once in her chambers, he did all he could to storm the citadel of her feminine grotto. She laughed at such feeble murmurings. But her restlessness was so fevered that even those euphemisms began to sound charmingly naive. Alistair was not compleatly without his merit. Indeed, his attempts to lure her to bed began to look inviting. Still, she held him at bay. (There was but one pair of arms wherein she wanted to revel and Alistair did not happen to own them.) Rather, she diverted him by divulging titbits from her tryst with her proposed lover in her carriage.

"He offered to spirit me from the country, but I refused," she related.

Alistair admitted that was proof indeed of her lover's concern for her plight.

He advised, "You must jingle the cage a bit. Send lovely billets-doux to remind him that you await his rescue."

Heeding his advice, she busied herself at her escritoire, writing page after page, tearing them in half and writing once again. One wafted to his feet.

It read, "You would not have to acknowledge the child. Of this, you have my promise, *Mon Cheri*. Indeed, it shall be our secret. If you cannot come to me and give me a child, I shall be put down as if a beast of burden which has passed its usefulness...."

Picking up a gold letter knife (one encrusted with gems), he sliced it in two. He approved of the general tone of her missive, but had further advice.

He called to her, "Sprinkle a little water upon the page so it appears to be tear-stained...."

"*Mon ami*, I do not have to resort to such trickery. My tears are quite real."

"Your lover is married?"

She shrugged, "Of course."

"With land, chattels...?"

Again, she nodded.

Holding the gold letter knife gingerly in his hand, Alistair gauged its weight. Her household was full of such treasures. It was important that he did not exclude his own suit for her affections.

He cautioned, "Your lover has much to lose and nothing to gain in aiding you."

Said she, "It was his marriage that separated us. It shall not again."

Indeed, it would not. She was no longer content for a single hour of pleasure. She wanted all of Darcy—man, arms, and sabre.

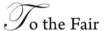 o the Fair

Geoff Darcy believed that embarking on a mission to purchase a horse for him was a superb notion.

He was too young to ride a full-sized, highly-bred animal on his own. However, he was not too young to prepare for that eventuality. Darcy wanted to do everything he could to encourage his son's already avid interest in all things equestrian. Although the finest of horses could be found in his own stables, he had not seen one of the proper temperament and age. A colt would be trained under his own exacting directions. By the time the horse was ready for Geoff, the boy would be ready for the horse.

In seeking this particular animal, Darcy's plans were quite unlike Lady Millhouse's. She might want to observe a circus, but Mr. Darcy did not want to attend, what might be considered, low entertainment. Perhaps, when the children were older and the times more settled, he might choose to take them all to the horse fair. As it was, he meant to return to the breeder where Elizabeth's mare, Boots, was purchased. The estate was the hithermost side of Maidenhead. As before, Fitzwilliam would accompany him. It was Fitzwilliam who convinced Darcy that the horse fair should not be avoided, as they would be in the vicinity.

"The likelihood that the fine animal I seek would be purchased from a gypsy is quite remote," Darcy grumbled. "But as you say, it would take little time to observe the stock there."

It was to be a trip of goodly length. Hence, they would employ the coach. Fitzwilliam's leg would not allow him to ride a horse as he once had. They would take their time and make a fine excursion of it. Indeed, by the time their plans had been framed, Darcy had become enlivened by the prospect. It was at Elizabeth's insistence that he relented upon betaking himself upon the journey at all. It was her contention that if he was to go, it would be better to go sooner than later. Later, she hoped to be with child. Later, she would not want him too leave her side.

"I hope that I may take to my bed with morning sickness at any moment. If you are to go, I would rather give you up now than when I am too unwieldy to take the stairs."

In truth, she hoped for her loving husband's distraction. As much as she desired her husband's company, she wanted him free—at least for a while—of the weight of Pemberley's daily burdens. It would do him good.

Upon the morning of their departure, Elizabeth flitted nervously about, suddenly not wanting Darcy to go away. She realised that she was hovering and therefore, making the leave-taking all the more unsettling. Geoff had begged his father to allow him to ride in the coach as far as the lodge-post. As the boy had been crestfallen to learn that he was not to accompany his father upon this journey, small favours were not to be withheld.

Whilst the coach was being loaded, Darcy stopped his meticulous watch over the activities to take his wife's arm. He led her away to the small alcove across from the portico.

Once there, he kissed her upon her forehead and said, "Before I take leave, I must tell you...."

He paused. Ever so propitious in word and deed, this moment was ill-timed, indeed.

After considering his words, he continued thusly, "Truth be known, I would never have stepped foot in her carriage...."

Thereupon, she realised that he was speaking again of his meeting with Lady Howgrave. Could he not just preface his discourse with that information?

Whilst she cogitated his exposition, he stopped again, pressing his thumb against his lower lip. His pauses were quite maddening. Between them, however, she understood that he was making a declaration of sorts. He was an educated man, capable of eloquence of address and superior elucidation. Why he could not just come out with it was becoming an increasing botheration. His last such advisement had not blessed her with unmitigated joy. Therefore, her anticipation of the information he was to offer worried the most precipitous reaches of her composure.

He chose to enjoy each pause in their discourse without daring to look in her eyes. Yet, she allowed him to gather his thoughts before completing his admission—if indeed that was what it was. Nonetheless, she feared that if he did not speak his mind soon, she could not be responsible for her actions.

Finally, he said, "Perhaps we should speak of this upon my return, when we shall be able to converse more freely—unconstrained by time."

"No," she said (far more abruptly than she meant). "You have had ample time to declare, assert, or profess what you are struggling to tell me at this moment. I shall wait no longer."

Clearly, his avowal was to cover the balance of the meeting he had engaged in with Lady Howgrave in London. As he was, if not to London, at least away in that direction once again, it did not bode well for her presumption that he was to have no further dealings with the lady.

"I had no choice, you see," he finally said.

"No choice?"

He answered, "To enter her carriage that night."

"You explained yours actions upon that occasion to me once before. Why do you persist...?"

He said, "I fear I must bring certain tidings to light now, lest delaying it might impede your future condition."

So, he had not told her all. It was quite apparent that he planned to relieve his conscience on the very threshold of his departure. Moreover, what he was to say was so injurious that, was she with child, it would befoul her pregnancy. His every word proved her correct.

"It is true that I did step into her carriage that night...." He stopped again, fretting, "I should not be speaking of it just now."

"No, you should *not.*"

Servants were hustling about, just beyond hearing.

She repeated her entreaty, "You should not—not *here*"

"*Mama,*" Janie called.

"In a moment!" Elizabeth responded (with uncharacteristic impatience).

He continued with singular determination, "You see, I encountered her in the garden. She was in want of speaking to me. It was my duty as a gentleman to escort her to her carriage. I had no intention of stepping inside it with her."

"But you did."

"But I did."

"So you said," she reminded him.

Folding her arms across her bosom, Elizabeth steadied herself.

"It is not what you might think. I could not take my leave, you see."

Closing her eyes, she said, "Then pray, *please speak*!"

He stood back on his heels, momentarily sputtering as if he did not know— not only how to explain—but what he must explain as well. She only dared open one eye to discern what caused this indignation.

Then at last, his exasperation erupted.

He announced, "She took my hat!"

"What?" Elizabeth responded. "Your hat?"

"My hat."

"She took your hat? What hat? Your umber one that goes so well with your pearl-grey waistcoat?"

"The very one," he replied.

"Pray tell, why in the world did she do that?"

"I can only fancy that she took it to obtain my attention—and thereupon, my cooperation."

Red splotches appeared high upon each of his cheekbones. Although they were rarely seen, they were quite recognizable for what they were—an indication of acute injury. If Lady Juliette Howgrave had the temerity to remove his hat from his person in order to gain his attention, she made a tremendous misstep. No one touched Mr. Darcy (save Mrs. Darcy). What might have been considered a small coquetry to another gentleman was to him an unparalleled affront.

"Did you retrieve your hat forthwith?"

His expression told her that he had, but he nodded as well.

"I was much in want of unkenneling this particular episode at the first possible moment. Why, I cannot explain. It is my duty to spare you these small indignities if at all possible."

She nodded, for she did understand. Just then, Geoff found his father's hand and began tugging him towards the coach. Excited to have one up on his sister, Geoff let go of his father's coat long enough to stick his tongue out in her direction. Janie stuck out her tongue in return. This sibling mischief was carried out beyond their parents knowing, for Mr. Darcy turned to Mrs. Darcy and kissed her.

Indeed, that kiss was not enough. Sinking against the wall of the darkened alcove, Mr. Darcy took Mrs. Darcy into his embrace, delivering unto her a kiss so penetrating that when he withdrew, she believed herself brought with child. She clasped his collar, urging him to kiss her again—but alas.

Janie pulled on her mother's skirt, "Mama! Poppa? Is Mama ill?"

As her husband released her, Elizabeth caught her breath long enough to say, "Kiss your Papa good-bye, Janie."

He leaned down to accept his daughter's kiss. She offered him a well-executed curtsy too. Pleased, he smiled at her.

To Darcy, Elizabeth asked, "Shall you see Lady Howgrave again?"

The question should have been beneath her. Her voice was betrayed by its urgency.

"No," he answered succinctly.

She nodded. Gathering herself, she reassured Janie, "Your father shall return before we know he has gone."

That was a compleat falsehood. She missed him ere the door to the coach was closed.

$\mathcal{J}$anus

It all came about because of greed. He should have known better. Once he had found himself a place within the warring political parties he should not have connived with a harlot to blackmail one of the aristocracy's favourite sons.

Politics was a delightful occupation. There was a minimum of gunfire and gobs of easy money. His rise from near death to having his middle finger upon the pulse of the nation had been precipitous. At last, his vast talents coalesced precisely with the opportunity to employ them.

As he walked the streets of town unmolested, he became evermore arrogant that he would never be recognised. As a matter of pride, he had always kept himself at arms length from his fellow man (near enough to borrow money; far enough away to escape grasping creditors). His few friends were fellow grenadiers. Most of them were now lying dead as mutton across the channel. His countenance had not altered remarkably, however his striking white hair concealed his true identity to anyone who might have been a casual acquaintance.

He had modulated his voice and, as he was surrounded by the patois of the street, soon became fluent in a variety of accents. His new persona had few collaborators and colleagues, for he trusted no one save dutiful Mrs. Younge.

On days when all went well, he even fancied that some day he might stand for Parliament. He certainly had the hair for it. Indeed, his silver mane was his defining characteristic. It offered his aspect a dignity that it had been lacking. When his flights of fancy caught up with him, he admitted that leaping onto the public stage might be a tad imprudent. It would beg questions regarding his family connections and military service. It was best simply to fade into the background. There was money enough to be made without the scrutiny.

When he had first taken the step from gentleman to man of commerce, the most convenient commodity to peddle had been female flesh. Mrs. Younge's rooming house had been ideally located, as Gowell Street had ample foot-traffic and was increasingly immersed in general bawdiness. It was quite easy to convince the retinue of emaciated harlots habituating the street that they were in need of his protection. (Should they be reluctant to pay this annuity, a local thug could convince them otherwise for a few shillings.) Soon, they were paying off with the regularity of a cuckoo clock. Mrs. Younge's qualms over being pressed into service as a procuress were eased by the jingle of coins as he dropped her share of the takings into her apron pocket. His severest test was not his conscience (Lord, no, not his conscience, that had shrivelled from disuse years before), but the incessant whining of females debilitated by the influx of their monthly curse.

Had he not been a man of ambition, he might have ridded himself of the entire enterprise for that reason alone. Quiet was not why he entered the resurrectionist trade, but it was an added inducement. Dead clients did not overmuch complain—not to say that profession did not have its drawbacks. Grave-robbing meant that one's goods went bad faster than day-old milk.

One of his finest qualities had always been timing. In his way, he was a visionary (whether one step ahead of a husband or the magistrate). As physicians uncovered the secrets of human physiology, surgeons flocked to anatomy classes. For every dissection, a body was required. Body-snatching was becoming an increasingly profitable profession. The relatively easy money meant any thief with a shovel and a sack was drawn to the trade. Increased competition for bodies not only cut into the profits, the influx of neophytes meant new grave-robbers had no finesse. Indeed, they were nothing but a gang of slack-jawed incompetents. It was one thing to hurry a death, quite another to knock youngsters in the head and drag them from the streets. The citizenry took notice when their children went missing.

Rubbing elbows with men whose aprons bore the stench of death did nothing to improve his attractiveness to the gentle sex. Indeed, ladies did not inhabit Gowell Street. That was what he missed most from his former life. He liked lovely-scented, enchantingly-coiffed, and divinely-demure ladies, not foul-breathed harlots with stinking quims and coarse ways. He could have any woman in that particular demimonde ten different ways, but the thought of such wretches made his stomach heave. Perhaps his unusual distaste for low women sprang from that little fray with the two little marmots. The recollection of the foul sluts was enough to put a man off lady-tail for good. Had it not been for ever-faithful Henrietta Younge, he might not have engaged in sexual congress whatsoever.

The dregs hanging about King's Bench were an improvement on those infesting the *Fortune of War*. He had conjured himself a fine life on the periphery of the law. Little by little, he rose in financial status. Time came about, however, for an improvement in his occupational environment.

Taken as a whole, his recuperation was remarkable, both tangibly and spiritually.

Well-schooled in many vices, becoming the local pimp had been a natural progression into moral corruption. His other sins were singular, a seduction here, a murder there; they had all served a specific purpose. To his mind, he was never a procurer. He did not lure customers; he merely served as a protector for a cut of the strumpet's sales. Moreover, he did not admit to body-snatching. He never put a hand on a dead body. He only brokered those transactions. His turn in various court facilitations exposed him to the legal profession's pettifoggers and prevaricators.

As all his various endeavours claimed the same trajectory, it was natural that his next step was into politics. (Granted, a leap from prostitution and grave-robbing into the political arena was more of a lateral move than a step up, still he made it with extraordinary ease.)

Always sniffing out ready money, he began to investigate political clubs. The Strand was crawling with outraged petitioners for reform, but none of them could obtain a consensus. Various shouting matches ensued—one evening was capped off by a stoning of the Prince Regent's carriage.

Suddenly, his ambition was reinvigorated. As easy as crossing New Oxford Street, he left the hawkers, harlots, and immigrants behind, ready to play the cards of decent folk again. For most, working both sides of the road was no easy feat. He knew, however, that the intricacies of such manoeuvring often involved little more than sporting a good pair of boots, well-attended side-whiskers, and the proper accent.

Thus equipped, he prowled the better boot shops and haberdashers surrounding Bond Street until opportunity presented itself. In less than the time it took to have his boots polished, he was befriended by a bored and semi-respectable lord.

He introduced himself humbly, "Alistair R. Thomas at your service."

Garrulous Lord Orloff had been the harbinger of an abrupt alteration in his situation. It foretold of an introduction into the finest sitting rooms in town. In doing so, he had become a trusted member of both sides of the political curtain. In no time, Sir Henry Howgrave became his newest and dearest friend.

When at last he won the honour of leading Lady Howgrave from speech to speech, he revelled in her company. There was no finer lady in all of London, much less evident within easy reach of tiresome lecture halls. Through dedicating hours upon hours to her amusement, he learnt that all was not well in the House of Howgrave. Clearly, each had been the other's trophy. Of the two, quite obviously Howgrave made the better bargain. It was clear that Lady Howgrave had come to that unhappy conclusion as well. Indeed, upon occasion she was very nearly morose.

She had good reason to be. One would only need to be in Howgrave's company an hour ere he would make the most lascivious comments regarding his wife's connubial attributes. Few men in politics could claim to be a gentleman. (It was not a profession that always called to the honest and the just.) However, Howgrave's remarks and vocabulary would have made a seafarer blush. Had Alistair not been so eagre to ingratiate himself to the man, he would have been happy to slap him across the cheek with his gloves.

Despite being married to a swine, Lady Howgrave literally radiated allurement. Some way, somehow, she managed to remain unwitting (or, in truth, in avoidance) of his own romantic overtures. The farther beyond his reach she was, the more eagre he became to climb the catacombs of her womanhood. The awful truth—that she was immune to his amorous leanings—was a brutal blow. A lesser man might have given up all passionate ambitions.

She rewarded his devotion with nothing but her friendship.

Of course, he made certain lovely Juliette learnt of her husband's despicable blabbering about her conjugal attributes. It was painful, but gave her leave to seek comfort in the embrace of a more discrete lover. Regrettably, he could not convince her to come to him.

Despite this setback (and during the brief lulls between orchestrating rioting factions), he re-dedicated himself to her. He had all but given up the seduction when, in a burst of candour, she told him of her plan to escape her husband. That was a bit of a surprise, but the desire was hardly astonishing. As he believed abetting unhappy wives the obligation of any true gentleman (they were always so very, very grateful), he steered their conversations towards intrigue and compromise. Beyond her fetching perfume, the danger was intoxicating. She only offered the details of her plan in halting fits and starts. Wine, intoxicant of the gods, helped her tell him everything.

Under the limpid glow of empty glasses and wilted candles, it looked as if his appeal for her to share her confidences would finally bear fruit. He poured her another glass of wine and did not have to make a pretence of being a great ally to whatever venture she was to undertake.

"Your husband is an ogre," he said. "I am at your service. What can I do to assist you?"

"No, *mon ami*," she demurred. "It is a great secret. I must not speak of it."

She did, however, speak of it. Secrecy, she had insisted, was essential; as a former lover was to come to her rescue. When he learnt the gentleman was not only rich, but married as well, he knew all was not lost. He encouraged her to write to her lover in the hopes of identifying him by offering to post her letter. She did not allow that. Foiled, but not defeated, he did not give up. He was determined to unearth, and thus, interfere with her machinations.

Night after night, he prodded her, "Who is this lover? Someone of your circle? A soldier? Is it Wellington?"

He laughed. She laughed, but she did not tell him his name.

"I cannot tell," she whispered.

"It is Wellington!" he invoked a faux gasp.

It was vital he learn the identity of her former lover beyond serving his own desire. For was her husband to learn of any of it, he would inflict the ultimate punishment. This would not come to pass by his own hand, of course. (Howgrave would have his lickspittles tend to the dirty business.) That would be a shame. Not that Alistair truly cared for Juliette. She was an exceptionally beautiful woman. His interest, however, was one of self-preservation. Was she taken to bed, or made her escape under his watch, Howgrave would certainly blame him.

Was he culpable, it was only fair that he have the pleasure of bedding her. For him to succeed, this gentleman-saviour had to be unearthed and besmirched beforehand.

Tickling her, he bid, "Is this knight in shining armour a man of my acquaintance?"

"I think not," she said. Her words were slightly slurred.

"Is he a man of the first circles?"

"Do not ask me of him, I beg you. He is a man of honour."

"If he is so honourable, why has he not yet saved you?"

"He is the best of men, but Darcy is seldom in town. Our plans are...."

Her head dropped forward, Alistair was uncertain if she had fallen asleep. He grasped her shoulder and shook her. She roused.

"Darcy?" he repeated. "Of Derbyshire?"

"You *do* know Darcy," she cooed, then slipped back into her dreams.

Had he spoken then, a simpering note would have insinuated itself into his voice—one long-buried. Instead, he spoke only to himself.

"Darcy, eh?" he marvelled.

"Well, slap my ass and call me George Wickham."

*H*orse Holiday

Sally Frances Arbuthnot's life was absolutely topsy-turvy.

Although she had learnt to keep her past penchants to herself, she was beside herself with excitement that they would all go to London. Indeed, she was unable to hide her delight. This was not because she missed the sickly yellow haze that passed for air and the cinereous film that covered every person, dog, or building—for she did not. Point of fact, the fresh air of the country had begun to grow on her.

The truth was far too simple.

Lady Millhouse had promised that she would take her to see an Italian opera at the Drury Lane Theatre.

"Tis just a repertory company, dear girl, but they give it quite a go!" her ladyship did enthuse.

Sally did not need the encouragement, for she had always longed to see a proper opera. All she had witnessed were street performances and puppets. She was well nigh giddy even before Lady Millhouse proposed that she be taken to a dress shop to purchase a frock to wear to the theatre.

"I would call my seamstress, but there just isn't the time. *Coccinelle* near Green Park is quite fashionable. Mademoiselle Fisher shall add lace and ribbons to the finest silk...."

"Yes," agreed Lord Millhouse. "My dear wife shall have you dressed to make a maypole blush!"

To look as pretty as a maypole was handsome indeed! Sally knew not what to admire the most. Her mind seized upon the possibility of silk stockings and that thought gifted her a sense of anticipation beyond any she had ever before experienced. It was so intense that, had she been a puppy, she would have waggled her tail. The Millhouse revelled in the part they played in bringing her such joy.

To poverty born and workhouse bred, Sally never fancied her chances of being doted on by anyone, much less favoured by persons of such vast means. She could not help but feel happy, but still a bit discomfited by the attention. Whilst in town, she prayed that she would not see anyone from the Dials.

They would call her a sham—and a sham she was. In truth, she was just a girl from the slums and always would be. No amount of scent and soap could make her a quality lady. That did not mean she would not go to the opera. No amount of taunting would stop her from going. She simply would not allow herself airs (even in silk stockings).

As they took their leave from Pennyswope, Sally reminded herself they would not be long in London. So long as she kept to the Millhouses coach and house, there would be little chance she would be see by any of her previous acquaintances

Such petty fears were put aside the moment they arrived at Newmarket. The crowd was enormous and the excitement was infectious. It was such an invigorating place that Sally knew not where to look first.

Purchasing rotational stock for the mines was as much an excuse to come to town as a mission. Lady Millhouse was a great admirer of the thoroughbred races. They were to tarry there and then on to London. Because of the Millhouse's enthusiasm for the three year-old fillies, they led her off to observe several of those contests before tending to business or fun. Their favourite placed a poor third, but Lady Millhouse was undaunted.

She asked her husband, "Dearest, do you recall in the year '14, when Byerley took the field for three year-olds! Was that not a year!"

"How can I forget, Winnie? We took near a thousand guineas home!"

Sally knew Lady Millhouse's given name was Winifred, but that was the first time she had heard her called by it. For quality folk, the Millhouses were as lovie as Billingsgate barkers. Their easy affection reminded Sally of the Gardiners.

Fully engaged, her ladyship roared, "We must not miss the classics for they are next! Oh, was I younger I should have loved to take a rail on a fast steed!"

As the start of the next race commenced, Lady Millhouse jumped up and down with the exhilaration of child. She asked Sally something, but the question was lost in the cheering of the crowd. It was difficult to listen to the Millhouses, as they detailed the regulations of each race and the pedigrees of each horse, for all the distractions.

As rousing as the races were, Sally was ecstatic when they went on their way to see the accompanying fair. She had never seen anything quite like it in all her born days (and she had once paid a penny to observe the mummified corpse of a two-headed pig). What with musicians and fortune-tellers, and pickpockets circling amongst the breeders and horse owners, the sounds and smells reminded her of London—on its best day. Someone had a monkey. It was shrieking either in hostility or fright.

"Oh, look there!" cried Lady Millhouse. "I spy the Bingleys!"

Holding out both arms in eagre anticipation, Lady Millhouse seemingly enfolded the entire family within them. With much talk of small worlds and an exchange of the condition of the roads, they were a merry bunch. Lady

Millhouse even introduced her to Mrs. Bingley who nodded and spoke to her particularly. That was a surprise and delight, but Mrs. Bingley was Mrs. Darcy's sister and both those ladies were unassuming and kind. Lady Beecher was with them and extended her hand to Lord Millhouse. Her wrist was limp as me auntie's and she showed a distinct distaste for everyone else, especially such riffraff as the Millhouse's lately-adopted waif. Sally did not give a frog's fart what that so-called lady thought.

Bingley still had his cane and favoured his gouty toe. (It said much for his recovery that he managed to wear his favourite boots.) He had a three year-old filly entered in the Epsom Oaks and they had brought their two oldest boys to watch. Bingley was quite pleased with his odds and wanted to share his enthusiasm with his sons. Their boys were more excited than usual, tugging upon their mother's arms, pulling her thither and yon to amusements that they had little chance to enjoy at Deering Lodge.

In his inspirited discourse with the Millhouses over the betting odds, Bingley's purpose for bringing his sons to the races was soon forgotten. It was left to Jane to keep them in check. Happy to have an excuse to see the sights, Sally took the boys in hand and they went to buy some ices.

Whilst her husband and Bingley exchanged their opinions upon various colts listed in the General Stud Book, Lady Millhouse was reminded of her original enterprise and invited Jane to accompany her in quest of the extra shift of ponies.

"After all, Jane dear, had you and Georgiana not informed me of the plight of the pit ponies, I would not be here now."

Thus, she insisted they take a turn about the grounds to see what was for sale. Not disposed to talk of race horses, Caroline followed them.

Despite gypsies and travellers begging their attention, Sally and the boys soon caught up with them. Lady Millhouse found the gypsies quite exotic. Her upbringing a bit more salty, Sally was less impressed. She finished off her ice with great rapidity, but the boys' were dripping down their chins. Jane attended them, but some messes are foreordained. As they ran screaming about their Aunt Caroline's satin skirts, she closed her parasol to use it as a weapon against them. Everyone but Caroline found the antics quite hilarious.

There were many people of all ilk trading horses in the area. Several claimed to have thoroughbreds, though most looked to be lame or excessively old to compete. Amongst them was a man with a string of ponies, noticeable for nothing more than each one of the beasts were more emaciated than the next. The owner claimed their condition was the result of personal privation and not gross neglect. His assertion was not supported by his well-tailored frock coat and ample supply of Geneva. This infuriated them all save Caroline (granted she may have been offended too, but she was loath to draw the long bow upon any injury not inflicted upon her personally). Lady Millhouse took it upon herself to express their collective outrage.

As she was rarely without her crop, her ladyship held it before her and then began a hearty bastinado across the man's shoulders.

"Fie upon you, sir! Fie, I say! A man who will starve a horse is no man at all!"

Instinctively, Sally caught the tail of her ladyship's coat and begged her to cease lest the constabulary take her away. She only quit her attack when the man was able to beat a retreat to the safety of the ground between his waggon's wheels.

Hastily collecting herself, her ladyship sent for her own men to fetch the poor ponies, bellowing to one and all, "There, you have it! Easy as that! Our ponies are bought!"

In fortune, their men had joined them, for the ponies had been spooked by the man's high-pitched squealing. It was left to limping Bingley, and ageing Lord Millhouse, to scurry to capture the end of the rope before the horse tore lose. The dull-eyed creatures were in no mind to follow anyone.

"Make haste!" Lady Millhouse called to her footmen, "Secure some grain from our stores!"

As they hurried off, she took hold of each pony's lead rope and one by one yanked each of them free. Bingley's boys were happy to help shoo the animals towards a nearby field. Initially reluctant, the ponies eventually allowed themselves to be herded. Then one shaggy, brown pony raised its nose and emitted a slight whicker. It was as if a call to arms. They trotted, then galloped until they all came sliding into the wet grass. The herd hastily dispersed into the tussocks and sedge as if a harvest feast had been laid out before them.

That stirring sight bequeathed another one. It was equally moving, but sweetly askew.

Lady Millhouse was taller than her husband, therefore when she rested her forehead against his shoulder she had to stoop when she wept.

Sally looked away, not because she believed the sight abhorrent, but because she did not. People were peculiar. Lady Millhouse would thrash a man and weep for animals all in a minute's time. Plain men and innocent babes starved in every corner of the country every day of the week, yet no one wept for them. She shrugged. What more could be done?

On the back stairs of Pennyswope, all manner of tales were exchanged. Most of the stories were nothing but a good-natured laugh. Unsurprisingly, Lady Millhouse's unguarded conduct was often the topic. She had been known to do more than swat dog-kickers; she took a crop to wife-beaters too. A woman so willing to right a wrong might take on the rest of the world's inhumanity as well. When the time came, Sally meant to have a word with her about that.

Settling everyone's nerves took a while. There were arrangements to be made to transport the ponies to Pennyswope. As these matters were attended, another, more peculiarly fractious raucity was heard. It was Bingley who interpreted it for what it was. He ran in the direction of the melee, employing his walking stick as a pivot, alternately waving it in the air as he could. Lord Millhouse was behindhand of him with her ladyship (skirts raised to her knees) fast over-taking then both.

Jane and her boys stood still. Caroline was struck dumb.

Sally told them all, "I will go see what's the matter,"

She then ran towards the ruckus.

Jane heard her husband holler, "Belay that Kneebone!"

She blanched and clasped her children to her. Caroline blindly dug into her reticule until she found what she wanted. She up-ended the silver flask and emptied it with one long swallow. With a gesture devoid of gentility, she wiped her mouth with the back of her glove.

Thereupon, she fainted dead away.

79

$\mathscr{S}$eed of Doubt

When Juliette was roused from her stupor, she heard Alistair speaking excitedly.

"I know the Darcys, they are a fine family," he said. "There is no finer gentleman than Mr. Darcy."

Unconvinced, she bid, "You are acquainted with Mr. Darcy?"

"The older gentleman, yes. He's now long dead," he said, very nearly falling into his oft-repeated tale of misuse. "The son is quite arrogant. I doubt he would recall me."

She was resentful of her lapse of discretion and suspicious that he had taken advantage of her inebriation. Moreover, it was morning, a time she disliked to be on display. This was most especially true if she had over-imbibed on wine the night before. All in all, she was in a bit of a snit. Alistair talked on, either uncaring or unwitting of her mood. What he had to say, however, was not to be denied.

"I know enough of the Darcys to say that he has Howgrave's fortune ten times over. You have been waiting for him to come to you for an interminable amount of time and he has yet to darken your door. I fear he has forsaken you, dearest Juliette. If he has, oblige him to reimburse you for your aggravation."

She said airily, "What I want of him does not demand anything but an afternoon—no, an hour of his time."

The implication was clear. In his astonishment, he had not recalled that she meant for this lover—Darcy—to impregnate her.

"Would you but desire an afternoon of amour for amour's sake? You do not need Darcy for that. I could please you in ways you have yet to imagine...."

"Silly fool!" she snapped. "I desire fornication, not an assignation. I need impregnation. Darcy is a man of vigour and vitality. His loins, they are...."

"Ah, yes. You must provide Sir Howgrave with an heir."

Why she wanted Darcy of all people to do the job meant only one thing. When the time was ripe, she would toss the name of the father of her child in her husband's face. Word had it that Howgrave was not to the manor born. Every man and potboy in Kympton knew that he was a child of the vestry called Freddy Dumpstitch. As bastard son of a maid, he had been a local joke.

To be cuckold by Mr. Darcy would be a particularly stinging rebuke. Howgrave would pay for her silence.

He said, "Should Darcy not be tempted, all is not lost."

Juliette's head rolled to the side, her eyes turned in his direction. Her expression was unwelcoming.

She said, "I have not given him up as of yet."

Endeavouring to keep the patronisation from his voice, he said, "You are right to keep that hope alive. But, if he does not come, so to speak, you must have an alternate."

She saw the wisdom in that, but was not altogether pleased at the offer she knew was to come.

She said, "I trust you want to do the job yourself?"

His scheme had not been as disguised as he might have hoped. That did not mean that it was a bad idea.

He rerouted the unveiling by announcing, "I have a grand notion."

Her expression was wan. She yawned.

"Imagine me with hair near-black in colour as it once was. Before I went to the wars my hair was black as the night. In height and form, I am Darcy's double,"

Unimpressed, she said angrily, "I want a child fathered by Darcy, not a garrulous nonentity without six-pence in his pocket."

"If that tryst does not bechance, do you not see that I am the next best thing to Darcy. I shall bootblack my hair and purposely be seen coming from your chambers." His words were coming faster, "Surely certain members of your circle had to have known of your affair with Darcy. That knowledge, along with well-placed innuendo and the world will believe that he is your lover still!"

She reminded him, "Darcy is hardly dull-witted. I dare say that if he has not come too my bed, he shall be unconvinced that he fathered my child...."

"What would he deny? There would be no open accusation. It would be nothing but gossip."

Her expression said she was pondering the possibility.

Wanting to clarify his design, he said, "No doubt, he would pay us handsomely for the rumours to desist."

She did not notice that his pronoun was now plural. Her shoulders were tense, her chin, elevated as she bethought the scheme. It was important for him to disrupt her obvious loyalty to Darcy. He saw no reason for it.

"You must see that Darcy is not the man you believed. Whilst you writhe under the cruel hand of your husband, he diddles his wife. He does not deserve your regard."

After a moment of thought, she bid him, "Do you know *her*?"

He hesitated before admitting, "Yes, I met her before her illustrious marriage. More of a wit than a beauty as I recall."

She announced, "His marriage was most unexpected."

"Indeed," he agreed. Then he could not help but crow, "She once set her cap for me. I saw nothing in her that I esteemed. I cannot account for Darcy's taste. He is a cold fish."

Alistair might be of his acquaintance, but she surmised that he did not, indeed, know Darcy.

"There is one certainty," she said. "The more I entreat him to come to me, the less apt he is to do so. I must desist."

Alistair's plan seemed flawless. They would play both sides against the middle. She would extort her husband to tell the world that he was the father of her child, and extort Darcy to tell them he was not. It was sheer brilliance! Tricky, but brilliant.

Abruptly, she recollected an unhappy fact.

She said, "The Darcy I know will not bow to extortion of any kind."

Alistair wilted. It was true. However proud of the Darcy name, it could not be presumed that Darcy would bend to threats. Fie! Foiled at every turn. Suddenly a thought occurred to Alistair, one of stunning simplicity.

"You lay with him how long ago? How would he know if you did or did not have a child by him then? I propose this: if he does not come to you now, your can claim a child from your prior liaisons."

Alistair seemed to relish concocting unscrupulous subterfuges. Indeed, he came up with them seemingly at will. It was no wonder he was so valuable to a politician. However, Juliette was losing her taste for it all. Still, she was so exceedingly determined to see Darcy again that she was grasping at straws. There was no method she would not employ if it would persuade him to come to her. She mulled over the notion of claiming a child by him. That was not a negotiation he would charge to his solicitor. She believed with all her heart that once he was within the comfort of her chambers, their previous association would be rekindled.

She said with finality, "My scruples look fondly on seduction, but become unwieldy at outright blackmail, especially if it is based on a lie. Should a man produce a bastard, it is only fair for him to compensate the mother. Conjuring this child from whole cloth does not suit my own particular notion of morality."

Alistair turned away. She could see that he was hiding his amusement.

Had he been of greater sensibility, she might have attempted to explain that, unlike politicians, some harlots had honour. No matter how hard, some hearts could be injured. The hurt she felt when Darcy turned her away had not faded. When she had come to him, the only help he offered was that which would be at no cost to his dignity.

Darcy must pay for that conceit, by hook or by crook—but not by Alistair.

When it came to revenge, it was best served cold.

𝒟uelling Duo

Sally had seen some marvellous things in her young life, but watching quality folk making big fools of themselves in broad daylight beat everything else hands down. She saw that right off.

When the shrieks of terror rang out, Bingley seemed to have known instinctively what was to occur. Although Beecher was half of the fray, Bingley did not call to his brother-in-law. Rather, he called to Major Kneebone, rightly assuming that, as the more dangerous of the two, he must be contained first.

Although she had seen many a fight, Sally had never witnessed a real duel. Still, she understood its governing principles. This was to be a gun fight (which meant it would be high on excitement but short on finesse). The rules for such an encounter were well known. The combatants were to stand back to back, walk a specified number of paces and on command, turn and shoot. If the first shot missed its mark, the second man was free to take his shot in his own time.

Whereas their group arrived just after the initial calling out, they only witnessed what came next.

Kneebone was clearly prepared to respect these time honoured stipulations; Beecher was of a different mind. Cowering, he refused to engage whatsoever.

Waving his pistol in the air, a very inebriated Major Hugh Kneebone screamed, "You cowardly snake! You adulterous wife-thief!"

Beecher responded, his tone wheedling, "I implore you sir! If I have offended, I beg leave to apologise."

The crowd about them was growing larger by the moment (plain folk, always happy as Sally, to observe two gentlemen behaving as if a pair of rakehells). Only when Bingley took charge of Kneebone's hand and the gun in it, did Beecher stand. Now out of immediate danger, Beecher's first attempt to ameliorate the accusations flung at him was to cast blame upon his diet.

"My reprehensible behaviour is, no doubt, the fault of my cook. I am fed a daily diet of truffles and oysters. I shall beat her the moment we return...."

Kneebone was not appeased by such nonsense. His cheeks flushed, his hair askew, his bony wrists protruding from the sleeves of his coat; he looked less like an officer in His Majesty's army than a farm boy done wrong at the fair. His eyes were glassy; his demeanour still menacing. Tugging on his arm, Bingley repeatedly called his name, but to no avail.

Only after resorting to slapping his cheeks, did Bingley at last obtain his attention.

"He is not worth the bother," said Bingley. "You must think of your family!"

Sally had seen men gone mad before. She observed such to Lord Millhouse.

"Off his napper, ain't he?" she said.

Lord Millhouse agreed, "No seeds in his pumpkin today... soused I'd say."

"Plain as Persia, dicked in the nob," she replied.

Lord Millhouse added, "All his dogs aren't barking...."

"If you *please*," cried Bingley.

They hushed themselves.

Sally could not resist one more aside. She whispered, "All foam, no ale."

Lord Millhouse nodded and they both watched closely as Kneebone slowly remembered himself. His chest did not quit heaving in rage and exertion, but he regained his senses. Once Kneebone's attention was averted, Beecher withdrew a small pistol from his waistcoat and aimed it at Kneebone. Gasps erupted from the crowd. The consensus was that Beecher was not much of a shot and the onlookers scrambled to escape possible gunfire. Other, more hardy types, stayed to watch it play out. Their patience was rewarded.

Beecher hollered, "Your wife is a strumpet, Major! It is all her part! Indeed, she seduced me!"

Bingley was infuriated at his aspersions (however dangerously true they might be).

To Beecher, he hollered, "How dare you sir! You are nothing less than a nefarious tosspot!"

It was no surprise when someone came from behind and hit Beecher over the head with a pot. The weapon was only a piece of crockery taken from a nearby hawker, however it was quite effective. Shards scattered as Beecher tumbled limply to the ground. His forehead dug into the mud; his hinderparts pointed skyward. As he fell (and for several seconds thereafter), he emitted an extended expulsion of gas. This incited a wild round of laughter from the crowd.

Having the honour of rendering him thus (and still holding the handle of the destroyed pitcher), Lady Millhouse asked them, "Do you think that feist was due to the truffles or the oysters?"

As Beecher appeared to be laid out of his senses, Lord Millhouse grabbed a tankard from an onlooker and threw the ale in his face. It did little to rouse him. Hence, it was left to the gentlemen to take care of him and he and Bingley each clasped an arm.

Bingley hissed to a footman, "Get the coach!"

With the utmost rapidity (and very little fanfare) Bingley's coach was drawn up. When the door flew open, it was not by a footman's hand, but Darcy's.

Bingley was exultant to see his friend, "Darcy, you seem arrive at the most propitious moments!"

Wasting no time with pointless questions, the moment he gained the ground, Darcy grabbed one of Beecher's legs (the other bobbed along the ground quite on its own). It was, after all, only fitting that such an odious duty was not left to servitors, but carried out by true men of honour. It was the least they could do for the reputation of an actual gentleman.

"I am here quite by chance," Darcy said as they walked.

As they had to struggle to lug Beecher's surprisingly obese person to the coach, Fitzwilliam held open the coach door. They did not speak again until the loathsome chore was done.

"On three," Bingley said. "One, two, and *three!*"

Beecher landed in the bed of the coach much as he had on the ground. This time when he landed, his rump emitted only a single "toot."

As the men dusted their gloves of any leftover residue of Beecher's person, they spoke as if they had just lifted a dirty hamper into the coach. Darcy did not inquire what came to pass.

Instead, he explained to Bingley, "It is Fitzwilliam who said we must observe what sort of stock could be found here. We were quite disappointed at Maidenhead. The man had no colts. Indeed, he had nothing but foals."

It was said that Lord Winton Beecher came to his senses halfway to town. The Bingleys abandoned Beecher and Caroline to ride alone to London. Taking a stand, Charles announced to his sister that his children would no longer be subjected to her husband's abhorrent behaviour. Having missed the accusatory portion of the conflagration, Caroline feverishly questioned her husband as to why Kneebone was so determined to have a duel. In the past, such events occurred due to financial transgressions. Stone-faced, Beecher kept his own counsel on the matter, only altering his slouched position when he was overcome by a retch.

Whilst Jane fretted over Caroline's public humiliation, Bingley washed his hands of it. He would not allow so small a thing as near-murder ruin his day at the races.

"Caroline made her bed...." he reminded Jane. "We have done all we can."

He and his family meant to stay in Newmarket the rest of the week, happy to be unencumbered by loutish relatives.

The last Sally saw of Kneebone was as he was taken away in Mr. Darcy's coach. It was a disappointment for her to see such a good and honourable man as the Major be driven to such ends, particularly through the agency of his inconstant wife. It was said that Mr. Darcy meant to return Kneebone to Chelsea. In the time he was there, Mr. Darcy took no notice of her. That was of no great surprise. That gentleman had much on his mind. It would fall to him to console and admonish Major Kneebone and, no doubt, censure Mrs. Kneebone too. A thankless duty that.

After Beecher's coach was out of sight, Darcy's coach, followed by the Millhouses, lumbered onto the road to London. On the seat next to Sally, Lady Millhouse sat in appalled silence, an attitude quite unfamiliar of her. Whaling away on a ne'er-do-well did not cause it. More likely she had time to recall the scandalous behaviour they witnessed and was displeased about it. For all her blustering, she had firm rules of conduct and they did not include roguery.

Lord Millhouse's countenance did not display the same disturbance as did his wife's. His sensibilities were not insulted by his wife's timely beaning of Beecher. Nor could his injury at her thrashing of the horse seller be put at no higher than "surprised." As for herself, Sally was rather impressed by her ladyship's gumption. She would be a force to be reckoned with should she ever take up residence on Dyot Street. That set her mind to thinking of the common folk.

In the quiet, Sally reminded herself that the first spare minute in town she would pay her respects to Nell. Such a walk would also keep her from forgetting whence she came. As if aroused by the son of Odin, Lady Millhouse suddenly thundered, "Dare not forget we shall betake ourselves to Drury Theatre!"

It was not Sally place to make the observation, but she thought it important all the same. Once in London, tides could turn. She might not have another chance to speak her mind.

She said to Lady Millhouse, "Y'know, buyin' more ponies won't make any difference in them mines."

Her ladyship did not look in her direction, but replied, "We must do what we can."

Sally said, "In the Dials folks do a lot worse in the name of 'feedin' their families.'"

Her ladyship was silent only for a moment.

Then, she said, "A pony now, the world, in all good time."

Sally knew to be satisfied by that.

When the outskirts of London were in sight, Lord Millhouse said, "I understand that London's limits can be seen from the topmost gallery of St. Paul's Cathedral."

Sally responded, "It doesn't look all that small when you're afoot."

He laughed at the truth of her remark. Lady Millhouse did too, announcing her interest in town reinvigorated.

"We shall go to Astley's to watch the equestrian performances," she said eagerly. "First we must get you a proper bonnet!"

"Yes'm," said Sally.

As soon as she could sneak out the garden way from the Millhouses' townhouse, Sally trudged up Ayliffe Street and through Goodman's Fields to the cemetery where her grandmother lay.

In the few years she had been gone from town, she found it much altered. Indeed, a menace overtook the streets unlike any she had known before. Doorways were darker than smut and crafty eyes hid down alleys causing skeletal cats and mangy dogs to fend for themselves on the thoroughfares.

Most unexpected were the black-clad men who sat upon the gravestones. They were armed with sticks, as if they feared the corpses might climb from their coffins to threaten passers-by with death. Initially, she was alarmed, certain these were the ghosts of suicides wrongly laid to rest in the churchyard. Everyone knew they had to have a stake driven through their heart and be buried at a crossroads so the devil would be confused.

One ghoul raised a hand in her direction, bidding her have a good day. That meant it was unlikely that they were apparitions from beyond the grave.

The truth was far worse.

$\mathscr{L}$ucifer Lies in London

Colonel Fitzwilliam was happy for a single part of the whole stink.
He said, "At least Kneebone has not sullied his uniform with such an unhappy performance."

Darcy did not reply. He was vexed. When he commenced upon his journey, he had promised Elizabeth that he would be only in the furthermost reaches of town. Now he was not only forced into Chelsea to return Kneebone to kith and kin, he was to suffer the abhorrent company of Lydia as well.

Fitzwilliam made another pronouncement. He would take upon his shoulders the task of scouring the countryside for the perfect colt for young Geoff. He left the coach to Darcy and went on his way with an air of self-congratulations. Darcy, however, was not fooled by such subterfuge. Fitzwilliam simply wanted to avoid the brouhaha. (Facing Napoleon's Imperial Guard would be a preferable to witnessing the guilt and recriminations of a marriage gone to the bad.) Darcy did not blame him. Kneebone was not his kin; Lydia was not his sister-in-law. (Fitzwilliam was not kin to Bingley either, but was happy to keep him company at the fair.)

Was that not his unhappy circumstance, Darcy would certainly not be toting a drunken cuckold back to his unadoring wife

During the journey from Newmarket to town, Major Kneebone sobered. His head hurt and he had a need to talk freely of his many tribulations. By inclination uninterested in another man's marital woes, Darcy found himself a captive to poor Hugh's unhappy delineation of the milestones in the deterioration of his unpropitious marriage to Lydia Bennet Wickham. Darcy was not entirely unsympathetic. She was a young woman he had detested from the very moment they had first been introduced.

Moreover, jealousy needed no explanation. Darcy understood why Kneebone went after Beecher. He was only curious as to how he came to find him when and where he did. Caroline and Beecher were constantly on the move, most often one step ahead of their creditors. In the erratic political climate, gentlemen were unable to carry a tab as they once had. His extravagances were only exceeded by Caroline's. It had been necessary for

Bingley to keep Caroline's money from them lest they squander it all.

"How did you come to know where to find Beecher?" Darcy asked.

"Mrs. Bingley told Lydia," Kneebone answered flatly.

Darcy replied, "Of course."

"I have a daughter," Kneebone said miserably. "If it was but me, I would have taken my leave long before now. I dare not leave a defenceless child in the sole custody of a mother who...." He paused and then said, "I beg forgiveness of all of my many shortcomings, for they have been on goodly display today."

Darcy gave a nod. He did not say more, fearing any comment might encourage further divulgements of an intimate nature. When such was made by anyone, he was always left with the uncomfortable choice of either commiseration or encouragement. As he was unused to offering them, when he did, his words sounded stilted and insincere. Upon those occasions, he could hear Elizabeth's voice gently chastising him to take the time practise that which did not come easy to him.

"Shall I take my leave of her, Mr. Darcy? I have just cause," Kneebone queried wretchedly.

Advice was not Darcy's strong suit either. This was not because of a lack of opinion (for he did have that), but his belief that offering another counsel should be the sole office of the clergy. In place of a recommendation, Darcy offered him only an observation.

"It has been my experience that even a bad mother is better for a child than no mother whatsoever. Protection from such ills is the foremost duty of a father."

"Is it that simple?" Kneebone replied.

"Simple? I think not," mused Darcy.

Kneebone grew quiet.

As they drew nearer to Chelsea, both gentlemen's thoughts were alike. It remained to be discovered whether Lydia was at home or had fled elsewhere. She might well have fled, for Kneebone said that he had spent many days drinking and thinking of nothing but her infidelity—and railing against the cur who connived to break his semi-happy home asunder. Alas, in the end, Kneebone took more of the blame upon his shoulders than he should have and lay none whatsoever on Lydia.

When they gained the steps leading to Kneebone's house, Darcy did not accompany him inside. Was he to do so, he could not trust himself to remain civil to Lydia. As far as he could discern, Major Kneebone had been a good husband to her. He had loved her well when she was inconstant. What sort of husband would he have been, had she been a faithful wife? He knew that Elizabeth had penned similar words of wisdom to her. Would that she had simply heeded them.

To Darcy's surprise, Lydia had not fled. She greeted her husband on the doorstep, her eyes bright with excitement.

"Hughie! Hughie, my love! How could you? You might have been killed! Did you do him harm? They shall take you away, you know—and where shall your poor wife and daughter be without you? I promise you never to drive you to such madness again! I *promise!*"

With that, the door was closed. It was just as well, Darcy had no interest in hearing those protestations and promises that were unlikely to be recalled from this day to the next. He also disliked knowing that the day's misadventure would have to be related to Elizabeth. She always despised the cost her family caused his dignity. He vowed to be more reassuring to her on that count.

Across the country from his family and without a horse for his son, he was in the one place he did not care to be. Gloom threatened his mood. It was late in the day. He vowed to leave London at first light. Although he did not look favourably upon an overnight stay, he resigned himself to make good use of his time. With the present unrest permeating all levels of society, he would satisfy himself that his own accounts were well-watched. That would mean a trip to Threadneedle Street. He would stop there first ere he betook himself on the road home.

Rapping his walking stick on the roof of the coach, he directed his driver to Mayfair.

As he travelled the familiar cobbles, he looked out the window impassively. Whilst he in no way felt menaced, there was an undercurrent of discontent apparent through placards and notices weighing down every fence and post along the way. From his vantage, London seemed even less orderly than it had been when he last occasioned it. For all its blathering, the government had done nothing to help, and managed to enrage the masses in the process.

He was still pondering that as he entered his house. It was a reassurance to think of his family safe in Derbyshire.

As his road-weary coat was taken, a footman extended a silver tray. Upon it lay several cards and a letter. The cards were of no interest to him. In some ways London was still not above a country village. Everyone in town still knew who had arrived and where they were to dine before the horses were unhitched. The letter caught his attention. It was addressed by the increasingly familiar hand of Lady Howgrave.

He gave an inward sigh. Whether it reflected badly on his manners or not, he meant to ignore Juliette's letter. No doubt it would contain more of the entreaties that he had hitherto turned away.

He had waffled far too long before (and in) telling Elizabeth of the business with Juliette and his hat. For all that, he still had not told her that Lady Howgrave had importuned him with a lewd request. Whether to add to Elizabeth's agitation troubled his conscience, his scruples, and his sleep. He abhorred speaking of such unsavoriness to anyone, much less to his wife. If he did speak of it to her, any further acquaintanceship with the Howgraves would certainly be compromised. To his mind, it had already been fractured.

Whatever Juliette's design, she must find a more willing accomplice somewhere else. He did not doubt for a moment that she would. Yet unopened, he dropped Lady Howgrave's missive onto on the table. There were more pressing matters at hand.

The next morning he had a quick cup of tea and girded himself to wade back through the street traffic.

Unsurprisingly, the town was not much improved from the day before. What he saw upon Threadneedle Street that day told him a great deal about the temper of the times. It was thick with coaches, but very few open carriages or lone horsemen were to be seen. (Darcy surmised that gentlemen were going to great lengths not to attract attackers.) Despite the congestion, he made good time. As he meant to be on his way, he too was in his coach. He alit from it just steps from the bank's offices. Before he could enter, he was hailed.

"Ho, Darcy!" said Sir Henry Howgrave. "I say, have you come to count your money? You must hurry lest they close the doors on you ere you are but half-way done with it!"

With great reluctance, Darcy spoke to Howgrave. He did not, however, inquire after the health of Howgrave's wife.

Howgrave gushed, "You must come with me tonight. I am to give a talk at Marylebone at half-past seven. I shall speak to the latest outrages in the countryside. I shall have my lovely wife by my side. She makes quite a fuss when she has to forgo one of my speeches. Alistair, that is my secretary, Alistair Reed Thomas, is very good with her for she can be a bit testy. I cannot say enough good about him. He was Wellington's attaché during the wars."

Darcy demurred, but did not suggest they meet another time.

Finding no offence at his refusal, Howgrave began upon his way. Abruptly, he stopped and turned about.

Said he, "By the by, did you hear? A man's murdered body was found behind White's at first light today. Likely throttled. Are we safe nowhere? Will these rioters not leave gentlemen one inviolable House wherein to be entertained? We shall not be denied. Boodle's will do. Perhaps you will join us there tonight? No? I understand."

Darcy bid him good day and did not think again of their conversation. After his business had been concluded, he obtained a newspaper from a street vender. He folded it, placed it under his arm, and did not read it until he reached the solitude of his coach. When he opened it, bold headlines heralded the heinous murder behind White's. The story related every grisly detail. He did not read it in its entirety. As he began to turn the page, he happened to catch sight of the victim's name.

It read, "Cyril Smeads."

That Cyril Smeads had come to an unceremonious end was unsettling. But then, Darcy knew that Smeads was the untrustworthy sort. Perhaps he had betrayed a man of a volatile nature, for the description of the crime suggested it was one of unusual ferocity. Somehow, the matter left him exceedingly uneasy. As he bethought the subject, bit by bit, he was further troubled.

Dead Cyril Smeads, Juliette and her new escort, the illustrious Alistair Reed Thomas.... When it came to him, those revolving thoughts coalesced as it lit by gunpowder.

Reed Thomas. Thomas Reed. The name Wickham had signed to the vellum....

Wickham.

₰he Devil & Cyril Smeads

Before the dust had settled upon their arrival in town, Lady Millhouse had Sally perusing Rowlandson's latest drawings as they were pasted onto the window of the print shop. This proclivity was due less to possible parsimony (they did not come cheap) than her ladyship's desire to be the first to see his next masterpiece. Sally did not read all that well, it was easy enough to decipher the cartoon's social comment without making out the captions.

After a good laugh they stopped at the confectioner's, then on to Berkeley Square. Just that bit of walking on the cobbles made Sally's feet hurt and she had begun to admire the thought of her ugly, but comfortable boots. Lady Millhouse urged her on, for she had a whim.

"Tomorrow we shall see 'Gentleman' Jackson's boxing saloon. Now, let us stroll down St. James Street. It is the home of a number of men's clubs and is therefore forbidden to ladies of condition."

It was as just as her ladyship promised. The windows of White's bowed outward. The chairs there were filled with snide-looking young bucks, brushed and shined like they were gentlemen. All of them had quizzing glasses and openly salivated at any young lady daring to pass nearby. As Sally and Lady Millhouse passed under their scrutiny, the ribbon of Sally's new bonnet chafed her and she ran her finger around it to loosen it a bit. Being eyed by young men of the ton (with clean fingernails and dandified airs) made her colour heighten. Lady Millhouse's contrariness was aroused at the sight of them. She hesitated only in deciding how best to upbraid them. In the end, she let them be, possibly of the belief that she had abused her good name quite enough just being there.

"I would take you inside, but his lordship fears for my safety, the dear man. I do adore him and, upon occasion, abide by his wishes. He belongs to all the clubs. As a man of the hunt, he prefers Boodle's. Serious gamblers favour White's. Indeed, they say White's has never known to blackball anyone."

Before Sally could protest, her ladyship had a change of heart. She caught Sally's hand and tugged her towards the door.

She said, "Let's have a peek. That could do no harm. I care little who mocks me behind my back, do you?"

Giddy by the adventure, they burst through the doors arm in arm—and much to the horror of the troglodytes of the beau monde. Sally knew she looked like what she was—a fancied-up malkin from over the way—and endeavoured not to care about their stares. Lady Millhouse flitted by the young nobs, uninterested in their attention or their opinions. Gaining a seat against the wall, she called out an order of lemonade for them both and looked about the place with great enthusiasm.

She said, "I have no idea why gentlemen enjoy such places. The ornaments are a bit dreary."

From the window seats came a cacophony of laughter. Amidst the subtle sound of dice, someone made reference to a "horse's godmother" which begat more giggles. There was little doubt of whom they spoke. Sally was indignant at such effrontery. Her ladyship could be accused of being a bit strong-featured, but for one who enjoyed the outdoors, her skin was unweathered. Indeed, she bore a healthy glow and a firm figure from her time on horseback.

"A bunch of over-bred twiddle-poops," Sally opined.

"Fops one and all," agreed Lady Millhouse.

Impatient and thirsty, Sally went to get their drinks for them. This was most likely ill-mannered, but as a servant girl, she felt it well within her domain to do so. As she passed by a man with a tray of drinks, she looked at him twice. His countenance looked quite familiar. When she returned with their lemonades, Sally sat silently sipping the refreshment. As she did, she continued to eye the server.

"Does that man look familiar?" she asked, flicking her head in his direction.

Rather than take a subtle glance, her ladyship turned compleatly about in her chair and pointed, "That one there, dear?"

The man was busy handing out drinks and did not see her. She knew him, however, and had a name for him too.

"He was cast out of Pemberley for gross misbehaviour. Smeads, I believe is his name."

It was. It *was* Smeads. Sally Frances recalled the first time she spied him. It had been upon her first foray into the land of the gentry. Looking to learn what befell her brother, she had gone to the Darcys' house in Mayfair and mistook Smeads, a man of considerable pomposity, as the master of the house. He was an oddly constructed little man, nothing less than a lascivious fusspot. Watching him take money from beneath the tables, Sally concluded that he did more than draw drinks for the gentlemen. She could not decide whether to make herself known to him or not.

That decision was made for her as he recognised the lady she accompanied. He gave her ladyship a tight little bow, but nary a peep came from his lips.

Indeed, Smeads had nothing to say to Lady Millhouse as she was quite witting of the particular nature of his dismissal. The old boot had some gall to come inside like that. It was obvious the lady did not care if she was deemed a lady or not. She and her little servant girl went on their way directly. She left a penny on the table just to vex him. He tucked it into his waistcoat all the same.

Another table tucked in a corner was filled with men in urgent conversation. From the ribbons pinned to their lapels, some had to be politicians. (When women and politicians came in a place at will, that club was clearly losing its cachet.) Although that sort was a bit niggardly in doling out gratuities, Smeads hurried to them anyway. They were good patrons of the other services he arranged (that of the company of women of the loose-legged variety).

Clean white cloth over his arm, he offered them his ear. In murmuring voices, specific orders were given. With great efficiency, he wrote down the details of the particular trysts he was to arrange. Within moments, Smeads recognised another personage from Derbyshire in White's. This one he had not seen in years, but as a servant he had kept close tabs on his various (and nefarious) doings.

Indeed, he had been presumed dead.

Always with a nose-open for a chance of money, Smeads took heed. Any man who was thought to be dead and was not, was begging to be extorted. (Smeads did not make the rules, he merely observed them.) The group was deep with back-slapping members of Parliament. Indeed, Sir Howgrave was a patron of all the clubs. Howgrave called George Wickham, "Alistair." Smeads was well aware of Howgrave's questionable lineage. Politics was a filthy business, the perfect place for men of compromised breeding. It was little wonder that Howgrave and Wickham were thick as thieves. Their ilk found their own level.

Smeads waited until their little conclave broke up before daring to speak to George Wickham candidly.

When he first addressed him, Wickham bore that slightly abused expression often employed by the aristocratic when their person was contaminated by lessers. As few gentlemen bothered to look at who served them, he did not immediately recognise Cyril Smeads. With the added bother of having to place a face out of its usual context, Smeads's identity came to Wickham with surprising rapidity.

"Why, Smeads good man. I thought you were still slaving under the whip of the Darcy family. Did you steal a spoon?" he laughed.

As Wickham spoke to him in a jovial manner, and Smeads responded in a servile fashion, most would not detect the machinations whirling behind each man's eyes. It would have been a test whose brain had the upper hand.

"Your hair is quite handsome, sir," Smeads dared to say.

As the son of Mr. Darcy's steward, Wickham was not Smeads better—at least not originally. Now that Wickham was skulking about with men of station, he had leapt a level or two. Hence, it was a precarious job employing just the correct amount of subservience. But he did. Wickham remained quite friendly until one of his companions called to him to follow them on to their next watering hole. It was Howgrave.

"Alistair," he called, impatience straining his joviality. "Shall you come with us, or do you prefer your present company?"

"In a moment," Wickham said.

As everyone knew Smeads arranged womanly favours, their discourse was not suspect. When Wickham was called by another name, the expression upon Smeads face barely altered. (Inscrutability was his particular talent.) The small alteration that did attend his features gave Wickham (who spent his life gauging such variations) a clear edge. Of this, Smeads was unwitting.

He knew only that for whatever reason George Wickham wanted these men (a man of Parliament, two lords, a judge, and a diarist) to believe him to be someone else. To Smeads's mind, that smelled of money. (Indeed, that which was obtained by exaction was the very sweetest kind.) Smeads, quite obsequiously, bid to speak to Wickham in confidence.

"Let us meet at ten," Wickham said agreeably.

Wickham's smile was brilliant. He even twirled his walking stick as he took his leave.

Preparing for battle, Smeads went over what he knew. Wickham was thought to be dead. If he was not, he was to be tried in court for desertion and murder. He was thick with men of means and well-imbedded into a scheme of national importance. Silence would be crucial to him. The only thing left was for Smeads to determine—what price did Wickham fancy his freedom was worth? It would be a matter of successive payments, of course. Blackmail is never a one-time expense.

Smeads retrieved a cigar from his waistband and lit it. Puffing away, he marvelled. What a treat! Two persons of his past acquaintance in one day.

One was just a nothing country lady. The second was to be the plunderer of a thousand pirates. Smeads went out the back, tore off his apron and cast it aside. If he played his hand correctly, he would not be in need that again—ever.

That was the single presage of the evening that he got right.

ℐoing Snacks

Sally's grand return to town was remarkable for its diversions. The daylight hours saw them tour Bond Street, insult propriety and buy her first lace-trimmed gown. That next night they took their amusement at Covent Garden. In between the two, she saw to Nell.

The gown Lady Millhouse bought for her was a lovely lilac. The lace scratched, her slippers hurt, and her new stockings drooped (causing her to dig at her petticoat every so often lest they fall down around her ankles). These sacrifices to fashion were made freely, for the thrill of silk far outweighed the cost in aggravation.

Was it possible, Lady Millhouse was more inspirited than Sally over the performances they were to observe.

Her ladyship told her excitedly, "Tonight we have an opera; tomorrow next we shall enjoy Grimaldi."

"Yes," interrupted Lord Millhouse who was a great admirer of the clown, "He has great fun at the audience's expense. It is a high time, indeed."

The particulars meant nothing to Sally, but the Millhouses' enthusiasm was enlivening. However, in a week brimming with surprises, forthwith of this discourse came another, even greater astonishment to Sally.

After molesting a horse-trader, crowning a gent, and brazenly intruding into unladylike venues on all corners of the West End without a by-your-leave, Lady Millhouse was reluctant to sally forth into the neighbourhood surrounding of Covent Garden without holding her husband's arm.

"We must take heed and allow Lord Millhouse to precede us through the streets, for Drury and Bow are notorious for persons of dubious repute."

Sally knew, in truth, she was of "dubious repute," and she was a bit miffed to be considered a peril to persons of peerage. As these particular gentlefolk were quite good to her, she meant to ease their qualms by assigning herself to mind them.

Taking the arm of each, she told them, "Let us have no fears, for now you shall be under my watch."

Lord Millhouse doffed his hat in acquiescence and they went unto Covent Garden, laughing like children. Their anticipation was well-rewarded. Her ladyship had been quite correct when she assured Sally that she would not need to understand the words. The music, indeed, transported her. Not only had she been bestirred by the opera, their seats overlooking the stage made the entire production all the more wondrous to her.

"It were as if they were singing just for me," she chattered happily as they exited the theatre.

It was near midnight when Lord Millhouse called for their coach. As the theatre goers dispersed, the gaslights cast eerie, elongated shadows from each figure. Sally was unused to the gaslights and the ghostly forms reminded her of those she had seen at the graveyard. She began to feel less like a guardian and more like quarry. Of the country for so long, she had forgotten how forbidding the streets of town could be. As they were much taken by the chore of claiming their coach to make their away, the Millhouses seemed unbothered. However, one murky form arrested Sally's attention—most alarmingly so. Indeed, had Winged Pegasus have lit in her path, Sally could not have been more astonished.

It may not have been a ghost, but sure as Sunday it was a wraith from her past.

Daisy Mulroney stepped onto the walkway in front of them. Wearing a bright red jacket, her hair was tucked away beneath a bonnet the size of a small waggon. Still, Daisy was easily recognisable. As Sally was compleatly flummoxed herself, she could not precisely gauge the Millhouses' expressions. She could tell that Daisy had caught their attention. Sally could sense Lord Millhouse prickling a bit. Indeed, he did not seem to like the look of Daisy— many did not—and he called again for his coachman. From his posture, Sally believed he knew not whether to nod to the female confronting them, or beat her away with his walking stick. Sally put out a hand, protecting whom from what, she was uncertain.

To Sally, Daisy said, "We need to jaw."

Without looking at Lady Millhouse, Sally nodded, thus following Daisy as if a siren up Bow Street.

At the last minute, her ladyship called out, "Shall we wait here for you?"

With false gaiety, Sally answered that she would find her way back herself. St. Giles, after all, was within yowling distance of where they stood.

"Tell 'em I got me a carriage," Daisy whispered. "I don't wanna be arrested for child-stealin."

Sally stifled the urge to argue that she was hardly a child and called back to the Millhouses, saying, "The lady's my friend and she has a carriage."

No further proof of gentility was needed than that one kept a carriage. (They were glad to hear from Sally that the undersized person, whom she claimed as her friend, was, indeed, a woman.) Hence, they quit their efforts to keep possession of their young friend. As they watched her go, however, their gazes were fondly apprehensive. Daisy's expression was a bit perplexed too. She glanced at Sally and frowned uncomprehendingly.

She said, "I wouldn't have taken ten to one that yer'd turned into a lady."

Sally retorted, "Yer came up a bit in station yerself."

Daisy snorted, "We don't got time fer catchin' up on each other's achievements. Seein's yer here, I got to tell you that yer got trouble."

"Me?" Sally asked incredulously.

Knowing Daisy was not one to exaggerate, Sally awaited her revelations—but no privacy to speak was at hand.

Indeed, the Millhouses were not the only stares Daisy drew. The opera-goers were dispersing, but rascals and round-heels had just begun their evenings and cast their eyes about for easy prey. Daisy grabbed Sally and made haste to her coach. Sally was well-impressed. It was a fine carriage (two seats, velvet upholstery) and it came with an impeccably-dressed footman, who hastily lowered the steps. Once ensconced and on their way, Daisy was ready to speak openly. It was no surprise that Sally knew what she would say before she uttered the name.

"Wickham."

Still, Sally protested the name, "No."

"Yes!" said Daisy.

"No!" Sally insisted, not wanting to believe that he had actually survived.

"Yes," Daisy announced with finality, thus ending the verbal impasse.

Sally finally admitted the obvious, "He didn't die. That rat."

"Nay," claimed Daisy. "He's alive and walkin' the streets with hair white as Lucifer's and sportin' a bad limp. He's called by another name but it's him fer certain. He's back to his old tricks too!"

Sally Frances Arbuthnot mused but a moment, before opining, "I guess I shouldn't have used that pea-shooter. A bigger gun would'a done a better job. Next time, I'll know. If you want to kill a snake, you chop of its head."

Turning to Daisy, she bid, "Is he after us?"

"Not that I know of, but you know he won't leave it. He's gettin' bolder by the day."

"You'da thought he'd take off across the waters—what with him wanted for murder and all. Where'd yer see him?" asked Sally.

Daisy said, "I built me a four-storey house up the way, but business took me to an alehouse called the Fortune of War—it's a real bucket of blood. Recent years have seen the place taking an even worse turn. Now it's used as a meeting place for resurrectionists."

Sally leapt to her own conclusion, "A grave-robber? Him? A brothel bully suits his scruples, but not his mettle."

Daisy replied, "I heard he was pimpin' women, so it wasn't no far jump to brokerin' bodies. He don't dirty his hands though. He paid others for that and he worked out the sale. Sold dead folks teeth too, he did."

Although she should not have been, Sally was confounded.

"Ain't he 'fraid of being seen, him being a known murderer? Aren't you afraid he'd see you? You ain't exactly easy to miss...."

"He's the one that needs to be scared," Daisy said defiantly.

"You ain't exactly hard to recognise," insisted Sally.

"So yer said."

Sally altered the subject, "I thought you took yer leave of town."

Daisy replied, "Town suits me better now I got some money."

That was an easy conclusion. Something else came to Sally.

"When I went to pay respects to my grannun's grave, it was watchers I saw."

Daisy told her, "Now that our Wickham's agitatin' rioters and the like, he's running with some foul types."

"Would you expect otherwise?" interrupted Sally.

"You better take care," advised Daisy. "He'd know me certain as sin, but he may recall you too."

Sally drew herself up proudly and, sniffing as if she was but one from a baronetcy, she replied, "I can take care of myself."

Daisy paid that cheek no mind. She laughed mirthlessly at Wickham's impertinence.

"Can you believe it—he calls himself Alistair Reed Thomas now," Daisy said. "He calls himself after my dead brother. What bollocks!"

Another worry crossed Sally's mind.

She said, "We best advise Mr. Darcy of it."

"He's up north, idn't he?" asked Daisy.

"No, he's meant to be...."

"You keep up wi' 'em then?"

Lost in other thoughts, Sally did not answer that.

She fretted, "We'd better tell him."

"Yer do what yer want," responded Daisy. "I got my own affairs to see to."

"Oh, yeah?" Sally said.

"Town ain't like it was. Vagrants don't go unmolested. Used to, if beggers got too thick they'd be rounded up by the parish constable. Most of the time, if they weren't hurtin' no one, he didn't bother with 'em. Now they went and hired a collector—a failed stay-maker from Highgate they say—who pinches 'em for ten shillings a head. Debtors what owe good money belong in gaol, not poor citizens who ain't got a hare's squat."

After her outburst, Daisy went silent. Sally directed her to the end of the block near the Millhouse mansion. As she leapt from the carriage, they gave no good-byes. Sally looked back once, but all she could see was the mist.

The streetlights gave the damp cobbles an unearthly sheen. A flower seller trundled her cart off down the street. It was very late, or very early. Sally had lost track of time. The bridge between opulence and decay was a short one. In the still air, the stench of the offensive trades wafted around her. The night soil man attended the chamber jars, the sight whereof made Sally wonder why Wickham could not be disposed of as easily. It would have been fair for his body to be laid out for anatomists, but then he would be too far gone to appreciate the irony.

Sally worried whether to tell Darcy about Wickham—and the Millhouses too. Her ladyship knew Wickham, both of them did.

To kill a snake, yer got to cut off his head.

84

The Boast

Darcy was aghast!

Wickham was not dead, but alive and well—no doubt living in extravagance at taxpayers' expense.

He not only walked the streets with impunity, but he had the unmitigated gall to employ the appellation of the man who had kidnapped Elizabeth! The mere thought of that indignation stole Darcy's breath. He endeavoured to collect himself, for much was at stake.

Had Smeads recognised Wickham? Did Wickham then do murder again? It was certainly feasible. He had killed before to conceal his foul deeds. The pieces of information fit together quite easily. Darcy could certainly perceive of Wickham infiltrating political camps. Such devilry as had passed for statesmanship of late stank of his interference. Moreover, if that cur had attached himself to Lady Howgrave, the acquaintance was not fuelled by altruism. (Wickham spent absolutely no extended amount of time with a woman without reward of some sort.) He held out hope that Juliette was not allowing him liberties. Was she, then she might be in grave danger. She was a woman of the world, but her troubles might leave her unusually vulnerable.

The missive she sent him still lay on the silver tray. That pricked his conscience.

Darcy considered, and then discarded, the notion of exposing Wickham to Howgrave that very moment. However, he could not be certain of their connection. It was quite probable that Howgrave would not recognise Wickham, for he came into his fortune after Wickham had been banned from Pemberley. There was little doubt, however, that Wickham knew Howgrave. Wickham kept abreast of (and revelled in) all the county gossip. Whatever their association, both men were manipulative scoundrels with accommodating morals. Howgrave might admire a man of Wickham's particular talents.

After considering all sides, Darcy decided that he would apprise Howgrave of his secretary's identity through a third party. However, he believed it best to warn Lady Howgrave directly. In this, he meant to be swift and discrete.

It lay undecided whether to confront this Alistair Reed Thomas himself. The man had nine lives.

Darcy could not trust himself not to take a whack at one or two of them.

"Word has reached me," Juliette announced.

Her inflection was soft, even forgiving, but her words were not. Alistair inspected his fingernails as she spoke.

She said, "Information had reached me of your boasts."

Without hesitation, he said, "Lies! Others envy my place with you."

Most unpropitously, he made his denial before the specifics of his transgression had been given. In a moment, he realised that and grew silent. Forming a steeple with his fingers, he pursed his lips. She sighed and then continued.

"You have boasted that I have afforded you favours in these chambers."

She felt as if she were scolding a recalcitrant child. However, it was vital that she persuade him to keep his silence about their affair. She had only deigned to accept him into her bed to salve her wounded ego. They had only been intimate upon a few occasions. He seemed not to care that they could both be killed. They both had reason to be exceedingly wary. Howgrave's marital rites had plunged into such degradation, she believed he would admire any excuse to smite her, her lover, and the horse upon which he rode.

Her state of affairs had done nothing but deteriorate since allying herself with the likes of Alistair Thomas. One must never allow a braggart privy to one's concerns. Bed him, perhaps—tell him secrets, never. That can only lead to vexation. (It was a lesson once well-taken—one that loneliness forgot.) Confidences were often exchanged in the somnolent afterglow of sexual congress; hers she yielded all too willingly. Juliette knew she must tread carefully. She had come to understand that Alistair was a man quite capable of the worst kind of betrayal—and a fool as well.

So far as she could determine, his boasts had not seeped beyond her particular circle of woman-friends. Alistair had been quick to infiltrate them.

"If others know, soon Henry shall know...." she fretted.

"I am as silent as the grave," he lied. "Your husband is a knave who cannot piss without filling his boots. He knows nothing of our attachment—and he never will."

"Attachment?" Juliette repeated incredulously before reclaiming herself. "I thought we agreed, *Mon ami,* we share nothing more than a flirtation. Each warms the other's body."

"If I recall correctly, we have a mission—that of impregnation," he simpered.

In listening to him, the folly of the entire gambit was obvious. She would have said as much, but Alistair was not listening. He was busy grousing about her husband.

"Two stone underweight, he is. I do not fear him! He is nothing but a pudding-headed son of a chambermaid! I am an superior marksman!"

Upon that assertion, Alistair flung himself into a chair and slung his leg over the arm, kicking his foot with exaggerated insouciance. Sighing, Juliette resigned herself to living out her days foisted between a fool's fodder and a laughing ass. Dashed was her faint hope that she might not need Darcy and his fertile loins. It had been an unmitigated disaster. For all his poking about, Alistair had not had any greater luck impregnating her than had her husband. She pondered the oft told caution that if one did not take pleasure in the act, one would not fall with child. She had always discounted that premise. An undue number of children were born of rape and indifference. She had come to believe, however, that coital exhilaration was a great advantage to beget a babe.

Although he went to near acrobatic lengths to hide it, Alistair's ball-sack was half-empty. That was quite obvious to a woman of her... experience. Due to her wellspring of lovers, she was quite witting of all sorts of genital abnormalities. His state could be attributed simply to a case of an undescended testicle. Perhaps, it caused his limp. Nonetheless, Alistair's procreative abilities were compromised by half.

The only advantage to abandoning her schemes was that she would not have to gird herself to betray Darcy.

Had he come to her just once, she would have asked nothing more of him. That one concession would have been triumph enough. It would have gone a long way towards healing the sting of his first rejection. Her recollection of that long past night was still fresh. She had employed every measure known to her (and her ways were many) to tempt him to her bed, but he had refused her. Once was a humiliation; twice an abomination.

When Alistair proposed the complicated deception, injuring Darcy's standing seemed the surest way to enjoy vengeance.

It was all nonsense, of course.

As it became ever more obvious that Darcy would not rescue her from her very present hell, rather than finding solace in Alistair's schemes, she forsook them altogether. Plucking through her bijoutier for bits of jewellery to sell, she vowed to fund her own way. There were many pieces that she abhorred. The gold letter-knife was vulgar—a gift from Lord Orloff. It would not be missed. Indeed, her plans were coalescing quite nicely. An old beau had offered her a villa in Venice. There, she would lick her wounds, happy to leave England and its satyrs and rogues behind.

Nothing exposed the truth of that observation more than the recumbent form of Alistair Reed. One by one, he was decimating the grapes from a delectable tray of fruit. Just as he tossed one into the air, she abruptly stood.

"My husband is come."

Startled, Alistair's mouth popped shut and the grape bounced off his forehead.

Her call was a ruse, one designed to watch how hastily Alistair could scramble away when he thought he might be caught where he ought not to be. Her husband would not return for hours. Soon Alistair would realise that, but at that moment he claimed his hat and walking stick with the same scurrying pace as a rat disturbed in the pantry. Before he took his leave, he made an attempt to engage her in a wet, tongue-probing kiss. She tuned her cheek, wincing at the thought of it. He seemed not to notice when she wiped his saliva away. Perhaps even then, he had designs upon another woman's bed. Good riddance.

Through the same door Alistair departed, came her chamber-maid. In her hand she held a card. It was offered with such reverence that Juliette rather hastily snatched it from her proffered fingers.

As she read it, she exulted, "Fortune shines! God in heaven has heeded my prayers—and me, a soul so rarely to church. Never again shall I question...."

Tucking the card into her bodice, she began to pace about the room. She stopped, placing her hand across her racing heart in an attempt at becalming herself. It was all she could do to catch her breath, for it had abandoned her the moment she recognised Darcy's hand.

At last he had come.

Had she time to change her frock? No, just a fresh petticoat. With great dispatch, she rid herself of her pantalets. (They were lined with lace and frills, but she wanted no impediment should passions be inflamed.) Pinching her cheeks, she called to her maid to help re-pin her hair. Always a wisp or two was left to trail down her neck to assure that there was nothing *rangé* about her coiffure. A daub of perfume and she was prepared for what ever might come to pass.

At last he had come. He had come for her.

ℱlux and Femininity

L ong, delicate fingers snaking through his thick, dark hair; naked legs entwined, writhing. His manhood, engorged by desire, lay thick and wanting against her white thigh. She rolled the flat of her hand across it admiringly. Against his ear, her plump, cherry-coloured lips whispered provocations.

"Take me, mount me! I beg for the nectar of your loins! I am yours!"

Fleshly treason pardoned by wet lips and urgent moans.

A breathless, feminine voice, proclaimed, "Once lovers have lain as one, it can never be forgotten."

Over his shoulder, she looked at Elizabeth and asked, "Do you not agree?"

"What?" Elizabeth said, groggy with sleep.

She sat up in her bed, bidding, "Who is there?"

Holding a candle high, she looked first in her bed, and then about the room.

Her bed was empty, as was the room—echoingly empty.

No one had actually spoken.

It had been a dream—a very authentic and, therefore, troubling dream.

The faces of those who inhabited the vision had been indistinct. That is not to say the persons in the image were unrecognisable. As it happened, the *penis in erectus* was exceedingly familiar to her. It was the very one her husband owned (and wielded so handsomely, bringing her to rapture upon innumerable occasions). Indeed, when circumstances kept them apart, explicit dreams of Darcy (and his virile member) were a great pleasure to her. Then again, in those past dreams, she had always been his lover. She could not fathom why she dreamt that some succubus was having her way with her beloved husband.

Indeed, it was quite... vexing.

Replacing the candle, she fell back into the bedclothes. As the air was heavy, it was some time ere slumber once again embraced her. When it did, hers was a restless, haunted sleep. Again the spectre came to her. This time, the lovers were tangled in the bedclothes, their limbs grating against one another.

Fingernails raked across his broad back, leaving garish, red streaks behind. He presses between her thighs and she accepts him with lusty passion. As he impales her, she cries out, 'Yes, Darcy, oh, Darcy, *mais oui, oh, Oui, Mon cheri!*'"

Elizabeth sat up again. This time, she was drenched with perspiration and her breath came in great, heaving (possibly indignant) gulps, she threw back the covers. The cool air hit her bedewed body and within moments, the exposure to the chill made her shiver. With compleat awakening, came another truth.

This time, there was no denying it. The voice in the dream was Juliette's. It still echoed in her head—words of such intimacy she blushed in recollection. It was as if her own mind had made her a voyeur to her husband's infidelity. A cold, grasping hand of dismay clamped upon her heart. It took several minutes to convince herself that it was a fiction and not a true portrayal of her husband. Still, she dared not sleep again. The pain she felt was palpable.

Dropping to the floor, she drew Darcy's robe about her. Fearing what vexation might next afflict her, she was tempted to go to the nursery and take the remainder of the night with her children. That would surely soothe her, but might awaken them. She decided against it. Taking a candle in hand once more, she repaired to her dressing-room. It did not take much light to find what she sought. She withdrew it from the drawer and hastily ran back across the floor and leapt onto the bed.

With great care, she unwrapped the soft, protective cloth from the ivory miniature. She did not realise that she had held her breath until she released a great sigh of relief. Just the sight of her husband's likeness gazing back at her was a comfort. Holding the candle high, she ran her fingertips reassuringly across his features. One by one, she took measure of his countenance—strong chin, straight, patrician nose, and a singularly seductive lower lip. In the miniature, however, his eyes were dispassionate. That was its one falsehood. But then, no painter could capture the lightening that roiled beneath Darcy's taciturn exterior. His eyes, though reticent, were, in truth, as dark and deep as an abyss.

Although she had not yet shaken off her dreams, she understood what provoked them. A missive from Lady Howgrave arrived just days before. In swirling, sophisticated script, it bore Darcy's name. Believing that its contents might need the immediate attention of his solicitor, she had forwarded it to Darcy the moment it arrived. Perhaps she should have read the letter before redirecting it. Another wife might have done so. However, she did not believe her husband's devotion was so weak that a letter from another woman would contravene it.

Nonetheless, the lurid nightmares had been annoyingly real and they had agitated her in a way she did not care to admit. As it happened, it was not Juliette's letter that provoked them. Most likely, they were aggravated by a post she had received that afternoon. It was from Darcy, apprising her that he would be delayed.

He was to London after all.

One thing was no longer deniable. Elizabeth recognised that her dreams were announcing what she would not. Lady Howgrave did not want Darcy's aide as a gentleman. She wanted Darcy—and not to just decorate her arm. She might well have been abused by her husband, but she did not need Darcy for her to leave him. It took a woman to recognise another's design.

"'Nectar of his loins?' How ridiculous!" she thought. "Who would speak such nonsense? A woman of accommodating morals?"

Knowing that the more she fretted over such imaginings, the more they would plague her; she put out the candle and crawled beneath the bedclothes. This time, she held the miniature near to her heart. And with it, came a dreamless sleep.

86

Forewarned

There was but a matter of seconds between the time Darcy was announced and when he strode to her. Had she the time, she would have girded her loins—for they were much in need bracing. When he was but an arm's length away, he stopped abruptly and, almost as an afterthought, offered a stiff bow. His scent, a musky blend of masculinity and leather, wafted over her like the tide.

That and the very vigour of his figure gifted her a frisson within her feminine cleft. It was one so fully engaged that all her senses screamed that she run from the room and interfere with herself libidinously in private. Choosing between that and standing her ground (and pressing her knees together), she could but chose the latter.

With great determination, she disallowed her thoughts to dwell upon her very present titillation and take measure of his expression. That, more than words, would betray his true mind. She had seen him but once since his child's death, and that was in the darkness of his garden. Then, he had been inscrutably curt. In the candlelight of her salon, she could see him quite clearly and believed that she detected an alteration in his countenance. Unsurprisingly, it was one of great subtleness. She did not think it attributable to age. (Men had a maddening ability to grow ever more handsome with time.) Shaking aside such deliberations, she endeavoured to put what time he might allot her to good use. Her eyes—the avenue to one's very soul—promised him all she had to give.

With a half-gasp, she cried, "I knew you would come!"

As she said those words, the weight of her long-felt tribulations overcame her and she, quite without sham of any kind, fell into his arms. Her milky shoulders shuddered against his coat as she struggled not to weep. However sincere her cri de coeur might have been, Mr. Darcy did not respond in kind.

"I fear you mistake my visit, Lady Howgrave. I am not come in response to your previous entreaties, but to offer a caution of extreme urgency."

She took but a half step backward, just far enough that she could still feel the warmth of his breath. Placing a delicately manicured hand upon his forearm and an expression of due diligence upon her face, she listened.

"I have good reason to believe that a gentleman of your acquaintance is an impostor," he stated.

She sighed. "If you are here to apprise me of the fact that my husband is not a gentleman, he has proven that nightly."

Juliette had been arranging her bracelets, her thoughts much engaged in how to guide their conversation into one of intimacy, when something in his voice made her cease simpering and pay heed.

He continued, "I have come to learn that the man that you know as Alistair Reed Thomas may well be Major George Wickham, army deserter, murderer—a compleat villain. There is no deed too nefarious for him not to consider. His likeness is similar to mine—a twist of fate that has allowed him to repeatedly use my name ill."

Juliette placed the first three fingers of her right hand against her lips. In doing so, she allowed herself time to grasp fully what he had said. She recalled the name. Major Wickham had been married to Elizabeth Darcy's sister. It was above three years since her friend, Marie-Therese Lambert had come to her in London asking that she contact Darcy on her behalf. Marie-Therese had known of Wickham's whereabouts and was obliged to tell Darcy of it. Juliette recalled it particularly because it was the last time she saw Darcy before her marriage to Howgrave.

To Darcy, she said, "I recall that we spoke of him in London. A lady friend of mine had information of him. It was my understanding that he is now dead."

"That was my belief as well," Darcy said. "Indeed, I cannot be certain until I see him for myself. Still, I felt it my duty to warn you of him."

His avid interest in her well-being bode well for a possible tryst. The likelihood, however, that Alistair was George Wickham was remote. A man of such a history would conceal his identity, not enter the public arena. That made no sense whatsoever. Juliette believed that Darcy might be using that as a ploy to see her. The worm may well have turned.

"You are so kind to worry for me," she said, lowering her eyelashes demurely.

Deep in thought, Darcy's eyes narrowed a bit.

He said, "A man who may have recognised Wickham was murdered just last night behind White's. Please beware."

Sensing he meant to take his leave, she bid, "Why did you come to me and not my husband?"

Folding his hands behind his back, his countenance bore a measure of discomfiture. Juliette raised her chin just a bit, begging an answer. She watched him closely as he formed his reply. What he was to say meant all to her.

"Wickham fancies himself a lover," Darcy said carefully, "I believed that, of the two, your dignity would be more apt to be compromised by his schemes."

Before her very eyes, all the hope she had heaped upon this encounter dissipated like a candle snuffed by the wind. One last flicker and it was gone.

"I thank you, Mr. Darcy, for your kind thoughts. Mr. Thomas means little to me no matter his true identity. However, he is secretary to my husband. I shall advise Sir Howgrave that he may have a mountebank in his midst— howbeit, I confess, he shall be difficult to discern —one from all the others."

Darcy appeared relieved, happy perhaps in the knowledge that she would not issue another plea like those which had been so futile in the past. If he harboured a lingering desire for her, he had managed to conquer it. Fit and handsome, he would head his coach homeward, without a backward glance or recollection of their time together.

Turning away, she whispered, *"Merci, Mon cheri."*

"I bid you good-day," he replied.

Before he quite turned to go, she said, "May I beg another moment of your time?"

Betraying a flicker of apprehension, he said, "Yes. Of course."

"When last we spoke I was *tres tristesse.* I was out of spirits. *Tres.*"

His voice a bit gentler, he said, "I have advised my solicitor to serve you in any way possible. He stands by even now."

"Does he?"

"Indeed."

"It is propitious that you have come here yourself to apprise me of Mr. Thomas's possible duplicity. There are other matters of an intimate nature upon which we must speak," she said, adding coyly, "Certain *impro,priétés* must not fall victim to the indiscretion of the pen."

His gaze was wary, but he did not speak.

"You shall have need of your solicitor's services."

Neither his posture nor his countenance altered.

Her chin dipped fetchingly, she said, "Am I to flee from my husband's beatings, I must be well-funded. Your previous offer, while helpful, was a pittance. I shall require more—much more."

Pursing his lips, he said, "I fear you have over-estimated my generosity...."

"Not only do I have to see to my own keep, I must attend to my child. Your son—*fils naturel*."

She turned and faced him. To his credit, Darcy did not appear to flinch. Under such a revelation, his reserve was quite remarkable. It was well-nigh a match for her persistence.

She continued, "He is attending Exeter and shall, no doubt, bring from thence all the stock English accomplishments. He resides under a friend's name. I seldom see him, but he has your length of bone. Indeed, he is handsome boy. In time, it may be necessary to reveal his parentage."

She could see Darcy's veil of hauteur reinforcing itself. He needed more prodding.

"The child is a remembrance from our last time together. I would never think of pursuing an portion of your estate, but he should most assuredly be kept in a manner befitting his bloodline—and well-away from society hens and prying dowagers. I have decided on Venice."

It was difficult to hold his gaze. After a moment, she looked away.

Her allegation had been carried out on impulse, a farce that she had not had time to thoroughly study. She wondered whether he recalled the specifics of their waning affair—how in the last year he came to her but once and refused her attempts to engage him in amatory rites. At the time, she had been both miffed and mystified. What she had not been was *enceinte*.

When she introduced her fabrication to him, she was prepared to weather his anger, denials, even (dare she hope) acquiescence. What she did not expect was to have her assertion be ignored. However, he spoke only to what brought him there.

He said, "If this man, Mr. Thomas is George Wickham, he shall make himself known in some foul way. Call your footmen immediately. You must take heed."

Without further comment, he made his away, leaving her flushed and aflutter.

Darcy had compleatly dismissed her ploy. Men of his station were wary of such traps. This time, pecuniary advantage had not been her true aim. She meant only to determine if he had forgotten those evenings—silent, fevered amours, not a dozen nights (but countless achievements). To him, it had been an arrangement; to her, an entanglement.

She sighed over what was and would not be again.

What to do concerning the snake she had allowed into her bed would come to worry her later.

Noblesse Oblige

Her husband stood in the darkened doorway. At last he was home! His countenance showed signs of grave displeasure. Elizabeth could not fully ascertain his mood, for she was wracked with labour pains. Her hands clutched and re-clutched the rungs of the headboard as the contractions ebbed and flowed. The effluence of toil soaked her hair and pillow. Next to her were a bowl of water and a stack of white cloths. Jane occasionally mopped her forehead. Darcy neither spoke nor came nearer to her than the doorframe. It was as if a line had been drawn and he was somehow not allowed to cross it. The contractions began to come stronger and more urgently. The ordeal would soon be over. Did his tortured expression betray catastrophe? She dared not ask.

From behind him, she spied Janie and Geoff peeking at her. Their little faces bespoke great apprehension. Why were they there? The rooms of Pemberley were beyond counting, the park, enormous. Could not one of the vast number of servants betake them from such a worrisome vigil?

"Margaret!" she called out. "See to the children! Take them out to play!"

Her poor children were frightened. Why had Darcy not seen to them? It looked as if his mouth was sewn shut. Another pain hit her and she turned on her side, agony overtaking her very being. Why could she not curb her own wails as she had in times past? Jane and Georgiana stood looking at her as if they were mute and she had gone mad.

"What is the matter with everyone?" Elizabeth mumbled, sitting up.

As she did, she realised that she had another, very exasperating, dream. However disconcerting, she gave brief prayer that she was no longer tortured by images of her husband cavorting with another woman. Labour was far less painful.

It was still dark out. Outside the door, she heard whimpering.

"Cressida?" she called.

Curled up in front of her door, the dog's tail flapped weakly against the wall. Graeme crouched next to her. When he saw Elizabeth, he stood.

He said, "She would have nothing but that I bring her here, m'lady."

'Oh, dear," Elizabeth said. "Poor dog."

It was well apparent that old Cressida was not long for the world. She had been growing weaker by the day. All they could do was to see to her comfort. Kneeling next to her, Elizabeth petted her a moment. Then she instructed Graeme to carry her to the kitchen (for it was the warmest room in the house). Once the dog was settled on a pallet before the fireplace, Elizabeth crooned one of the children's favourite lullabies to her. Cressida's death would be both a great loss and immense relief to everyone. Watching her creep about was nearly as painful as it must have been for Cressida to bear it. Indeed, of late the children pulled her about in a waggon.

Cressida intermittently whined and whimpered. In time, she only panted.

When daylight came, Elizabeth called for the children. The twins had a number of speckled spaniels and two whippets with which to play, but they always favoured the old wolfhound. The other dogs were soft as butter and licked their faces. But eventually, they would all squirm away when pressed into service for various indignities. Only grizzled Cressida would allow any humiliation with good-natured forbearance.

When the children arrived, they sat next to her and took turns brushing her coat and scratching her behind the ears. Directly, Elizabeth had them make way for Graeme. He knelt next to the dog, placing a hand on her head. He then, quite hastily, quit the room. Elizabeth did not fault him for that. She suspected his countenance was wavering and he stole away lest the children see him weep. She could not keep from that herself.

Cressida's imminent passing also begat a number of questions from the children in regards to dying in general.

"Why must she die, Mama?" Janie cried.

"She is old, dear," Elizabeth replied.

"Why do we die when we get old?" inquired Geoff. "Why can we not live forever?"

Elizabeth began to relate of the various frailties that dotage assigns all the world's creatures and why death was often a kindness.

Listening politely, Janie said, "But William was just a baby and he died."

At first, Elizabeth was caught unawares. She dared not show that the observation troubled her.

"William was taken ill, dearest," Elizabeth reminded Janie. "He was just a baby and not strong enough to survive such as that."

"We must die if we are too young, and we must die if we are too old?" Geoff asked worriedly.

An explanation was not at hand just then, so Elizabeth drew her son onto her lap and kissed the top of his head. Janie's greatest care was that Cressida would go to heaven. Soon after they discussed all possible variants of the great beyond, they fell silent and each took turns petting Cressida until her last breath was taken. Everyone wept unashamedly. Elizabeth drew her children to her breast, patting and crooning to them until the worst of their grief eased.

When it became obvious that the dog was to be buried with the other family pets behind the stables, both children were dismayed. They wanted the dog to be laid to rest next to William to keep him company. Had Darcy been home, Elizabeth doubted he would have approved of such a plan. Just then however, Elizabeth approved of any design that might soothe her children's broken hearts—never mind hers.

The children mourned for some time, but by mid-afternoon they were back at play. Elizabeth did not regain her spirits quite so easily. She felt the loss of Cressida most keenly when she returned upstairs. Every time she had heard Cressida slide to the floor outside their bedchamber, it had been a comfort. The absence of that sound was painful—indeed, she muffled her tears in a pillow for several hours.

Such a show of grief was uncommon for her. No doubt, the dog's death had rekindled grief over dear, little William. Nothing else could account for it— unless it was the loss of sleep during her odd, nightmare-filled night. Perhaps, that had made her more susceptible to lewd dreams and melancholy turns.

A nap would have rejuvenated her. She was disinclined to take one lest she be beset again by obscene visions. Elizabeth most fervently wished Darcy home. She wanted to be held, reassured, soothed—just as she had done for her children.

A knock upon the door announced a missive from Darcy. It said that he would be home by the following night. Again, she began to weep copiously.

Such tidings should have caused her joy. Her spirits were wildly capricious— quite beyond her reason or control. Was her state of flux attributable to the loss of a dear, canine companion or was she missing her dear, lusty husband? Perhaps it was both. Then, in the midst of her weep, she began to laugh.

A singular thought arrested all her emotions: Her husband was not the only thing that she missed.

$\mathcal{I}$nterview with a Wench

Juliette composed herself from her wretched meeting with Darcy with singular ease.

Although she had been near brought to her knees with despair, one who happened upon her just after Mr. Darcy's visit would not have detected it. However resilient was her countenance, her heart saw no reason to go on. Her plan to repair to Venice, once so full of promise, now twirled emptily before her, a vast and endless gloom.

Ensconcing herself upon her favourite settee, she called for a carafe of wine. There was no longer reason to abstain. In the morn, she might draw the drapes. But for this night, she meant to become quite drunk.

Before the footman returned, her quiet was broken by the sudden appearance of her husband. He gained the room in a huff, but she paid him no heed. Therefore she was taken by surprise when he walked over to her, drew back his hand, and slapped her hard across her cheek.

Startled by pain and humiliation, she covered her cheek with the back of her hand and looked at him incredulously.

"Husband!" she cried.

Both knew this kind of attack was not part of their agreement. He stood over her, stout and snorting, like a bullying boar. Hastily recovering her composure, she refused to ask him why he struck her. It was his to explain. Hand trembling, she took a dainty sip of her wine. Through sheer will, she did not spill a drop.

He snapped, "I spied Mr. Darcy leave these apartments just moments ago!"

With a deadly gaze, she replied, "Indeed?"

Enough time had passed that she knew that what he said was not true (unless he had a drink at Boodle's between that time and this). Someone had given him that information. It was not difficult to fathom who carried the tale. Although Howgrave brought back his hand as if to strike her again, she did not allow herself to cower. Rather, she rose and walked to her escritoire and daintily picked up the letter-knife, making a great pretence of opening, and then inspecting, her latest invitations. As she dug the point of the opener

against each seal, she saw that vulgar knife as embodying what her life had
become—tasteless, dull, and passé. However, Howgrave had not ceased his
tirade.

"I know it all!" he cried.

"I have no idea to what you refer," she sniffed. "I readily admit that Mr.
Darcy was here. His visit was a matter of business. It is the first time I have
seen the gentleman in some months."

"That is a bloody lie," he hissed. "He has been coming here clandestinely
whilst I attended meetings!"

"What *bêtise!*" she scoffed. "Mr. Darcy has not been in town for months.
Ask for yourself—do not rely on malicious gossipmongers."

"Then why was he here? This day? I met him earlier and he made no
mention of a visit."

"I shall share that with you when you have reclaimed your temper. For now
I must prepare for the theatre. Shall you accompany me?"

Juliette was not yet prepared to recount Darcy's odd allegation. She was
in want of considering the prospect without fear of a scene (such as the snit
her husband had just displayed). Had she her heart's desire, she would have
shaken her husband until he gibbered. Indeed, had she not so much to lose,
she would have screamed the truth in his chubby, little face.

"Darcy was once my lover, *mon cochon!* Had I my way, he would be yet. He
is no flaccid, ineffectual brute. He is strong, worthy—and potent."

However much she would have liked to watch Howgrave squeal, she dared
not speak such heresy. Rather, she stood, smiled coquettishly, and extended
her hand. In it, she held Darcy's card.

"Would a lover leave his card?" she asked.

Howgrave came to her side to nuzzle apologies against her neck.
Imperceptibly, she dipped her knees to accommodate his bussing. Such ego-
salving measures had not been a particular bother in the past. Now, everything
concerning the endomorphic beast annoyed her. At least Alistair was tall and
trim-figured. At the thought of him, she took another sip of wine.

Darcy's unexpected visit had left her in a muddle of disappointment and
regret. Hence, all that he told her of George Wickham was slow to come to
mind. As she bethought his words, she recollected Darcy saying that he and
Alistair were said to resemble each other. She puzzled over that statement, but
only for a moment. Then she recalled Alistair saying much the same thing.
She saw no true resemblance save for height. That hardly seemed proof of his
identity. Alistair was a bit of a rogue, but a murderer? She thought not. He was
a scoundrel, nothing more. She was far too worldly to be so easily fooled. Her
thoughts, however, were arrested by her husband's interminable whine.

"We do not have to bear another bloody Italian Opera, do we dear?"
inquired her husband patting his hair.

"No, my dear," she replied, "Tonight, Grimaldi."

By the time they were fitted in finery and had gained their carriage, the pretence of a happy marriage was once again in place. By Juliette's design, they were late arriving at the theatre. Their box was near the stage and every patron watched them as they found their seats. Used to such scrutiny, Juliette was quite at ease. Howgrave preened momentarily and then he introduced her to new acquaintances, Sir Louiemac and his wife, Majorca. Neither had any hint of breeding but they were not ill-mannered because of it. They had lately come into money, by way of the Smithfield Stockyards. Their fortune, however, had not the stench of whence it came. Indeed, their wealth had reached an apogee that allowed the aristocracy to overlook its taint. (Since the wars and the reversal of fortunes in all levels of society, the upper class was far more accepting of those who had ready money.)

Louiemac's cuffs were more out of fashion than his wife. Majorca's manners were gauche and her face was uninspiring. Juliette did not mind. When nothing else could cheer her, her mood could be improved by sitting with an unhandsome woman. Basking in the glow of unadulterated admiration of those around her, she was soothed. Indeed, she was lulled into self-congratulatory complacency until she happened to spy Alistair peering over the backs of the gentlemen hovering about her husband.

He winked.

She pretended not to see him, but gave an inward shudder. A rogue in disguise or not, the thought of his company had lost its appeal. The only tell-tale sign of her unease was a slight shifting in her seat towards Sir Louiemac. Once positioned, she did not move until the intermission. The production had been quite amusing. Most of the spectators laughed uproariously. Juliette covered the lower half of her face with her fan more than once, but she did not find it as droll as did the others.

When the men adjourned to attend their bladders, she breathed a deep sigh of relief. Therefore, when she heard the rustle of silk, she turned to look upon what female dared invade her box. As she did, she was arrested by the sight of a most alarming personage. Indeed, the wench was so quaintly painted that Juliette momentarily believed her to be a juvenile member of the cast.

"How'dya do?" said Daisy Mulroney.

She offered her hand and her name. Juliette accepted neither.

Lady Louiemac was well-occupied by peering at other ladies' gowns through her quizzing glasses. The strange creature before Juliette seemed to be speaking only to her. Desperately looking about for the men of her party, Juliette nodded curtly. Many strangers claimed her acquaintance—some of them even less acceptable than the one before her.

Not mincing words, Daisy said, "The tall feller—the one with the white hair—he's with you?"

Juliette looked furiously about for someone of authority, hissing at Daisy,

"You do not belong here. Leave, now."

"Beg pardon, sister, but you ain't no better'n any other strumpet in this town," Daisy replied. "I should leave yer be, but I ain't that kind of female."

"Convent Garden hobby-horse, I'd say," Juliette snapped back in an inflection that was far more Wapping than Mayfair.

At this, they both smiled. Daisy even laughed that the lady was that accomplished a mimic. More annoyed than angry, Juliette took a better look at the sassy girl. She saw immediately that she was not a girl, but a woman—five and twenty years if she was a day. She was dressed in the finest of gowns, but her ensemble was atrocious. Suddenly, recognition wafted over Juliette. This little woman harboured many political meetings. Her house was enormous, but furnished with disastrous discernment. Daisy Mulroney had come into money too late in life for it to improve her taste. Juliette's countenance hastily regained its placidity, not giving a hint of repugnance. Before she could ask what she wanted, Daisy began to chatter away. What she had to say was flabbergasting.

"The white-haired feller is a ponce, a resurrectionist, and a murderer, but not in that order. He came with his silk nose-wipes into the Fortune of War every day. You do best to stay clear of him."

There were any number of questions that Juliette wanted to ask this wanton sprite, foremost amongst those inquiries was why she was warning her against Alistair.

Before she could ask her that, the demoiselle urged, "Watch out fer 'em, I tell yer. He's hard to kill. We shot 'em and he didn't die."

"You shot him?" Juliette repeated daintily.

"Yea, in the knackers," Daisy said flippantly. "He has ones of stone—or did."

Colour drained from Juliette's lovely complexion. Daisy did not notice that, for she was on her way lest she be seen.

Her last remark was over her shoulder, "If yer don't believe me, ask ol' George if he's still got teeth in his pockets."

$\mathcal{F}$ortune Fails

Upon the carriage ride home from the opera, Juliette had to withstand the company of the stiff-rumped Majorca along with her pressing personal concerns.

The men chatted on like storekeepers in knuckle-dabs, but Juliette did not care to converse. She could do nothing but wonder where Alistair Thomas was at that moment and would he return to apply for more of her time. If he was guilty of the crimes of which he was accused, she contemplated how best to unmask him. Should she go to her husband, or to the authorities?

That, she supposed, was putting the cart before the horse. Above all else, she had to determine who he truly was. The wee strumpet at the theatre said Alistair was a procurer and grave-robber—and that he was a habitué of a disreputable house called the Fortune of War.

Abruptly, Juliette asked, "Pray do you know of an establishment called 'The Fortune of War?'"

Majorca looked at her blankly, but both men bore gazes of such astonished abhorrence that Juliette was taken aback by their alarm. Fluttering her fan, she begged their pardon, saying, rightly, that the name was mentioned at the performance.

"Infamous place," Howgrave said gruffly. Betokening the time-honoured expression of displeased spouses, he decreed, "We shall speak of this in private."

She was satisfied to do so. Nonetheless, Sir Louiemac did not shrink from scandal.

"If your husband is too mannerly to speak of it, Lady Howgrave," said he, "May I explain our surprise and disgust?"

She nodded.

"They say that the Fortune of War is one of the vilest places in town. It looks to be a common drinking house, but word has it that grave-robbers do their business there." He turned to Howgrave, offering, "Grave-robbing has become quite a lucrative activity. It is something Parliament must address, Howgrave."

Lady Louiemac became quite animated, inquiring as to why anyone might possibly want to dig up a corpse.

As Lord Louiemac was now rich, he only visited Smithfield on market day. (Lady Louiemac came not at all.) Although his fortune was made by tallow and hides, the filth and mire of the lanes oozed so deep, even he avoided it when he could. To endure the air, befouled by fresh-killed carcasses and their entrails, he covered his face with a handkerchief lest his lungs be stung by the acridity. Indeed, Louiemac was less sequestered from the baser doings in London than even the likes of Henry Howgrave.

Louiemac told them, "The anatomy classes are filled with surgeons in want of learning the skills necessary for their occupation. They are in constant need of fresh dead to dissect."

"I think I shall be ill," said Lady Louiemac.

The thought of such deeds was grisly to Juliette as well. However, unlike Lady Louiemac, she had withstood grander misfortune than stench of sewage. In Paris, she had the questionable pleasure of observing any number of heads being lopped off. (In her opinion, witnessing the death throes of headless bodies squirting blood trumped the mere thought of a day-old corpse quite handily.) The newspapers alluded to suspicious removals from cemeteries, but as the dearly departed were rarely disturbed once they were committed to their graves in the West End, few investigations were made.

Thinking of the yellow-haired pigmy, Juliette looked out the window at the wide, clean streets. As she pondered the woman's nebulous aspect, she recalled only that her hair was gold and her name was Daisy. The portion of her discourse regarding grave-robbing had already been proven true. It had been her experience that if part of a story was genuine, the likelihood was greater that the rest was accurate as well. And, if a man would stoop to stealing corpse, he would not scruple against soliciting on behalf of harlots. It was only by fortune of her uncommon beauty that she had not fallen prey to one of London's pimps. As it was, she answered only to herself—at least until she had taken the idiotic notion to marry.

That little doxy was literally dripping in pearls and emeralds, but was certainly not of station (not even a maid to a person of station). How she came so recently into money was quite a mystery, but from her coarse articulation, she was not a few years out of the rookeries bordering the Thames. No doubt, that was how she learnt of Alistair's dreadful doings. She knew his name to be "George." It remained unclear as to why she shot him—or said she did. Perchance, in his past occupations their paths crossed. If he was shot, he was fortunate to survive it. If the wars taught them nothing, it was that few lived long after being shot, and if they did it was not without severe scarring. Alistair bore no scars or wounds, just a limp.

Daisy, the wealthy wench, said that she had shot George in the groin. Alistair was one ball shy and sporting a limp. At that moment, she realised it all must be true. The moonless night obscured the expression of clarity and fear that overspread Juliette's lovely countenance. Shortly thereafter, another, surer expression slipped from the corner of her eye. It was one both cunning and content.

Juliette's mind had always been quite sharp. Once she was certain of the issues at hand, she moved with near vulpine stealth. Now fully informed, she no longer feared Alistair, be he pimp, body-snatcher, murderer, or George Wickham. Information is all. That was something that anyone who lived by their wits knew well. More importantly, such tidings were far more useful when they were owned by just one party.

George Wickham had no idea that he had been exposed.

Surely, he did not believe that he would remain undiscovered. Was he that arrogant, or that stupid? With men, she knew, oft-times it is a mixture of both. The question was, how could she use him to her own ends?

Above All Else

Having discharged his obligations, as he saw it, to defend his countrymen from the auspices of a truly wicked (and possibly deranged) man, Darcy made ready for home. Just knowing that Wickham was alive, and given to the worst kind of criminality, meant Darcy would make fast to protect those dearest to him. Indeed, a pang in the pit of his stomach reminded him that the cur had been at large for these past years and could have easily made his way to Pemberley to do them harm.

That he had not, only meant one thing—he had not yet.

Darcy could have allowed the matter drop after Wickham's attempt at extorting money from him failed, but he had put his faith in the wheels of justice. The tale he had to tell of Wickham was quite astounding and, had another citizen come to authorities with such a story, it might have been met with disbelief. Coming from Mr. Darcy, not known to be prone to drink or hyperbole, it was seen as gospel. Therefore, it had been reasonable for Mr. Darcy to expect Wickham to be immediately apprehended three years past.

Darcy had hied for Pemberley then under that understanding. As he was never apprised that Wickham had been remanded, he had believed him either dead or absconded.

Not only had he not been arrested, Wickham had walked the streets of London unmolested, free to wreak mayhem and harm at will. The notion of it left Darcy angry and appalled. As his ire remained barely contained, he prepared to take his leave of London still brooding over the matter. Hastings had seen to it that his personal items were carried to the coach. Darcy picked up two missives—one from Juliette and the other in a hand of execrable penmanship. He placed them in his coat pocket. He did not then, nor all the way across the country to Derbyshire, read the one from Juliette.

When he arrived home, Elizabeth had greeted him with genuine enthusiasm. She withheld full effusiveness until she could put it to good use in private. Before their family number had improved, she might have leapt upon him forthwith of closing the door. Now, there were greetings to be made to Geoff and Janie before passionate embraces could be shared. He had purchased small gifts for each of them from the horse fair. Despite its rusticity, Janie was quite pleased with her doll.

However Geoff was not even a little happy with the crudely-carved horse he was given. It was obvious that he would not be satisfied with anything less than a full-sized steed. In his young mind, he envisioned it as a black horse identical to Blackjack (he had not specified that, but it had been his secret wish). Darcy did not welcome his son's lack of gratitude. It was ill-mannered.

Darcy remained silent, that alone disclosing his disapproval. The pout upon his son's countenance did not fade with any rapidity.

Mr. Darcy would not have it. At least, that had been his initial response.

Beside length of bone and a firm chin, Darcy knew that he had bequeathed his son with other attributes. He recognised obstinacy in his son and knew that, however unwittingly bestowed, it was inherited from him as well. He was but a small boy who, at that moment, was quite chapfallen.

Darcy waited. After a moment, Geoff knew what was expected of him.

A bit begrudgingly, he said, "I thank you, Papa. It is a fine horse and I like it very much."

It was the first of many untruths that he would have to tell in the name of politesse and his father was proud of him.

Placing a hand on his shoulder, he assured him, "Colonel Fitzwilliam is still in search of a colt as for you even as we speak. I promised you a horse and you shall have it."

Knowing that the promise of a horse was not negated, just postponed, Geoff scrambled happily on his way. Janie, however, remained. Seeing his sister did not follow, Geoff stopped. Then, he came and stood by her side as she tugged at their father's sleeve.

"Papa," she bid.

Seeing that her expression was unusually solemn, Darcy knelt.

"Pray, what is the matter?" he asked.

Thereupon, her chin quivered and her eyes filled with tears. (Geoff did not cry, but, then, he would not look at his sister either.) Darcy pressed his daughter to his chest and patted her back. As Janie was not forthcoming about what troubled her, he looked to Elizabeth for further elucidation.

Although she knew Darcy would notice Cressida's absence, Elizabeth had not wished to tell him of his dog's death forthwith of his return. When she tried to speak, grief silenced her. Darcy stood; his expression was one of distress.

Prolonging his unease would have been unconscionable. Hence, Elizabeth managed to say only, "Cressida."

His countenance altered. True sadness softened his features. Directly, he regained his composure. That was quite necessary, for only in containing his own sorrow was he thereby able to sooth his family's.

He took his wife in his arms, whispering against her ear, "She is at peace."

In a moment, Elizabeth gathered herself, saying, "It was I who meant to solace you."

As Elizabeth contained her weep, the children then came to their parents. Darcy lifted Janie into his arms and kissed her cheek. Geoff hugged his father's knees, reminding Darcy that his heart needed comforting too. Hence, Darcy stood Janie down and drew Geoff into his embrace as well.

Darcy told them, "You were very good to Cressida and we shall miss her."

Janie wrapped her arms about his neck and wept for a moment longer. This time, Geoff patted her, repeating the same words his father had just employed.

"You were very good to Cressida, sister," the boy said. "We shall miss her."

After a time, everyone's senses were settled enough that the children went off to play with their new toys, thus allowing Elizabeth to alter the subject from what had occurred at Pemberley as to what actually happened at the horse fair.

"How was Mr. Bingley's toe?" she asked, thus advising her husband that gossip of the melee had preceded him.

He replied, "It is much better."

Elizabeth could not wait for greater privacy to inquire, "How did you leave Major Kneebone? Was he well too?"

Darcy glanced at her inquisitively, but did not hold her gaze, as he said, "I see word of the escapade has reached Pemberley."

Word of the altercation, and the miscreants involved, had arrived, but not the resolution. She nodded once.

He said, "Major Kneebone was the worse for wear, but ultimately reconciled with your sister."

"No one was injured?"

He replied, "Only the dignities of gentlemen who should know better.

Bingley's toe is quite improved."

Naturally, Elizabeth wanted a more detailed accounting of the entire fracas, he promised her that. Both knew the telling should take place in the quiet of their chambers. He did not think of Juliette, or her missive to him again, until Goodwin removed his well-travelled coat and prepared it for a good dusting. As always, Goodwin checked the pockets for any stray papers. From the breast pocket, he withdrew Juliette's letter. Without the appearance of looking at it, he placed it on the tableside. Only then did Darcy note something that he did not initially observe. Juliette's missive had come by way of Pemberley. He recognised Elizabeth's hand redirecting it to the horse-breeder at Maidenhead. From there, it was forwarded to London. Such a circuitous journey for one letter, he thought.

As Darcy had spoken to Juliette subsequent of its arrival, he saw no particular reason to read it.

At dusk, he repaired to his study. He did so with great purpose. Sitting at a writing table, he laid the poorly penned missive he had received in London before him. It was from Sally Frances Arbuthnot. Upon any other occasion, he would have been unable to imagine what might cause her to write to him. The events of the past week opened all manner of possibilities. He was then, neither altogether taken aback by her misspellings, nor by what her letter alleged.

Standing, he strode to the bookshelves to locate a piece of vellum from its upper reaches. Returning to the desk, he unrolled it. At the bottom it had been signed in Wickham's hasty, but curlicued, scrawl.

Thomas Reed.

Closing his eyes (with either resolve or dejection—he knew not which), he took a deep, purging breath.

Wickham was alive.

Darcy was then satisfied that he had taken the precaution of leaving a letter with his solicitor in London for Howgrave. In it, he apprised him that his secretary might well be an impostor and, if he was, he was both dangerous and desperate. A confrontation might be deadly. It was all he could do at the time. It was his plan to send emissaries to make inquiries and alert the authorities, but his first duty was to keep his own family safe.

He blew out the candle and went to his wife.

𝒫rometheus and the Eagle

H ow about a little love-poke, m'lady?" cooed Alistair.
Juliette snapped, "Dare not speak to me in such a fashion."
With each passing hour, the very thought of Alistair (by whatever name) had become ever-more irksome. A political party was much in evidence downstairs. The cackling laughter was not a comfort. She had little time to conjecture whether Alistair would dare steal his way up to her chambers, ere he did. It was obvious that he was intent on continuing with their farce of an affair. Time was at hand to unmask him.

Alistair cajoled, "Darling, what have I done? Nay, what can I do to make your lovely lips smile?"

"Darcy called upon me today," she announced.

"I beg pardon?" said he. Clearly discombobulated, he gathered himself with great haste, quipping, "You then have hitherto been serviced?"

She did not allow his remark to chafe her. Rather, she imagined Alistair squirming like an eel when she confronted him with his duplicity.

Airily, she said, "Mr. Darcy came here upon a matter of business. He reports that there is an impostor in our midst."

"I fancy then he apprised you of my little ruse," Alistair replied.

Juliette did not respond. It had been her experience that, if left alone, the voluble sort usually spun their own nooses. As if proving the point, Alistair continued to talk.

"Darcy has always envied me—no doubt, he envies me now. It is he who set the magistrate upon me, thereby forcing me to assume another identity. One could say that any blame lies with him."

He then quit the subject of his lies and misrepresentations to attempt to flatter her, "I must say I was altogether astonished to learn, not only that Darcy had once taken a lover, but that he had bedded possibly the most exquisite creature in all of London."

Alistair then tipped his glass of wine in her direction before continuing, "To think, all that came to pass without me learning of it until now. I had been quite certain that Darcy was... prim upon matters of amour. Did he happen upon you whilst on some drunken debauch?"

She laughed, "I assure you he did not."

Alistair laughed too, but it was bit hollow.

Recalling her first meeting with Darcy, Juliette thoughtfully twirled a tendril of her hair between two fingers.

Lost in that moment, she said, "The conditions he required—even to deign an introduction—were quite rigid. To engage him one had to be inviting, but not forward, witty, but not cutting, vivacious, but not eagre. His demands were far too complicated for some middling chit to manage. The reward, however, was quite...."

Juliette told Alistair far more than she meant to about Darcy's taste—in conversation and congress. To be so forthcoming was quite unlike her. She blamed her lapse in discretion upon Alistair. His smugness had begged comeuppance. The expression upon his countenance was one she could not quite gauge. It seemed an odd mixture of jealousy and conceit. Alistair quickly righted himself. Indeed, he raised his arms to her.

"Come to me, my pet. If Darcy did not requite your every dream, I am here for you."

As she did not move to him, he divested himself of his wine and went to her. From behind, he slipped his arms about her, encircling her just below the bosom. His breath hot on her ear, he said, "You did not believe Darcy's lies, did you? He is determined to have me silenced. In truth, I am...."

Just as he began to repeat his usual inventions, half-truths, and outright prevarications, the door was opened. Sir Henry Howgrave stood in open-mouthed disbelief. He had meant only to invite his wife to meet new contributors—his way of apologising for his earlier accusations. He found his wife and his secretary in an attitude that left little to the imagination. Indeed, Howgrave's fleshy jowls trembled with outrage and a vein in his temple throbbed. In a trice, he saw that he had not erred in accusing his wife of adulterous conduct, only the identity of her paramour.

To Juliette, Howgrave said, "It isn't that damned Darcy who is the rutting-dog after all!"

To Alistair, Howgrave howled with injury, "Alistair? How could you?"

His little game was exposed, but Alistair (a veteran of weathering husbandly outrage) was quite indifferent to that fact. He threw his head back and cast out an irrefutable indictment of Sir Henry Howgrave—one that cut the poor man to the core.

He said, "Ahoy! If it is not Freddy Dumpstitch!"

With that singular insult, full recognition hit Howgrave. His mouth was agape, seconds passed by ere he could utter more than affronted grunts. When at last, he spoke; he knew exactly whom he addressed.

"George Wickham! They said you were dead! Yet, here you are, still nothing but a worthless mutton-monger! And a wolf in sheep's clothing to boot!"

Howgrave's metaphors might have been a bit imprecise, but his appraisal of his secretary's duplicitousness was exceedingly accurate. Moreover, with his husbandly pride gouged in the worst possible manner, Howgrave was out for blood. In appearance, word, and deed, he was no longer the impotent cuckold Wickham had so often belittled. Indeed, Wickham suddenly realised that he may have baited the wrong bear. Hence, he shifted seamlessly from perpetrator to victim.

"It was her!" said Wickham, pointing at Juliette. "She begged me, appealed to my vanity, saying that you cannot satisfy her. I defended your honour, but her wiles are many. I was putty in her designing hands!"

Howgrave turned his wrath upon Juliette. Pinning her against her escritoire, his hand came down across her mouth, splitting her lip.

Wickham continued to prod him, "She denigrated your manhood whilst fondling mine. Pray, what man can contain his lust against such ways?"

Howgrave hit his wife again. As if a puppeteer, Wickham cast an aspersion and Howgrave slapped his wife. It was a test as to which man's passion was more inflamed. It was Wickham, however, who had the misjudgement of allowing his gleeful grin to come within Howgrave's eye-line. This redirected that man's rage from his faithless wife to his faithless friend. Gurgling with fury, he lunged at Wickham. Easily the more nimble of the two, Wickham dodged him, scrambling just beyond his grasp. Wickham made a vain attempt to steer him back to Juliette, but he caught his toe on the edge of the carpet.

Although Howgrave was shorter, fatter, and unarmed, Wickham truly feared for his life. Abruptly, it was no longer a game. Perspiration formed on his forehead as he looked desperately about for a weapon, but to no avail. Howgrave's bulging eyes looked as if they were to pop out of his eye-sockets. He flailed wildly at Wickham, who put up his hands in a futile bid to deflect his blows.

Suddenly, Howgrave's rage-red eyes protruded further. A bit of pink froth foamed from his mouth. He then dropped to his knees. As Howgrave had continued to crawl towards him, Wickham scrambled to his feet and engaged in a hopping dance to remain just beyond Howgrave's reach. Defeated, Howgrave fell into a motionless heap.

Wickham cried incredulously, "Is he dead? I never touched him! It must be apoplexy! What luck! But, then he had the neck for it."

As Wickham bent over Howgrave, he saw the oddest thing. Obtruding from Sir Henry Howgrave's side was the gold handle of a very vulgar letter-knife. It was imbedded to the hilt and a great pool of blood was collecting beneath him.

Juliette stood silently just beyond her husband. With great haste, Wickham understood what had come to pass.

He said, "My sweet, my princess, you rescued your true love!"

As if by instinct led, Wickham began to plot. First, he appraised Howgrave's corpse. The man was beyond saving, but the letter-knife was worth a hundred pounds. Wickham quickly grabbed it and wiped the blood from it on the side of Howgrave's trousers.

With Howgrave still leaking blood onto the carpet between them, Wickham crowed, "We are free of him! Come with me now! This letter-knife alone will buy our passage wherever we chose to go. Collect your jewels, for we shall have need of them...."

He looked about, searching for other items to scavenge from the room.

"George," Juliette said quietly.

Taking no notice of the name she employed, he answered, "Yes, dearest?"

"Do you have teeth in your pocket?"

Unconsciously, Wickham's hands went to his pockets. The expression that then overspread his countenance was not one of contrition. He bore the unadulterated manifestation of a guilty man.

It was true. Ponce, grave-robber, murderer, thief. She knew it. He knew it. He blanched, but reached for her penitently. As he had so many times before (with so many women), he knew he could convince her that he was not the blackguard that he truly was.

Ingratiatingly, he told her, "I am of Darcy's blood and he will pay what I ask."

Uncertain how this information was taken, he watched her countenance with exceeding care. Her lovely rosebud lips pursed, seemingly beckoning a redemptive kiss. He took a step towards her, and, as he did, her mouth, so lush and moist, formed a perfect "o."

At first, she emitted a single lilting note, one that hung prettily in the air. Then slowly, stealthily, it altered. From the back of her lovely throat came a sound that was other-worldly. What had been a lovely and provocative intonation transmuted into a howl—unlike one he had ever heard. It was a raging, moaning shriek.

Whilst her cry still hung in the air, Juliette then reached up and clawed at the diaphanous fabric of her bodice. As she did, it shredded. Of the belief that she had keened and then rent her gown in grief, Wickham stood absolutely transfixed. He was so taken by the sight that he was not roused until the room was descended upon by a hoard of Howgrave's men.

Observing the bloody tableau, all fell silent.

Suddenly, Wickham was quite aware that he happened to hold the letter-knife in his hand. Upon that knife, most conspicuously, was the blood of a Member of Parliament, a landowner, and a gentleman. Was that not accusation enough, Lady Howgrave extended a trembling forefinger directly at Wickham. Thereupon, she swooned.

Wickham was nonplussed. Normally, so adept at slipping into whatever character was required, his mouth opened, but nothing came out.

This was unfortunate.

In that void, every man who stood before him believed that they had just disturbed the ravagement of a fair lady and the murder of her devoted protector. Fuelled by alcohol and offended masculinity, they saw in George Wickham, a singularly guilty man.

To Sleep, Perchance to Dream

By the time Mr. Darcy slipped in beside his wife, he felt the deep respirations of her sleep. He could have serried himself behind her and drawn her to him, but he did not. Rather, he propped his head on one hand and gazed at her in the candlelight. Only within his wife's cathartic presence did he set aside the disorder of the past days.

He also did a rather common thing.

The placket of her gown lay open. That unbuttoned vee exposed a good portion of her delectable, white breast. He had been gone half a fortnight— long enough for him (bridegroom or not) to be brought to arousal by the very sight of his wife's bare skin. Indeed, he blatantly ogled her. As he did, he exhaled a great sigh of appreciation.

Without moving a hair or flicking a finger, she opened one eye. Caught in salacious admiration, he gave a start. Half-awake, but sensing discombobulation, Mrs. Darcy gathered the fabric of her gown in her fist and clasped it to her bosom.

He caught her hand, saying with a small laugh, "You awaken, only to find a strange man in your bed?"

Embarrassed, she did not want to recount the nettlesome dreams that had been plaguing her nights. Instead, she reached out and stroked his face.

Then, she employed her most fetching smile, "A 'strange' man, you say? Perhaps I should entertain that thought.... Ouch!" she gasped.

His pinch was quite unexpected and she slapped playfully at his hand.

"What ungentlemanly behaviour!"

With an exchange of a single look, all teasing was forgot. Wrapping her in his arms, he rolled atop her. The loose braid she often wore to bed was not in evidence. Indeed, her hair cascaded across the pillow most alluringly.

Gliding his knee between hers, he looked into her eyes, and said, "There is much to tell you...."

Placing her forefinger against his lips, she whispered, "Can it not wait until the morn? I have so longed to have you all to myself."

No other words could have been half so admirable just then. It was not by great design that he had moved his knee in such a provocative fashion. However unintentional, he credited it with obtaining her acquiescence to set aside his journey and all that had passed therein until another time. His foremost desire was to lie with her in unfleeting splendour until the dawn.

Her body, which had been taut, becalmed within his embrace. She took his face in her hands and covered it with happy kisses. As she did, his fingers parted the placket of her gown reverentially. Suddenly overtaken with a rare bout of diffidence, she closed her eyes and turned her head in such a way that stole his notice.

"Pray, why do you not want me to admire you? It is my particular pleasure." he asked quietly.

His voice was not critical, but curious—and possibly a little hurt. As he spoke, he brushed his fingers across her cheek. She opened her eyes. He was gazing at her closely, his long fingers burrowed into her hair, thumb stroking her chin. The redolence of his hand (and the specific placement of his knee) recalled a union long past—one quite singular.

That memory arresting all her thoughts, she bid, "Do you often recall our nuptial night?"

An odd sound erupted from his throat.

He said, "Do I what? Why, pray, would I ever do that?"

She meant no offence, nor did she think he could have taken her inquiry as such. Taken aback, she very nearly let the subject go to the side. However, that was not her nature.

She prodded, "I simply wonder if our recollections of the event are alike."

Clearing his throat, he said, "Allow me a moment.... Yes, to be sure. I have certain recollections."

She waited.

"Our memories may be quite different," said he. "This is particularly true if you only recall the event as singular. My recollection was that it was not just the evening, but the night, the dawn, the morning and, if memory serves, twice in the coach ere arriving here."

His directness did him credit, but turned her crimson. Still, she sighed in remembrance of it all. There was one niggling memory, however, that kept her reminisces of their wedding from being altogether laudatory. It was one that had no part in their amatory rites. It pertained to the carriage ride thither. Just bethinking it, her brow knitted.

She asked, "Do you recall how reticent you were upon the journey from

Meryton to London? You did not speak two words together until we arrived in town."

Her inquiry was met with silence. Perhaps it was too obscure to remain in his memory, she reasoned. Just as she concluded it was thus, he surprised her. When he spoke, it was with uncharacteristic openness.

"In truth, I was apprehensive."

She blurted, "You? If anyone should have been anxious it should have been me—a simple virgin wrested from the bosom of my family by a gentleman of dour opinions and huge... estate."

Although she immediately regretted having interrupted him, she understood why she did. His answer was altogether astonishing—and a bit off-putting. It was far easier to jest than believe that he regretted their marriage. As a worldly man, he could not have been apprehensive on any other account. True, she had been quite restless and somewhat agitated on the road to town, but, she had not been truly afraid. Granted, there came a time that night when she was a bit askance that what was supposed to come to pass between them was, in fact, feasible. (Indeed, his member was greatly engorged and she knew not quite where he meant to put it.) Passion quickly overrode such hesitation. After that initial mingling of bloods, she could think of nothing but the next.

The memory of the first night they took as one had always been her particular pleasure. Perchance, her happy recollections were false. It was possible that she had not pleased him as he had pleased her. He had so eloquently convinced her of his gratification, she had never once considered it was otherwise.

Suddenly, all that she believed about that passionate time was in question. She looked at him, but he did not return her gaze. Indeed, he lay on his back, his forearm across his eyes. It was quite obvious that he was more inclined to speak of the recent days in London than of those long past. She endeavoured not to take offence. A singular image (forever imbued with a specific fragrance) would always remain with her from that night. Indeed, was she granted but one memory of her husband, it would be of him as he stood barefoot, casting rose petals across their bed.

Even before she had convinced herself that she was in no way vexed, he removed his arm and turned to her.

He said, "You say I was reticent in the landau after our vows. If I was, I beg you forgive me. For, you see, I was engaged in a great struggle. I longed to remove your glove, but I was but a glance away from compleat want of conduct. I dared not trust myself with so small a liberty, lest I surrender to abandon altogether."

That admission was one she valued beyond all telling. She kissed him lovingly, fully prepared not to speak of it again. Whatever her limitations as an unlearned bride, she believed she had overcome them. Nothing else was of importance. Upon this occasion, however, he was the one to pursue the subject.

He reached out for her, drawing her beneath him again. Taking her face in his hands, he spoke with uncommon candour, articulating rapturously of what she had no notion that he recalled.

Said he, "Apprehension quite overwhelmed me. Indeed, when we reached London, I trembled at the very thought of lying next to you. Your skin was alabaster; your eyes were limitless pools of wine. The embroidery on your gown, the way your hair fell across your shoulder, the turn of your countenance, all conspired against my restraint. Your very touch shattered me. And when you spoke my name, I was struck dumb."

His voice remained a whisper, but took on the huskiness of penance as he said, "When we were at last one, I was tormented by guilt at the pain my lust, my ardour caused you. Yet, I could not govern my own passion. My will was stolen—along with my breath, my mind, and my heart. If I do not speak of it, forgive me—for it is what I cannot forget that strikes me silent."

As she listened, she was still as the night. He had recollected the embroidery on her nightdress (the pattern of pink flowers that she herself had sewn). When she thought she was beyond being surprised by him, she was once again astonished. The clamour of her heartbeat left her breathless. Gathering herself, she clasped his face in her hands, searching his eyes. In them, she saw not regret, but appetence. Wild with abandon, she covered his mouth with hers. Unable to slake herself of him by that alone, she paused but a moment before taking his lower lip between her teeth. She did not bite down, just enough to tug on it a bit.

"Do you happen to recall the first time I did that?

Said he, "The oak."

In a trice, her gown was in twain, the gossamer fabric no real challenge to a man who was intent on taking his wife. Ere either took a breath, his hand encircled the back of her knee and he stole between her thighs. The familiar frisson of hunger overspread her legs (a week's worth of ardour stored within them), demanding his repair. As he pierced her very being, she fell back in compleat surrender. Words then came from her lips that she did not mean to share.

"I beg the nectar of your loins!"

In the miniscule portion of her mind not overborne by desire, she feared that that ill-chosen phrase had broken the spell that transported them. (She held out hope that he had not heard her, for he did not hesitate in his passionate ministrations.) Then and thenceforward, he performed acts of exhilaration upon her person that were both sure and insistent, each stroke deeper than the last.

He, master of the crescendoed duet, and she, apt pupil, came to amour's zenith together—with a minimum of conversation and utmost satisfaction.

Indeed, as he rolled from her, she was left in leg-quivering gratification, but prostrate from exhaustion. Looking lovingly in his direction, she reached out and laid her hand upon his chest. So still was he, she thought (as was his want) that he had fallen asleep. He had not.

"The nectar of my loins?" he repeated incredulously.

For the second time that night, a rubescence spread upwards from her bosom to her throat and brightened her cheeks. Providentially, there was no window light to lay bare her embarrassment.

He rose upon an elbow and inquired, "Where did you ever hear such an expression?"

With compleat candour, she answered, "The words came to me in a dream—a most provocative dream."

𝒟ead Reckoning

George Wickham once again found himself standing in the Old Bailey, he was not there to cadge, filch, or prevaricate—well, not on someone else's behalf. From the court, laughter could be heard reverberating from the King of Denmark Inn across the street. From the gaol, the sound of raucousness did not cheer him.

No matter how loudly he protested, he was taken into custody whilst Howgrave's blood had yet to coagulate. No investigation was carried out. There seemed no reason to bother. Nonetheless, Wickham insisted that he had been arrested on false charges. At first he screamed; eventually he merely rasped. Never had he begged for his life more sincerely. Eventually, he forsook his pleas and sent word of his arrest to two people. He sent word to Lord Humphrey Orloff and Mrs. Henrietta Younge to come to his aid. To no one's great astonishment, Mrs. Younge hied to his side directly. Lord Orloff did not come, but he offered to pay whatever legal obligations were incurred by Alistair R. Thomas. Although he accepted the man's generosity readily, Wickham was not at all grateful.

"How can my friends desert me in my time of need?" he cried.

"You haven't any friends, Georgie," reminded Mrs. Younge.

"Hush," he hissed.

He quickly explained to her that he had not quite decided which name he would adopt insofar as the trial ahead of him. Indeed, that would be an exceptional challenge. Wickham had always kept his identity... fluid. Whilst employing what, one must concede, was a masterpiece of factual manoeuvring, Wickham explained the choice of his identities to his solicitor, Mr. Blackbird. The solicitor conferred with the barrister, Mr. Paret. Both concluded that of the two, Alistair R. Thomas's crimes were more defendable—and as payment was made in Alistair's name, preferable. Wickham could but agree, believing that he would have better luck being tried for a crime that he did not actually commit. In this, he was mistaken.

The charges were Murder and Attempted Violation of a Lady.

When word of the heinous crime was announced, court watchers were stirred into a frenzy of eagre anticipation of the trial. Newspapers regaled the general public with tales of the murder and hinted broadly at its lascivious aspects. It did not take great powers of deduction to conclude that the lady whose honour had been near-defiled was none other than the much-admired Lady Howgrave. Staunch widow that she was, her ladyship eschewed anonymity, vowing to bear witness against her husband's murderer. Hence, the man who killed Lady Howgrave's husband had to endure general loathing from those in all walks of life.

"I am an innocent man!" he declared again and again. "Howgrave meant to kill me! Indeed, she is the murderer! I am an innocent man!"

Wickham was not unaware that his alternate persona was the talk of the town. Ergo, in the many days that he spent before the bench, old bugaboos troubled him. Most of all was the inability to obtain proper barbering. If he was to stand quite prominently before the multitudes, he demanded tonsorial consultation and was outraged when it was refused. Fussing with forelock made him late for court.

Moreover, he was manacled during the proceedings and he would not wear his good hat to court lest some scoundrel snatch it from his head and make off with it. He sent it home with Mrs. Younge for safekeeping. However dedicated she was to Wickham, Henrietta Younge had a practical side. Instead of holding his hat in protective custody, she sold it to a used clothing exchange, raking in a goodly sum. (It was, after all, a handsome hat.) In return, she brought him some tri-cornered monstrosity (and an insect-infested remembrance of a lately hung felon). He wore it only once, and within the week, he insisted she exchange it for a remedy for lice. Regrettably, his vanity brought him as much notoriety as his crime.

By then, the newspapers had labelled him "The Vain Violator."

Had he just kept his hat on, his head down, and his mouth shut, Alistair's aspect might have not been recognised by past cohorts. Old Bailey was just over the street from the Fortune of War. Still, it was not unreasonable for him to believe that those who knew him as a procurer and a body-broker would not come forward. Few of his former conspirators liked to draw unnecessary attention from the magistrate. Indeed, Wickham held out hope that his past life would not overlap his present predicament. However, citizens of the nether-society were no less impressed by notoriety than gentlefolk and sallied forth with lurid tales of his past misdeeds.

Newspaper hawkers did not need to scream the headlines to create sales. In the time it took before the case was finally heard, all of the known world (and half the Dark Continent) knew of the particulars of the horrible crime and were baying for blood.

Alistair's defence was negligible. He was observed by a half-dozen men standing over Howgrave's corpse with the blood-dripping murder weapon in his hand. Most regrettably for him, the newly-dead gentleman's lovely widow stood next to them, announcing her assault and pointing to Alistair as the culprit. Because of this, even his solicitor did not believe that Lady Howgrave was the murderer. Wickham saw his only recourse was for the blame of the whole mess to be foisted onto the victim instead. This took a bit of fancy footwork. It also required him to quit avowing the truth.

Instead, he insisted, "Oh, heavens above! I loved Henry like a brother. Lady Howgrave has simply been too distraught to recall the incident accurately. This was a true accident. I fear Sir Howgrave was overtaken with drink. In truth, we were all a bit fuddled. Poor Henry happened to fall upon his sword—er, letter-knife."

Alistair also forgot to address the little allegation of attempted defilement. If any one testimony sealed his fate, it was that of Lady Howgrave. When she entered the court, an awed hush overspread the room. A black veil was artfully draped from her hat to her shoulders. (It was just thick enough to imply the convulsive torment of her grief-stricken heart, but translucent enough to display her unrivalled beauty.) Her voice was soft, her French accent peculiarly indistinct. It was the intonation particular to a woman of culture and station. Indeed, her voice was so soft that the spectators had to strain to hear her.

After she sat to offer her testimony, she meticulously arranged her skirts. Then, with exaggerated care, she turned back her veil. Against the raven garb, her lovely face was pale as moonlight. Murmurs of admiration hummed from one end of the courtroom to the other. It was determined that her declaration would be unassailable ere she opened her mouth to speak.

She prefaced her telling of the event by relating that Mr. Thomas's position of secretary to her husband was one of great trust. Hence, when he came to her sitting room that night, it was under pretence of obtaining her signature.

"Once he gained the room, the man went mad! He attempted to kiss me and demanded... other favours! He tore at my gown! I cried out, but the knife he held at my neck... it... it frightened me!"

Overcome with emotion, she stopped. Gasps, even moans, erupted from the onlookers, believing her ladyship might swoon. Whilst the court was quieted, Juliette dabbed at the corner of her eye with her handkerchief. (Those who were familiar with her husband's speeches should have recognised the gesture, but no one did.) Clearing her throat, tears still troubled her. Duteous as she was to her husband's memory, she made herself continue. Her voice trembled at the recollection.

"Just as he overpowered me, the villain was thwarted when my dear, brave husband came upon the terrible scene and put himself between us."

Pointing to Wickham, she said, "That *démon* then plunged the weapon into my dear Henry's heart!"

Howgrave was stabbed in the side, but the prosecutor did not want to taint her testimony by mucking about with trivialities. The victim was dead as mutton and the accused held the bloody knife in his murderous hand. Nothing more need be said. The *coup de' grâce* was employed regardless.

Voice quivering with sufferance, Juliette continued, "I hurried to my husband and pressed my handkerchief to his wound in an attempt to stanch the blood, but in vain!"

At that moment, she withdrew from her bodice another handkerchief, this one stained with her dear, dead husband's blood. She waved it once and laid it across her skirt. The red stain, the white of the handkerchief, and the black of her mourning dress was more an accusation than her pointing figure.

"I did what I could, but my husband died in my arms," she said, thereby being overcome by grief.

All eyes flew to Wickham. (He was not actually hit, but recoiled as if he had been.) Weeping uncontrollably, Juliette stood, Lord Orloff rushed to her side and led her down the steps and away. It was quite fortunate that burning at the stake was no longer a penal option. Had a poll been taken, it would have been reinstated on the spot.

"She lies!" Wickham cried indignantly. Forgetting the agreed upon testimony, he yowled, "She did it! Not I! Not I!"

As Lady Howgrave was escorted from the court, a queer roaring erupted behind her. Indeed, catcalls and outraged howls became a maelstrom of denunciation—a melee quite reminiscent of the one she endured on her aborted trip to the guillotine lo those many years ago. If that came to her mind, she gave no notice of it. Another far greater ovation arrested her attention the moment her black ensemble was spied at the door. Indeed, as Orloff helped her make her away, a great surge of humanity enveloped them. Some were merely admirers; others were reporters from newspapers as far away as Vienna. All of them cried out inquiries, hoping against hope that she might make a noteworthy quote.

She had but one inexplicable statement, before stepping majestically into her crepe-draped coach.

"*Vouloir, c'est pouvoir.*"

"What did she say? What did she say?" was the cry.

The interpretation was swift, but unhelpful.

"Where there's a will, there's a way."

It was just vague enough that each writer could make what they wanted to of it.

Indeed, thereafter not only were newspaper pages dedicated to speculation about Juliette, but a variety of biographies appeared. A small volume of poetry, effusive admiration of her great allurement, was published anonymously. It sold well. Lady Howgrave, however, remained concealed. Some said that she sold what she could of her husband's estate and, over-wrought by the tragedy, repaired to the north of Italy with Lord Orloff.

Her former paramour was not so fortunate.

In the face of conflicting statements by his client, Wickham's solicitor gave up any pretence of his innocence and told him to throw himself on the mercy of the court and plead that his had been a crime of passion. However, another suspicious death had been uncovered, the victim last seen in Alistair's company. That, taken with allegations of the most reprehensible behaviour, meant justice was not generous. Gentleman or not, the man who smite a Member of Parliament must be duly punished.

In the end, it was deemed that Newgate or Coldbath Prisons were not punitive enough for such as him. When he was consigned to twenty years on the penal ship, Discovery, now moored on the Thames at Woolwich, Wickham suffered a fit of incontinence. He blamed that on the gaol's constant diet of maize and oatmeal—a diet that would not improve once he was ensconced in the decommissioned warship's hull.

The town gaols were horrid, but a man with influence or money could improve his keep in them. The rotting ships had been often used to take prisoners to Australia. Overcrowded prisons meant they had to house the overflow of prisoners from Newgate and the like. Prisoners upon the ships were chained to their cots each night lest they slip ashore. During the day most of the fettered inmates were condemned to hard labour in the maze of warehouses along the southern shore. Those who did not were subject to daily floggings.

Wickham wrote countless letters, imploring everyone he knew to speak on his behalf. In the end, no one came forward. He was truly bereft. To his solicitor, he cried, "Why am I abandoned in my great hour of need?"

"You were hardly abandoned," replied Blackbird.

"Whatever do you mean?" inquired Wickham.

As Blackbird gathered his papers to leave, he said cryptically, "Why do you think you were not hung? As much as I would like to have the credit, leniency did not come about through my defence—or your lack of contrition.

Your death sentence was commuted to twenty years. If your behaviour is beyond reproach, you may well be considered for a pardon—although that may require you to leave the country."

Leave England? Wickham pondered that possibility, but gave no more thought who might have interceded on his behalf.

As Wickham awaited Alistair's transfer, he had little to entertain himself save for a snuff box with a risqué vignette of Anthony and Cleopatra inside the lid. It was enamel with insets of mother of pearl and rubies. Lydia had sold all his other possessions. It was the only thing of any worth that he had kept through his travails (and a rather thorough frisking by his gaolers). It was a wonder that he had still possessed it. Through admirable sleight of hand, he was able to pass it to Mrs. Younge. She nodded her head and said not a word.

He counted upon what that box would bring to save him from floggings, fleas, and pestilence in his future abode.

Convicted of murder and mayhem and identified as a body-snatcher and pimp, Alistair Reed Thomas, the assumed name of Major George Wickham, murderer, deserter, and general all-round cad, was carted off to the Discovery penal ship. He was not taken in a coach, but sequestered in a barred, wooden-wheeled tumbrel. Accompanying him were two prostitutes (one who claimed an acquaintance), several thieves, and a man who had done business with him at the Fortune of War. One of the men reached out and pinched Wickham on the buttocks, giving him a wicked smile.

"Dare not think of that, you worthless turd," said Wickham airily.

With great haste, all of the other passengers hovered on the far side of the conveyance from Wickham. Not because of any particular distaste for his crimes. But, as they travelled down the street, he was called the most despicable names and pelted with the rotted leavings of the costermonger's bins. Being consigned to a pillory would have been worse, but just barely.

"I am a gentleman and cannot be treated in this manner," he cried. "I owned a carting business!"

In the crowd observing this small parade was poor Mrs. Younge. She did not relish the notion of walking down to the stinking wharves, only to wave at poor George through a porthole. From the sum she obtained for the snuffbox, she bribed the gaolers for him to have a boiled egg, an extra blanket, and an additional bowl of jack-stir-about every day. What was left from the sale, she felt right in keeping against his debt to her. There was little enough chance that he would pay on it in the near future.

Amongst the many spectators that day were Lord and Lady Millhouse. Knowing the full history of the man, they had special interest in being assured that he was, indeed, consigned to prison. Sally Frances Arbuthnot stood next to them. As the fare to Old Bailey was two shillings, she dutifully paid the Millhouses for their trouble of bringing her. (Lady Millhouse refused her money, insisting that seeing ol' George Wickham get his just desserts was payment enough.)

"One evil at a time, child. One evil at a time."

As Sally watched Wickham being taken to serve his penance, she did not hoot. Indeed, she was unusually quiet. Her prayers had been answered and she gave thanks for that. At long last her dear brother's murderer had been brought to justice. The sentence may not have been carried out in her brother's name, but it was good enough for her. By whatever name, George Wickham had committed unspeakable crimes. She looked on the sight before her with great pleasure, but could not quite forget that the snake still had its head.

From just behind her, a garishly-dressed, undersized damsel leapt forth. No taller than a ten-year-old boy, she had an enormous bonnet and pretty fair aim. Indeed, she landed a decaying tomato squarely in Wickham's face. The crowd cheered.

Thinking that he recognised the culprit, George Wickham was aghast.

Rotten tomato parts streaming down his face, he screamed, "There she is! There she is!"

Mrs. Younge, poor deluded creature, believed he called only to her.

he Dance

News of Howgrave's murder arrived well-nigh synchronous to Darcy apprising Elizabeth of the likelihood that Wickham had resurfaced. He showed her Sally Frances Arbuthnot's letter, but not the vellum. She recalled the name nonetheless.

The Darcys had not truly wished Wickham dead, but would not have mourned if he was. Darcy had not dallied about when he told her all that came to pass in London.

Despite his particular dislike of the man, Darcy was most distressed when he learnt of Howgrave's murder. It was his initial belief that the murder may have occurred due to Wickham's unmasking. Inquiries made it clear that, despite the event occurring close on the heels of Darcy's visit, it was entirely unrelated. Everyone in their circle knew that Alistair and Juliette were lovers.

Alistair was becoming ever-bolder. It was a matter of time ere Howgrave caught wind of the affair. No one, not even her closest confidants, believed Juliette murdered her husband.

Despite the goings on, Darcy wanted to be fully assured that Alistair Thomas was actually George Wickham. He was determined to do it himself, but Fitzwilliam disagreed, insisting that he be the one to make a clandestine visit to the gaol to discover the truth.

"I daresay you will draw far too much attention in that part of town, cousin," Fitzwilliam pointed out.

"You are hardly indistinguishable from the masses yourself," Darcy replied wryly.

Upon most occasions that would have been so. However, wearing a modest cloak and a hat pulled low, the patch over his eye gave him a roguish look. Delighted to be able to engage in a bit of stealth, Colonel Fitzwilliam fitted himself out for Darcy's approval before he set out for London. By observing him through the bars of his cell, Fitzwilliam made an immediate identification without Wickham being any the wiser.

He reported to Darcy, "His hair has gone white. It is his most notable feature—no doubt how he managed to avoid recognition for as long as he did."

The only other thing of note was who happened to be visiting Wickham that day.

Fitzwilliam asked, "Do you recall the companion of Georgiana's—the one with whom Wickham first conspired...?"

Indeed, Darcy did. Neither wanted to speak of that long ago (but not forgotten) betrayal. He nodded, therefore sparing Fitzwilliam the distasteful task of repeating the particulars of it.

"Mrs. Younge," said Darcy.

"Yes, Mrs. Younge," repeated Fitzwilliam. "I was able to observe Wickham because he was conversing with a woman. I am quite certain it was Mrs. Younge."

"Is her dedication to him born of loyalty or love?" Darcy observed. "Neither is wise nor true."

Shaking their heads, neither had more to say about such an odd, lasting affair.

When they learnt that Wickham was to be tried as Alistair Thomas, Darcy, Fitzwilliam, and Bingley engaged in lengthy discussions whether it would be right to interfere with the proceedings or not. The consensus was that they would not make his true name known unless he was found not guilty of Howgrave's murder. They would only speak if he was once again free to prey on society. As there was no refutation save Wickham's, Darcy knew he must believe that the murder took place as Juliette described. If his letter to Howgrave exposing Alistair's true identity was read by him, Darcy never learnt of it.

For weeks, the letter Juliette posted to Darcy, upon the days prior to those events, lay unmolested (and routinely dusted) upon the table where Darcy had left it.

It did not remain unnoticed by his wife. As Darcy continued to ignore it, in time, curiosity got the best of Elizabeth. She picked it up, looked at the seal, and (to her great embarrassment) was gratified to see that it had not yet been opened. It was peculiar that Darcy had brought it all the way back with him. It troubled her not to think of a reason why he did. (Nor did she admit to herself that when she admired her husband's bare back that she was relieved to see it unscarred by anyone's fingernails but hers.)

Holding the letter to her nose, she took a small whiff. Perfume still clung to the paper, a reminder of Lady Howgrave's tenacity.

"Shall you read it?" Darcy asked.

She had not heard him approach and he gave her a start.

Turning about, she bid, "Is there a reason for me to do so?"

"Only to satisfy one's curiosity."

"In the tale, something untidy befell that inquisitive cat," she observed.

He replied, "In your own home, it is my advice to do what pleases you."

Taking a candle, she held the corner of the letter to it until it caught fire. Then, she laid it in a porcelain bowl and watched it long enough to see that it would burn. Her only regret was that the flame might mar the finish of the bowl.

Steeling herself, she said, "I beg one question and, I freely admit, it is one that is beneath me."

The only display of concern upon his countenance was a slight furrowing of his brow.

With a slight catch in her voice, she asked, "In your time with that lady did you ever call her, *mon cheri?*"

He seemed taken aback, but only for a moment. As the question hung in the air, it sounded quite ridiculous to her. Indeed, it was not only a silly inquiry, but one that was ultimately pointless. Was he to answer, however, she knew that he would not lie. Both eagre and apprehensive, she awaited his reply. His answer was succinct.

"No, I did not. I have never spoken a word of endearment—in any language—to another woman."

It would seem that time would never be quite right for him to apprise his wife of Lady Howgrave's scandalous request. Some incidents are so peculiar one can only set them aside; in time, to be forgotten by all parties concerned. It was Darcy's opinion that to tell Elizabeth of that aberration would serve nothing but his conscience. He had the strength not to speak of it to her.

Their time and thoughts were much engaged elsewhere during the days of the trial in London. When Alistair Thomas was convicted of murder, the general populace, for once, came to a general agreement; all concerned believed that The Vain Violator's sentence was not harsh enough. Soon the newspapers found other, far more important events to report. Mid-winter, the old king finally died. Decrepit, demented, and despised, he was buried almost as an afterthought.

Epilogue

It was a crisp evening, the sort of winter's eve that the moon shone most inviting. The house was full of people. Their time had been so taken with their guests that Elizabeth hoped to escape them for a while.

In the music room, someone played the pianoforte. It might have been a waltz. Her mood was romantic and she did not want her husband's to be compromised by music that she knew he believed to be loathsome. Tossing a shawl across her shoulders, she took Darcy's hand, whispering to him that she would like to take a bit of air. She was surprised that he agreed to it so readily.

They escaped onto the promenade. The air was brisk, possibly too cold to linger. She shivered. He drew her to him, the warmth of his arms quite appealing.

As she placed her cheek against his chest, he held her more tightly.

She sighed.

He stepped back, and with a slight twinkle in his eye, inquired, "Has someone come between us, Lizzy?"

She opened her mouth to answer, but laughed instead.

She answered, "Never between us—an addendum, perhaps—be it boy or girl."

Taking her again in his arms, she was caught a bit off-balance. As a dancer, Darcy was not the most proficient. That hardly mattered. When he began to twirl her around in the steps of the waltz, he astonished her once again.

To be in his arms was pure rhapsody.

As he swept her about, she allowed her head to fall back with abandon. Closing her eyes, she was lost in that moment—and all those yet to come—dancing to only music they could hear.

The Ruling Passion, be it what it will,
The ruling passion conquers reason still...

About the Author

With almost 350,000 copies of *Mr. Darcy Takes a Wife* and *Darcy & Elizabeth* sold, Ms. Berdoll remains the reigning Jane Austen sequelist to date.

Her other books include the historical romance, *Fandango* and a humorous look at euphemisms, *Very Nice Ways to Say Very Bad Things.*

Linda Berdoll is still happily married to her high school sweetheart and lives outside Austin, Texas.